**P9-CBS-303**

"A legal thriller so savvy and well written it's hard to believe it's a first novel. The dialogue is literate, often funny, and all the characters live and breathe."

—*Kirkus Reviews*

"A fast-paced, intriguing, multifaceted tale."

—*Publishers Weekly*

"Move over John Grisham, Esq. Watch out Scott Turow."

—*Lawyer's Journal*

"A witty, intelligent journey through big firms and prosecutors' offices that should be familiar to any lawyer."

—*Virginia Lawyers Weekly*

"A towering achievement!"

—*Massachusetts Bar Journal*

"A book you can't put down; exciting, full of twists and turns, it is a fast-paced thriller."

—Barry Reed, author of *The Verdict*

# A CINDERELLA AFFIDAVIT

———◆———

# MICHAEL FREDRICKSON

**TOR**®

A TOM DOHERTY ASSOCIATES BOOK
NEW YORK

This is a work of fiction. All the characters and events portrayed in this book are either products of the author's imagination or are used fictitiously.

A CINDERELLA AFFIDAVIT

Copyright © 1999 by Michael Frederickson

A Tor Book
Published by Tom Doherty Associates, LLC
175 Fifth Avenue
New York, NY 10010

www.tor.com

Tor® is a registered trademark of Tom Doherty Associates, LLC.

ISBN: 0-812-58013-3
Library of Congress Catalog Card Number: 99-21740

First edition: May 1999
First mass market edition: July 2000

Printed in the United States of America

0  9  8  7  6  5  4  3  2  1

For Jolly and Zeke

Lying is impossible.
—Gregory Bateson

# *Foreword*

This is a work of fiction. The novel owes its origin, however, to a Boston murder that was the subject of a celebrated trial known as *Commonwealth v. Lewin.* I have appropriated, if you will, the structure of the situation. The early parts of the book track the main events of the murder and the quandary in which the police found themselves. Indeed, the affidavit set out in chapter six is taken almost verbatim from the document that was so stormily central to the *Lewin* case.

But there the resemblance ends. The real-life case was just a springboard for the story, and once aloft the book stays there or crashes on the strength of fabricated events and imaginary characters. I wish to stress in particular that I know nothing about the people who lived through the actual events, and no one should infer that anything I have invented here is meant to describe them. The *Lewin* case brought suffering, in some instances tragedy, to many of the people it touched. It was never my intention to intrude in their anguish by presuming to write about their lives. Any resemblance between them and my fictional characters is, as they say, coincidental.

I have also adapted a snippet from the transcript of an actual arraignment before an Australian court. This short episode, which begins chapter thirty-nine, is available on the Internet. Forgive me. It was just too tasty to pass up.

There are many people I must thank for their help and encouragement during the writing and publication of this book. First and foremost is my wife, Jolly, who was a constant source of support as well as sound and blunt advice. I literally could not have done it without her. I am indebted to Jim DeGiacomo and Dan Crane for sharing their legal expertise to keep me from exposing too much ignorance of criminal law; notwithstanding their advice, experienced practitioners will detect that I have taken some small liberties with criminal procedure in the pursuit of dramatic effect. Tellis Lawson, Tina Fernandes, and Bill Farwell gave me technical advice on weapons, salt cod, and computers, respectively. Richard Alfred, Jim Brink, Mark Fredrickson, Steve Gallos, Lynn Goldsmith, Bill LeDoux, Martha Lynch, Steve Schaffran, Samuel Shem, Ruth and Dvora Tager, Connie Vecchione, and Tom Weist were my first readers and valuable critics. I stole an embarrassingly large number of jokes and quips from my old friend Nick Ruf. Matt Zuckerbraun and Ken and Gussie McKusick extended lavish hospitality when I needed a quiet place to work on the manuscript. I am grateful to Jerry Cohen, Bob Gleason, Noah and Lorraine Gordon, Sam Pinkus, and Gene Winick for reaching out to help a neophyte in this most peculiar business.

Finally, there's my mother, Evelyn Fredrickson, whose infectious love of books it was impossible not to catch when I was growing up. A savvy reader, she is the only person so far who guessed the ending of this one. But, then, she always could see right through me.

# *Prologue*

Francis X. Dunleavy laid the old service revolver next to the Delft sugar bowl. It was a gift from his mother-in-law, who had pressed it into his hand with both of hers during one of the few quiet moments of his wedding reception. Its chrome-plated finish even now as sleek and unpitted as a baby's cheek, the gun was the dowry settled on his bride as she was passed from one cop's family to another's.

Dunleavy took his dinner plate from Doreen. With his free hand he carefully swept to one side the items from the kit he had used to clean and oil the revolver. He set the plate down where they had been.

Fish sticks, for Christ's sake. Dunleavy looked glumly at the plate. He picked up the catsup bottle sitting beside the open box of cartridges and slapped its bottom with the heel of his hand. Fucking fish sticks. Instant mashed potatoes. Frozen peas dyed the same improbable green, and presenting as much promise of flavor, as the vinyl siding that clad his house. Dunleavy took a bite and chewed listlessly.

"So when will you be back?" asked Doreen, accusation in her voice. Standing over the sink, she briskly shook bread

crumbs off a cookie sheet under running tap water. It crack-
led like the tinny thunder in a high school play. "I thought
you were working days this week anyway."

"I don't know," Dunleavy replied. His fork, cradling a
golf-ball-sized nugget of potatoes studded with peas, was
halted in midair. "We go in about eight and if we score I'll
be doing paperwork till at least eleven."

Dunleavy shoved the fork in his mouth. He dispiritedly
surveyed from the rear his wife's square shoulders and thickening hips. The blue cardigan and the beige wool skirt she
wore to school every other Thursday made her look dowdy.
A knot of reddish hair at the back of her head bobbed up
and down as she scrubbed furiously into the corners of the
cookie sheet. She rinsed the pan and shut off the tap and slid
the pan into the drainer. Wiping her hands on a towel, Doreen turned to face her husband.

"I just wish someone could explain to me why you have
to work tonight. When you're supposed to be working days.
Are you telling me the union doesn't have policies about
this?" Her schoolteacher's voice now.

"Look. I told you. Ray and I have been working on this
for weeks. It's ready. We gotta do it." Dunleavy bit into a
piece of fish. It was still cold in the center. He pushed his
plate into the middle of the table with his thumb and looked
at his watch. Almost seven.

He picked up the revolver and swung out the cylinder. It
wasn't regulation—they issued Glocks and Sigs these days—
but it had always brought him good luck. He began slipping
cartridges into it, one by one. When it was loaded, he snicked
the cylinder back into position with a lateral flick of his wrist,
eased the hammer down on an empty chamber, and stood
up. He lodged the gun into the holster behind his back.

Dunleavy was a big, burly man, over six feet tall, and
Doreen had to step aside to let him edge past her in the tiny
kitchen. He laid his plate in the sink and ran water over it
briefly.

"Well, we need to talk," Doreen said to his back. "You
can't keep this up. I can't keep this up. The kids never see
you and Kevin is getting out of hand."

Dunleavy winced. At seventeen his oldest son was way

beyond "out of hand," and Dunleavy did not need Doreen to remind him that something had to be done.

A honk. And just in the nick. He grabbed his overcoat and bolted, hatless, for the door. "Don't wait up," he called as he barreled out the door and skipped down the stairs two at a time. He grinned. Like a kid out of school, he thought. Doreen, God love her, was a good mother and a good wife, but my Christ she had the knack for making you feel like one of her eighth graders.

Francis Dunleavy stepped out onto the stoop. The swooping wind was so cold he stopped for a moment and took a careful breath. Then he hurried to the blue unmarked Plymouth idling next to the curb. BAD COP, NO DONUT, said the bumper sticker. Dunleavy didn't get the passenger door closed before the car lurched away from the curb.

The air in the car was a suffocating mix of tobacco smoke and beer farts. "Mother of God, Ray, it's a fuckin' gas chamber in here," Dunleavy said. He cracked his window with exaggerated haste and craned his head toward the opening. The cold air bit his cheek. He suffered the cold long enough to make his point and rolled the window back up. "Did you get the warrant?" he asked, turning to the driver.

Detective Lieutenant Raymond Carvalho was a thin swarthy man with a nose you couldn't miss: long and tapering before ending in a bulbous knob, it looked for all the world as if its demented maker had deliberately pulled it away like taffy before the flesh had set. Carvalho slipped his right hand into his worn tweed sport coat. With thumb and forefinger he pulled out a folded set of papers just far enough to give Dunleavy a glimpse. "All set," he said.

Leaving South Street, the peeling wooden triple-deckers of Jamaica Plain cowering in the bitter cold, Carvalho eased the Plymouth up Centre Street and then cut over to the Jamaicaway toward downtown Boston. The last of the rush hour traffic was flowing thickly through the dark in the other direction.

"Piscatello and Kelleher are gonna meet us at the diner," Carvalho said. "I even got your hammer, you being such a hunk and all."

"Aw, Jesus," groaned Dunleavy. "Not Kelleher. Every

time you're out sick or whatever, I end up getting stuck with him." He gazed out the passenger window.

"Hey, I hear you," said Carvalho. "The guy could fuck up an earthquake. I figure we leave him outside to cover the alley. That way, he steps on his dick, we won't be in the way." Carvalho stuck a cigarette in his mouth and lit it with a disposable lighter. Dunleavy opened his window again and stared out the window in silence for a while.

Later, he said, "You had any second thoughts, Ray? About the Tung On, I mean. We could ruffle some feathers upstairs."

"Let 'em ruffle," said Carvalho, expelling smoke through his nose. "They can't prove we heard anything about Tung On involvement. So far as they know, we just got a tip on a retail outfit. Nothing to do with Vu and his gang. And it could turn into something pretty interesting if your guy is right about Vu. Why should Organized Crime get all the goodies?"

"You trust Gogarty to back us?" Captain Oliver Gogarty was head of the Drug Control Unit of the Boston Police Department.

"Gogarty wouldn't back his sainted mother if he thought there was any political risk in it. But there's nothing to prove we knew this bust might involve Vu, so he's safe and so are we."

While they talked, Carvalho wheeled smoothly through the Fenway and threaded his way onto Huntington Avenue and then east on Stuart Street. At Washington Street, Stuart turned into Kneeland Street. The corner of Washington and Kneeland made up the southern terminus of the Combat Zone, a decaying quarter to which zoning law confined most of the city's porno cinemas, adult bookstores, and nude bars. The sleaze was dwindling, however, as the Zone was failing to hold the line against advancing development from the north. The Zone now lurked in the shadow of the new Hotel Adams complex, a towering vanguard of urban renewal that threatened to eradicate the Zone.

The Plymouth continued down Kneeland, past the lights of Chinatown winking bleakly on the left, and crossed the entrance to the Fitzgerald Expressway. Two blocks later,

Carvalho turned left on South Street and immediately pulled over on the right next to a hydrant.

Across the street on the corner stood the Blue Diner, an artifact from the 1930s in the inevitable shape of a railroad car. The diner gave off glints of zinc and cobalt blue in the wash of the streetlights, its windows festooned with strings of tiny white lights. Once a greasy spoon serving workers in the Leather District, the diner had undergone gentrification in the mid-1980s, when new management pitched its menu to stockbrokers and lawyers with a craving for the comfort food they had forsaken as health-conscious professionals. The line outside the diner was daunting during lunchtime, but at night the joint returned to its roots as truckers, cabbies, and insomniacs stopped in for coffee and homemade pie.

The policemen crossed the street and walked toward the diner. They were joined by a short, barrel-shaped man wearing a baseball cap and a Boston Bruins jacket.

"Hey, Ray," said the man. To Dunleavy, he asked, "Doreen let you out, eh, Frannie?"

"Hi, Sal," said Dunleavy, as he opened the door to the diner. He let the others enter ahead of him. "How's the diet?"

"Thriving, Frannie, thriving. It's *me* I worry about."

Detective Salvatore Piscatello's doctor had ordered humiliating, tectonic changes in his celebrated eating habits, and Piscatello was as vocal about his suffering as he had once been about his gustatory exploits. Not that he could argue with the doctor. His orders had come hard on the heels of tests showing that Piscatello's cholesterol level had finally overtaken Wade Boggs's lifetime batting average. He squinted bitterly at the daily special scrawled on the blackboard behind the counter. Meatloaf with mashed potatoes and pan gravy. He trudged on behind Dunleavy.

They followed Carvalho to a wooden booth at the far end of the diner. There a red-haired man sat with a glass of tomato juice in his hand. He was younger than the others, thinner and much taller, his eyes such a cool bachelor-button blue that Dunleavy felt a flicker of regret that they had been wasted on a man.

"Hey, you're late," the redhead said in cheerful greeting as he slid over to make room for Carvalho. Piscatello and

Dunleavy joined them on the other side. "This is my third juice."

"Fuck your juice, Kelleher," said Carvalho. "Can we get some coffee over here?" he called to a passing waitress, moving his index finger in a tiny circle over the table. He sat back and lit a cigarette. He looked at Kelleher's glass.

"Do you ever eat or do you live off that shit?" he asked.

"Course I eat," said Martin Kelleher. "I just happen to like juice. It's healthy and I like it." He took a sip, then examined his glass. "I'd like more variety, but tomato is better than nothing."

"With vodka, maybe," said Carvalho, blowing smoke in his direction. "Which reminds me. Who's for a few pops at the Cork when we're done? We can catch the tail end of the Celtics."

"Not me," said Dunleavy. "Doreen's gunning for me as it is."

"Too much free bar food," said Piscatello.

"Who's playing?" asked Kelleher.

Carvalho didn't answer him. The waitress brought three mugs of coffee and, unbidden, another glass of tomato juice. Kelleher smiled at her.

"OK," Carvalho said, tapping his cigarette against the rim of an ashtray. "Word is the Chinks just got a whole new load of shit. If we catch 'em with enough they may roll over. So here's the order of battle. Any minute now we should get word on a successful drop. That the inventory is in. Then we take a little cruise up the street and park over on Kneeland. The building is number sixteen, a three-story walkup halfway up the block on Tyler. Apartment number four, third floor, on the right side of the hall. We—"

"Left," said Dunleavy. Carvalho looked back at him in puzzlement. "The door's on the left side, Ray."

Carvalho paused a moment, then, nodding to Dunleavy, he went on. "Correction," he said. "The door on the left is the one. You'll be able to tell 'cause it's been reinforced to slow down any party crashers and it has a special, like, mail slot cut into it just under the eyehole. The customer sticks the money in the hole and the dope gets shoved back out.

Wrapped in a lottery ticket. Nobody ever sees the dealer. Slicker than snot on a doorknob."

"So it's a no-knock?" interrupted Kelleher.

"No, Kelleher," said Carvalho evenly. "We're gonna doll you up as the Avon lady and see if you can sweet-talk us in. Of *course* it's a no-knock, for fuck's sake. No, wait. I take that back. Frannie's gonna knock—with the hammer. Once he's through the door Piscatello and I go in. And you, Kelleher, you're positioned in the alley so you can take anybody coming out down the fire escape."

Kelleher reached for the juice glass but Carvalho snatched it away. "And if you drink any more of that goddamn juice, you'll be off shaking the dew off your lily just about the time it all goes down."

"How many inside?" asked Piscatello. He poured fake sugar into his coffee and stirred.

"Only one, so far as we know," said Dunleavy.

"A piece of cake," said Carvalho. "Our friends of the yellow persuasion never try to get rough with cops. And besides—"

A beeper went off. Dunleavy reached down to his belt and shut it off. "That," he said, "would be my man. Back in a second." Dunleavy got up and walked over to the pay phone by the men's room. While the others drank, Carvalho watched Dunleavy. Dunleavy looked back at him as he talked into the phone. Then he hung up and gave the thumbs-up sign to Carvalho. He returned to the booth.

"The shit's there. He wants twenty minutes so he can get into position to cover his ass," said Dunleavy.

Carvalho looked at his watch.

"Fuck him," he said. "I don't have all night."

Carvalho took a last sip of coffee and stood up.

"Mount up," he said. "We ride."

Five minutes later, they got out of two unmarked cars on Kneeland Street and walked casually toward Chinatown. As the others headed for Tyler Street, Kelleher peeled off to the left and entered the alley. A large black dog that was nosing about the garbage cans loped away as Kelleher made the turn.

It was too cold for much foot traffic, even in Chinatown,

but the policemen still attracted little notice. Spanning Tyler Street a faded banner with Chinese characters luffed in the chill wind. WELCOME TO CHINATOWN, it said in English. Hunched into the wind, Dunleavy walked stiffly and deliberately, the head of the sledgehammer jammed up into the armpit of his overcoat.

Fourteen Tyler Street was just a few doors in from Kneeland. It housed Ho Yuen's Imports, a shabby storefront on the left with dingy windows displaying Taiwanese crockery and cheap jade carvings. The shop was closed. Just past it were five cement steps leading to the unsecured entrance to the apartments above Ho Yuen's.

Number sixteen.

Carvalho climbed the steps quickly and opened the door. He held the door as Dunleavy and Piscatello stepped inside. Glancing up and down the street one last time, Carvalho turned and followed them, pulling the door shut behind him.

The stairway was unlit. The only illumination was the dim reflection from a naked bulb hanging in the second-floor landing around the corner above. The three men climbed, quickly and silently, making the turn at the landing and proceeding up the next flight to the third floor. This landing, too, was lit by a single bulb, as was the narrow third-floor hallway into which the men moved single file.

They stopped at number four, on the left. They heard the muffled sound of a television, its voices and canned laughter seeping out of the apartment across the hall. There was no other sound.

Dunleavy looked at the door to number four. It was reinforced, all right. Steel. The bright brass of a new Yale lock. The jamb was made of fresh two-by-eights, nail heads still gleaming in the weak light. And there in the center of the door, below the spy hole, was the money hole. It was a crude job, someone using a small drill bit several times to gouge out a hole that was less than an inch in diameter. Dunleavy could see nothing looking into it. Must be some kind of flap on the inside, he thought.

Dunleavy watched as Carvalho moved to the far side of the door, near the doorknob. Once in position, he released the trigger guard on his nine-millimeter Glock, which he gripped in both hands and raised beside his cheek. Piscatello took up a position on the other side, clutching a Mossberg shotgun to his chest. Dunleavy opened his coat and removed the hammer. He spread his legs and assumed a striking position. He looked over at Carvalho.

Carvalho nodded.

Dunleavy swung the hammer and brought it down with all his force at the lock above the doorknob.

The sound of the hammer blow was sudden and shockingly loud in the tiny hallway. Dunleavy felt no give in the door. His ears ringing, he swung again, and then again, keeping his eyes on the lock. It seemed about to give. As he swung the hammer back to strike a fourth blow, he noticed for the first time a hole the size of his fist in the metal just above the hole.

Dunleavy stopped swinging now, listening for the sounds that a few seconds earlier had thundered off the walls. He heard nothing. His gaze fixed on the door, he watched as another hole silently appeared a few inches from the first one. Then a thin splash of red streamed across the holes like paint from a spray can.

Dunleavy looked over at Carvalho in confusion. Carvalho's face was contorted and he was screaming at him, but Dunleavy heard nothing in the swaddling silence.

The hammer fell from his hands and Dunleavy tried to move in Carvalho's direction. His feet did not follow at first and when they did Dunleavy began to spin, wheeling slowly back toward the door. The red stream went before him, spraying the door again. Like tomato juice, he thought.

Then his knees gave out and he slumped to the floor. Lying on his back, Dunleavy looked up at the water-stained ceiling tiles in mute wonder. He was faintly aware of the floor sliding beneath him, then realized he was being pulled by the ankles away from the doorway. Carvalho was kneeling beside him.

Dunleavy watched Carvalho moving his mouth in urgent speech. But the silence would not release its grip. Dunleavy heard only the silence, which swelled in a pulsing crescendo—so loud the pressure made his temples pound. Then it stopped and he heard nothing at all, over and over again.

# I

———— ✦ ————

# LIES

## DR 6-101.   Failing to Act Competently

**(A)**      A lawyer shall not:

**(1)**      Handle a legal matter which he knows or should know that he is not competent to handle, without associating with him a lawyer who is competent to handle it.

—American Bar Association
**Code of Professional Responsibility**

# 1

---

# The Deposition

Objection," said C. Morton Atwater.

"Objection," said Laura Amochiev.

"Objection," said three other lawyers, almost simultaneously.

"Objection," said Matthew Boer, a beat behind the others.

"Should I answer?" asked the witness, looking to Atwater on his right. The witness was a potbellied plumber named Antonio Salvucci. He had followed the erratic bounce of objections by swinging his befuddled and suspicious gaze up and down the conference table like the victim in a game of keepaway. Which, in a way, he was, thought Matthew Boer.

"Just a minute," said the stenographer, who was struggling to match objection to attorney. She had no need for concern, since everyone (including Matthew, who hadn't even heard the offending question) had climbed aboard Atwater's initial objection. Whatever had prompted it.

Matthew turned his chair slightly to hide the *New York Times* crossword he was working from behind a yellow pad propped up on his knee. He folded a page from the pad back over the puzzle and entertained a fervent wish that he were somewhere else. Anywhere. He looked around the room.

At the far end of the room, Atwater had silenced Salvucci, his client, by raising his left hand a few inches off the cool cherry of the conference table. Atwater's flunky, a young man in his twenties named Scoville, sat on Atwater's right and took notes furiously. The stenographer rubbed her temples and then returned to fiddling with her machine. Atwater waited patiently.

The anchor of the litigation department at Royce & Bell, the largest law firm in Boston, C. Morton Atwater was a patient man. He was tall and soigné, with thick, wavy hair the color of galvanized metal and smartly cut to fit the contours of his scalp like the shoulder feathers of a raptor. His gray herringbone suit, butter-soft over a blue cotton shirt with a crisp white collar, was perfectly matched to a dark silk tie so understated you had to stoop over it to discern its flecks of red and gold. Atwater would have thought the tie daring ten years earlier.

When the stenographer nodded to indicate she was ready, Atwater swiveled his chair slightly toward his client. "Go ahead and answer the questions, Tony. Ignore the objections. They are made to protect the record. If I think a question shouldn't be answered, I'll tell you. Now, Ms. Hallowell," he said, smiling at the stenographer, "would you read back Mr. O'Boy's inartful question?"

Holding aloft the ribbon of paper that extruded from her machine, the stenographer read, " 'Directing your attention to—' "

"Fuck you, Mortie," said Billy O'Boy from across the table, his face reddening. "That's off the record," he added, glowering at the stenographer. He turned back to Atwater. "Just tell him to answer the goddamn question, OK? It's too late in the day for this shit."

"Billy," said Atwater, his hand raised in a gesture of seignorial indulgence. "I apologize. Please go on."

Billy O'Boy settled back in his chair. He was a big, bluff man with thin white hair above a plum-colored face etched with rum sores. The pink flesh of his neck and jowls spilled over his collar. His green club tie fell off to one side, seeking its way to his belt by taking the Great Circle Route around a big belly that strained at the placket of his shirt. Like some-one left him out in the corn too long, thought Matthew.

O'Boy represented an elderly Virginian named Felter, on whom Antonio Salvucci had landed just as Felter was hand-ing his keys to the valet parking attendant at the swank new Hotel Adams. Unfortunately for Felter, Salvucci was not alone. With him fell two plumber's helpers, eight hundred pounds of equipment and materials, and most of the ceiling of the porte cochere sheltering the entrance to the hotel. Sal-vucci and his crew had been rooting around in the crawl space above the ceiling while upgrading the plumbing for a new barroom on the hotel's mezzanine, just above the porte cochere.

All of this, and especially the severity of Felter's resulting brain injuries, constituted what O'Boy liked to call "good facts." A canny old trial horse and stalwart of the plaintiffs' bar, he had leapt at the opportunity to represent Felter—or his court-appointed conservator, to be more accurate, since Felter himself could no longer walk or even speak. O'Boy had hit all moving targets. He sued Tocco Corporation, the giant mechanical contracting firm for which Salvucci worked, as well as the hotel and all those involved in its original construction four years earlier. Today he was taking Salvucci's deposition. Atwater, Tocco's counsel, was de-fending Salvucci.

Matthew Boer represented the hotel. Well, actually, Ben Fleishman, a senior partner at Daphnis & Clooney, repre-sented the hotel, and Matthew reported to him. Matthew's role during depositions was to show the flag, take notes for reconnaissance reports to his superiors, and eventually ask questions after the principals—in this instance, O'Boy and Atwater—had done battle. Of course, it was understood that once important employees of the hotel actually became wit-nesses, Fleishman himself would take charge, as Atwater had done today. Only five years out of law school, Matthew was not yet ready for such robust duties.

The stenographer opened her mouth to read back the ques-tion.

"I'll rephrase the question," O'Boy interrupted. "Mr. Sal-vucci, directing your attention to the work order that was previously marked Exhibit One-thirty-seven, do you recognize that document?"

Salvucci glanced at the piece of paper in front of him. "I don't know," he said, glancing over at Atwater. "You just handed it to me. Can I take a look at it?"

"Be my guest," said O'Boy.

The room was silent as the witness perused Exhibit 137 at an agonizingly glacial pace. Matthew finished the upper right corner of his puzzle. Finally, the witness raised his head and looked at O'Boy.

"OK," said the witness.

"So you do recognize it?" asked O'Boy.

"I didn't say that."

"Are you telling us you never saw it before?"

"No, I'm not telling you that either."

"Well, what *are* you telling us, Mr. Salvucci?" O'Boy sounded exasperated.

"I'm telling you, OK, I finished reading it."

"Perhaps you'd like us to wait while you rest your lips," said O'Boy, whose own store of patience, obviously smaller than Atwater's, had been depleted.

"Mr. O'Boy," said Atwater with uncharacteristic sharpness, "you are getting out of hand. If you abuse my client again, I will terminate this deposition at once and explain the circumstances to the court."

"Well, then, can you answer my question? Have you seen the document before?"

"I don't know."

"Mr. Salvucci," said O'Boy, his baritone sinking to bass. "Isn't that your signature at the bottom of the work order?"

The witness flipped to the last page and peered intently. He looked up and glanced at Atwater, then back at O'Boy.

"I'm not sure. It could be. It looks like my writing, but I can't be sure."

"Mr. Salvucci, how many people at Tocco go around signing your name to things?"

"Uh—" said Salvucci.

"Objection," said Atwater.

"Objection," said Laura Amochiev, counsel for the architect who had designed the hotel, and the ceiling.

"Objection," said the lawyer who represented the general contractor that had built the hotel.

"Objection," said counsel for the structural engineer.

"Objection," said the lawyer whose client had manufactured the straps by which the porte cochere ceiling was hung.

"Objection," said Matthew Boer, with a dying fall.

"It is obvious," said Atwater, "that Mr. Salvucci has no present memory of having signed the work order. I will not have you badgering him because he can't recall."

"He hasn't even told me *that*," said O'Boy. "And now that you've signaled how you want him to answer, let me at least get it on the record. Mr. Salvucci, do you recall—"

"Please, Billy," said Atwater, sighing, "that wasn't worthy of you."

"Do you recall," O'Boy pushed on, "signing the work order marked as Exhibit One-thirty-seven?"

"I'm not sure. I could have. I don't recall."

Matthew's attention drifted and he soon lost track of the questioning again. He could no longer remember how many depositions he had attended, but he had quickly tumbled to their awful, ill-kept secret. They were dead boring. Skull numbing. Stupor inducing. Proof against all stratagems for maintaining concentration. Even the witnesses couldn't take the tedium. If not totally terrified, they started out with bounce and bonhomie, delighted with a day or two off from their regular duties. But the carnival mood rapidly gave way to a snarling hostility, after which they sank into the surly torpor of a teenager asked to account for her whereabouts the night before. And as for the lawyers . . . ?

Matthew stared out the windows of the Royce & Bell conference room, looking east into the icy chop of Boston Harbor, which was weakly lit by the setting sun. *A doom with a view,* he thought grimly. He let his mind drift to the sleek horseshoe-shaped bar at the Cayenne Social Club, where he would meet Ira Teitelbaum after work. He could almost taste the first margarita, that perfect prism of a drink refracting a rainbow of flavors—salt, sour, sweet, and the rushing heat of chilled tequila. Then bubbling, fiery enchiladas and Teitelbaum's mordant take on the practice of law.

He mentally shook himself back into focus, forcing himself back to work.

Nineteen down: *Absquatulate*—seven letters starting with *v*. Matthew frowned, his pen poised over the puzzle.

"Vamoose," Laura Amochiev offered in a whisper over his shoulder.

Startled, Matthew jerked his head around. Laura started, too, as others up and down the table were looking at her. Her whisper had apparently come out louder than she intended.

"My sentiments exactly," said Atwater. He replaced the cap on his fountain pen with an audible snap. "Enough for today. My client is tired and so am I." He pushed his chair back and looked at O'Boy. "Billy, I'm sorry but we need to reschedule the resumption of Mr. Salvucci's deposition. I have a partners' meeting I can't miss on the fourth."

O'Boy sat up straight in his chair and glared at Atwater. "I'm not putting this over because you have a partners' meeting," he said.

"It's about compensation, Billy," Atwater said with a wide grin, as if this explained everything.

"I don't care if it's about peace in the Middle East. It's not a legitimate conflict that should screw up our deposition schedule. Get your boy Scoville to cover for you."

Scoville blushed.

"I'm afraid I can't do that," said Atwater, a chill in his voice now. "And neither Mr. Salvucci nor I will be here on the fourth." Then his face softened and his smile was back. "You are free," he added, gesturing toward the table like a hostess showing the way to the salad bar, "to use the conference room . . ." With a touch of malice, he allowed his voice to trail off.

"The deposition is going forward. I'll get an order if I have to."

Atwater sighed and let his hand fall to his side. "You do what you must, Billy," he said. Then, moving with catlike languor, he reached into his coat pocket and took out a small black book. It fell open obediently in the palm of his hand to a page marked with a gray ribbon, like a missal. Atwater flipped indolently through the pages. Without looking up he said, "How's the sixteenth?"

But of course March 16 was no good for someone, and after rejecting a number of dates, the lawyers were able to settle on March 24. Salvucci was not consulted. O'Boy, who did not participate, brusquely gathered his papers, walked to the door, and jerked it open.

"So," said Atwater, "we seem to be agreed on the twenty-fourth? Billy," he called to O'Boy's retreating figure, "should we pencil you in as undecided?"

The door banged against the stop as O'Boy marched up the hall.

"Well, he's sold," said Atwater. The others laughed as they stuffed their briefcases.

"I'm sorry," said Laura a few minutes later as she and Matthew emerged from the elevator. Rounding an indoor fountain, they walked through the forested atrium of the office tower that housed Atwater's law firm. "I couldn't help myself. You looked stuck."

"I am stuck," said Matthew, grimly. "But at least you got us out of there." As he ducked under the branch of a ficus tree, he wished he'd brought a machete.

"God, it *was* awful, wasn't it?" said Laura.

"Listening to Billy O'Boy is going to drive me crazy," said Matthew.

"That's a short trip, lover," Laura said, squeezing his arm. She smiled, showing large, straight teeth that lit up her Slavic face. She had thin blond hair that hung straight to her shoulders before turning in fashionably, and her gray eyes were hooded by eyebrows so pale they were barely visible. Her silk blouse, dyed the reddish pink of a rabbit's eye, accentuated the pallor of her skin. *So pretty,* thought Matthew, *but touch her anywhere and you leave a mark.* Seized by a sudden flare of affection, he smiled back at her.

"See you Friday night?" he asked.

"I'm looking forward to it," she replied.

They said good-bye at the door without touching.

Walking into the bitter wind, Matthew trudged the two blocks back to Fort Point Towers, the office complex where Daphnis & Clooney leased three floors of office space. The complex comprised four separate towers of wildly differing heights and shapes—a rectangular tower that shot up fifty stories alongside a squat tubular structure with a conical copper roof, and an octagonal tower of medium height abutting a shorter gabled one—all shoved together in a flamboyant jumble of architectural styles. Built in the developers' heyday of the mid-1980s, the structures were finished with pink granite panels and fake Palladian windows that looked painted on like the ersatz shutters of a Ligurian villa. Security guards, caparisoned in uniforms right off the Love Boat, roamed a vast, marble-columned lobby that wanted only Samson in chains and Cecil B. deMille to achieve its full potential.

Fort Point Towers was the brainchild of an internationally renowned architect who had once brushed it off, during an after-dinner speech, as "a postmodern trifle that should have been built in Houston." Perhaps inevitably, it was known ever after as the Trifle Tower, but it was still high-end office space, commanding almost forty dollars a square foot in a soft market.

As Matthew stepped off the elevator on the thirty-ninth floor of the cylindrical tower, he felt the familiar thinness of the hardwood flooring under his feet. The lawyers charged with overseeing the build-out of Daphnis & Clooney's space had chosen a lavish Brazilian hardwood for the floors. The wood proved so extravagantly expensive they had had to economize by cutting back on the thickness of the flooring. It looked beautiful, with its burnished, variegated browns, but underfoot it felt and sounded downright tacky. The law firm responded by forbidding the wearing of high heels (not by clients, of course, who could wear cleats if it struck their fancy). Then the firm bought bales of Oriental rugs—showy Isfahans, subdued Masheds, coarsely woven Bokharas—to scatter about the common areas and in partners' offices, all to muffle the hollow-sounding rap of leather heels on the flimsy flooring. This did the trick, but only if you hopped from carpet to carpet.

Matthew stopped briefly at his secretary's cubicle to gather the small pile of pink message slips that awaited him. As usual, Sally was nowhere to be found. He flipped through the messages as he entered his office. Call Rowell Falk. A flicker of fear. Got to finish that settlement agreement. See Fleishman first thing in the morning. Should have taken notes during that plumber's deposition. Call Nachman Weiss. Urgent. Oh, Christ, not Weiss. Three messages to call Danny. Who? No last name, just a number. Teitelbaum had to cancel for dinner. Shit. Annual performance evaluation set for Thursday afternoon. Terror. Nausea.

Matthew shut his office door, sat down at his desk, and directed his attention to the slips fanned out in his hand. Determined to stick to his latest stress-reducing regimen, he stacked the slips in descending order of probable unpleasantness. Then, breathing deeply, he picked up the top one and called Falk's extension. Voice mail. Relieved, Matthew left his message, pushed the disconnect, and tossed the slip.

Taking another deep breath, he picked up Weiss's message and dialed. Known as Miami Weiss to his detractors (and their number was legion) because he was seldom in the state during the winter months, Nachman Weiss was the lawyer on the other side of a messy contract dispute. Mindlessly disputatious at every turn, Miami Weiss was the most disagreeable lawyer Matthew knew. So far, he reminded himself.

"Weiss here," said Weiss.

"Nachman," said Matthew. "This is Matt Boer returning your call."

"Thank you. Look. I don't want to fight about this," said Weiss brusquely, "but I will if I have to." Matthew closed his eyes and waited. "I want your assent to postpone the hearing on my motion for summary judgment. I have to be in Coral Gables next Tuesday for a client who—"

"That's OK with me, Nachman," Matthew interrupted, relieved that it was just a scheduling issue. In truth, Matthew had never met a continuance he didn't like. "When do you want to reschedule?"

Weiss fell silent. Two seconds. Three. Then, suspicion seeping into his voice, he asked, "Why are you agreeing to this?"

"What?"

"You heard me. Why are you agreeing to this?"

"I don't know. You asked. I got no problem with it."

"Don't get evasive with me," said Weiss, his voice a hiss. "I demand to know why you're agreeing to this."

Matthew felt the back of his neck flush in anger. OK, he thought. "I'm not telling you, Nachman." Snotty.

"You smartass bastard," said Weiss. "You think you and your fancy firm can push me around? Well, you've got another think coming. I'm calling the clerk to make sure we're on for Tuesday. And if you're not there, I'll have your ass!" He hung up.

Matthew stared at the phone in wonder. Jesus, he thought. The ultimate litigator. Someone who won't take yes for an answer.

He picked up another slip and dialed again. "Is there a Danny there? This is Matthew Boer returning his call."

"Matt? Matt, it's me, Danny. Danny Li. You remember?"

"Oh, yes. Of course," said Matthew, warily leaning back in his chair. "Sorry. There was no last name on the message. How have you been? I haven't heard from you in—"

"Matt, listen. I'm in the shit. You gotta help me. You know that cop, the one that got shot? I'm in it, man. Deep. They will be looking for me. I gotta talk to you. Listen, OK?"

Matthew was listening. And way in over his head.

# 2

---

## IT

Sarah Kerlinsky had wanted to be a lawyer from the time she was nine years old. She could trace it to the evening her father, vanquished once again by her relentless arguments at the dinner table, had turned toward Uncle Solwyn, rolled his eyes to the ceiling, and said with mock weariness, "My daughter, the lawyer." Uncle Solwyn laughed at his brother's spin on an old joke, but for the first time she learned there was a name for what she wanted to do, and she had never looked back. As she sat waiting to be called in the Superior Court for Suffolk County, it struck her that all of her professional life since then had been but a preparation for this, the biggest case of her life.

And no doubt about it, the defense of Michael Chin was a big one. Bigger, she suspected, than any Massachusetts murder case to come along in the almost twenty years she had been practicing law. When she put it that way she felt a tiny needle of doubt. Was she up to it? A moment's further reflection told her she was.

Sarah had grown up in Lawrence, Massachusetts, a large industrial community some fifty miles north of Boston.

Lawrence had been sinking economically and socially all her life. Everything about it looked worn and tired and grimy. Beirut with bad schools, her uncle called it. Her father was a high school history teacher who had never wavered in his fidelity to the leftist politics he had absorbed growing up on the Lower East Side of New York during the Great Depression. This devotion had not been easy; Norman Thomas and causes like socialism and unilateral disarmament were greeted with ugly suspicion and hostility in his community. But Simon Kerlinsky had cradled the guttering candle of his faith, defending it, often without hope but unflaggingly nevertheless, against all comers in the faculty lounge. Not to mention the hooting derision of his brother Solwyn, a successful businessman who made a handsome living by trading in used office furniture.

Uncle Solwyn, God bless him, took his brother's wry remark and Sarah's aspirations seriously. Childless himself, he stepped in to do what his brother could not. He saw to it that Sarah had the wherewithal to attend Brandeis and Harvard Law School. This, of course, left the brothers to debate whether Sarah would go to work for one of the big Boston law firms (the running dogs of the corporations, Simon called them) or pour that fancy education down the drain by joining the National Lawyers Guild to give aid and comfort to Simon's goofy left-wing causes.

Sarah disappointed them both by announcing she was interested only in criminal defense. Defending those accused of crimes, she insisted, would allow her to practice constitutional law on a daily basis, with the odds stacked against her, and that was what she wanted to do.

The brothers were speechless. But not for long.

"Like Edward Bennett Williams!" cried Uncle Solwyn, the first to recover. "The man's made a fortune in criminal law. Look at the law firm he's built for himself. He even owns a baseball team!"

"She should help him defend Republican mobsters like Hoffa?" said Simon incredulously. "People that sold out the labor movement to hoods? Why don't you just tell her to go help Nixon fight his impeachment? Not my girl." Turning to Sarah, Simon softened his voice. "Sarah, listen. We'll call your cousin David. He has a friend in the Movement who knows William Kunstler. What he did for the Chicago Seven—"

"Kunstler!" It was Uncle Solwyn's turn to wax apoplectic. "That hooligan! For such a radical I hocked my business?"

"At least he's a criminal lawyer with a social conscience," said Simon. "Not Mr. Hired Gun for the big shots."

But Sarah disappointed them both again. She took a job in Boston working for next to nothing at a small general practice firm known as Beckman & O'Reilly. The firm was owned by two women whose own law school credentials paled next to hers. Sarah liked their practice and their politics and being part of an all-woman law firm.

When she wasn't handling tasks for her employers, Sarah had hung around the district courts of Suffolk County, where she cadged appointments to defend indigents against misdemeanor charges. She soon made the jump to major crimes in the Superior Court and gradually built her reputation as a tough, tenacious, and, above all, thorough trial lawyer.

Then, in the early 1980s, she defended a young woman named Michele LeDoux, who had shot her longtime boyfriend in the head as he lay sleeping beside her in a drunken stupor. Sarah amassed evidence that the boyfriend had abused her horribly for years, and she called experts to testify that the woman's judgment was impaired by post-traumatic-stress syndrome. The prosecutor ridiculed her defense, but the jury bought enough of it to reject first-degree murder in favor of manslaughter. By then a cause célèbre in feminist circles, Michele LeDoux served only two years before Governor Dukakis pardoned her. And Sarah Kerlinsky had made her bones as a figure to be reckoned with in the criminal defense bar.

"Commonwealth versus Chin, et al.," cried the clerk, and Sarah jerked to attention. "Third call. Are counsel present?"

"The Commonwealth is ready," said Jeremiah DeMarco. The chief of the Homicide Division for the Office of the District Attorney for Suffolk County pushed aside the wooden gate in the rail and stepped into the inner sanctum of the courtroom. Dumping an accordion binder of documents on the table to his right, he sat down. As he was arranging papers, he looked up and watched as Sarah strode purposefully to the defense table on his left. She smiled to the clerk and sat down. From the lockup the bailiffs led four manacled Asian men, who shuffled to their seats in the jury box.

The clerk raised her head and peered about the courtroom. "And Mr. Morrissey?" she asked. The room was silent as lawyers and reporters turned to scan the room. The clerk shook her gray head and handed a file up to the Honorable Robert Corrigan Doyle.

As the judge opened the file, the clerk intoned, "The next matter is Commonwealth versus Michael Chin, et al., Your Honor. Number nine-five-one-three-four-two. Appearing for the Commonwealth is First Assistant District Attorney Jeremiah DeMarco. Appearing for defendant Michael Chin is Sarah Kerlinsky. Appearing for defendants Lai Huong, Warren Liu, and Dai Cheng—"

Suddenly the rear door to the courtroom banged open and a chubby man in a rumpled chocolate-brown suit hurried up the aisle, crossed the bar, and lifted his battered briefcase up onto the defense table beside Sarah. Scowling over his half-glasses, Judge Doyle had watched his approach.

"Is James Morrissey," the judge finished for the clerk. "That will be fifty dollars, Mr. Morrissey," he said, looking down once again at the file in front of him.

Morrissey stood up quickly. "I beg your pardon, Your Honor?"

"I said that will be fifty dollars. You missed the first two calls of the list and you were late for the third. I'm fining you fifty dollars for tardiness."

"I apologize, Your Honor," said Morrissey, his tone measured, "but with all due respect, I was not late. I had a change of plea on another matter over in the Dorchester District Court, and I so informed the clerk."

With an inquiring air, Judge Doyle leaned over theatrically in the direction of his clerk. She shook her head.

"I left my secretary with instructions to inform the clerk, Your Honor," said Morrissey, sounding defensive.

"Late," said the judge, shaking his head. Sarah saw that he was enjoying himself now. The presence of reporters in the courtroom had not escaped him. "No notice to the court or counsel. And you know a district court matter does not trump a commitment in this court. Fifty dollars, Mr. Morrissey."

Morrissey lost it. "What?" he cried. "That's outrageous! Listen, I remember, Judge. I remember back when you were only part-time on the bench and you used to recess from ten-thirty to one o'clock, making everybody wait, 'cause you were over in the registry doing real estate closings. And you have the nerve to fine *me* for being late?"

Doyle's eyes narrowed, the fun gone out of them. "You're up to seventy-five dollars, Mr. Morrissey."

Morrissey glared back. Then he reached into his pocket and whisked out a handful of bills. Ostentatiously, he thumbed through them in the hushed courtroom. As he neared the end of his count, he said without looking up, "Tell me when I get to a hundred."

"You just did."

"Fine," Morrissey snapped. He stomped up to the bench and thrust a fistful of bills at the embarrassed clerk. Then, turning his back on the court, he strode to his place at the table. He sat down beside Sarah again.

"Now, Ms. Kerlinsky," said the judge, settling back in his chair. "I believe you have a motion?"

She smiled shyly as she rose. "I do, Your Honor, but I had hoped to find you more charitably disposed to the defense. I trust I won't get fined if you deny my motion."

The courtroom went dead quiet again as Judge Doyle stared at her in something akin to disbelief. She held on grimly to her smile, gambling. Then a huge grin broke across Doyle's face and he threw back his head and laughed. Sarah let out her breath. The other lawyers laughed along with him, partly out of relief, partly in admiration for Sarah's cheek, but mostly from habit after years of toadying to men in black robes. Only Morrissey was unsmiling.

"Let's get on with it," said Judge Doyle.

Sarah cleared her throat. "Your Honor is no doubt aware of the tragedy that brings us before you. On the evening of February 7th, Detective Francis Dunleavy was killed by two gunshots fired through the locked door of an apartment in

Chinatown while he was attempting to execute a warrant to search for illegal drugs. That warrant was issued on an application sworn by Detective Lieutenant Raymond Carvalho. Carvalho's affidavit is based on information he received from a confidential informant. My motion is to compel disclosure of the identity of the informant.

"The reasons for disclosure are straightforward and compelling. The Commonwealth claims the shots were fired by my client, Michael Chin. But no one saw the shooter. By the time police officers had forced their way into the apartment, it was empty. Their search eventually led them down the fire escape and into the second-floor apartment immediately below the room from which the shots were fired. There they found four men and a pistol under a mattress."

"Must have been pretty crowded under there," said Doyle, grinning in the direction of the reporters.

"Apparently not as much as my syntax, Your Honor," Sarah said, a deferential smile flitting across her face. Then she banished the smile and went on. "The Commonwealth contends the fatal shots were fired from the pistol. All four men were arrested and charged with various offenses, including the murder of Detective Dunleavy. One of them is my client, Michael Chin.

"Now, it is my understanding that the Commonwealth intends, perhaps even today"—Sarah looked over at De-Marco—"to dismiss the charges against the other three defendants in exchange for their cooperation. 'Cooperation,' Your Honor, means giving testimony that my client was alone in the apartment when the shooting took place and that he then ran into the room below with the gun, as they testified at the probable cause hearing in February.

"Now, these three gentlemen, Your Honor—well, let's just say that there is nothing in their criminal records that bolsters their reputations for truth and veracity."

"I can imagine," said Judge Doyle, with exaggerated weariness. "But that doesn't give you the right to endanger confidential police informants."

"No, it doesn't, Your Honor," Sarah continued. "And if we were just concerned with charges of drug dealing, you would be right to deny my motion. But this is not a suppression hearing to determine whether the police had probable cause to secure the search warrant. This is a murder case now, and the informant's testimony will be critical to my defense at trial. Under the cases cited in my papers, the informant's right to anonymity must give way if his evidence is relevant to my client's defense. And the informant's evidence is more than relevant. It is crucial. If I may, Your Honor . . ."

Sarah reached down and retrieved a paper from the table. "Let me direct Your Honor's attention to Detective Carvalho's affidavit. You should have a copy attached to my motion."

Judge Doyle flipped through the documents before him. "Yes," he said after a few seconds.

"Detective Carvalho, as you can see, sought a warrant to search apartment number four on the third floor of sixteen Tyler Street. In his application he swears to have received information from, and I quote, 'a reliable informant' referred to as 'IT' in the affidavit."

She pronounced it "eye tee."

"Carvalho establishes his informant's reliability by listing two other cases in which his information was useful. Now, Carvalho says, IT reported that he had been in the apartment two days before the shooting. The affidavit refers to the apartment as the home of one John, 'a CH-slash-M'—which I take it stands for 'Chinese male,' since the officer later tells us John is of 'Chinese extraction.' He is further described as thin, about five feet eleven inches in height, and in his late thirties. Detective Carvalho relates that the informant said he had seen John packaging cocaine in Massachusetts lottery receipts. IT also told Carvalho that John had rebuilt the door to the apartment 'making it an extremely heavy door to break down,' and that John sold cocaine through a hole in the door without opening it."

Sarah paused, placed the paper back on the table, and turned toward the jury box to her left, where the four prisoners were seated. "Stand up please, Michael." One of the prisoners stood.

"You see my client before you, Your Honor. Now, I grant you he is of 'Chinese extraction,' to use the officer's infelicitous phrase. But, as you can see, he does not fit the informant's description of the occupant of the apartment—this John—in any other way. Mr. Chin is not thin. He is barely five feet tall, not five eleven. And he is only twenty-six years old. He is not John.

"So where is John, Your Honor? Is he one of these other defendants, none of whom is named John? Extremely doubtful. I would venture that none of them is even close to five eleven."

"What good does John do you?" interrupted the judge. "Do you intend to portray him as the shooter?"

"Oh, I don't want John, Your Honor," Sarah answered. "I want IT. He possesses material and exculpatory information. Remember, no one saw my client in the apartment from which the shots were fired. In fact, nobody saw *anyone* in the apartment on the day of the shooting. The Commonwealth's theory of prosecution at the probable cause hearing was that Mr. Chin was the *only* person who lived in the apartment and sold drugs from it, and the only person who was in it when Dunleavy was shot. At the probable cause hearing, all three of the Commonwealth's key witnesses were adamant that Mr. Chin, and only Mr. Chin, had been dealing out of the apartment for the last two weeks before the shooting.

"But IT's statements contradict, categorically, the testimony given by the Commonwealth's witnesses. IT can testify that someone—someone who obviously was not my client—had actually been living in that apartment and was there two days before the shooting. IT's testimony would be very harmful to the Commonwealth's case. Because it tends to impeach the testimony of key prosecution witnesses, his testimony is clearly exculpatory. And that testimony is backed by Detective Carvalho, who has vouched for IT's credibility and reliability. IT is vital to my client's defense. I ask for an order compelling the Commonwealth to disclose IT's identity."

As Sarah sat down, Judge Doyle swiveled his chair slightly to his left. "Mr. DeMarco?" he asked.

She watched Jeremiah DeMarco rise and button his suit coat with his right hand. DeMarco cut a commanding figure in the courtroom. Six feet three inches tall, he was still at his playing weight when, some twenty years earlier, he had been an all-Big East tight end for Boston College. He stood with his powerful legs slightly apart, his chest filling his corduroy jacket. He glanced briefly at Sarah and then looked directly at the judge.

"I think Your Honor put your finger on the critical issue when you mentioned the dangers implicit in Ms. Kerlinsky's motion. This is a murder case. And a particularly vicious one. She's been paging disrespectfully through the sworn affidavit of Detective Carvalho, a highly respected police officer whose partner and best friend bled to death in his arms. And why? Because Michael Chin chose to shoot a policeman through a door rather than face arrest for drug trafficking. What is such a person likely to do when charged with first-degree murder, especially to the informant who ratted him out in the first place?"

Sarah shot up. Furious, she said sharply, "My client has been denied bail, Your Honor. He has been convicted of no crime. He is an immigrant with no history of violence. In fact, his record is cleaner than any of his accusers'. It is odious to insinuate that Mr. Chin is somehow a threat to anybody's safety."

"Not necessarily Mr. Chin personally, Your Honor," said DeMarco, backing off somewhat. "Mr. Chin was not alone in all this. As Your Honor will appreciate, no business of this nature gets carried out in Chinatown without approval from higher-ups in the criminal world. This little vending machine for cocaine addicts was obviously just one dealership in a larger chain of illegal enterprises. So even if Mr. Chin were a low-level retailer and completely innocent of the murder charges against him, an informant stripped of his anonymity would be in grave danger from Mr. Chin's superiors."

"Perhaps," interrupted the judge, "but that's why he has police protection. If his testimony is as critical as Sar—Ms. Kerlinsky says, she's entitled to the disclosure."

"Its usefulness is marginal at best, Your Honor," said DeMarco. "I don't need to remind Your Honor that drug dealers selling out of an apartment often use an adjacent

apartment for their backroom operations. As a place to secure
their cash and inventory away from the retail activities in the
first apartment, in case it gets raided or robbed. Here, obviously, the backroom operation was set up in the apartment
immediately below the one the officers raided. Traffic between the two was via the fire escape. And the lower apartment was where the other defendants were situated when
they saw Chin burst in carrying the gun he used to kill Detective Dunleavy.

"Now, if Ms. Kerlinsky wants to attack their credibility in
this respect, she doesn't need IT. She has the affidavit. She
can use it to argue to the jury that someone else—this John,
presumably—was in the room and could have fired the shots.
She has all she needs to impeach their testimony. And to
whatever extent a live witness might be more useful to her
than the affidavit, well, that is more than outweighed by the
personal risk to the informant and by the chilling effect it
would have on the flow of information to the police. I fail
to see how IT's testimony can be considered 'crucial' to her
defense.

"But there's another, more serious flaw in the logic by
which Ms. Kerlinsky deems IT so 'vital.' John obviously
wasn't on the scene at the time of the shooting. I don't see
anywhere in her affidavit a suggestion that John is invisible.
So why wasn't he arrested with the other defendants? This
is smoke, Your Honor. I urge you to deny the motion."

Judge Doyle turned toward the defense table. "What do
you say to that, Ms. Kerlinsky?" he asked. "How could John
have been there when the shooting took place?"

Sarah stood. "Well, let me say first that I'm gratified the
Commonwealth has conceded the admissibility of the affidavit." She smiled at DeMarco. "But it's not enough. This
is my case and I'd like to try it my way, not the district
attorney's.

"Second, it is anything but 'obvious' that John was not
present when the shooting took place. According to the police report there were four officers on the scene. Detectives
Carvalho and Piscatello were at the door of the third-story
apartment where Detective Dunleavy was killed. The fourth
officer, Detective Kelleher, was outside in the alley, watching

the rear door of the building and the fire escape. In his state-ment Kelleher indicated that he heard someone come partway down the fire escape. He didn't *see* anyone. The police in-ferred, logically enough, that the person Kelleher heard en-tered the second-story apartment through the window from the fire escape.

"But that means no one was watching the front of the building, Your Honor. And no one was watching the door of the second-story apartment. According to the police re-port, the arresting officers did not get to the second-story apartment until several minutes after the shooting. In the meantime, anyone in that apartment—including John—could have simply walked out the door, down the stairs, and stepped into the street. He could have disappeared before the police finished breaking through the door and followed the killer's path down the fire escape. There is a real possibility that a fifth person, matching the description of John found in Detective Carvalho's affidavit, did the shooting and walked away."

"Your Honor, if I may respond," interrupted DeMarco. "This business about John running through the room and out the door is nothing but speculation. I've got three witnesses who say it never happened. And that there was no John pres-ent on the day of the shooting."

"Yes, I know," Sarah interjected, with some asperity. "The three codefendants. I heard them at the probable cause hear-ing."

"She's got a point," DeMarco conceded. "They're not ex-actly nuns, I admit. But what has she offered against them? Aside from rank speculation, that is. She has the burden of demonstrating a need to know the informant's identity. IT's testimony that John was there the day before doesn't prove he was there the day of the killing. Now, if Mr. Chin wants to take the stand and tell us that John *was* in the room . . ." DeMarco trailed off with a smile in Sarah's direction. "Well, the Commonwealth would welcome an opportunity to test his veracity on the matter."

Sarah felt her anger rise again. "Mr. DeMarco knows my client is not going to waive his Fifth Amendment rights by taking the stand. This is ridiculous. And my position is based on much more than speculation. At the time the arrests were made, the police swabbed the hands of all four defendants—including Mr. Chin—to detect traces of gunpowder. The tests all proved negative. Now, I see Mr. DeMarco is about to protest, no doubt by claiming that gunpowder residue tests are often inconclusive. Let me save him the trouble. I agree with him. I only wish he would voice such skepticism when they come out the other way. The point remains that the negative test results lend considerable force to other evidence suggesting that the killer need not have been among those arrested at the scene.

"But let's return to the point, Your Honor. We're getting pretty far afield here. After all, viewing John as the shooter is a bit of a red herring. I've shown that he's a possibility, and so are any of the other three men arrested on the scene. But I don't need that possibility to justify the order I seek. I repeat: IT's statements flatly contradict the testimony of the Commonwealth's three key witnesses. They say Chin was the only one working out of the apartment. IT says otherwise. That makes him the only witness who can directly impeach their testimony. And unlike the Commonwealth's witnesses, he's a disinterested third party whose veracity has already been vouched for by a police detective. Therefore, under the relevant case law, his testimony constitutes material and clearly exculpatory evidence that outweighs the need to preserve his anonymity."

She leaned forward toward the judge. "Your honor, IT's testimony is the best, the *strongest,* evidence by which I can attack the prosecution's case that Mr. Chin was the shooter. Any trial without him would not be a fair trial."

Judge Doyle watched abstractly as Sarah took her seat. "Mr. DeMarco," he said at last, "is there some reason you can't reveal the informant's identity in private, just to Ms. Kerlinsky? I have to tell you, while I haven't read the papers yet, she seems to have the more compelling case."

"Your Honor," said DeMarco, "I have the greatest respect for Ms. Kerlinsky's discretion. But given the publicity surrounding this case, the risk of a leak to the media would be too great at this stage. At the very least, her motion is premature. If it is to be allowed, it should be done closer to trial, in order to minimize the potential for disclosure."

Judge Doyle sighed. "I'll take it under advisement. Anything else?"

"Yes," said Morrissey, rising. Sarah noticed that he waited a few seconds for the absence of the customary honorific to sink in. Judge Doyle gave him a look to curdle milk as he continued. "Defendants Huong, Cheng, and Liu move to dismiss all charges against them. The Commonwealth has assented to the motion."

"That's right, Your Honor," DeMarco added. "In exchange for their cooperation."

"Is this a dismissal with prejudice?" Although he did not shift his gaze from Morrissey, the judge's question was addressed to DeMarco.

"No, Your Honor," said DeMarco. "The Commonwealth has made certain promises, but it wants to see how cooperative these defendants are before dismissing the charges forever."

"I'll allow the motion. The charges are dismissed."

Sarah was on her feet again. "I trust, Your Honor," she said, "that the Commonwealth will disclose all the details of these promises?"

DeMarco flushed visibly. "Of course we will make the proper disclosures, Your Honor. I resent counsel's insinuation that we would not."

"Enough," said Doyle. "Next case, Margaret."

# 3

## Curse the Darkness

The walk from the Drug Control Unit to Homicide wasn't a long one—just straight down two flights of stairs—but Raymond Carvalho needed a rest along the way. He left the stairwell one floor above Homicide and ducked into the men's room.

There was only one other occupant, a uniform Carvalho had seen around but didn't know. Feet apart, he was combing his hair in front of the mirror with both hands. Carvalho nodded to him and proceeded to a urinal. He made a show of unzipping his fly and, supporting himself with his left hand flat against the wall, he leaned into the urinal and waited.

When the other man left, Carvalho zipped up and walked over to the sink and turned on the tap. Stiffly, he leaned over the sink, bending with his back as much as possible and doing his best not to move his neck at all. He filled his open hands with the cold water and brought them up to his face. He doused himself several times and then straightened up and stared bleakly at his dripping reflection as he groped for the paper towels with his right hand.

"Jesus. Fucking. Christ." Carvalho's voice rang off the grimy plastered walls. The bags under his eyes were almost purple and he swore he could see, actually *see,* the skin over his temples vibrate like a drumhead from the throbbing inside them. He wiped his face with a paper towel, then another, stiffening as the pain shot through his neck when he accidentally flexed it.

Carvalho remembered little from the night before, and a fat nothing of what had happened between one in the morning, when he left the County Cork, and five-thirty, when a rap on his window had jerked him out of a dreamless sleep. Lifting his head from the steering wheel, he had opened his eyes and blinked into the glare of a state trooper's flashlight: *Think,* he thought, as he rolled down the window.

"What the hell are you doing?" asked the trooper. He couldn't have been over twenty-five. Clean-shaven. Neatly creased trousers. A tightass.

"Detective Lieutenant Carvalho," Carvalho said, marshaling a smile. "Boston PD." He pulled his badge from his coat pocket and handed it to the trooper. The trooper held the badge under his flashlight and then looked up in puzzlement at Carvalho. Too young and stupid, thought Carvalho. Never heard of professional courtesy.

Try candor.

"The truth is," Carvalho said, "I had a couple bumps more than I meant to last night. I'm driving home when I realize this, 'cause I'm getting too sleepy to drive, you know? So I figured the best thing to do was to sleep it off." Grinning (sheepishly, he hoped), he raised his eyebrows and shoulders in a half-shrug. He waited.

"Is that right," said the kid. It wasn't a question. "Well, next time you might pull off the road first."

Carvalho looked out his windshield and saw that he could sight right through the hood ornament and pick up the broken white centerline of the road.

Sweet Jesus.

"Wait a minute," said the trooper. "Carvalho . . ." He paused, light dawning on Marblehead. "Aren't you the guy whose partner went down in that Chinatown bust?"

Ah. So it's solidarity, then. Carvalho nodded sadly, dropping his eyes. Five minutes later he was on his way.

So Carvalho's day had started. Dealing with tightass schmucks with his neck aching. Well, not his neck so much as the muscles just above it on the back of his head. Every time he was stupid enough to move his neck they sent pain streaming up the sides of his head to flood his throbbing temples. And that was just the crick from sleeping hunched over the steering wheel. The crick's confederate, the hangover itself, was methodically chiseling out the bone behind his left eye, apparently in an effort to gouge out and enlarge the socket. It felt like it was succeeding.

Carvalho left the men's room and went down the stairs and on into Homicide. The squad room was quieter than Drug Control, no sniveling junkies or screaming crackheads, just phones ringing and cops talking into them. The quiet life, thought Carvalho. He walked to the far end of the squad room to a corner office with pebbled glass walls. The door was open.

"Captain?" he said from the threshold.

Seated behind a battered metal desk, Captain Kieran Joyce had a telephone receiver wedged between his chin and right clavicle as he scribbled on a notepad. He looked up and pointed first to the door, then to a chair in front of his desk. Carvalho shut the door and sat down.

"Uh-huh," said Joyce into the phone. "Yeah. OK. I got it." Then he listened in silence for a time. Carvalho wanted a cigarette, but he was afraid his hand would shake.

In his midforties, Joyce was built like a linebacker, though his big frame was broadened through the middle by years behind a desk. Joyce had flat brown eyes that squinted out of narrow slits cut into an Irish pudding of a face, white and puffy beneath a stack of hair whose pitch-black color fooled no one. He was chewing gum.

Carvalho looked around the room at the photographs arrayed on the walls. Joyce with Mayor White. Joyce with Mayor Flynn. With Congressman Kennedy. With the Senate president. With Jackie Crimmins, the Suffolk County DA. Gotta hand it to him, the guy got around. No wonder Joyce had made division chief. Carvalho remembered how, three, maybe four years earlier, there had been a major upheaval in the department over who would become the new chief of Homicide, Joyce or a black dude named Meggitt. Meggitt had departmental citations and a lot of support on the city council. Joyce had his connections going for him, especially with Crimmins, and a lifelong friendship with the commissioner. The appointment quickly took on the character of a political campaign in the grand Boston manner, marked by racial innuendo, ethnic rivalries, and old grudges. When the mud settled, Joyce had won by a snout.

Joyce hung up the phone, clasped his hands behind his head, and leaned back in his chair. "That was DeMarco," he said. Cocking his head to one side, Joyce seemed to take in Carvalho for the first time. "Are you gonna open that eye?" he asked.

"What?"

"Your left eye. It's closed. Almost, anyway. You look like buzzard puke. What gives?"

"Nothing. Just a headache. I'll live. What does DeMarco want now?"

"Listen, Ray." Joyce leaned forward and put his hamlike arms on the desk. "I know Frannie was your pal and all, but this is no time for you to be laying into the sauce again."

Carvalho opened his mouth to object, but Joyce raised both hands and cut him off. "Hey, don't bother," he said. "I don't wanna hear it. I've seen your personnel file. You were calling in sick too much even before the shooting. The fact is, we're gonna need you at your best if we hope to nail the gook that shot Frannie. The press is gonna be all over you like brown on shit. Maybe you should go back to those meetings. If you're gonna do what you need to do, you gotta be clearheaded and not dragging your knuckles. You understand me?"

"Give me a break, Kieran," Carvalho said harshly. "I don't work for your unit. I work for Gogarty."

"Fuck this line-of-command bullshit, Ray. We're not talking *units* here and who reports to who. The whole department is in this. You wanna keep nursing all the jerk-off gripes between units, fine. But not now. Not on this one. Dunleavy was ours, goddamn it, and he went down. And went down stupid, if you ask me, standing right in front of the door like some asshole rookie. Why the hell weren't you guys wearing Tevlak, anyway?"

"Vests?" Carvalho snorted. "They were *Chinese*, for Christ's sake. When was the last time you heard of slopes shooting it out with cops?"

Joyce just shook his head. "Let me ask you something else. It's bound to come up sometime, so we better clear it up right here. Where did I put your inventory from the bust? Here." He picked up a single sheet of paper and read from it. "Found in upstairs apartment: shell clip from gun, three spent shell casings, small bag of powder, jar of lactose, one attaché case (empty), a set of gram scales. Found in lower apartment: gun, three stacks of old lottery tickets, four bags of powder, two syringes, yadda, yadda. Only four bags? You brought all this down just to seize four little bags of dope?"

"Sometimes the haul is less than you expected. You know that."

"Oh, I know that. I'm just bringing it up 'cause somebody may try to make something of it. Especially in conjunction with an empty briefcase."

Carvalho straightened up in his chair. "Are you inferring we stole the product?"

"I'm not *inferring* anything, Ray. I'm just telling you how it might look to outsiders. Particularly the defense. Do you know who's the lawyer for the shooter? Sarah Kerlinsky. She's replaced Morrissey."

"I know. She was at the probable cause hearing."

"Isn't she the one who ate your lunch for you in the Fallon case? Remember?"

Carvalho remembered. Augie Fallon was a middle-management player for the South Boston mob with a mean streak as wide as Kansas. Carvalho had finally caught him with enough cocaine to ensure conviction and a mandatory minimum at Walpole—until Sarah Kerlinsky moved to suppress the dope. Carvalho could still see her, a tall sharp-looking broad in granny glasses, standing primly behind the defense table in Suffolk Superior and firing off dozens of short questions in the flattest of voices, without a hint of emotion or innuendo. She had pecked him apart like a raven with roadkill, and he hardly felt it. No probable cause; Augie skated.

"What's she want?" Carvalho asked.

Joyce took the gum out of his mouth and threw it into a wastebasket beside his desk. It made a soft ping. "Everything—and yesterday," he answered. "She's been all over your warrant application. She wants the name of your informant and copies of all your buy logs. DeMarco says she's got a right to the logs for sure, and she'll probably win on her motion to get the informant. He's fighting it, though. So you better get the shit together and talk to your snitch. Make sure he's gonna be around."

"I'm not burning my snitch," said Carvalho as he straightened up, his neck suddenly forgotten. "I'm still using him and he'd never live to testify anyway."

Joyce leaned back again and tapped the eraser of his pencil on the desk blotter as he eyed Carvalho through the slits of his eyes. "Ray," he said at last, "there wouldn't be any creative writing in that affidavit, would there?"

"No."

"Listen, I used to work drugs. I know how it works sometimes, Ray. You gotta be straight with me. If this is a Cinderella you better—"

"I told you—"

"Shut up and listen. Now, if it was a Cinderella, and if it was me who signed it—and there was a time when it coulda been, you know what I'm sayin' here?—then I'd be hoping like hell the snitch did not live to testify. 'Cause if he don't exist, I couldn't afford to produce a live informant, being as whoever I found would never stand up in court. And then I'd really have my nuts in the wringer. You with me?"

Carvalho nodded noncommittally.

"So I'd want a dead one," said Joyce. "Lots of scumbags die every day in Boston."

Carvalho frowned. "You're not suggesting—"

"That you kill one?" Joyce laughed out loud. "Oh, Ray, that's rich. Not that we all wouldn't like to now and then. The way I see it, it's better to light up one vandal than to curse the darkness. But no, Ray. I got piles of dead candidates right here." He picked up a handful of file jackets from the left side of his desk and brandished them under Carvalho's nose. Carvalho pulled back instinctively and his neck spasmed. "All I'm saying is, you need a dead snitch, I probably got one. Right out of central casting. This is Homicide, remember. Capeesh?"

Joyce paused. Carvalho didn't answer.

"But, of course, you don't need a dead one 'cause you've got a live one—which you better make sure you can find when the time comes. Meanwhile, Kerlinsky wants your buy logs. DeMarco says get them to him so he can make the production. He doesn't want the judge to think we're dragging our feet making discovery. Now," Joyce said, picking up the phone again, "if you'll toddle off back to your *unit*, I'll attend to mine."

He was dialing before Carvalho was out the door.

Back at his desk in Drug Control, Carvalho washed four aspirin down with a couple gills of Seagram's V.O. from the bottle he kept in the middle drawer. *Think,* he thought.

But nothing came to him but memories. Memories of losses. Of Dunleavy. Of Rosa, his ex-wife, and the flat bitterness in her eyes when she loaded the car to move back to her mother's in New Bedford. Or his son, whom he hadn't seen in seven, eight months now. He thought of his childhood home, the ground-floor apartment of a shabby two-family on Marney Street in East Cambridge. It had been demolished to make way for a Dunkin' Donuts a few years after his father followed his mother into the cheap seats at the cemetery over on the west end of town. His seven brothers and sisters were scattered evenly over the eastern seaboard, as if their careful spacing might ensure that nothing would disturb the benign indifference that allowed them to coexist in peace.

Carvalho hauled himself heavily to his feet and made his way to the evidence room. Its entrance was a set of Dutch doors, the lower half closed. Behind the door sat a middle-aged clerk named Lurleen Daniels, a mountainous black woman given to wearing the reddest lipstick and nail polish Carvalho had ever seen.

"Morning, sweet thing," Carvalho said as he picked up the

clipboard. It lay on a shelf that was screwed onto the lip of the lower half-door.

Lurleen flashed him a smile of vermillion and ivory. "Good morning, Ray." Then she frowned, her brow suddenly home to a cocoa-colored worm that twitched with concern. "How you doing, hon? God, that's rough, about Francis. You OK?"

"I'll make it," he said without looking up from the clipboard. "I need to have a look at the buy logs. The DA wants copies." He scribbled his initials on the board and handed it to her.

"Sure, you'll make it," she said, putting the clipboard back on the shelf and reaching into the top drawer of an old wooden desk behind her. She extracted a heavy, ledgerlike volume and handed it to Carvalho. "But it's still rough."

As he took the book, Carvalho looked hard into her huge brown eyes. They were bottomless pools that seemed to well up with compassion, and for a moment, just a moment, Carvalho considered whether to let himself sink into that sympathy. Then he broke the look and, smiling grimly, thanked her and walked away.

There was no one in the small lunch room, which doubled as a photocopying station, and he was able to copy the relevant pages without interruption. Setting the copies on the lunch table, he opened a bottle of white-out and, leaning over the copies, he painted over all the log entries except those that recorded controlled drug purchases made at 16 Tyler Street. He blew the erasures dry and made six copies of the redacted copies.

As he was slipping the finished product into a manila envelope, he straightened up and caught his reflection looking back at him from the surface of a small mirror near the coffee machine. He locked eyes again, as he had with Lurleen, and stared.

"Ah Jesus, Frannie," he said aloud. "What a fuckin' mess."

# 4

## I Talk, I Die

Danny Li's volatile career as a restaurateur had blown up in his face when his manager, one of the four co-owners of the restaurant, was caught dipping into the till. Danny and his other partners fired the thief, a tiny immigrant from Hong Kong named Mai Sum. Mai Sum responded by suing them all for freezing her out of the small corporation through which the four partners owned the restaurant. Matthew Boer had represented Danny and his partners in the litigation. He took little pride in the work he had done on the case.

Matthew's involvement had begun three years earlier when Ben Fleishman wandered into his office. Fleishman was the firm's star litigator. He was brilliant, sophisticated, a devotee of German opera, which he was known to hum to himself while holed up preparing for trial. When he talked, you could hear semicolons.

At the time, Fleishman was the chairman of the firm's Associates Committee, the body charged with assigning, training, and evaluating Daphnis & Clooney's armada of associates. He had struck Matthew as an odd choice for the position. While capable of great charm and affability, Fleishman was known as a mercurial boss, given to black moods, inexplicable icy snubs, and spectacular tantrums when things didn't go his way. Matthew generally tried to stay out of it.

Fleishman had popped into Matthew's office without warning or knock. He picked up a chair, spun it around, and sat down facing Matthew, his long arms folded across the back of the chair. Matthew stiffened at first, then relaxed when he recalled that he was not currently assigned to any of Fleishman's cases and thus could not be berated for some tardy or shoddy work.

"How's it going?" asked Fleishman, showing his loopy, wolfish smile. "We working you to death yet?" With his thumb and middle finger, he smoothed back his signature eyebrows. Black, bushy, and beetling out a full inch over the base of his massive brow, they were so luxuriant that they knitted together seamlessly above the bridge of his nose.

"Not too bad," said Matthew, "and not quite to death." He smiled back.

"What are you working on? I hope I'm not interrupting."

"No, not at all. I'm doing a brief on this complicated federal jurisdiction issue. Pretty dry, actually." Actually, Matthew thought it was pretty interesting, but he was reticent to confess a fascination for abstruse legal doctrine to a meat-eating trial lawyer like Fleishman.

"Ugh," Fleishman said, recoiling in mock horror. "I guess. Well, I have something that might interest you. Something with a little more bounce." Fleishman smiled and waggled those kudzulike eyebrows. "It's the kind of situation that would benefit from your maturity and judgment."

*Bullshit*, thought Matthew. *He's shopping the case.*

"Might even get you into court," Fleishman said. "You interested?"

Matthew was interested. After almost two years at Daphnis & Clooney, he had yet to stand before a judge or be entrusted with any tasks more exciting than drafting pleadings, doing legal research, or sifting through cartons of business records.

"I don't know much about the case," said Fleishman, "except that it's a corporate freeze-out involving owners of a Chinese restaurant in Waltham. You know the *Donahue* case on shareholders' duties in small corporations?"

"Of course," Matthew lied. He made a mental note to check with Teitelbaum.

"The client—" Fleishman fished in his shirt pocket for a yellow Post-it and consulted it. "The client is named Danny Li. Actually, there are three clients, counting the other two shareholders, but Li seems to be their point man. They've been represented by some guy named Callahan. He defended the first day of Li's deposition. Now he wants a different lawyer. So he went to Lo Fat."

"Low Fat?"

"I kid you not." Fleishman raised his right hand as if taking an oath. "L-O, new word, F-A-T. President of the Chinese Betterment Association and a mover and shaker over in Chinatown. He's also a long-standing client. He referred Li to us. So we'd be doing Lo Fat a favor by helping him out."

"I'm definitely interested," said Matthew.

"Good. Call Li and arrange to get him in here. See what you can find out from Callahan. Also call this, ah, Henry Tun, who represents the plaintiff. Tell him you've just signed on and need some time to get up to speed before resuming the deposition."

Matthew started scribbling.

"And get a transcript of what's taken place so far in the depo. Feel free to ask me for advice as you go along. Meanwhile, I'll open a new case and get you on the books. I'll be the RA."

Fleishman used the argot of the firm's compensation system. Daphnis & Clooney had been one of the first of the major Boston firms to scuttle the old lockstep compensation scheme under which partnership profits were divided almost exclusively on the basis of seniority. The more senior you were, the bigger your cut. When Daphnis, Whitbread & Smith had negotiated its merger with Clooney, Badger, Stone & Parker some twenty-five years earlier, it became necessary to reconsider compensation issues for the newly constituted Daphnis & Clooney. The younger partners demanded a system that adequately rewarded those partners most responsible for the financial success of the firm, namely the rainmakers, who brought in the business, and the drones, who did the work.

The upshot was a compensation system designed to reward contributors to the bottom line. In addition to hours actually spent rendering legal services, credits were awarded for fulfilling certain roles on each case. The attorney who brought the client to the firm was called the OA, or originating attorney, and the one in charge of managing the case was the RA, or responsible attorney. Values were assigned to these categories according a complex formula, and fees collected on a particular case were then allocated in accordance with the formula. At the end of the firm's fiscal year, its powerful Compensation Committee would apply the formula and calculate each partner's split of the profits.

"Let me know if I can be of any help." Fleishman wiggled his brows again, as if promising great fun, and made his exit. Matthew found himself alone in his empty office holding a Post-it with several names and Danny Li's phone number. Maybe it would be fun.

It wasn't. The first thing he discovered, on reading the deposition transcript, was that Danny was lying all over the place. Why, Matthew couldn't tell, but the lies were obvious and self-contradictory. They were equally obvious to Henry Tun, the lawyer who represented Mai Sum. Tun had fed rope to Danny so that he could be trussed up for ultimate slaughter if the matter ever went to trial. So the first question of substance Matthew asked Danny, when they finally met, was why he had been lying.

In his late twenties, Danny Li was a slight man with a wispy goatee and an almost pathologically restless manner. He greeted Matthew with a flaccid handshake and copious thanks, but his eyes were always elsewhere. Taking in the decor of the firm's reception area. Peeking into other offices as he walked down the curving hallway. Checking out the prints in Matthew's packing crate of an office. Even confined to a chair, Danny could not sit still, his legs shifting from knee to knee, his eyes skittering away from Matthew's.

"Lying?" he answered, looking wounded at the suggestion. "Why you think I lie?"

"Well, for one thing, you keep changing your story. Especially about the finances of the restaurant. Something's going on here. If I can detect it just from reading the transcript, what do you think a judge is going do when he sees it? If I'm gonna help you, I need to know the truth."

Danny stopped fidgeting for a moment and actually looked Matthew full in the face. He seemed to consider the problem. "Everything I tell you is secret, yes?" he asked finally.

"Everything," said Matthew firmly. With a glow of satisfaction, he felt the sanctified heft of his oath of office. To hold his clients' confidences inviolate. This was what being a lawyer was all about.

"Yes?"

"Yes. Not even the court can make me tell."

"OK." Danny smiled and started fidgeting again. His hands fluttered like birds before him. "At the restaurant we cheat on taxes. We keep cash. Not report."

This in itself was hardly earth-shattering. But as Danny talked, Matthew was introduced to the mysteries of a systematic, if small-time, tax evasion conspiracy at the Lotus Blossom in suburban Waltham, Massachusetts. It was not confined to the occasional plucking of cash receipts. The Lotus Blossom had an institutionalized system for depriving the state Department of Revenue of its seven-percent bite out of every meal served. Each evening for a prearranged time—say, between eight and nine-thirty—the waiters would put aside their regular pads of sequentially numbered meal checks (Danny called them the number 1 tickets) and write orders on a new pad (the number 2 tickets). These cash receipts were stashed, along with their corresponding number 2 tickets, in a small box behind the bar. The cash box was entrusted to Mai Sum, who, as bartender and manager, did not take dinner orders. If the customer paid by credit card or asked for a receipt, the order was copied over onto a number 1 ticket and the number 2 ticket was thrown away. That way, there were no breaks in the numerical sequence of number 1 tickets, all of which recorded sales that would be reported to the state, and the number 2 tickets provided the owners with records of unreported cash taken in.

But the scheme did not stop with the accumulation of unreported receipts—or even, for that matter, at the doors of the Lotus Blossom. Every Chinese restaurant and supplier operated this way, Danny insisted. For almost every reported expenditure the restaurant made, whether for foodstuffs or equipment, even for wages paid to the waiters and kitchen help, there was a shadow transaction, a cash kicker from the box behind the bar. At the end of the week, the four owners would tally up what was left in the box and split the skim equally among themselves.

Equally, that is, until Mai Sum unilaterally determined that her share was not commensurate with her duties and, through the alchemy of resentment, transmuted some of the cash in the box into a merit bonus for an underappreciated manager. The others became suspicious when the weekly skim totals dropped off, but they could prove nothing. As long as she removed the number 2 tickets corresponding to the amount of cash she pilfered, Mai Sum destroyed the evidence that the restaurant had ever received the cash she stole.

Then Danny, with the soul of a comptroller, figured out how to catch her. He secretly instructed the waiters to give him all the number 2 tickets that would otherwise be discarded if the customer paid by credit card. When these tickets were compared to those in the cash box, there should then be no breaks in the numbering of number 2 tickets. When breaks showed up anyway, the partners knew that Mai Sum was stealing and Danny could prove it.

Except he couldn't. Not in a court of law. Not without revealing the partners' tax fraud. Their intricate scheme for skimming cash required two sets of books, which bespoke a studied intentionality that made jail time highly likely if the Department of Revenue ever learned of the scheme. The public books were handed over to Dennis Callahan, a twenty-seven-year-old storefront lawyer who did the owners' corporate work and prepared their tax returns. The owners kept for themselves a private set (in Chinese), which reflected the complete transactions. What had turned Danny's deposition into a flimsy tissue of perjuries was Callahan's understandable but mistaken belief that the fight was over the numbers in the public books. Both Tun and Danny, the corporation's treasurer, knew otherwise, and even Danny's febrile imagination failed him when he tried to justify the public numbers under questioning by Tun.

Matthew thought to take the news to Fleishman, but he

was on the phone and two other tense associates were loi-
tering outside his office in hopes of an audience. Matthew
walked two doors down to see Teitelbaum instead.

Ira Teitelbaum clapped his hands together and howled
with delight. "Hoo boy!" he said. "Fleishman promised you
fun and you got it!" Grinning, he leaned his three-hundred-
pound hulk back in his chair, which groaned in protest.

Teitelbaum's office was, as usual, an impossible mess.
Files and books were stacked everywhere, and the desk itself
was piled with pink phone slips, manila file folders, loose
papers, Styrofoam cups, and the sinister remains of a sub-
marine sandwich. Tiny yellow Post-its covered the telephone
console and the glass shade of his desk lamp. The only ornament was a bumper sticker taped to the window which
admonished visitors to ESCHEW OBFUSCATION. The walls
were completely bare, and the office otherwise contained no
individuating appointments, unless the squalor alone might
serve to identify its inhabitant.

With his shirttail out and his tie loose and askew, Teitelbaum certainly seemed at home in such an office. His most
salient feature, apart from his gargantuan size, was the thickness of his wire-rimmed glasses, which had the effect of
magnifying his brown eyes to cartoonlike proportions. He
sucked a cold pipe in grudging deference to the smoke-free
environment the firm had recently declared for itself. Which
was just as well, thought Matthew, since Teitelbaum seemed
to accord the firm so little deference in everything else.

Matthew said, "Fun? They could go to jail. And I can't
represent Danny at his deposition when I know he's perjuring
himself. He has to either straighten out the record by admitting he's been lying or I can't represent him. I can't participate in a fraud on the court."

"Oh, it's worse than that," Teitelbaum interjected with relish. "If he purges himself of perjury by correcting the record,
he'll end up exposing all over the deposition transcript that
he's engaged in a criminal conspiracy against the Department
of Revenue. It's a splendid mess. But relax. It'll never come
to that." Teitelbaum beamed a seraphic smile and put his feet
up on the desk, knocking the half-eaten sandwich onto its

side. Mayonnaise oozed out onto a yellow pad and glistened in the sunlight.

"How do you know that?"

"Because everybody's in on it. Even the plaintiff. They could all go down for tax fraud. It's in nobody's interest to let this stuff become public. Tun's just playing a clever game of chicken. His client, as the shareholder of a small corporation, has a right to continued employment in the corporation's business. The courts are very skeptical when a shareholder is fired. Her job is one of the only ways she can recoup her investment. There's not exactly a bustling market for her stock in the—what's the name of the place?"

"The Lotus Blossom."

"Food any good?" Teitelbaum's question seemed to remind him of the sandwich on his desk. He picked it up and examined it with distaste and then dropped it into a wastebasket, staring gloomily after it.

"Who knows? I just met the guy. So she can't sell her stock on the open market."

Ira looked up at Matthew. "Right," he said, focused once again. "So your clients have to show they had a damn good reason to fire her, but your defense—that she's a thief—is one you can't raise. Because what she stole were the proceeds of an illegal transaction. That's what brother Tun's betting, anyway. So here's what you do. You call Tun and tell him your client is going to correct his testimony if the deposition resumes, and that the corrected testimony will implicate both of your clients in a criminal conspiracy. Suggest that the two of you sit down and settle the case instead. But first you have to clear all this with your client. Or clients. They all have to agree before you can proceed."

They did, but Tun would have none of it. His client, he insisted, would deny any involvement in the tax fraud.

"Come on," said Matthew. "She was the manager. She and Danny did the books. No one is going to believe she knew nothing about it. Don't be naive."

"Hey, I'm from Chinatown," said Tun. "I worked my way through Suffolk Law waiting tables in Chinese restaurants. I know how it works. So when that dope Callahan kept showing me his books to prove that her stock in the company wasn't worth what she should get to settle this case, I knew he didn't know the real finances."

"Well, what are you going to do when I take her deposition and she perjures herself?"

"I told you. My client says she knows nothing about skimming and I plan to represent her on that basis. And anyway, right now we're taking *your* client's deposition, not mine."

Matthew could almost hear the smile at the other end of the phone.

So Danny returned to the deposition and proceeded to describe in detail the partners' scheme for cheating on their taxes and how he had caught Mai Sum stealing from the cash box. Tun took careful notes as he questioned Danny. A squat, pock-faced Chinese man with a comfortable paunch, Tun methodically tightened the noose with each incriminating answer. The deposition proceeded painfully in this manner for more than an hour. Then Tun abruptly altered course.

"Mr. Li," he asked, looking up from his notes, "since the date the Lotus Blossom opened for business, have you acquired an ownership interest in any other restaurant?"

Danny looked over at Matthew. "No," Danny answered.

Taking his cue from Danny's look, Matthew said, "I don't see the relevance of this line of inquiry."

"Well," said Tun, "he has admitted to skimming the corporation's cash. My client didn't get it. If it's been drained off somewhere, I have a right to find out where it went." He turned to Danny again. "Have you acquired an ownership interest in any real estate since the Lotus Blossom opened for business?"

Danny looked at Matthew again, then back at Tun. "Can I talk to my lawyer?" he asked.

"No," said Tun.

"Of course he can," said Matthew, standing up. "Off the record," he said to the stenographer. "We'll just step outside for a moment.

"What's going on now, Danny?" Matthew asked when he and Danny stood alone near the elevators in the hallway outside Tun's office suite. Danny was uncharacteristically motionless, his features giving away nothing.

"I will not talk about other restaurants or real estate," he said evenly. "Others are involved."

Matthew frowned.

"I talk, I die," said Danny. "Or Mai Sum die."

Matthew stared stupidly into Danny's blandly expressionless face. After a long pause in which neither spoke, Matthew nodded and led Danny back into Tun's conference room. They sat down.

Matthew nodded to the stenographer. "The record should reflect," he said, "that my client will answer no questions regarding his personal financial situation or about his personal investments outside the Lotus Blossom. The questions are not relevant. They're not reasonably calculated to lead to the discovery of admissible evidence. He won't answer."

"And let the record also reflect," said Tun, angry now, looking toward the stenographer, "that the questions posed are directly relevant to the uses to which the defendants have put cash revenues siphoned off from the corporation. I have the right to trace those funds, wherever they may be now. Therefore, I am suspending this deposition while I seek a ruling from the court ordering Mr. Li to answer my questions. The stenographer is requested to prepare a transcript of today's testimony on an expedited basis so that I may put it before the court."

Tun gathered his papers and pushed back his chair.

"I think we should talk, Henry," Matthew said.

"What's to talk about?" demanded Tun.

"Indulge me, Henry." Matthew stood up. "Danny, why don't you wait for me out in Mr. Tun's waiting room. I'll just be a minute."

Tun settled back in his chair. Matthew closed the door behind Danny and the stenographer. He sat back down.

"We got a problem, Henry," he said. "My client says that if he answers your questions, either he or your client will end up getting killed. Now, I don't have the foggiest notion what that's all about. You probably know better than I do, since you knew to ask the questions in the first place. Whatever. It doesn't matter. I'm not gonna let him testify. You don't want him to testify either. So it doesn't matter what the judge says. He's not gonna testify. We gotta work this thing out."

And they did, eventually. The next morning Tun and Matthew agreed fairly quickly that Danny and the others would buy Mai Sum's stock, but they could not agree on its worth. Matthew defended Danny's cash flow projections for the corporation against Tun's claim that Danny was low-balling him. Danny, Tun insisted, had based his projections on the rather static profits indicated in the public books when the cash box totals indicated the restaurant was experiencing more marked growth. Matthew felt queasy.

"Doesn't it bother you," he asked Tun, "that the two of us are sitting here arguing over who should get what from the spoils of an ongoing tax fraud?"

Tun laughed. "A little," he said, "but what else am I supposed to do?"

"You're right to be bothered," said Teitelbaum later that day. "You've got two officers of the court busying themselves at cutting up the skim. It stinks. It might be OK if the clients agreed to stop skimming cash. At least then you wouldn't be implicated in an ongoing crime. But even then you'd want to be sure they'd quit skimming. *Missouri* sure."

Matthew shook his head in despair. "They're gonna love that," he said. "From what I can tell, the restaurant only makes it into the black because they don't pay all their taxes."

Teitelbaum flashed his grin. "Hey, you wanted to be a lawyer, didn't you? Sometimes you gotta bring 'em the bad news."

About five o'clock that evening, as he drove out to Waltham, Matthew was roiled by guilt and dread. He believed he was, in a sense, about to complete the betrayal of his own clients. Having advised Danny to confess to perjury and tax fraud (under oath, no less), he had left his clients at the mercy of anyone (the stenographer?) who might decide to drop a dime on them. He might even have endangered Danny's life by exposing him to Tun's questions about other business interests—a risk Teitelbaum dismissed as hysteria, but who knew? And now he had to advise them that, after exposing them as he had, he would have to withdraw as their lawyer unless they agreed to start paying all their taxes, a step likely to hasten the financial ruin of the restaurant he had been hired to protect. Some lawyer.

Some restaurant. The Lotus Blossom was the sole occupant of a small, squat, concrete-block building off Moody Street in Waltham. Once a filling station whose windows had been bricked up, the building stood alone in the middle of a pockmarked parking lot. Inside, except for an enormous urn filled with genuine, if wilted, chrysanthemums in the tiny entryway, there was little to distinguish the restaurant from scores of other low-rent Chinese restaurants: lots of red on the walls, Formica tables, a short bar painted black like fake ebony, dragon prints on the walls, and the smell of cooking fat and soy sauce. There were customers at only two of the tables.

When Matthew entered, Danny came out from behind the bar and greeted him effusively.

"Matt," he said, shaking his hand with enthusiasm. "We are waiting for you. What you like, man? Beer? Mixed drink? We have full license."

Matthew took a beer and followed Danny into the kitchen. It was filthy, with vegetable refuse underfoot, the sink piled high with dirty pots. A teenage boy was pulling the skin off the neck of a naked chicken. Sitting around a small table at the back of the kitchen were a man and a woman, whom Danny introduced to Matthew. The woman was folding wontons. This was the first and only time Matthew met his other two clients, Danny's fellow shareholders. They all smiled politely. Matthew quickly forgot their names.

Matthew gravely broached the subject of the restaurant's tax evasion. When he mentioned that the skimming had to stop, Danny interrupted him to say that the partners had already reached the same decision themselves. Henceforth, the restaurant would pay all its taxes. This, Danny said, was necessary if the restaurant was to grow into a successful and respectable business, a goal all the partners shared. The others smiled and nodded their approval as Danny spoke, though Matthew doubted their limited command of English permitted them to comprehend much of what was said.

Relief soaked into Matthew as he listened to Danny. Their

business soon concluded, lawyer and clients turned convivial, and before the evening was over Matthew had downed five or six more beers and a crab Rangoon so vile he would have to warn Teitelbaum. He could still taste it the next morning.

Two days later Mai Sum and her erstwhile partners reached agreement on their own as to the financial terms on which they would sever their joint interests. Matthew and Tun negotiated the wording of the documents that gave effect to the settlement, and the lawsuit was dismissed. The day the settlement documents were signed and a check payable to Mai Sum was delivered to Tun, all copies of Danny's deposition transcript were handed over to Danny. The stenographer, so far as anyone knew, never told a soul.

Danny and his partners made good on Matthew's fee, which they paid off in installments over several months. Matthew never ate at the restaurant again, but he did occasionally drop in for a drink and listen to Danny describe one supposedly surefire—and usually shady—entrepreneurial venture after another. Danny's girlfriend, Julie, joined them sometimes, sipping tea while seeming to ignore the substance of their conversation. Tiny, pretty, and sharp-eyed, Julie had lustrous black hair long enough to graze the curve of her buttocks. But Danny's schemes were lustrous only in contemplation and, like the restaurant itself, they were always empty. Finally, about a year after the case had settled, the Lotus Blossom withered like its chrysanthemums and closed its doors. Matthew assumed his client had moved on to some new, and probably illicit, venture. He heard nothing further from Danny Li.

Nothing, that is, until Danny called, some two years later, to talk about the murder of Francis Dunleavy.

# 5

## The Gobbet

Detective Salvatore Piscatello shoved open the door to the County Cork. A frigid gust of wind swept in ahead of him, and he suffered silently the glares of a foursome who shivered at the table nearest the door. He shut the heavy door behind him and picked his way through the tables toward the bar.

The County Cork, in pointless homage to a drunken epiphany that once called the owner's attention to the pun in its name, actually stocked a couple of red wines that did not come in screw-top bottles. But this was no up-market wine bar, and those fancy clarets macerated unmolested on the top shelf behind the bar. It was the beer and the Jameson and Old Bushmills that moved here, as the County Cork remained the sort of meat-and-potatoes Irish bar that its name more plainly promised the regulars.

Raymond Carvalho sat at the far end of the bar. He had a cigarette in one hand and a bottle of Harp in the other. Across the bar from him stood the bartender, a lean, hard-looking man called Trubs, whose black hair was gathered in a greasy ponytail over his collar. They were both looking up at a television set that was cantilevered out over the entrance to the kitchen. In the foreground of the screen were two talking heads whose remarks could not be heard above the din in the bar. Behind them ran footage of O. J. Simpson at the defense table as he huddled with a sampling of his lawyers.

"He'll walk," said Piscatello as he reached the two men.

"Yeah?" said the bartender. Neither turned around. "What about the DNA? That looks pretty solid."

"Horseshit," said Piscatello. "What about the jury? It's pretty solid, too. Solid black. You just wait. That nigger's gonna walk."

"Guy did it, though."

"Course he *did* it, Trubs. Since when did that matter?"

"It's a waste, then."

"You won't get an argument outa me."

The bartender finally turned away from the screen and faced Piscatello. "You want something, Sal?"

Piscatello grimaced. "Nah. Well, maybe. Gimme a tonic. Diet Coke."

The bartender scooped up ice in a beer glass and filled it from a hose. He let the foam subside, topped off the glass, and set it down on a cocktail napkin in front of Piscatello.

"You know what's really a waste, Trubs?" Carvalho spoke for the first time, his attention still fixed on the screen.

"What's that, Ray."

"It was the wrong guy. I mean, if some football-star-turned-sportscaster has to kill his wife, why couldn't it be Frank Gifford?"

Trubs slapped the bar to punctuate his laughter, and Piscatello went into a coughing fit when he sucked a mouthful of Coke into his nasal cavities. Trubs thumped him on the back and continued to laugh.

"I mean," Carvalho continued, "have you seen her lately? She's beggin' for it. I'm telling you, she's enough to drive you to *Barney*."

Carvalho turned toward the others. He smiled to see them laughing and handed his dead soldier to Trubs, who replaced it with a fresh Harp.

"Oh, Ray," said Piscatello weakly, when his coughing subsided. The fizz had made his eyes water and he dried them with the damp napkin. "It's good to see you getting back some of the old snap. I was starting to worry about you there."

Carvalho abruptly picked up his coat from the adjoining barstool and stood up. He said to Piscatello, "Let's grab the booth back there and talk some business."

"Let me hit the head and I'll be right over," said Piscatello. "Oh, Kathie Lee!" he brayed to no one in particular. Then he laughed again as he ambled toward the men's room in the rear.

Carvalho slid into the booth and took an abstemious sip of the Harp. So Piscatello was worried about him. Well, he'd have to take a number. Worry didn't even begin to describe his own state of mind. It was more like dread, but of what he was unsure.

He had awakened, some twelve hours earlier, to the sound of a strange female voice humming in the shower. He did not know the voice, which was worrisome enough, but his alarm heightened when he failed to recognize the bedroom as well. And his clothes were nowhere to be seen.

Carvalho had lain there for a moment, straining to recall how he had gotten there—wherever he was. He drew a blank. Then the shower stopped running. He jumped out of bed and, wrapping himself in the top sheet, hustled out the bedroom door.

He found himself in a tiny paneled living room, equally unfamiliar. The room was just big enough for a couch, two wicker chairs, a television set, and a coffee table. The table was strewn with women's magazines and an empty bottle of Matteus Rosé. He found his clothes scattered around the table. Hurrying, he started pulling on his pants, stuffing his shorts into his hip pocket.

"Ray, are you up?"

The voice from the bathroom made him jump.

"Yeee!" he answered, as he caught the glans of his penis in the zipper. While he was gingerly freeing himself, he realized he wasn't going to make it out in time. God, who was she? And where the fuck was he, for that matter? He looked around the room for clues. On top of the television was a framed photograph of three laughing young women in colorful ski outfits. Carvalho didn't even know which one it was. He plopped onto the couch.

The magazines.

He flipped over an issue of *Cosmopolitan*. The mailing label identified the subscriber as "A. Beasely"—a fat lot of good that did him—and gave an address in Easton, a town well to the south of Boston. What the hell was he doing in Easton?

Suddenly, she was standing in the doorway, pink and steaming from the shower as she knotted the sash of a baby-blue terry-cloth robe. She was slight and dark, kind of pretty in a timid way, he thought. Damp brown curls clung to cheeks that dimpled as she smiled. "Good morning," she said shyly.

Carvalho spread a broad grin over his turmoil and decided to bluff it out. "Hey, Beasely," he called as airily as he could manage. "How you doin'?"

Her smile evaporated in confusion, which gradually gave way to pain as her eyes brimmed up and her shoulders sagged.

"Aw, shit," said Carvalho.

A tear began to slide down her cheek.

"You got a roommate, don't you?"

She nodded.

"Shit."

"I don't believe this," she said to nobody in particular. "This has got to be a new low."

Carvalho noticed with chagrin that the wine bottle really was empty. Looking away from the woman weeping silently in front of him in the crummy little apartment (her name, it turned out, was Donna Something), Carvalho glimpsed just for a moment a secret and repellent chunk of himself. It was only a fragment, a lump that he had never encountered so clearly before. You couldn't see it head on, but only out of the corner of the eye, like a floater flitting across the edge of your field of vision. Then it was gone, slipped back beneath his view, an unspeakable gobbet bobbing and lolling in the putrid sump of his consciousness.

Then, mysteriously, his self-loathing receded and he was overtaken by an unexpected sadness on her behalf and by the sumptuous softening of a heart long since tanned to shoe leather by liquor and the horrors he had witnessed on the job. He sat with her, held her hand, and told her about the blackouts. He had never told anyone about them before, but he knew no other way to explain himself or to make her feel better. Besides, he knew he would never see her again.

It was not until he was well on his way back to the city that he realized how shaken he was by the whole episode. It wasn't as if these dead spots in his memory were a novel experience. He could recall any number of occasions when, with Dunleavy driving, he had searched for his car by tracing ever-widening circles out from the bar in which he last remembered drinking. Or pretending to recall some drunken escapade his friends taunted him about, even as he worked slyly to winkle out of them the details he needed to maintain the charade. Once a blackout had scared him so bad he had gone off the hard stuff for more than a month. That was the morning he discovered that something—or someone—had stove in the right front quarter panel of his car. For the next two weeks he pored over reports of unsolved hit-and-runs at the department, afraid of what he might find in them. But no deaths surfaced and his dread slowly lifted. Canadian whiskey soon resumed its rightful place in his life.

But this time it was different. He had seen the gobbet, and he was not ready for a personal reckoning with that turdlike piece of himself. He didn't know what it was or what it meant, but it spooked him. All he knew for sure was that it had some connection to the drinking.

So Carvalho backed off. No hard stuff. Just beer. Maybe a little wine with food. He would pace himself. He took another sip of Harp.

"Hey, Ray." It was Piscatello slipping into the booth across from him. "I thought of who else it shoulda been."

"What?" Ray looked up, confused.

"Who killed his wife. Instead of O.J.?" Piscatello was grinning in anticipation. "You ready?"

Ray smiled.

"Ahmad Rashad," said Piscatello expectantly.

Ray frowned.

"You know," Piscatello explained, "he's married to that

ballbuster plays Cosby's wife on TV? Phylicia Rashad."

"The one who's pissed off all the time?" Ray smiled now.

"Yeah. Her."

"Maybe. I'm still with Frank, though."

"Yeah, me, too. I gotta admit you're right." Piscatello gnawed at his lower lip. "So. You working tonight?"

"You could say that. It's about Frannie's case. We got a bit of a problem."

"The way I hear it, it's you who's got a problem. Like no witness. That right?"

"Sort of. I just had a talk with DeMarco. He thinks the judge is going to make us burn the snitch we used to get the warrant. DeMarco suspects we can't produce him."

"Fuckin' lawyers," Piscatello spat bitterly. "First they fuck everything up so we can't do our jobs. For all the pissant rules we gotta look out for. Then they screw you over if you actually get something done."

" 'Ray,' he says to me." Carvalho sucked his manhood into his larynx to mimic DeMarco's baritone. " 'My old man was a cop. I understand these things.' "

"What a jerk," said Piscatello.

" 'If there's a problem with the paper, Ray, I can live with it. I can take the hit.' "

Piscatello snorted. "Big of him."

" 'The case can survive a little bad news—*if* we get it out on the table right away.' "

"Oh, sure," said Piscatello. "Long as it's not *his* dick on the table."

" 'But if the paper's bad, Ray, and you try to bury it, you're gonna poison the well. And you'll hand the defense what they need to put Frannie's killer back on the street.' "

"What did you tell him?"

"I told him the paper was good. I told him I wasn't gonna burn a working snitch. And I expected him to convince the judge to see it our way."

"Damn straight." Piscatello paused and looked at Carvalho. "But what if he can't, Ray?" he asked finally. "What if you got the judge ordering you to burn him?"

"I don't know yet. Joyce keeps dropping hints I should burn a dead one. You know, like make out the snitch is some dead junkie already on the books as an informant."

"I like that. Can't be any shortage of likely candidates."

"It's too risky. Too many dates need to match up just right to make it work. I used my guy a lot. You could never be sure it would hold up. Suppose the dead guy was inside or something at a time I've got him making a buy?"

"I see what you mean," said Piscatello. "It's a bitch."

"Joyce also keeps bugging me about the empty briefcase we found in the apartment. Like he thinks maybe it wasn't empty after all."

The two men looked at one another.

Piscatello said, "Well, we were both there. I know I didn't have no time alone with some briefcase. Did you?"

"No. It's not like we had a lot of time to do anything, with all the screaming and running and getting cuffs on those guys. I just wish Joyce would leave it alone."

The two men were quiet again, thinking. Carvalho finished his Harp.

Then Piscatello said, "I thought it was Frannie had the snitch on this anyway."

"He did. But you know Frannie. Doreen was giving him shit about being away so much. So he calls me up and gives me the details he got from the snitch and asks me to get the warrant. Which I do."

"SOP," said Piscatello. He frowned. "Wait a minute. Then there is a real snitch, right? Just the wrong officer swearing out the warrant?"

Carvalho nodded.

"You know who it is?"

"No. Frannie kept this guy to himself. Probably because it's Chinatown and we maybe got the Tung On in this. Or maybe the snitch made him promise to keep it extra quiet. You know Frannie. That Catholic conscience of his."

"He was a man to keep his word, that's true."

"But even if I did know who it was I wouldn't dare produce him. He'd have the same problems with the dates a dead snitch would have—worse, in fact, 'cause they could cross-examine him and he'd crumble."

"I see what you mean."

"Truth is, if I knew who he was, I'd be out there puttin'

the fear of God in him. Make sure he got his ass out of town till this thing is over with. To Toronto or wherever these people like to go."

They were quiet again. This time it was Carvalho who broke the silence.

"Doreen called me this afternoon."

Piscatello looked up, his eyes wide open. "Jesus. What did she want? How's she holding up?"

"Like an iceberg. And so full of rage you can feel the hum through the phone. She don't come right out and say it, but it's plain she thinks Frannie's death is my fault." Carvalho started peeling the label off his empty. "Like it was me told him he should plop himself smack in front of the fucking door and keep whaling on it. Anyhow, she goes on about how she knows Frannie's best friend won't let anything get in the way of putting his killer away."

"Sounds like DeMarco's been talking to her about the snitch business," said Piscatello.

"Well, duh," said Carvalho with disgust. "Didn't you see her on the tube with Crimmins last night?"

"No."

"And Frannie's brothers? Four of them are cops, you know. It was some show. Crimmins cranking out sound bites about the sacrifice of one of Boston's finest and the need for a governor with the balls to fight crime. And Doreen, standing in front of a wall of suffering Dunleavy menfolk, saying she's confident the entire department will work together to convict the killer." The outer surface of the Harp bottle was stripped clean now. Carvalho looked at the foamy residue in the bottom and set it down.

"They're putting it on you, Ray."

"Trubs!" Carvalho called out irritably. He held up the dead soldier. Then he turned back to Piscatello. "Of course they are," he said. "I can't really blame them, either. So I gotta handle this in a way that won't flush the case and my pension down the toilet."

Carvalho paused and looked at Piscatello.

"Don't stop now, Ray," Piscatello said at last. "Drop the other shoe."

"I need to engineer a hunt for the snitch. It's gotta be well documented, believable. And in the end, unsuccessful. But if I do it alone, they won't believe me. On the other hand, if I got a fellow officer working with me, and coming up empty like me, what can the judge do? Hey, we tried to comply with his order, but the witness obviously got spooked and split. So they'll all just have to do without him."

"And you want me to be the fellow officer?"

"I'll understand if you want out. It could get pretty hot. But I was sort of hoping you would. I figured you wouldn't want Chin to walk any more'n I do."

Piscatello's stomach growled as he looked down at the floor beside the booth. Then he looked up at Carvalho.

"We'd probably have to pull a lot of overtime, wouldn't we?" he asked with a grin. "To do a thorough search and all?"

"It wouldn't surprise me," said Carvalho, smiling back at him. Trubs arrived with a fresh beer.

"Trubs," said Piscatello. He scooched over to put his back to the wall and one leg up on the bench seat. "Bring me a couple of monsterburgers and an order of fries, will you? And a pitcher of Rolling Rock. Looks like Ray and me got some detecting to do."

Carvalho took a healthy hit of the Harp.

# 6

## Irons

Matthew Boer was lucky. He found a well-lighted parking place on Beacon Street right in front of the Cao Palace, where he was to meet Danny. He shut off the Honda and looked around.

He was in Allston, a Boston neighborhood known for its low rents and the transience of its inhabitants. One of the few fully integrated neighborhoods in the city, Allston attracted Jamaicans, exiled Russian Jews, Asian and Hispanic immigrants, Boston University students, and slumlords. Through its heart ran Beacon Street, a soiled ribbon of storefronts, tough bars, weather-beaten apartment buildings, and Third World restaurants. As a storefront Vietnamese restaurant, the Cao Palace fit right in.

All of which made Matthew smile, for it reminded him of his first meeting with Ira Teitelbaum, some five years earlier, when Ira had been assigned to introduce him to the alien environment of Daphnis & Clooney.

"I'm supposed to take you to lunch," Teitelbaum had announced. "You don't wanna go to one of those mahogany-walled chophouses that look like boardrooms, do you?"

Matthew had grimaced in sympathy.

"I figured from your credentials that you'd be a kindred spirit," said Ira, unerringly picking Matthew's resume from among the slops on his trough of a desk. "I also see you're a fellow émigré from the academic world. St. Olaf College, whatever that is. Shooed unfledged from the nest, were you?"

Matthew laughed. "I guess you could say that. After twenty years of schooling and two years teaching English, I discovered I didn't like my work all that much. Which was just as well, since my department chairman didn't either. So here I am. You, too?"

"Philosophy," said Teitelbaum. "I spent three years teaching Great Thinkers to the overprivileged at Williams. God, talk about death's dream kingdom." Teitelbaum feigned a shudder. "I fled to BU Law School. What was your field?"

"Well," said Matthew, flinching inwardly, "my dissertation was on the poetry of Owen Felltham."

"Felt who?"

"Felltham. There's no reason you should have heard of him. No one else has. He was a seventeenth-century poet and essayist. His *Resolves* were much admired by Charles Lamb." Matthew felt immediate disgust at having taken refuge in this pathetic defense. Just for a moment it brought back the chill of the grotty apartment where he had hunched over his desk, for three bleak years, writing the desiccated epic that became his thesis. Never, he felt certain, had so much pain and ennui been shed in the taking of such barren ground.

"Jesus," muttered Teitelbaum, his sympathy genuine. "No wonder you got out. I can sympathize. My thesis was on Moritz Schlick."

"You're ahead of me there," said Matthew. "At least I've *heard* of Schlick. But I always get those Viennese guys mixed up. Was it Schlick or Rudolph Carnap who got shot by his student?"

"It was Schlick. And not a moment too soon. But you gotta tell me, is there really such a place as Sleepy Eye, Minnesota?"

"Yup. My hometown. Thirty-five hundred souls."

"Wow."

Teitelbaum, Matthew learned, had grown up in Brookline, an urban, predominantly Jewish community grafted onto the southwestern haunch of Boston. Teitelbaum's father was a merchant who commuted daily to an industrial section of Boston known as Bay Village. There he struggled to keep his creditors from dismembering Teitelbaum Home Furnishings, a discount warehouse that sold substandard furniture on easy credit. (FEATHER YOUR NEST WITH A LITTLE DOWN, said the outsized sign above the plate-glass windows.) After his teaching stint at Williams and the completion of law school, Teitelbaum had spent four years as a prosecutor in the Suffolk County district attorney's office before joining Daphnis & Clooney at age thirty-six. Four years later, and six months before Matthew arrived, he had been made a partner in the firm's litigation department.

As for lunch, Teitelbaum had offered a choice between a trendy French bistro called Catherine of Tarragon and Pancho Shapiro's, a tiny taqueria near North Station. Matthew's decision to opt for the latter established a foothold for what became an easy, solid friendship. Despite their divergent backgrounds, they shared the ruins of their academic careers, and Ira became Matthew's de facto legal mentor as well as his guide through the Byzantine byways of the law firm. For his part, Ira gained a companion willing to join him in defying salmonella in the ethnic dives he sought out with a collector's passion.

Like the Cao Palace, thought Matthew, as he checked his watch. Ten minutes early. Better read the damn thing again, he thought. He reached over and picked up the briefcase lying on the passenger seat. He flicked on the overhead light and popped open the briefcase. He shuffled through the papers he had copied several hours earlier at the courthouse. All were labeled *Commonwealth v. Michael Chin, et al.* The papers included a docket sheet, the indictment, several discovery motions and orders allowing them, an inventory of objects found in the two apartments, a police report on the catastrophic bust. Shunting them all aside, Matthew scanned the order allowing Chin's motion to compel disclosure of the identity of a confidential informant. Finally, he found what he was looking for. He pulled out photocopies of two single-page documents.

The first was entitled "Application for Search Warrant." Docket Number 9462. The applicant, identified as Raymond A. Carvalho, Boston Police Officer, Drug Control Unit, sought a warrant to search for

Cocaine, a derivative of the Coca Leaf, a Class B Controlled Substance, and all articles used in the cutting, weighing, packaging and distribution of a Controlled Substance. All personal papers and keys tending to show use, occupancy or control of the premises (16 Tyler Street, Boston, Mass. apt. 4) and all ledgers, books or papers tending to show dealings in a Controlled Substance(s); all monies derived from the unlawful sale of a Controlled Substance(s) and any other illegal Controlled Substance(s) that may be found therein.

The application identified the premises to be searched as occupied by or in the possession of "JOHN, CH/M, late 30's, @ 5'11." The application was signed by Detective Lieutenant Raymond A. Carvalho.

The second document was an affidavit that had been submitted in support of the application. Matthew read it carefully.

### AFFIDAVIT

In Support of Application for Warrant
Trial Court of Massachusetts

Your affiant Detective Lieutenant Raymond A. Carvalho has received information from a reliable informant, hereafter referred to as "IT," who has proven reliable in the past by providing your affiant with information that led to the arrest and now pending case in the Suffolk Superior Court of one Lamont Lovelady for Trafficking in Cocaine, Possession of Class D with Intent to Distribute and unlawful Possession of a firearm, also for the conviction in the Suffolk Superior

Court of one Maria Rovario for Possession of Class B with
Intent to Distribute.

"IT" now tells me that for the last three weeks and more
recently within the last two days, "IT" has been present at
#16 Tyler Street, Boston, Mass. apt. #4 on the third floor
of a multi-unit dwelling above a retail store in Chinatown;
that being the home of a CH/M (thin, @ 5'11", late 30's)
known to "IT" as JOHN; and while there "IT" observed this
CH/M (JOHN) engaged in the cutting, weighing, packaging
and selling of paperfolds of white powder, believed to be
COCAINE. "IT" further tells me that JOHN packages his
POWDER (street term, referring to COCAINE) in Mass. Lottery Receipts in order to keep himself away from what JOHN
refers to as "having possession of drug paraphernalia items"
(such as glassine bags) in the event of his house getting
busted.

"IT" goes on to say that JOHN has rebuilt the door to the
apt. thus making it an extremely heavy door to break-down.
JOHN deals his POWDER through a hole (@ 1") in his door;
never opening the door to anybody. JOHN believes this to be
a safe and secured system giving him an edge in case of a
Police raid on his apt.

As a result of the information received, I responded to the
location and at diverse times over several days did set-up a
series of covert surveillance posts; and while doing so, I observed an unusually high amount of foot traffic leading up to
the apt. I further observed these various persons knocking
on the door of apt. #4, located on the right side of the hall
viewed from the front stairway, and asking for "one fifty,"
"one," "an eight-ball," etc., while rolling their monies and
pushing it through a small hole in the door; these persons
would then receive a paperfold through the same hole. I also
observed these persons examining the contents of the paperfolds and I observed the contents to be a white powder,
believed to be COCAINE.

Two days ago I went to the location and knocked on the
door; a CH/M (suspect's Chinese extraction identified by the
accent of his speech) asked me what I wanted, I then replied
"an eight-ball"; I was then told to place the money through

the hole and received one lottery slip paperfold containing white powder believed to be COCAINE.

Yesterday, again I went to the location and again knocked on the door; the same CH/M asked me what I wanted, and again I responded "an eight-ball"; I was again told to place the money through the hole and again I received a lottery slip paperfold of white powder, believed to be COCAINE. On both occasions I used official BPD funds; marked monies.

As a result of the information received, the observations and investigations concerning this location (including the two separate drug buys at this location) and further based on your affiant's experience in the illegal drug field; your affiant does believe that large amounts of COCAINE, a Class B Controlled Subst., are being secreted and sold from this location; I further believe this to be an "on-going" illegal enterprise and that the drug laws of Massachusetts are being violated at this location; and due to the type of drugs involved and their easy destruction as well as to maintain a safety factor for the officers involved, a no knock warrant is hereby requested.

Your affiant has been a Boston police officer for fourteen years; has served in various Special Enforcement Teams, has worked undercover, has made undercover drug buys and is personally responsible for hundreds of drug related arrests, finally your affiant is currently a member of the Drug Control Unit.

> Signed under the penalties of perjury,
> Raymond A. Carvalho

When he had finished reading the affidavit, Matthew tucked the papers back in his briefcase, snapped it shut, and got out of the car and locked it. He carried his briefcase into the restaurant.

The Cao Palace sold fish. The odor that greeted him when he opened the door bluntly announced the fact. A long counter running along the right side of the restaurant was broken by a white enameled display case filled with fresh fish arrayed for retail sale. Six wooden booths lined the wall on the other side for those who wanted theirs cooked for them. Danny Li and Julie, his girlfriend, sat side by side in the third booth, facing the door.

Danny had a cigarette in his left hand. Matthew shook the other one and sat down across the table from them. He set his briefcase on the bench beside him.

Danny spoke briefly to Julie in Chinese. She rose and smiled at Matthew while she waited for Danny to make way for her to slide out of the booth. She was, Matthew observed, an attractive woman, very fetching in her aloof way, even if it would not have occurred to him to describe her as beautiful. As she headed for the door, he turned his attention back to Danny.

Danny's goatee was gone and his English, he remembered from the phone call, was better. Otherwise Danny hadn't changed since Matthew had last seen him. He wore charcoal-gray slacks and an oversized white dress shirt, wrinkled but clean and buttoned at the collar, which sagged loosely away from his neck. His longish hair was parted in the middle, and two black forelocks fell symmetrically across his forehead like parentheses. He still couldn't sit still.

A waiter appeared and set a veritable cauldron of steaming soup in front of Danny. Danny picked up a ceramic spoon and leaned over the bowl. "You should try some, Matt," he said. "Best fish in Boston."

"I've eaten," said Matthew. "I'll have to take your word for it. How are you?"

Danny swallowed a spoonful of soup with great delicacy. "Good. How long I stay good is your job. You go to the court?"

"Yes. You heard right. The court allowed Chin's motion to reveal your identity yesterday. Have you heard anything from the police?"

"No." Danny took another spoonful. His eyes flicked toward the front door, then the counter. "What did Dunleavy say?"

"Dunleavy?" Matthew looked about the room, considering whether he should order after all. The soup smelled wonderful. He turned back to Danny. "What are you talking about?"

"Dunleavy," Danny said. "The dead cop. That's why you

are here, right? What did he say about me to get the search warrant?"

Matthew was confused. "Dunleavy didn't apply for the warrant. Or if he did, his isn't the warrant at issue. The affidavit that's got everybody in a tizzy was signed by a cop named Carvalho, not Dunleavy."

Danny stopped eating and looked Matthew full in the face. "Carvalho? I never talk to Carvalho. I heard of him, but I never talk to him. He is bad news. I stay away from him."

"Scroll that by me again," said Matthew. "The cop you gave information to was Dunleavy? Not Carvalho?"

"Yes."

Matthew leaned back and smiled. "Well, then, you can relax. You're off the hook. It's not Dunleavy's informant they want produced. It's Carvalho's. Here." He lifted his briefcase onto the table and opened it. He handed Danny the papers he had read in the car. "Look for yourself."

Danny put down his spoon and took the photocopies from Matthew. As he started to read the documents, Matthew signaled the waiter and asked for a bowl of the soup.

False alarm, thought Matthew. If Danny had talked only to the dead cop, then Danny's exposure had died with him.

But it was soon apparent that Danny did not share Matthew's sense of relief. By the time Danny flipped over to the second page his hands were trembling. He finished reading and looked at Matthew. Then he pushed the bowl toward the middle of the table and laid the two pages side by side in front of him. He looked from one to the other and then up at Matthew.

"This is wrong," he said. "Crazy."

"I don't understand."

"Me either. Some of this I told Dunleavy. Some I did not. It doesn't make any sense."

Matthew considered. "So what?" he asked. "Maybe Carvalho had his own informant who gave him some of the same information you gave Dunleavy. There's a little overlap. That's not unusual. The point is, you're not Carvalho's informant. No one will be looking for you."

"No, no. You do not understand. I am IT."

"It? What is this, a game of tag?"

"IT. I-T. What Carvalho calls the informant."

"Look," said Matthew, mildly exasperated as he spun one of the sheets around and examined it. "Did you give information that led to the arrest of Lamont Lovelady? Great name. I'll bet you *he's* not Chinese. And Maria Rovario?"

"No. I never heard of them. But some of that stuff in there I told Dunleavy. And Carvalho did not hear it from somebody else."

"What do you mean? And how do you know that?"

"Because I made it up."

Matthew said nothing while he tried to absorb this. "Let's go back to the beginning," he said at last. "You talked to Dunleavy. When was that?"

"The last time? A few days before he was shot. That is when I told him these things."

"What 'things' did you tell him?"

"All that stuff about how John sold drugs through a hole in the door. But I never told him John's name and I—"

"Whoa. Slow down. What else did you tell him?"

"You think I'm gonna tell him who lived there? No way. So I never told him a name and I made up a description. How many five-eleven Chinese do you know?"

Matthew considered. He said, "So Dunleavy must have passed along what you told him to Carvalho, and Carvalho put it in his affidavit."

"Yes. But Carvalho put in extra stuff I did not tell Dunleavy—like John's name. And the door is on the wrong side of the hall. And the other cases he said I informed about—Lovelady, these people. Before this I did not give Dunleavy information. What is happening, Matt?"

The waiter brought Matthew's soup, but he ignored it.

"I'm not sure. Does Carvalho know you?"

"I don't think so. I told you, I never talked to Carvalho. He is crazy. Crazy mean. But if Dunleavy told him what I said, maybe he told my name too. Matt, you must fix it. I cannot go to court."

"Hold on," said Matthew. "One step at a time."

"I talk, I die," said Danny softly. He smiled, but he still looked scared.

Matthew did not smile back. "I remember," he said. "But

this is a little different. This is not a private dispute between owners of a restaurant. It can't be finessed by cutting a deal. A cop was killed. You can't just make it go away. They're going to do everything they can to make you talk."

"No," said Danny. "You must fix it. I cannot talk. I cannot go to court."

"Look. First off, we don't even know if Carvalho knows who you are. Or if anyone in the Police Department does, for that matter."

"If Dunleavy told Carvalho anything, he told my name, too."

"Maybe yes. Maybe no. Let's not jump to conclusions. But if they do know who you are, you will have to testify. I don't see how we can avoid that."

"No. I cannot talk. You do not understand the people involved."

"Drug dealers, apparently," said Matthew dryly.

"More. Much more. You remember the flowers at the restaurant, Matt? Very big ones?"

"The chrysanthemums." Matthew pictured them drooping pitifully in the foyer of the Lotus Blossom.

"Yes. Why do you think the restaurant buys such a very big amount of flowers? And you saw the books. You know the restaurant paid a lot of money for these flowers every week. A *lot* of money. You think it was for flowers? For such a small restaurant? No, Matt. It was for friendship. It is dangerous not to have the friendship of people like these. You understand?"

"Protection. I get it."

"Those people are involved here, Matt. I cannot talk."

"You would have police protection, Danny. There is even a witness protection program, if you need it. They can give you money, a new identity. Relocate you."

"No. I cannot leave. You do not understand these people. You can't hide. For Chinese people America is a small place. If they want to find you, they will find you. Besides," Danny smiled at him, "I have irons."

"Irons? What the hell are you talking about, irons?"

Danny seemed to withdraw, to pull back into himself. "Irons," he said. "You know. In the fire."

"In the fire." Matthew shook his head. "I don't get it. One minute you tell me your life is in danger if you testify. But if it turns out you have to, you refuse to accept protection. Because you have 'irons.' What am I supposed to do with that?"

"I cannot leave Boston. You must tell them I will not talk. Tell them I have no evidence. I must stay out of this. You fix it. I can pay you."

"Suddenly you've got money?"

"I told you. I got irons." Danny smiled, reaching for his soup spoon and pulling the bowl toward him again.

"If you're so flush, what were you doing selling information to a narcotics cop?"

Danny looked down at his soup. "I got busted. Dunleavy told me he would drop the charges if I give information."

"When was that?"

"Five, six weeks before the shooting."

"Busted for what?"

"Heroin. I was holding."

"Simple possession?"

Danny nodded.

"Look, unless you were caught with enough dope to raise the bust to intent to distribute, the most you'd get was a fine. Did Dunleavy threaten to charge you with dealing?"

Danny shook his head.

"Then I don't get it. There was nothing to make it worth your while to become an informant. Especially given your fear of talking. Why didn't you just plead to possession and tell Dunleavy to go screw? You just said you can afford a lawyer."

But Danny's fugitive eyes would not meet his. They were quiet for a while as Danny ate his soup.

Then Matthew said, "I never thought dope was your scene anyway. What's going on here, Danny?"

"This is not important. It is important that you fix it so I do not talk in court. Will you help me?"

Matthew put the photocopies back in his briefcase and snapped it shut. He compressed his lips and looked at Danny.

"I don't know what I can do. I really don't. But I'll look into it and get back to you. I'll call you. Meanwhile, if the cops approach you, tell them nothing and say you want to talk to your lawyer." Matthew took a business card from his wallet and scribbled on the back of it. "Here. I've added my home number. Call me if you hear from the police. OK?"

Matthew stood up and dropped a ten-dollar bill on the table next to his uneaten soup. He picked up his briefcase and started for the door.

"Hey, Matt?" Danny called to his back.

Matthew stopped and turned halfway toward the booth, looking back at Danny. Danny still had the spoon in his hand. "Yes?" Matthew said.

"You still feel bad because the Lotus Blossom closed after we stopped cheating on taxes?"

Matthew said nothing for a moment. This was new ground for the two of them, and Matthew was unsure of his footing. It was as if his exasperating relationship with a client he had never understood was suddenly shifting under him and moving to some other, unknowable plane. Finally, he let himself slide with it. "A little bit, sometimes," he answered. "I didn't really have a way to help you much."

Danny shot him a wide grin. "Don't feel bad, Matt. We never stopped."

# 7

## The Clerk

Sarah Kerlinsky awoke to find the bed empty. She could hear Maury and the girls moving about downstairs in the kitchen. She groped for the clock. Seven fifty-five. Shit! The school bus would be pulling up in fifteen minutes. She whipped the covers off, sat up, and hooked her wire-framed glasses around her ears. Getting to her feet, she stepped into her slippers and pulled on her bathrobe.

"Morning," she called as she shuffled hastily down the stairs.

"Hi, Mom," sang the girls in unison.

Rounding the corner into the kitchen, she saw Maury smiling at her from behind the kitchen island, the coffeepot in his hand. Maury Jacobs was a large moon-faced man in brown horn-rimmed glasses. He was tall and heavy with sloping shoulders and clothes that hung gracelessly on his awkward frame. But he was intelligent, genial, and patient, qualities that endeared him to his more physically striking wife.

"Are you feeling rested?" he asked as he poured a cup of

coffee and held it out for her. "You seemed so wasted last night, I thought I'd let you sleep."

Sarah took the coffee with one hand and rubbed her eyes with the thumb and forefinger of the other. She shook her head to clear it. "Oh, boy," she said, blinking and breathing deeply. "Was I dead! Thanks."

"Dead?" said Rebecca. "Alison's cat is dead. Alison's mom said he got electrishooted."

Sarah shot a look of concern at her five-year old, but Rebecca's pudgy face was untroubled. She looked at her mother with mild interest.

"Not that kind of dead, sweetie," Sarah said. "I just meant I was very, very tired this morning. I was *so* tired, I didn't even hear you guys get up."

"It was a telephone pole," Rebecca explained.

Sarah frowned. "A telephone pole?"

"Where he got electrishooted. Alison's mom said."

"Electro*cuted*," Leah corrected her sister. Three years older than Rebecca, Leah was tranquilly examining the box of Cocoa Krispies in front of her as she ate her cereal.

"That's what I said!" rejoined Rebecca, her underlip jutting out.

"No, you didn't. You said electrishooted. That's not a word."

"It is, too!" Rebecca's lip quivered.

"So you *did* say it?" Leah demanded, pouncing on her sister's shift of ground.

Rebecca squinched up her face, her eyes disappearing behind the cheeks. "Daddy," she called in a querulous voice that threatened tears.

As Rebecca turned toward her father, he was already there to hold her against his soft belly. "It's okay, honey," Maury said soothingly while he stroked her head. "Leah's just honing her trial skills." He looked back at Sarah and smiled. Rebecca snuffled quietly. Leah rotated her cereal box to read the end panel.

Sarah smiled bravely back at her husband. A swell of sadness lapped against her as she watched her daughter reflexively reach out for comfort to Maury instead of her. She had witnessed similar events before. It was Maury, she had observed, to whom the girls first brought news from school. It was Maury they usually asked to read to them at night. And if she and Maury argued in front of them, they seemed always to take his side against her. Now, for the first time, these impressions took shape in her mind and left her feeling shunted off, almost imperceptibly, to a subtle remove from her children. With a shock she realized her husband had supplanted her as the primary focus of the girls' emotional life.

*Is this what men feel?* she wondered.

Because, like the men she knew in her business, she had her work to blame for her inability to be as present, physically and emotionally, as Maury could. Maury, sweet Maury, with his relaxed life as a professor of anthropology, could afford to be available, and he was. She could not. Not, anyway, if she wanted to pursue the kind of practice she relished.

Not that she was consumed with guilt over it. A little, yes. But she loved her work, couldn't imagine doing anything else. She just wanted both, and it saddened her when she glimpsed, like the shadow of a dark wing, the tiny sacrifices she was forced to make to keep them both.

Maury's voice broke in on her mournful reverie. "Girls, get your lunches. It's almost time for the bus." He turned to Sarah. "Can you still pick up Rebecca after her gymnastics class or do you want me to?"

"Jesus." Sarah closed her eyes and pressed the heel of her hand to her forehead. "That's right, it's Thursday. I forgot." She ran her hand through her hair and looked at her husband. "Could you? I gotta go through files at the clerk's office. I need to find—"

"No problem. I can do it," he said with a smile.

She felt a burr of resentment. Maury's kind safe eyes were devoid of accusation, but its very absence seemed all the more accusing, as if his generosity itself brought home and made more intolerable her own shortcomings.

But all she said was, "Thanks."

She intercepted the girls on their way to the front door and hugged them good-bye. From the picture window she watched as they climbed aboard a Newton school bus. Rebecca's face appeared at one of the windows and they waved to one another as the bus pulled away. She followed its course until it rounded the corner and whisked her babies away.

An hour later Sarah was striding briskly across Pemberton Square, the redbrick crescent that separated the courthouses from an arc of commercial offices known as Center Plaza. She was headed for One Center Plaza, at the northern end of the square. There the Suffolk County Clerk's office for criminal cases had been banished a couple years earlier when the courthouses ran out of space.

There was something about Raymond Carvalho's affidavit that gnawed at her. She wasn't sure why. It had to do with the names of the defendants who had been arrested on information provided by his snitch. Lamont Lovelady. Maria Rovario. And now Michael Chin.

One African-American (she felt reasonably certain).

One Hispanic.

And one Chinese.

Now, wasn't that interesting?

She decided to run it down. Sarah smiled grimly at her own unregenerate compulsion to do just about everything herself, even, like today, the routine task of reviewing files in the clerk's office. Her friends called her insecure, compulsive, incapable of delegation, anal retentive. She couldn't really disagree with them. She just never felt comfortable with a case unless she personally handled every piece of paper and satisfied herself that she had missed nothing. Her comfort level was even less sustainable when she was in the throes of preparing a big case.

Trotting down a set of cement steps with the unseasonably warm sun on her back, Sarah entered One Center Plaza at the mezzanine level. The criminal clerk's office was the first door on the left. Conceived as temporary quarters, the office had no counter like those in other clerks' offices. Instead, she found herself standing before a standard-issue steel desk set diagonally to cut off access to a haphazard warren of cubicles.

The clerk behind the desk looked up and smiled when he recognized her. Sarah silently thanked Margaret O'Reilly, her first mentor. "Greet every clerk like you slept with them the night before," was O'Reilly's advice, and Sarah had never regretted following it. Not that she found it a burden. To the contrary, she relished the camaraderie with court personnel, and she found herself intrigued as much by the twists and turns in their own lives as by their perspective on the legal system.

The clerk was a lugubrious man Sarah knew only as McFeeterson. He had a round, reddish face with bags of billowing purple flesh under his eyes, and he laid his bare arms across the *Boston Herald,* a sensationalistic tabloid spread on the desk in front of him. No heavy lifting. As always, Sarah had to struggle not to stare at his hair. McFeeterson had not accepted gracefully the baldness that had crept inexorably up his scalp. Instead, he had let his hair grow long at the back, where it was still thick, and beginning all the way back at the very base of his skull, he combed it straight up and over the top and sides, then down again over his forehead before stopping just short of his eyebrows, where his barber had rounded it off into a forced smile. A perm gave it body and held it precariously in place, and the total absence of sideburns made McFeeterson look like a man in a graying bicycle helmet. Sarah could never look at it without wondering how spongy it would feel to the touch.

"Good to see you, Sarah," he said.

"Mac," Sarah said. "How are you?"

McFeeterson lifted his hands in a gesture of weary helplessness and nodded toward the *Herald* in front of him.

He said, "Ah, Sarah, as good as I can be. It's an evil world, you know."

"It is indeed, Mac," said Sarah. "What's got you down?"

"Oh, it's not any one thing. It's the accumulation of little cuts."

"Yes?"

"You know. Like Bosnia. O. J. Simpson. Oklahoma City. Kids machine-gunning kids. Now the military has to give out combat boots even if you're light in your loafers, if you comprehend the trend of my drift. And then you got a president can't keep his business in his pants."

He dropped his chin to his chest and peered up at her. "I hope I'm not being offensive here."

"Hey," she said with a shrug.

McFeeterson said, "What kind of leader is that? Don't misunderstand me, now. I may have voted for Reagan, but I'm a lifelong Democrat. I could handle a president I don't always agree with. But I don't have a *clue* what he stands for. Does *he,* for that matter?"

"He does tend to go with the flow."

"Flow? I tell you, Sarah, the man is a goddamn wind sock."

Sarah grinned, letting him run with it.

McFeeterson said, "You remember when those conservatives used to go around crying, 'Let Reagan be Reagan'? Every time they thought his advisers were pushing him too far to the left? Well, can you imagine anyone ever saying, 'Let Clinton be Clinton'?"

Sarah was laughing now. "No, I can't," she admitted.

"Of course not. Because nobody knows what that would mean. Am I right or am I right?"

"Well, Mac, nobody ever asked Nixon to be Nixon either."

McFeeterson snorted amiably. "That's because we all *knew* he was evil down deep. Better to stay on the surface. With Clinton, though, there ain't no 'down deep.' "

"There's no 'there' there?"

"Right. But enough. What can I do you for?"

"I need to have a look at a couple of files. I don't have the docket numbers, I'm afraid. Just the names."

"Shouldn't be a problem," said McFeeterson, directing his attention to the computer terminal on his desk. "Let's have 'em."

"Lamont Lovelady is one. That's an open case. The other is Maria Rovario. It should be closed."

McFeeterson watched the computer screen as he pecked at the keyboard. "There we are," he said, jotting numbers down on a pad in front of him. "It'll take about fifteen minutes. You wanna have a seat in the hall and I'll bring them out to you?"

While waiting at a wooden library carrel in the hallway right outside the clerk's office, Sarah used the time to look over the summer camp brochures Maury had stuffed in her briefcase on her way out the door. Summer would soon be upon them and they had yet to settle on day camps for the girls. She was still comparing swimming schedules when McFeeterson handed her the files.

Neither file was thick. She picked up the thinner of the two, *Commonwealth v. Lovelady*. The docket entries indicated that a motion to suppress had been brought and denied, and she flipped quickly through the papers until she found the search warrant affidavit she was looking for. It was Carvalho's, all right, and the snitch was identified as IT, as she expected. But it was the first paragraph of the affidavit that caught her attention:

Your affiant Detective Lieutenant Raymond A. Carvalho has received information from a reliable informant, hereafter referred to as "IT," who has proven reliable in the past by providing your affiant with information that led to the arrest and now pending case in the Suffolk Superior Court of one Maria Rovario for Possession of Class B with Intent to Distribute, also for the conviction in the Suffolk Superior Court of one Martin C. Reardon for Trafficking in Cocaine, Possession of Class D with Intent to Distribute.

Sarah frowned as she read it. Then she compared it to the first paragraph of Carvalho's affidavit in the *Chin* case. Different names, slight changes in the offenses charged, but otherwise absolutely identical. Of course, the use of boilerplate was understandable. A cop couldn't be expected to reinvent the wheel each time he filed an application for a search warrant. But now she had another file to pull. *Commonwealth v. Martin Reardon*. She wrote it down.

An Irishman to add to the list of IT's victims.

This guy was pretty versatile.

Sarah felt a tingling in the hinges of her cheekbones as she thumbed eagerly through the other file. She quickly found the affidavit used to bust Maria Rovario. And there, in a clone of the same introductory paragraph, were the names of two more dealers whose busts Carvalho had recounted as proof of IT's reliability. She added their names to Martin Reardon's and asked McFeeterson for all three files. While she was waiting for them, she set a yellow pad in front of her and broke the page into four columns by drawing vertical lines. After labeling each column, and leaving blanks for information yet to come, she entered what she had discovered so far:

| Docket No. | Defendant | Date of Warrant | Site of Arrest |
|---|---|---|---|
| 95-1342 | Michael Chin | 2/7/95 | Chinatown |
| 95-0226 | Maria Rovario | 1/6/95 | Jamaica Plain |
| 94-8975 | Lamont Lovelady | 2/11/94 | Dorchester |
| _____ | Martin C. Reardon | _____ | _____ |
| _____ | Larry Bratsos | _____ | _____ |
| _____ | Jorge Herrara | _____ | _____ |

With her elbows on the carrel desk, Sarah steepled her fingers and rested her chin on the tips of her thumbs as she stared at what she had written. She was still staring ten minutes later when McFeeterson appeared with the three new files under his arm.

"You finding anything interesting, Sarah?"

"Very interesting, Mac. I have the feeling I'm going to have to impose on you a lot today."

McFeeterson shrugged. "Hey," he said.

"You're a dear, Mac. I need to call my office to cancel an appointment for this afternoon. Is there a pay phone near here?"

"Use the phone on my desk."

*Thank you, Margaret O'Reilly,* she thought.

# 8

---◆---

# The Daisy Chain

Four hours later, Jeremiah DeMarco took her call.

"Good afternoon, Sarah," he said pleasantly. Sitting at his gunmetal-gray desk with what he promised himself was the last coffee of the day, he pried the plastic lid off the Styrofoam cup.

"Jerry," Sarah Kerlinsky replied. "Good of you to take my call."

"An old habit. I can't seem to break it. So, are you calling to beg for a deal? I might consider murder two." He took a sip of his coffee.

Sarah laughed. "Another old habit you can't break. No, thank you. I'll wait for the acquittal."

"You're awful cocky today."

"I've got good reason. And how goes the department's celebrated dragnet for your missing informant? You're not going to disappoint me and actually produce one, are you?"

It was DeMarco's turn to laugh. It always surprised him that he liked her so much. "I'm gonna do my best," he said. "If this weren't such a god-awful case, I would be savoring the ironies. In particular, that we both want precisely the opposite of what we pretend in front of the court. But you didn't call up just to revel in that, did you?"

"As a matter of fact, I did. That, and to ask your opinion. I've got more bad news for the department, but I can't tell who it hurts more, you or me."

"Yeah?"

"I ran a check on the cases Carvalho says IT provided information on in the past. You remember. *Lovelady* and *Rovario*?"

DeMarco felt his stomach muscles tightening. "You're telling me they don't check out?" He should have checked himself.

"Oh, they check out all right. That's just the problem. They check out *too* well."

"I'm not following you."

"I pulled the search warrant affidavits in the *Rovario* and *Lovelady* cases and, sure enough, Carvalho named IT as the informant on each of them. The trouble is, each of those affidavits refers in turn to yet another case in which IT was the snitch. And guess what I found when I ran down *those* affidavits?"

"Still more affidavits." DeMarco felt sick.

"Bingo. It seems we have a daisy chain of warrant affidavits involving the ubiquitous IT. A whole bouquet, in fact. Fifty-two in all. And I use 'ubiquitous' advisedly because IT supplied probable cause to do raids on drug operations in every conceivable neighborhood in the city. Dorchester, Back Bay, Charlestown, the North End, Southie—you name it, he was there."

"Son of a bitch," DeMarco said softly.

"And the level of detail IT has at his command! It's staggering, Jerry. Not to mention the ethnic diversity of his connections. There aren't many snitches who enjoy the trust and confidence of black, Irish, Chicano, and (need I add?) Chinese dealers. This guy is such a thoroughgoing multiculturalist there ought to be a place for him on the National Endowment for the Arts. Or at least the faculty at Penn. Are you still there, Jerry?"

"I'm here. What an asshole."

"I hope it's the detective lieutenant you're cursing, because this informant is obviously a godsend to the war on drugs. But to get back to where I started: Is this good news for me or bad? Obviously, I'd prefer you never produced the snitch, but does it help my case if it's clearly established that he never even existed? What do you think?"

"I think I would have been happier if Jimmy Morrissey was still representing Michael Chin. He'd be squabbling with Doyle over whether he was late for court instead of rummaging through the clerk's office."

"I'm not sure of that," Sarah laughed. "You've always underestimated Jimmy."

DeMarco did not otherwise share his speculations on how the new information affected her chances. He extricated himself from Sarah's gently mocking queries as gracefully as possible and sat quietly for ten minutes. Then he picked up the phone again and called the department. Carvalho was not at his desk. *He's probably out hunting for his snitch,* DeMarco said to himself with disgust.

DeMarco got up and walked down to the big office suite at the end of the hall. When he opened the door, he was greeted with a smile by Lorraine, the redoubtable matron who regulated the flow of supplicants to DeMarco's boss, the district attorney for Suffolk County.

"Is he alone in there, Lorraine?" DeMarco asked. "I need to see him."

"He's just on the phone. Go ahead."

DeMarco rapped on the inner-office door and opened it without waiting for a response. He stepped into the room and shut the door behind him.

The office was a long rectangular cavern with dark gumwood paneling. At the far end, behind an enormous oak desk, Jackie Crimmins sat in his shirtsleeves looking out the window. He had his back to DeMarco and a phone to his ear. Jackie spun slowly around to take in DeMarco but did not otherwise acknowledge his presence.

Jackie was a small man, under five foot four, and the size and shape of the office made him look even smaller. DeMarco found it odd that Jackie seemed unaware of the effect, since he was usually preternaturally alert to situations in which his size might be shown to disadvantage. Perhaps it was just an instance of one occasion for vanity—the possession of a majestic office—blinding him to its impact on another. Rather like Dukakis riding on that tank.

"No, Patrick," Jackie said into the phone. "No media. This is supposed to be a quiet fund-raiser, for Pete's sake. A tasteful soiree. It's money we'll be needing now, not coverage. You don't expect me to actually *carry* Louisberg Square in September, now, do you?"

There was just a hint of the Old Sod in Jackie's voice, a lilt that gave away his insular upbringing in South Boston—far away from the gaslit gentility of Louisberg Square, a cobblestone piazza on Beacon Hill that was the ritziest address in the city. Jackie was obviously raising funds there.

A Triple Eagle (Boston College High School, Boston College, and Boston College Law School) with ferociously loyal supporters in the city's blue-collar neighborhoods, Jackie Crimmins had risen rapidly through the Democratic ranks, first as a foot soldier in the war against school busing in the 1970s, which propelled him to a seat on the Boston School Committee and later in the state House of Representatives. Six years earlier he had upset a heavily favored incumbent to become district attorney, and his grip on that position was widely viewed as unshakable.

All of this Jackie had done despite his celebrated disdain for the media and the intensity with which it was requited. With his diminutive stature, ruddy cheeks, Johnny Unitas haircut, and flashy ties with matching show hankies, Jackie was the easy butt of caricature and editorial sarcasm. His stance in favor of traditional neighborhood schools and his unapologetic refusal to allow a television set in his own home (they discouraged reading, he insisted) only seemed to confirm that he was out of touch with the times. Why, the man attended Mass every morning.

But whether you were a political opponent or a media mogul, you underestimated the district attorney at your peril. Jackie Crimmins was no ignorant ward heeler. He read Greek and Latin for pleasure, and he had been known to hold his own in conversation with the likes of Elie Wiesel, Susan Sontag, and the Dalai Lama. A gifted mimic and a stand-up comic when it suited him, he gloried in heaping scorn on creatures of the media. "I had dinner with a *Boston Herald* reporter the other night," he once told a Rotary Club in Brighton. "It was a near-life experience." When Eddie Felch, a prize-winning reporter for the *Globe,* described Jackie as the only man he knew who could strut sitting down, Jackie thanked him publicly for the compliment on his posture but insisted the credit go to the discipline of his saintly mother. His only regret, he said, was that people might think his back was as stiff as Felch's prose. Felch later got even with a corrosive exposé of hiring and promotion at the DA's office, employment practices the reporter ridiculed as "majority set-asides for people without color." Jackie was unruffled. He knew that most of Felch's readers, professionals in high-end neighborhoods like Newton and west Cambridge, could not vote in Suffolk County anyway, and the backhanded allusion to his well-publicized discomfort (his own carefully chosen word) over affirmative action would serve only to stoke the fervor of his supporters in the city's neighborhoods.

But whatever his opinion of the press, Jackie Crimmins now needed to live above the fold. He was wheeling his guns in another direction and would have to broaden his base. The sagging Republican governor had announced his retirement, and Jackie had launched his own run to succeed him in the fall elections. Historically, Boston city politicians were an ethnocentric breed who had difficulty making the jump to statewide office. Jackie's strong public image as a crime buster and spokesman for traditional schooling, along with the careful forging of ties with district attorneys and police unions in the western and southern counties, had done much to unsettle conventional thinking on that score. A recent poll showed him leading the field among potential Democratic contenders.

All of which was just fine with DeMarco. He had moved into Jackie's slipstream during his first campaign for DA, and that support had earned him the opportunity to head the Homicide Division. Not that anyone could claim DeMarco did not deserve the job. He had already tried more murder cases, and more successfully, than anyone in the office before Jackie became DA, and DeMarco's record since then had reflected nothing but credit on Jackie's decision to elevate him.

And if Jackie made it to the State House? Well, DeMarco expected to move up, too. Perhaps as counsel to the governor. Maybe even as the next district attorney, since it would fall to the new governor to fill the vacancy created by his own election. Whatever his new position, DeMarco intended to see that it served, in turn, as an entree to one of the city's major law firms, none of which would have him when he graduated from law school.

DeMarco could still feel the sting of the penury that had disfigured his childhood. Nor could he forget how he had watched the spirit bleed out of his mother as she struggled to hold her family together in the projects of East Boston after the death of his father—like Francis Dunleavy, a policeman slain in the line of duty. The pension she received from the state in those days was mockingly inadequate to meet the needs of a widow with six young children, and to make up the shortfall she had taken the train every day to clean the fashionable homes of the rich on Beacon Hill. To this day, he could not bring himself to hire a cleaning woman. Much to his wife's dismay. No matter how he looked at it, it would feel like a betrayal of his roots and his mother. Fortunately, his two teenage daughters were of an age to help Brenda around the house.

Yet with his children's imminent coming of age also came the prospect of college educations he could never afford on the salary and savings of a county prosecutor. Not to mention—it pained him to consider it, but there it was—the need to provide for his old age. All these concerns would evanesce if he were to join one of the posh, white-shoe firms that had spurned him fifteen years before. He would come on board as a full partner, of course, whereupon he could luxuriate in the more genteel craft of defending white-collar criminals for the kind of money no one in his family had ever seen. And, frankly, he felt he deserved it.

"Jeremiah," said Jackie as he hung up the phone. "You seldom come to me with good news. Surprise me."

"I wish I could," said DeMarco, meaning it. "But not today. I just had a call from Sarah Kerlinsky. She represents the guy who killed Francis Dunleavy."

"A tragic, bestial business," said Jackie, shaking his head. "Thirty-seven years old. I've been doing what I can to console his family. His wife's a remarkable woman. Very strong."

"I saw you and Doreen on TV. It was pretty effective, I thought."

"Did you now? I'm glad to hear of it. I knew the boy's father, of course. God rest his soul. Out of Saint Monica's parish, he was. A real policeman, raising a whole family of policemen. How many are there, now?"

"Four of his brothers are on the force."

"If they are anything like their father, they will demand justice. Now, you're not going to tell me that their justice is in doubt, are you, Jeremiah?"

"No, I don't think so. We've got the three witnesses who were arrested with Chin. They're not exactly angels, but their stories are at least consistent."

"They'll stand up. The Chinese always stand up."

"We've also got one of Chin's prints on the murder weapon, but then it's got a partial belonging to one of our witnesses as well. And I've got a cellmate who will testify that Chin bragged about doing a cop. Pretty solid, on balance. It's just this damn snitch business. It's gonna get real messy before this is over."

"You mean that detective—what's his name? The one with the two-pound nose?"

"Carvalho."

"Yes. I knew it was a Portuguese name. East Cambridge, I reckon. Whatever. You're not suggesting he would defy a court order to protect this informant in a case involving the murder of his own partner?"

"No. Not at all. These guys never think twice about burning a snitch. They could care. And, obviously, even less so when a cop's been killed. So Carvalho has every incentive to produce the informant. I'm just afraid he won't be able to."

"Disappeared, you think?"

"Worse. I don't think he ever existed. I think Carvalho

made him up to get the warrant. I've suspected as much for some time. His obstinacy makes no sense otherwise. Not long after the court ordered him to produce his snitch, he showed me a police report on the suspicious death of some junkie. 'This is what happens to snitches that get burned,' he says. I told him that wouldn't do, we already lost that battle and he's got to produce the guy. That was three weeks ago. He hasn't said 'boo' since.

"And then this afternoon Sarah tells me Carvalho relied on the same snitch more than fifty times, and all over the city. It's inconceivable that a single snitch could have done all that. And sooner or later, I'm afraid, the press may pick up on it. I figured you should know, so you won't get blindsided when it does."

"You're right. Kerlinsky is bound to leak it."

"Oh, it won't come from Sarah," DeMarco said. "It's not in her interest to do so."

"Of course it is," said Jackie. "She'd love see to us embarrassed over this."

DeMarco should have expected this. For all Jackie's intelligence and savvy, he was not a trial lawyer, and it was often difficult for him not to view what went on in a trial through the prism of his political sensibility. What went on in a courtroom often was political, but just as often it wasn't.

"I don't think so, Jackie," said DeMarco. "At least, that's not the kind of embarrassment she has in mind. You need to keep in mind the peculiar dynamics of this issue for Sarah and me. It's almost amusing, really, when you think about it."

Jackie did not look amused. DeMarco decided he'd better explain.

"Look at it this way. Sarah asks the court to order the police to produce the snitch because his description of John, the occupant of the apartment, doesn't fit Chin. That means the snitch can contradict the testimony of our witnesses, who swear Chin was the only person to use the apartment. So the snitch's testimony would be exculpatory.

"Now, as for me," DeMarco continued, "I suspect from the beginning there is no snitch—no IT, as Carvalho calls him. Carvalho's adamant insistence that IT be protected feeds my suspicions. So I oppose her motion. The last thing I want is to have charges of police misconduct and to see the credibility of my police witnesses called into question by a clear showing that Carvalho perjured himself in the warrant affidavit. I want the judge to deny the motion and make us go to trial without IT. But no way. Doyle allows her motion."

"Doyle is not a reliable judge for a case like this," said Jackie. "I knew him when he was in the House. He was a poseur. A trimmer. Always ready to fall in with the prevailing westerlies. And he's ambitious. There comes a time—after a judge has heard his four-hundredth possession-with-intent—that he begins to pine for a seat on the Appeals Court. Doyle passed that point years ago. I can see him sniffing about for an opportunity to come across to the judicial nominating committee as a Courageous Jurist Doing the Right Thing in the Teeth of Public Pressure. Well, I'd love to see him come to me looking for an appellate judgeship. I'll tickle his catastrophe."

"I'd like to be there to watch," said DeMarco. "But I can't say he was wrong on the law on this one. The motion probably should have been allowed. Anyway, things changed once he issued the order to produce the snitch. I desperately want IT to exist and for Carvalho to produce him. At least then there'd be a chance that IT, if he exists, could explain away some of the questions raised by Carvalho's affidavit. Sarah, on the other hand, does not want him produced. She wants to make hay with the department's failure to produce a police agent who is supposed to be vital to her defense. Then she can use the empty chair defense. You know: 'Where is the witness, ladies and gentlemen of the jury? Why hasn't the Commonwealth produced him? What are they afraid he'll say? And where is John? What are they trying to hide?' She might even have a crack at getting the indictment dismissed for misconduct on the part of the Commonwealth.

"But," DeMarco continued, "her strategy is all based on the premise that IT actually exists and the police are refusing to produce him. If it's demonstrated that IT never existed and that Carvalho made it all up, all of Sarah's arguments about a missing key witness go 'poof.' Because if IT never existed, there's no reason to disbelieve our witnesses. So Sarah is not about to leak anything that might undermine her strategy. She wants Doyle and the jury to believe IT is alive and well—preferably hiding out with John in Carvalho's spare bedroom."

Jackie was quiet for a moment. "So what should yourself and I be doing?" he asked at last.

"We wait for Carvalho to either produce his snitch or come up with a report explaining why he can't. Assuming it's the latter, we'll be before Doyle again. Carvalho's report would come under sharp scrutiny and he would be cross-examined on the measures taken to locate the informant. Sarah will probably move to dismiss the indictment because of misconduct by the Commonwealth. Remember, police misconduct would be imputed to the Commonwealth."

"That," said Jackie, "is precisely the kind of opportunity you do not want to dangle in front of the likes of Robert Corrigan Doyle."

"I agree," said DeMarco. "But we're stuck with him on this one. I just wanted you to know that it's likely to come out, at some time in the future, that Carvalho has been lying about his snitch. So you won't be caught flat-footed when it happens."

"Ah, that's one of the reasons you're such a treasure to me, Jeremiah," said Jackie, without much irony. "For was I not there to give you this job when you proved your worth and loyalty? But you know," he added, rubbing his chin and looking away from DeMarco, "there just might be a way to turn such news to our advantage. Politically, anyway. The courtroom fallout I leave to you."

Jackie looked out the window as he spoke. "Picture it this way. Carvalho's not so much a villain as he is a symptom of a criminal justice system gone awry. All because the courts have spun out ridiculous technicalities that must be followed before you can get a search warrant. If the officer screws up on any of the trivia, if he fails to cross one *i* or to dot one *t*—"

"Well, not quite," DeMarco interposed with a grin. He regretted it immediately.

"What?" Jackie looked bewildered.

"You had it backwards."

"Oh, right. You dot the *i*'s. And cross the *t*'s. Where would I ever be without you?" Jackie seemed irritated by the interruption. Then he smiled. "You don't suppose," he asked, "that's why Carvalho named him IT? No, I'm getting silly. Let's get back to my peroration. The officer drops a stitch and the pusher is back in the schoolyards peddling his poison. So the pressure takes its toll on hardworking policemen trying to do their jobs. It breeds contempt for the law. And tempts our centurions with the understandable urge to cut corners just to get the job done. Mind you, I said understandable, not excusable.

"And the moral? Massachusetts needs a governor who will appoint the kind of judges who will clear out all the mindless technical underbrush, the debris that impedes the fight against crime. Remember, three of the seven justices on the Supreme Judicial Court are scheduled for mandatory retirement in the next six years. The right governor can make all the difference."

Jackie's voice had picked up speed and conviction as he talked, and when he finished he sat back with a smile and looked squarely at DeMarco. "With such a spin, Jerry, who knows? We might be able to turn it around."

"Maybe," said DeMarco. He tried to sound more convinced than he felt. He decided to change the subject. "There's another aspect of this case you should know about."

Jackie raised his eyebrows but held his smile. "There's more?"

"Yes. It's the Chinatown piece. I've talked to a cop I know in Organized Crime. He confirms my own impression that a retail drug operation like the one Carvalho busted could never have done business in Chinatown without the knowledge and approval of the Tung On. No one would have dared poach on the gang's turf. And that, as you know, means Herman Vu would have a piece of it."

DeMarco paused briefly. Jackie did nothing to fill the pause.

"Now, I know," DeMarco continued, "that you're getting a lot of political support from businessmen in the Chinese community. Especially since you've made such an issue out of programs to raze the Combat Zone."

"Indeed, I have," said Jackie. "If the obscenity laws can't do away with the smut, we'll have to do it with economics. I will urban-renew that moral grease stain right off the map. Naturally, as the Zone's closest neighbor, Chinatown stands to benefit from its demise. So, naturally again, they support me. Especially the businessmen who hope to participate in the commercial development that will replace it. And you know my campaign finance chairman is one of them. But I'm afraid I don't grasp your point, Jeremiah. What has all this to do with the Tung On?"

"Just a heads-up, Jackie. My pal in Organized Crime says there is almost nothing that goes on in Chinatown that Vu does not have his fingers in. It's like the wiseguys in the North End, except the Chinese are a tighter community than the Italians. I don't have to tell you how it works. There's legitimate business and then there's 'legitimate business.' " DeMarco made quotation marks in the air. "And you never know exactly who you're dealing with or where the money comes from. So all I'm saying is, be careful. The media already smells the chum in the water around the *Chin* case, and in the feeding frenzy somebody may stumble on something that might embarrass you and the campaign."

"You'd not be holding something back on me now, would you, Jeremiah?" Jackie's pale blue eyes were fixed on DeMarco's. "Do you—does your policeman friend—have anything specific I should know about any of my supporters or contributors? Because if you do—"

"No, Jackie. Nothing like that."

"If you do, let's get it out and deal with it. I know there were stories a few years ago about Lo Fat 'mysteriously' overcoming financial difficulties when he was just starting to develop the hotel. Nothing came of it then, and I went over it in detail with him when I asked him to handle the campaign finances. He's clean. And he's done a tremendous job raising money for us."

"I've heard nothing to suggest you're wrong, Jackie."

"I've known Lo Fat for more than fifteen years. Every

bone in my body tells me that the likes of Herman Vu is not his cup of green tea."

"I'm glad to hear it," said DeMarco. "And I'll leave you alone. I'd better get back to tracking down Carvalho. It would be nice to know what to expect next. He's out, of course."

"Given how his informant gets around," said Jackie, "he's probably looking for him in Louisberg Square."

Jackie never cracked a smile.

# 9

## The Cinderella Affidavit

As always, it was a mistake to ride with Teitelbaum. Matthew cowered in the passenger seat, his left hand clutching his shoulder belt and his right arm braced against the dashboard. Ira jerked the Saab into the left lane of Congress Street without checking his rearview mirror. He ignored the angry horn of the taxi he cut off.

"So I looked at the papers you pulled in the *Chin* case," Ira said a moment later, after he had deigned to stop for a red light at State Street. "I also logged onto NEXUS to read the newspaper coverage. Looks like your man Danny has got himself in quite a pickle."

Matthew was breathing easier now that the car was stationary. "That," he said, "I figured out for myself. So did Danny."

"Do you know what a Cinderella affidavit is?" Ira continued.

"A new Robert Ludlum novel?"

"It's a phony affidavit signed by a narcotics officer so he can get a search warrant. The narc is a creature of the streets, you see, and from what he picks up through rumor and instinct and a trained eye, he knows in his bones when he's fixed on a site where he's gonna find drugs. But he can't make the bust unless he has a search warrant. His gut instinct is not going to convince a magistrate that he has probable cause to issue a warrant. Even if he did find such a magistrate, he knows a court would throw out the warrant and then suppress all the evidence gathered in the search."

"The confiscated drugs being the fruit of the poisoned tree and all," said Matthew. "I remember that much from law school."

"Good boy. You may also remember that you can get a valid warrant on the strength of information supplied by an anonymous snitch. But only if the officer seeking the warrant can demonstrate two things in his application.

"First, he has to show that the informant knows what he's talking about. Obviously, a snitch who says he heard a rumor that someone is running a crack house at an address on Blue Hill Avenue won't do. This is called the 'basis of knowledge' component. That was met here by IT's eyewitness account of watching dope being packaged for sale in the apartment.

"The second component is the veracity requirement, something that tells the magistrate why he should believe the snitch when he tells him he saw the coke being packaged. Cops often meet the veracity requirement, as Carvalho did here, by showing the snitch proved reliable in the past. That's why the affidavit refers to those cases where this IT is supposed to have been helpful."

"You mean *Lovelady* and *Rovario*," said Matthew. He stiffened when the light changed and the Saab surged past Fanueil Hall in the direction of Cambridge Street. They were headed for the Longfellow Bridge, which crossed the Charles River and fed into the city of Cambridge.

"Exactly," said Ira. "That's one way to nail down the veracity component. So Carvalho's affidavit has both of the components necessary to show probable cause based on a tip from an anonymous snitch. But Carvalho went well beyond what was required. Just in case, he has added other information, independent of that provided by his tipster. To corroborate what IT told him, Carvalho says he made his own observations at the scene and, best of all, personally made controlled buys at the apartment. Like wearing his own belt with IT's suspenders. Add it all up and—shazaam!—he's established probable cause. With a righteous warrant that's pretty much bulletproof on a motion to suppress."

"Except it's all a lie," said Matthew.

"That it is. And it happens more often than the DAs and judges want to admit. So often, in fact, that the cops and the prosecutors even have a name for them. And that would be . . . ?" Ira looked over at Matthew and pointed an inquisitive index finger in his direction.

"A Cinderella affidavit?" Matthew filled in the blank, wishing Ira would keep his eyes on the road. The Saab had drifted toward the guard rail during the pop quiz. Matthew looked out over the bridge and into the Charles River Basin.

"An apt pupil!" Ira exclaimed. "You see, at a pretrial hearing on a motion to suppress evidence seized in a raid, the courts won't make the cop produce his informant. The defense is not going to get to cross-examine the snitch to show he didn't know what he was talking about. At that stage of the proceedings, remember, you're only concerned with whether there was a lack of probable cause. The courts are not going to make the police burn a snitch, thereby spoiling a valuable resource for law enforcement and even endangering his life, just to resolve a side issue over probable cause. It has nothing to do with whether the defendant will get a fair trial. The ultimate issue—is the defendant guilty or not?—is going to be determined by whether the defendant was in possession of the drugs, period. On that issue, the snitch's testimony is irrelevant. So the narc feels pretty comfortable about inventing information to put in his affidavit. Nobody's gonna make him produce the snitch who's supposed to have supplied the information."

"Except Judge Doyle," Matthew reminded him.

"Ah, but that's different," said Ira, cocking his eye. "You see, when Dunleavy got killed during the raid, everything changed. Suddenly what the snitch knew became *very* relevant to Chin's guilt or innocence. According to the affidavit, the snitch saw somebody who looks nothing like Chin in the apartment a couple days before the shooting. In fact, he says the guy lived there and ran the business out of the apartment.

So the snitch's testimony bears directly on whether it was Chin or somebody else who fired the shots through the door. Under those circumstances, the defense is entitled to question the snitch and, if his testimony seems useful, put him on the stand to rebut the Commonwealth's case that Chin was the shooter. Without his testimony, there is a serious question whether Chin can get a fair trial.

"Which brings us back to Cinderella. Carvalho can dress his affidavit up in that bogus finery and haul her to the ball in the pretty coach. There she can waltz her glass slippers off—but he's got to her out of there before midnight. Unfortunately, the gunshots that tolled for Dunleavy were the clock in this fairy tale. They broke the fairy godmother's spell and stripped off her ballgown."

"And Carvalho," Matthew added, "turns into a pumpkin."

"We have heard the chimes at midnight, Master Boer." Ira arched an eyebrow in Matthew's direction.

Matthew grinned. "That we have, that we—*watch out!*"

Ira hit the brakes hard to keep from rear-ending a Federal Express van.

"Jesus *Christ,* Ira!" said Matthew. "You don't want to die on your forty-fifth birthday. What would I tell Hannah?"

Ira ignored him as he barreled past MIT and the high-tech companies of Kendall Square. "Unfortunately," Ira continued, "all this leaves Danny Li in a very precarious position. And the irony is that Kerlinsky might not have had much of a motion if Danny hadn't played it so cute by inventing the description. He hasn't told you whose description he so carefully altered, but I'll bet whoever it was looked a lot like at least one of the four people the cops arrested. It's the possibility of a missing six-foot Chinaman that gave Sarah so much to work with.

"Now, maybe Danny gets lucky. Maybe Dunleavy never disclosed his identity to Carvalho or anyone else on the force. If so, Danny can just lie low till it all blows over. But I suspect he's right that *somebody* besides Dunleavy must know who his snitch was. Or can figure it out. The department keeps records on confidential informants."

"OK," said Matthew, "let's assume that Danny's name surfaces and he is picked up as a material witness. I've told him to say nothing till he's allowed to talk to me. But what do I do then? He's too scared to testify and he says he won't accept protection if he's forced to testify. He claims he has something cooking—one of his schemes, no doubt—so he refuses to consider leaving the area. How can I help him under those circumstances?"

"Well, for one thing, you can see that he's not browbeaten by DeMarco or the police. Or just plain beaten. And you can get him out of police custody, if that's what he wants. After that, you'll just have to feel your way. See what you can negotiate with the DA and Kerlinsky."

"You know her?"

"Indeed I do. She's as good as it gets. Very smart and *very* tough. That's not to take anything away from DeMarco, who's a shrewd and hard-nosed prosecutor, if a bit of a hot-head. But Sarah's as tough as an old badger."

Matthew couldn't help smiling. "What does a kid from Brookline know about badgers?"

"Only what I read," said Ira. "Let's just say she can be hell on heels if she decides she's getting jerked around. She will not be easy to deal with."

# 10

## The Invisible Hand

Moments later, Matthew was able to relax as Ira turned into the entrance of a parking ramp and plucked a ticket from the machine. He drove the Saab up the ramp and circled in quest of a parking slot. He finally pulled into one on the roof. After shutting off the engine he turned toward Matthew.

"You know, this could be a terrific opportunity for you," he said. "Monday morning, you file a new case form on this so you'll be ready to roll if you get a frantic call from Danny from a jail cell somewhere. But don't try to go it alone. Be sure to list me as the RA."

"Don't you think," asked Matthew, "that I should be listed as the responsible attorney on this? The rap on me at my performance review last year was that I should be managing cases more instead of just doing the grunt work for more senior lawyers. I think it would help to have the RA credit on this one."

"It would, but there's more to it than that," said Ira. "When the Management Committee learns what case this is, they're gonna shit nickels. It's too high profile. If it looks like you're out there on your own, they might just take it away from you. But with a former prosecutor as RA, nobody will squawk too much about your inexperience in criminal law. And when the time comes, I'll see that you get the credit for running the case. Remember, even the Lone Ranger had Tonto. Hey, you'll be coming to me anyway. Think of me as *your* IT. I mean, we've got the same initials, right?"

Ira shambled like a bear toward the parking elevator as Matthew hurried after him.

"How," Matthew asked, "do I identify the client on the new case form? Once I list the Commonwealth and Chin as adverse parties, the whole firm is going to know what case we're talking about. And with all the press coverage, they'll probably guess what Danny's role is. It's bound to leak out."

Ira pushed the button for the elevator. "Easy," he said. "On the form you identify the client simply as 'a third-party witness in a criminal proceeding.' You go to Central Files and tell the Venerable Beadle you want to do a conflict check, and you want to do it yourself. Given the nature of this case, you won't find any conflicts. D&C doesn't do a lot of blue-collar criminal defense work, in case you hadn't noticed. Plus he's a former client, so he was checked when you first represented him, what, two years ago?"

"More like three," said Matthew, stepping into the elevator.

"OK, three. You won't find any conflicts, but check anyway. Then you file your sanitized new case report with Mrs. Beadle. And you send a copy of it to the Management Committee along with a confidential memo. In the memo you reveal your client's name, describe the nature of the representation in detail, and report that your search turned up no conflicts. That way the committee can still feel like they're in charge and can satisfy themselves that there is no conflict—and Danny's identity will remain a secret to the rest of the firm. But make sure that Danny doesn't pay his retainer with a personal check. You don't want somebody in bookkeeping to spot his name on a check."

Matthew barked a laugh. "Not to worry. With Danny, it's always cash."

The elevator doors slid open and they found themselves standing in front of the entrance to Aporia, a fashionable bistro off First Street in east Cambridge. The name buzzed in sleek blue neon above the door.

Ira shook his head. "Oh, Hannah," he said as if to himself. "You know this ain't my cup of meat."

They went inside what had once been an industrial space, a warehouse perhaps. It had extremely high ceilings, from which was suspended the oversized ductwork for its heating and air-conditioning systems. The severity of the foyer, its surfaces all black iron and bleached oak, set an Apollonian tone that extended to all the appointments of the restaurant. Hungry as he was, Matthew hoped that such austerity did not reach the kitchen.

They were greeted by a slim maître d' in a black turtleneck who led them to their table. Despite his youth, he moved and spoke with an air of sepulchral gravity. As they followed him, Matthew felt a poke in the back. He turned and smiled to see Laura Amochiev following them.

Her gray eyes danced as she squeezed Matthew's arm. "Is this the birthday boy?" she asked, nodding in Ira's direction.

Ira stopped and put his finger to his lips. "Shhhh," he whispered, his eyes wide. "Talking's not allowed when you're not at your table. Do want to get us thrown out?"

Laura laughed. "Happy birthday, Ira."

The maître d', who was several tables ahead of them, had interrupted his glide and was frowning back at them.

"Couldn't you figure that out from how quiet everybody is?" Matthew asked Laura, slipping his arm around her waist and propelling her forward.

"Quiet?" said Ira, as they caught up with the maître d'. "They're all eating in some kind of sacramental hush. Is somebody sitting *shiva* or what? I mean, what kind of food commands such reverence?"

Matthew spotted Hannah, Ira's wife, waving at them from a table for six in the back. He felt the usual surge of affection on seeing her, and he basked in the warmth she threw off wherever she went. She was so tiny, weighing well under a hundred pounds, that Matthew could never see her with the gigantic Ira without having to fend off grotesque images of the two of them together sexually.

With Hannah was another couple Matthew recognized as

the Goldens. Frizzy-haired and petite, Emily Golden was Hannah's best friend and a colleague at the mental health clinic where they worked. Her husband, Barry, whom Matthew had met only once before, was a wildly successful high-tech something-or-other who had made a bundle when his company went public. He had developed a gizmo that automatically monitored the viewing habits of cable television subscribers. Barry was tall and slender, with a rapidly receding hairline and a stolid manner. Humor, Matthew recalled, gave him a wide berth.

Hannah rose to greet the late arrivals and introduced Laura to the Goldens.

"Come Friday night," said Laura as she took her seat, "it feels good to be in any gathering where the lawyers don't outnumber everyone else. A fifty-fifty split is at least an improvement."

"Fifty-fifty is just right," said Ira, shaking out his napkin with a snap like a maid with a bedsheet. "Like my marriage. A lawyer and a shrink, which is a good mix. She thinks I'm evasive and I think she's intrusive."

"Would *I* be intrusive," asked a black-clad waitress who appeared out of nowhere, "if I asked the new arrivals what they would like to drink?" Pretty and efficient, she took their orders—a margarita for Matthew, a Beefeater martini for Ira, nothing for Laura—and disappeared.

"Hannah, how could you pick this place?" asked Ira a few minutes later as they were looking over the menus. "The guy who seated us had no spikes in his EKG, and I don't recognize anything on the menu."

"I suggested it, actually," said Barry in a dogged tone. "Aporia has been getting raves and you have to book a table two months in advance. The veal is supposed to be miraculous."

"Veal?" said Hannah, alarm in her voice.

"Don't get excited, Hannah," said Ira. "This is Cambridge, after all. No one slaughters calves here without their informed consent."

"He's right, Hannah," said Matthew. "They have to sign living wills." He pointed to the menu in his hand. "And it says right here that they only serve free-range veal and chicken."

"Well, I'll pass," said Hannah. "I think I'll have the grilled vegetable platter."

"Murderer," said Ira out the side of his mouth. "And listen to this. 'Baby lamb chops over a bed of tiny French lentils freshened with cinnamon, and plated with enoki mushrooms and a tempura of Swiss chard.' What do they mean, 'plated'?"

"I think it has something to do with electrolysis," Matthew offered.

"That's what I was afraid of. Probably gives you vinyl meningitis. How come," he asked Hannah, "we never get to go to any of those ethnic places Matt and I like? Matt, what was the name of that great Thai place where we had lunch on Tuesday?"

"Son of Siam."

"Right. Good stuff, too. Hotter than a pistol."

Hannah looked at Ira over the top of her menu. "Ira, you're being rude," she said lightly. "Barry recommended Aporia. And besides, I think the menu is intriguing."

Barry changed the subject. "Tell me, Matt, are you lawyers all supporting Crimmins for governor? To get another lawyer back in the State House?" Barry's smile was mirthless.

Matthew pressed his lips together and considered the question. "Well," he said, "he's not my first choice. But if he's nominated, I'll vote for him. He's got to be an improvement over what we've had up there. How about you?"

Barry looked disappointed. "He's too much of a throwback liberal for my taste."

"Liberal!" exclaimed Laura incredulously. "The guy wants to bring back the electric chair!"

"Well, not so much on social issues, I grant you. But on the economy, he's just another lunch-bucket Democrat. This state can't afford another antibusiness administration, messing with the economy and raising taxes. It would just hasten the exodus of business to the South."

"Barry's a great believer in the free market," Ira explained to Laura in a stage whisper. "Adam Smith's invisible hand and all that. Just like Newt Gingrich."

"I suppose I am," said Barry. He sounded resolute in the face of impending ridicule, like someone who's been told he is old-fashioned for defending marriage or Shakespeare.

"I understand Crimmins has a lot of support among lawyers at your shop," Laura said to Matthew.

"He's got Fleishman and Falk thumping the tub for him," said Matthew. "They're holding a fund-raising breakfast for him at the firm on Monday, in fact. But I don't know how deep his support is throughout the office."

"When you see it from where I sit," said Barry, ignoring this sideshow, "it's plain that interfering with the economy just fosters harmful inefficiencies and waste. Left to its own, the market will bring the greatest prosperity to the largest number of people. Call it the invisible hand if you like, but it's certainly better than the alternatives."

"Beware the politics," said Ira portentiously, "of a man who's been jerked off by the invisible hand."

An embarrassed silence fell over the group as everyone feigned absorption in the menu. It was Laura who finally broke the awkward stillness.

"Isn't it terrible," she said, "what they did to Joan of Arc?"

Everyone laughed. Even Barry.

"We don't get out much," said Hannah wryly as she patted Barry's arm.

"Sorry, Barry," said Ira. "Sometimes I can't help myself. I see someone lob a big fat gopher pitch like that and I wanna hit it out of the park. I'm working on it in my polarity therapy, you know. I'm beginning to get in touch with my inner lesbian. I call her Crystal."

Emily raised her glass. "Happy birthday, Ira!"

The others joined in the toast.

"Now, wait," said Ira, "before anybody starts singing, you should bear in mind how dangerous that can be. Right, Matt?"

Matthew frowned his perplexity.

"Tell them," Ira said slowly, "how you earned the undying enmity of Rowell Falk with the mere mention of a song."

"Falk?" said Hannah in wonder. "What did you do, Matt?"

"Ira's exaggerating," said Matthew. "At least, I hope he is."

"I'm not kidding," said Ira. "The guy bears a grudge."

"Who's Rowell Falk?" asked Emily.

"He's a corporate lawyer at Daphnis and Clooney," Matthew explained.

"A corporate lawyer?" exclaimed Ira. "That's like calling Bill Gates a programmer. Falk *is* the corporate department at Daphnis and Clooney. He's built up this huge practice representing high-tech companies."

"I heard Falk at a seminar," said Laura. "He was very impressive."

"Ain't no flies on him," Ira acknowledged. "He's as smart as they come and he knows his field better than anybody in town. His liberal political credentials are impeccable—Lawyers' Committee for Civil Rights and all that. Oops. Sorry, Barry. But at least you'll be pleased to hear he's computer literate. Despite his years, he's got a reputation as something of a hacker, at least for a lawyer. And he can play the bon vivant when the mood strikes him. But he chews up a secretary every six months, and he abuses the associates who work for him. Not to mention his partners. All in all, he's a proctologist's dream—a perfect asshole. But he is a formidable power in the firm."

"What could you sing that would alienate the great Rowell Falk?" Laura asked Matthew with a smile.

"I didn't *sing*," said Matthew with a touch of exasperation. "It was nothing, really. We were having cocktails before the firm's annual dinner a couple years ago and he was talking to me about poetry. He's a great admirer of Robert Frost."

"Tell me you didn't trash him." Her smile broadened.

"No, no. Not at all. He was extolling the virtues of 'Stopping by Woods on a Snowy Evening' and I let it slip that the poem could be sung to the tune of 'Hernando's Hideaway.'"

Ira started singing, sotto voce, his shoulders rolling with the beat:

"Whooooose woods these are I think I know [cha cha cha]
 His house is in the village, though. [bap bap bah]
 He will not see me stopping here
 To watch—his woods fill up with snow. Olé!"

On the concluding syllable, Ira held his hands beside his left ear and snapped both sets of fingers. The couple at the next table struggled to ignore him.

"Try it, I dare you," said Ira. "Just *try* to scour that out of your brainpan. Poor Rowell will never be able to read his favorite poem again without hearing it sung to a tango. Is that what it is, a tango? Anyway, it's like Bert Sugar's definition of an intellectual: someone who can listen to the *William Tell Overture* without thinking about the Lone Ranger. Can't be done. He hates you, Matt. No matter how nice he comes on to you, remember: he hates you."

"He doesn't *do* nice," said Matthew. "Not with me, anyway."

"Who's Bert Sugar?" asked Barry.

The food turned out to be pretty good after all. Ira had the lamb chops.

It wasn't until much later that evening, when they were in Matthew's bed, that Laura raised the question again. "So who," she mumbled, "*is* Bert Sugar?"

"Didn't your mother tell you not to talk with your mouth full?"

Laura laughed and looked up at him. "My mother never told me *anything* about this."

"Don't stop," he pleaded.

"I'm waiting," she said.

"He was the editor of *Ring Magazine*," Matthew explained. "Just keep doing that."

"Ring? Like in boxing?"

"Yes. Please," he begged.

"How disgusting," Laura said. And she resumed her ministrations.

Matthew laid his head back on the pillow. "Mmm," he said, way back in his throat. Laura's short blond hair hung down over her face, blocking his view. He closed his eyes and drifted.

Later, they lay quietly in each other's arms for several minutes before either spoke. It was Laura who broke the silence.

"I like Hannah a lot," she said. "She's a love. Ira too, but is he always so flip?"

"Not always. I think the martinis got to him tonight. He's not much of a drinker."

"Well, he must be fun to have around the office."

"Oh, thank *God* for that," Matthew said with conviction. "I can't imagine how dreary it would be without him. They would drive me around the bend."

Laura put both hands around his left arm and snuggled into his shoulder. "You're not very happy there, are you?"

"I'm not even sure that's the way to describe it. Some of it's OK. Even exciting, like this business with Danny and the *Chin* case. Other times it's just dreadful. And I just seem to stumble through it. It's like I'm just following my life around."

"By the way, did you read Eddie Felch's piece on Judge Doyle in the *Globe* this morning?"

"The one about the undistinguished jurist with his moment in the sun? Kind of snide and denigrating?"

"That's Eddie, right down to his socks," said Laura.

" 'Eddie'? You know him?"

"A little. I used to run into him when I was with the *Ledger*."

The *Patriot Ledger* was a Quincy-based newspaper with a large circulation in the suburban communities south of Boston. Laura had been a reporter before attending law school.

"I'm sorry," she went on. "I got you off track. You were telling me how fulfilling you find your life at Daphnis and Clooney." She was smiling, full of mischief, her left breast bobbing as she lay on her side with her head propped up on the heel of her hand.

"Mostly it's the mind-numbing tedium of the work," he said, watching her breast sway as she settled herself. "Like covering depositions. *Please,* God: when I die let it happen during a deposition. That way the transition from life to death will be less noticeable."

"You make an unconvincing cynic."

"And documents. Interrogatories. Requests for—"

"Hey, I know. I'm in the same business, remember?" Laura worked for a medium-sized firm that specialized in insurance-defense work. Like defending the architect in the *Felter* case, which they never discussed because, technically, they were adversaries in the case. Their clients had sued one another, each claiming the other was responsible for Felter's injuries.

"What about all the hostility? Doesn't it get to you?"

"What do you mean?" she asked with a look of mock confusion.

Matthew grinned. "Yeah, right. Though you *do* seem to thrive on it. Me, well, every time the telephone rings I get performance anxiety. Like Tuesday, when I had this lawyer screaming at me because my client was sending his alimony checks to Attila the Hen."

"You're kidding." Laura was laughing now, her breast jiggling. "He actually put that on the checks?"

"Oh, no." He reached out and cupped her drooping breast in the hollow of his hand. "He's too cute for that. He just puts it on the envelope. Last month it was the Bitch of Buchenwald. And I have to keep a straight face when her lawyer calls. Do I need this? And yet I get this feeling I'm supposed to win every phone call."

She clasped her hand over his. "I thought D and C was supposed to be laid back and associate-friendly. A more humane environment than the other big firms. You know, kinder, gentler. With people who are interested in things besides just law?"

"So did I. Well, maybe that's true for some of the partners, but I sure don't experience it that way. All those young associates are driven like salmon heaving themselves up the fish ladder on a dam. Maybe I'm just cut out to be a fat, sleepy lake bass. Unfortunately, the partners know the pool where I lurk."

"Like Falk?" Laura was grinning now.

Matthew grimaced. "I went to see him earlier this week about a settlement agreement I had drafted for him? Like always, he makes me feel like a piece of shit—in his sophisticated way, of course. I mean, I'm a good writer, a damn good one. Everybody tells me this. So I'm sitting there, admiring his gorgeous rug, and he's telling me my draft is the work of a mere scrivener."

"He called you a scrivener?"

"Not exactly, though he did use the word. The effect was clear. It always is. The first time I ever did any work for him, he told me I had misused the word 'comprise.' 'You will never get ahead in this firm,' he says to me, 'until you learn that the whole comprises the parts and the parts compose the whole.' That was four years ago, and I haven't used the word since."

"But surely that was his idea of a joke," said Laura.

"In a way. But in a way it wasn't. This is the guy who, when I went to ask for more details on one of his assignments, raises his eyebrows and asks, 'Was my memo unclear?' You know what I mean? How do you answer a question like that?"

"Pretty crummy," she agreed. The fingers of her right hand combed through the hair on his chest. "I can see why you'd want to stay away from him. So why don't you? He's not a litigator."

"No, but he uses a lot of them to service his clients. It's kind of ironic, actually. He loathes litigation. The 'zero-sum people,' he calls us. But he's one of the principal feeders of the litigation department. His clients are always getting sued. And he's the kind of guy who likes to stay on top of his cases. A couple times a week he makes the rounds through the halls like he's walking a trapline, keeping tabs on his client's cases."

"Swooping down on unsuspecting associates?"

"Exactly."

"An interesting verb, swooping," she said, nuzzling against his neck. "I've been known to do a little swooping myself." She slipped her hand under the sheet and slowly slid her fingers down his chest to his belly.

"It's a participle, not a verb," he whispered hoarsely. Inanely.

"And you're a pedant, not a scholar," she whispered back as her hand hit home. "But at least yours isn't dangling."

Matthew reached out and touched her cheek lightly as her lips neared his.

"Oh God," he murmured just before he kissed her. "Not the invisible hand again!"

# 11

## Chickens

The thirty-ninth floor of the cylindrical tower at Fort Point Towers was laid out in a series of concentric circles like the rings on an archer's target. Lawyers' offices made up the outer circumference, separated by a hardwood hallway from an inner band of secretarial cubicles. Further inside, tucked between the secretaries and the building's service core, was an enormous doughnut-shaped room. This odd space was the home of Central Files, the windowless repository of Daphnis & Clooney's case files, some open but not currently being worked by a lawyer, others closed but not long enough to qualify for off-site storage.

Central Files also housed the firm's data bank for identifying conflicts of interest. The courts had a simplistic way of deciding whose client was whose in a law firm: everybody's client was your client, period. As a consequence, with more than 150 lawyers, Daphnis & Clooney had so many clients, past and present, that a lawyer taking on a new case could not possibly know whether the representation might clash with the interests of another firm client. The lawyer needed to clear the names through the firm's centralized system for detecting conflicts.

Matthew had learned this the hard way. During his first year at Daphnis & Clooney, he was asked by his landlady to bring a small claims action against a Volvo dealership that had overcharged her for repairs. Eager to proceed with his first real client in a case all his own, Matthew had filed his complaint with dispatch—only to see his office doorway darkened, two days later, by the ungenial visage of Rowell Falk. He was dangling a document at arm's length from his thumb and forefinger like some disgusting bit of offal. Stepping forward, his sour face set in a look of gelid distaste, Falk said exactly nothing as he let Matthew's complaint flutter down on his desk. Then he left. Matthew needed no explanation, for it sank in with sickening swiftness that the dealership was one of Falk's clients. In the eyes of the law, Matthew had sued his own client.

To prevent such problems, the firm had developed an elaborate system for detecting conflicts of interest. Actually, there were two systems. One was an oak cabinet with drawers full of five-by-seven index cards. Dating from the 1950s, it looked remarkably like the card catalog for the town library in Sleepy Eye, Minnesota, complete with those little brass drawer pulls that curved down over your finger so pleasingly when you opened a drawer. When a new case form came in, the name and address of the new client was transferred to an index card, along with the name of the case and the initials of its originating and responsible attorneys. A clerk would then make up separate index cards for each name the lawyer identified as an "adverse party" (an opponent) or as someone whose interests might otherwise be affected by the case (called an "interested party"). After the names were checked for conflicts, all the new cards would be stuffed in the cabinet for use in determining whether a subsequent case raised a conflict.

About three years before, the firm had reached the belated decision to automate the process and created a second, electronic data bank. Information was now also entered directly onto a data base in the firm's computer system. Read-only access to the data could be had from computer terminals on the firm's area network. The terminal devoted to inputting data directly onto the system sat on a desk next to the oak cabinet. Although Central Files maintained that all the old data had been transferred from the index cards to the computer, careful lawyers—and those who had been burned, like Matthew—still insisted on running names through both data bases just to make sure they didn't step on the toes of one of the firm's thousands of clients. As a further precaution, Central Files circulated a weekly new case report, which summarized information about new matters. Lawyers were supposed to peruse the reports to spot any problems too subtle for detection during the conflict check, but most read them to keep tabs on who was bringing in what kind of business.

Central Files was the musty domain of Mrs. Miranda Beadle. Mrs. Beadle was a big, square-shouldered woman in her early sixties. She wore her tartan skirts long, her gray hair in a taut chignon, and her reading glasses on a chain around her neck. Possessed of a tart tongue and a fearsome sense of entitlement, Mrs. Beadle was a staunch keeper. She was especially loath to let anyone meddle with the apple-pie order of her files. She let it be known that requests for files or conflict checks were best made in writing, and she preferred that the cards be touched only by the listless clerks who toiled under her. Whenever someone mustered the temerity to insist on running his own conflict check, as Matthew needed to do today, Mrs. Beadle's eyes never left him, lest he cavalierly disturb the sequence of the cards.

From his computer station Matthew had already determined that Danny was neither an adverse party nor an interested party in any other firm matter, and it appeared the firm was not representing any of the other parties or witnesses involved in the *Chin* case. He wanted to check the hard data on the cards to make sure.

"Good morning, Mrs. Beadle," said Matthew with a timorous smile. It was scarcely 8:15, but the matron was at her post. He slid a single sheet of paper across the counter toward her. "I've got a new case form for you and I need to confirm a conflict check on the cards."

Mrs. Beadle obliged him with the brief show of a smile as she donned her glasses. She glanced at Matthew's report and quickly looked back at him. "There is no client's name," she said accusingly. Her brow was furrowed as she peered over her half-glasses.

"I know. The client's identity is confidential. That's why I need to run the name myself."

Mrs. Beadle removed her glasses and held them by the crossed temples. "Mr. Boer, the firm must know the names of its clients," she said. By "firm" she obviously meant herself.

"And so it will," answered Matthew. "I will disclose his identity to the Management Committee. My client is adamant that I preserve his anonymity, even from others at the firm. Meanwhile, I need to run his name through your records."

Mrs. Beadle scowled at him while she considered this. Then she put her glasses back on and looked at the new case form again.

"I see you've listed yourself as originating attorney," she said without looking up. "And there's that Ira Teitelbaum as RA. I'm just looking at the list of adverse and interested parties. The Commonwealth, the Boston Police Department, a Detective Carvalho. And a number of what appear to be Chinese names. May I assume we can be trusted to search for matches on those names at least?" She looked at Matthew again.

"Of course. I only need to run the client's name myself."

"You're sure you don't want to check *them* yourself as well?" she asked with a sense of injured merit.

"Mrs. Beadle, I'm sorry. This has nothing to do with you. Your granite discretion is known to everyone. I just happen to have a very nervous client. He's quite specific about the way he wants this handled. And if you knew his situation, you would understand."

"Oh, it's none of my business how you and Mr. *Teitelbaum* choose to 'handle' this. I just need to know what it is you want me to do. Well, come on. Scurry on back here. I've got other work to do this morning."

Matthew scurried.

He quickly found the card for the lawsuit over Danny's restaurant and then satisfied himself that there was no other listing in the name of Danny Li. The cards confirmed the electronic data—only one card was found in Danny's name, for the Lotus Blossom case. As the computer had indicated, no one else at the firm was representing a client with interests that might conflict with Danny's.

When Matthew returned to thank Mrs. Beadle, she crisply advised him that she had already cleared the other names listed on his new case form. He was up and running.

Matthew hurried back to his office. He banged his knee against the stacked cartons of documents he had received from the owners of the Hotel Adams three weeks earlier. They were there for his review before producing them in the *Felter* case. Billy O'Boy's third document request had targeted information on the ownership and development of the hotel, no doubt in quest of other deep pockets to sue. Matthew had dipped briefly into the cartons when they arrived. They presented a bewildering and depressingly complex series of ownership entities, with limited partnerships within limited partnerships, interlocking shell corporations and nominee trusts, plus a klatch of lenders and investors taking pieces of the deal at varying stages. It would take hours to complete the dreary task of sorting out who was who, and when, and why. Matthew had called O'Boy and obtained an extension of time for making production. The cartons had sat undisturbed ever since, but Matthew felt a stab of guilt and dread every time he looked at them. Which, of course, was often since they were piled up next to his desk.

He checked his watch; 8:35. He grabbed his suit jacket off the back of his desk chair and rushed out the door and down the hall. His coat only half on, he ducked into the library and, trailing fabric like Loretta Young, swirled his way down the spiral staircase to the thirty-eighth floor.

By the time he reached the firm's lunchroom, it was already packed with lawyers. Most of them were from Daphnis & Clooney, but Matthew recognized some from other firms, like Morton Atwater. Ben Fleishman was still introducing Jackie Crimmins. After quickly scanning the room, Matthew despaired of finding a seat at one of the tables. He filled a cup from a coffee urn on the buffet table and went to stand at the back of the room. He found himself next to Robolawyer.

Rob O'Leary, as his mother called him, was a litigation machine. He had no outside interests Matthew knew of, just an all-consuming passion for the rules of evidence and civil procedure. The year he broke the 3800 barrier in billable hours, his wife had taken the kids and left, but he developed bionic endurance and worked even harder. All of which made him, at only thirty-four, a rising star in the firm. Ira had rechristened him, and the new tag was like a tin can tied to a dog's tail ever since. Their exchange of good-morning nods was interrupted by a spattering of applause that greeted Jackie Crimmins. Jackie was buttoning his jacket and walking toward Fleishman.

"Such an introduction!" Jackie said, smiling as he shook hands with Fleishman. "Most of you know that Benjamin and I go back a long ways—back, I might add, to times when no one would ever have accused us of seeing eye to eye on anything, let alone on who should become governor."

Jackie made a show of looking up at Fleishman from his tiptoes, mocking their great disparity in height. He got a few chuckles from the audience.

"But despite our hard-won friendship," Jackie continued, "and the embarrassing enthusiasm of his introduction, I could not help thinking, as I listened to him, of President William Howard Taft. He was a Republican, you know. So I guess that makes this the bipartisan portion of my remarks this morning."

A few more chuckles.

"President Taft was once introduced by a prominent New York lawyer named Chauncy Dupree." Jackie lengthened the vowels of the name just slightly and it came out *Chawncy*. "Now, Chauncy Dupree, in recounting the various offices Taft had held—senator, president, chief justice—pointedly referred to each position as 'pregnant with power.' No doubt he was poking a little fun at Taft's size. He was, as you know, a man of great girth—much like my old friend and former colleague here. Good morning, Ira."

Teitelbaum waved amiably from one of the tables near the front.

"Today, I suppose," Jackie went on, "we would have to call him circumferentially challenged. At any rate, Taft got up, thanked Dupree, and broke the news that he was indeed pregnant. 'If it's a boy,' he promised, 'I'll call him George. If it's a girl I'll call her Martha. And if it's just hot air, I'll call it Chauncy.' "

Fleishman led the laughter.

"It's flattering to see such a turnout so early in the morning. And I am especially gratified to see the faces of two people who have already done so much for our team. I refer, of course, to Rowell and Petina."

Matthew could see Petina Stong beaming back at Jackie. Falk's concentration seemed unbroken.

"As counsel to our committee, Rowell has been our bulwark against those niggling bureaucrats who administer our state's mysterious campaign finance laws. Would that our judges had the judgment and common sense of a Rowell Falk!"

Matthew and Robolawyer looked at one another and raised their eyebrows in unison. Rowell Falk on the bench? Matthew couldn't imagine Falk, with his mordant distaste for litigators, ever sitting through a whole trial, let alone presiding over one. As a business lawyer, the man hadn't so much as sniffed at the rules of evidence since he got out of law school, and he had a shorter affability span than Leona Helmsley.

"And as for Petina," said Jackie, "well, let me tell you. I came to her about a year ago with a half-baked notion of using private enterprise to eradicate the Combat Zone. Using her legal expertise in real estate financing, she has fleshed out my notion into a detailed redevelopment plan which will scrub that stain off the face of our city."

Jackie paused briefly and looked around the room. "Now, I know what you're all asking yourselves. What are these three intelligent, cultivated liberals—a Beacon Hill Brahmin like Falk, a director of the Anti-Defamation League like Benjamin, and a fire-breathing feminist like Petina—what are these people *doing* consorting with a hidebound old Mick like me?

"Well, let me tell you a little story.

"Most of you are too young to remember when my South Boston neighborhood wasn't quite as urban as it is today.

But when I was a boy it was not so uncommon for immigrant families to raise a little light livestock. Poultry. A goat or two now and then. My grandmother, God rest her soul, kept chickens. She sold the eggs to supplement her food budget. And it was my great delight, as a six-year-old boy, to help her feed the hens and gather the eggs.

"Now, it happened that Grandmother's hens were not respecters of private property. They liked to wander next door into Mr. McLaughlin's garden and work their mischief on his vegetables and flowers. Mr. McLaughlin was a choleric old darling who liked a jar of porter, and he railed bitterly against the feathered Visigoths. Nowadays, I suppose, he would have hired one of you and my grandmother would have retained Royce and Bell.

"Well, instead Grandmother got my father and my uncle to build a small run for the chickens. It was then that I observed something very curious. All day long the hens would walk back and forth, back and forth, along the fence, looking for a way out." Jackie's fingers scuttled across the table in front of him. "And then, every night, they would roost on that fence." Jackie held up both hands like a man hanging from a ledge. Laughter spread across the room.

"Now, what is it, I ask you, that is missing from the neurological makeup of a chicken that it can't escape the conditioned reflex of always hopping back down inside its own cage?" Here Jackie used an index finger to turn an imaginary screw into his right temple. "When all she needs is to look straight ahead and jump out of the deep-ditched pathways of whatever passes for thought in a chicken, and she can have her way with Old Man McLaughlin's flowers?

"Hey, don't get me wrong. I'm not here to malign the liberal wing of my party (you should pardon the pun) by comparing them to a flock of silly hens. After all, I'm here this morning because, like my grandmother, I need the eggs. No, it's my profession, *our* profession, I'm talking about. It needs desperately to crack out of the calcified shell of its old ways of looking at problems that just aren't going away.

"Take smut. Well, you take it. I'm against it. Always have been. It's an abomination. But I have to tell you, I've *had* it with going toe to toe against you First Amendment types over the enforcement of our pathetic obscenity laws. Because, frankly, I've been getting the bejesus kicked out of me. The Public Morals division of my office just ends up wasting precious manpower in endless legal battles we never win. Censorship may be good politics but it's bad policy. It doesn't work. And it's time somebody got honest with the public and acknowledged the fact.

"But." Jackie poked a finger in Petina's direction. "Create a partnership of government, neighborhood activists, and private developers and you can use law and economics to do what law alone could never do. Under Petina's plan the state's power to undertake urban renewal will be harnessed to the energies of private development. We will revitalize Chinatown and the communities that adjoin the Combat Zone. And we will bulldoze those smut merchants right into Fort Point Channel.

"Take our failing schools. Blame it on forced busing, if you like. Or on white flight, if you find that ideologically more palatable. We've had that battle. Or you might, if you're like me, point to the erosion of traditional values at home and in school. Take your pick. But at least let's agree on the state of things, which is that our public schools are an unmitigated disaster.

"Now, I'm the product of a parochial school, where I learned the value of discipline and hard work. I'm not some fruitcake pressing to replace biology with creationism, and I don't intend to kick off some witch-hunt to oust homosexual teachers. I'm on record as favoring voluntary school prayer, but that's another fight I'd just as soon leave to others because I don't think it would make one whit of difference to the quality of our schools. Again, let's work with what we can agree on. And I know two things about education that I'm betting the voters of this state are going to agree with me on: our schools need to go back to teaching basic educational skills and they deserve increased funding through a nickel-a-gallon surtax on gasoline.

"One last example that speaks most distinctly to our profession. It's about crime. The two wings of my party have been singeing each other's pin feathers off for thirty years over this one. And in vain. I confess that I favor a somewhat more capacious view of what constitutes probable cause than the one currently held by our Supreme Judicial Court, but these are details. Stuff at the margins. I have something bigger and yet more doable in mind. I intend to overrule *Mapp v. Ohio.*

"I'm sure that most of you haven't given much thought to the *Mapp* case since law school—if you recall it all. It's the Warren Court decision that gave us the exclusionary rule. You know, the one where the constable blunders and the villain goes free because the evidence gets thrown out? That is a travesty. That is the exaltation of technicality over justice. Ask anybody on the street and see if they don't agree with me. The rule has done more to breed public contempt for the criminal justice system and the legal profession than any single event, juridical or otherwise, of the last half-century.

"And when I'm governor, I'm going to overrule it."

Jackie paused and smiled. "How, you ask, could a governor 'overturn' a decision by the United States Supreme Court? Well, let's back up a minute. Why does the rule exist? Because, let's face it, it's the only game in town. The Supreme Court realized that there was nothing at all to deter overzealous policemen from trampling on the constitutional rights of citizens to be free from unreasonable searches and seizures. 'Gee willikers, Your Honor. You're right. I should have gotten a search warrant. But look at the evidence I found. He's guilty, isn't he? No harm, no foul.' So the Court established a disincentive to illegal shortcuts by the police. Do it by the rules or we won't hear your evidence.

"For a generation now those of us in law enforcement have been battling those of you who want to protect the constitutional rights of individuals. We've been fighting bitterly over whether it's right to exclude the evidence. And there's an air of unreality about it all. Because we shouldn't be arguing about whether illegally seized evidence should be admitted or not. Remember, the exclusionary rule is only supposed to be a means to an end, a tool to encourage respect for the law of search and seizure. In that, it has failed miserably. Far from making lawmen respect the law, it has made cynics out of them as they watch the villains walk. And policemen get credit for collars, not convictions, so the 'deterrent effect' of the rule is largely illusory. There's got to be a better way to do the deterring.

"In fact, the Supreme Court in *Mapp* anticipated the possibility. It indicated it would abrogate the rule for those states that came forward with an effective alternative deterrent. We've all been so wrapped up in the battle over the wisdom of the rule that no one has taken up the Court's challenge.

"I tell you, the Court these days is open to suggestion on this issue as never before. We've got a lot of smart, high-priced legal talent in this state. In this very room. I want to put it to work and see if we can't come up with our own alternative. What I have in mind is a review board that would compensate the victims of deliberately illegal searches and seizures in some fixed amount—say, a thousand or fifteen hundred dollars. At first blush, that doesn't seem like a lot of money. But when you consider that the compensation would be paid by the offending policeman, I'm sure you'll agree that it would be a much more powerful deterrent than suppressing the evidence.

"I've been working with the leadership of the policemen's unions and associations, as well as conferring with my fellow district attorneys across the state. I think it can be done. To head the committee that will draft the necessary legislation, I've put the touch on Benjamin here. Morton Atwater of Royce and Bell has agreed to cochair it with him. Hey, I had to have one Republican, right?"

Jackie put his hands in his jacket pockets. "Pornography. Education. Crime. My friends, we don't have to be that hen on the fence, caught up forever in self-defeating habits of thought. Don't just hop back down into the pen and peck away at the same old ideological chicken feed. Come on outside with us and we'll all head for the flowers."

The speech was loudly applauded. But Matthew noticed that Jackie Crimmins had not once mentioned the death penalty.

# 12

───◆───

# IT Call Home

Just a couple more questions to wrap up, Detective. You've told us that until you were ordered to produce your informant, you were confident that he would make himself available, is that right?"

The question, which Matthew heard as he was entering the courtroom, was put by a man he recognized as the prosecutor, Jeremiah DeMarco. Testimony was being taken on Michael Chin's motion to dismiss the indictment against him on the theory that the loss of critical exculpatory evidence—namely, the identity and whereabouts of a confidential informant—was the result of deliberate misconduct on the part of the Commonwealth. Matthew wasn't sure if he should be rooting for Chin or DeMarco.

Matthew shuffled quietly toward the front and slid into the second row of pewlike benches outside the rail. Across the aisle to the right was a gaggle of what Matthew assumed were reporters, some writing in little notebooks, others smiling and whispering to one another. A single television camera had been set up in the jury box. With its station's call letters shouted in a chemical fuschia from its metal barrel, the camera was a sinister and alien intruder in the dark wood-paneled courtroom.

DeMarco looked relaxed and fit as he stood behind the prosecutor's table. Quietly taking notes at the table to his left sat a tall attractive woman with closely cropped brown hair. Sarah Kerlinsky, Matthew said to himself. The judge, his eyes half closed behind yellowed lids like cheese parings, was gazing idly at a pigeon that preened its feathers on the ledge outside the window.

"It's like I told you," Carvalho answered. "The guy was always reliable and he never gave me any reason to think he wouldn't show if we needed him to testify."

"And how did he feel about having to testify?"

"Objection," Sarah said without looking up.

"Sustained," said Judge Doyle blandly, his eyes never leaving the pigeon. "Rephrase the question, Mr. DeMarco." Evidently, Judge Doyle could attend to more than one thing at once.

"Did the informant say anything that led you to suspect that he might be concerned about testifying in this case?"

"No. Not at all. He said he had no problem with it."

"And that's why you didn't feel the need to take his statement?"

"That's right."

"Or to learn his identity and address?"

"Right."

"In retrospect, don't you think it would have been better to have gathered that information, just to make sure you had it if you were ordered to produce him?"

"In retrospect, sure. It woulda been a good idea." Carvalho looked up at the judge, but he was still watching his pigeon, so he turned back to DeMarco. "But you gotta remember, this guy never told me his name before, or where he lived, or anything—and I never asked him. That was our deal. He gave me information; I didn't ask personal questions. That's the way he wanted it. So I figured, I start asking him now, he might get spooked and disappear."

"And when you learned of the court's order to disclose his identity, you conducted—and I'm quoting from your report now—'a diligent and comprehensive search for the informant.' Is that correct?"

"Yes. Like I said, I looked through mug books. Nothing. I cruised Jamaica Plain to look for him. But I couldn't. So we looked pretty much all over the city. He never surfaced."

"You and Detective Piscatello?"

"Yeah."

"And were all these efforts made in good faith?"

"Absolutely."

"Is there any doubt in your mind that you are unable to produce this witness at this time?"

"None whatsoever. The guy just disappeared."

"He's gone?"

"Like smoke."

"Thank you, Detective. That's all I have for the moment, Your Honor," said DeMarco. He took his seat.

Sarah Kerlinsky did not look up. "If I may have a moment, Your Honor," she said, still scribbling rapidly on a yellow pad in front of her.

When she spoke, Matthew heard a sharp intake of breath from a woman seated in front of him between two hulking policemen in uniform. A solidly built redhead in her late thirties, the woman wore a sensible gray suit and a maroon scarf. What struck Matthew about her was the terrible intensity with which she watched Sarah Kerlinsky. It took him a moment before he realized what it was that fired her intensity. It was hatred. She gave it off in waves of such fervid incandescence he had to stifle an urge to move away from her. Then he recognized her from press photos. She was Dunleavy's widow. And the officers must be his brothers. What was her name? Dorothy? Something like that. Taught social studies at a middle school in Hyde Park.

Sarah Kerlinsky put down her pen and stood up. She aligned the yellow pad in the center of the table. With the fingers of her left hand tapping a stack of papers next to her, she looked up, first at the judge and then at the witness.

Raymond Carvalho, who had been looking around the room, met her eye when she stood. He twisted his body slightly and settled himself comfortably, his hands drooping loosely over the arms of the witness chair.

"Detective Carvalho, we met at the probable cause hearing in this case, did we not?"

"Oh, we met long before that, Counselor." Carvalho smiled.

"But I'm referring only to the hearing that began on February 27th. Do you recall answering my questions at that hearing?"

"Vividly." He maintained his smile, relaxed but a little combative.

"Good," she said brightly, ignoring his manner. "Then you remember testifying about the two drug purchases you made at the apartment where the shooting took place?"

"Of course."

"One on February 4th and the other on February 5th, is that right?"

"I don't recall the dates, but if that's what I said, that's when I made the buys."

"On both occasions, when you made the buys, you asked for someone by name, did you not?"

"I did."

"And that name was John, wasn't it?"

"I asked for John, yes, but the person who—"

"You didn't ask for Michael, did you?"

"No. I asked for John."

"And the reason you asked for John instead of the defendant, Michael Chin, was because your informant had told you that someone named John lived there and ran the business out of the apartment?"

"Yes."

"And when you asked for John, did anyone behind the door tell you there was no John there?"

"No."

"No one refused to sell you drugs because you had given them the name of somebody they didn't know?"

"Believe me, they didn't care."

"But you did make a point of mentioning John's name, didn't you?"

"Yes, but I coulda told him Janet Reno sent me and he woulda taken my money." Carvalho smiled at his joke and looked out at the crowd, but it remained tense and silent.

Sarah turned her head toward the bench. "I move to strike everything after 'yes' as not responsive to the question."

"Strike it," said the judge, in a bored tone.

She turned back toward the witness. "At the probable cause hearing you also testified that IT told you that he had been inside the apartment two days before the shooting. Isn't that correct?"

"Yes."

"And he told you he saw John there then, didn't he?"

"Yes, he did."

"Did IT tell you he saw anyone other than John in the apartment when he was there?"

"No."

"Did he ever mention anyone other than John as working out of the apartment?"

"No, he didn't."

"In fact, IT never mentioned anyone else at all in connection with the operation at sixteen Tyler Street. The only person he ever mentioned was John, isn't that right?"

"That's right."

"OK. Now, let's back up a minute. You testified earlier today that you first received word sometime in early January that drugs were being sold out of sixteen Tyler. You got a tip from IT. And in your affidavit you describe observations you made at the site in order to confirm the tip." She looked up at him and waited.

"That's right," Carvalho said, finally realizing that an answer was expected.

"You testified that you personally 'surveilled,' to use your word, activity at sixteen Tyler Street between six or seven times before you applied for a search warrant, isn't that right?"

"The way I remember it, I said I didn't recall how often I did surveillance at the apartment."

"I'm just taking this from the transcript of your testimony, Detective. You said, and I quote, 'I surveilled the location many times, maybe six or seven times, before I tried to make a controlled buy.' Was that your testimony?"

"If that's what it says, yes."

"Do you wish to change that testimony in any way?"

"No, no. I just don't know exactly how many times I did it, that's all."

"But would it be fair to say, even today, that your best recollection is that you observed activity at sixteen Tyler at least half a dozen times before you sought a warrant?"

"Yes."

"And in the course of this extensive surveillance, you saw people buying drugs through a hole in the door?"

"Yes."

"And you saw people coming in and out of the apartment itself as well?"

"Yes, I did."

"Did you ever see Michael Chin go in or out of the apartment?"

Pausing, Carvalho brought his thumb and forefinger to his mouth, as if to pick at a piece of skin on his lip. He looked at the lawyer in front of him.

"I'm not sure," he said at last.

"Detective, would you like me to read again from your testimony at the probable cause hearing? Because there you stated flatly that you did *not* see the defendant at the scene at any time before the shooting. Has something happened to shake your confidence in that statement?"

"Not really. It's just that—well, I don't know any way to say this that don't sound, you know, like prejudiced? But they're all Chinese, you know what I'm saying?"

Sarah Kerlinsky smiled. "They all look alike?" she asked.

"Objection," said DeMarco.

"Overruled," said Judge Doyle.

"We're waiting, Detective," said Sarah.

"I'm just saying it's hard to be sure I didn't see him."

"But you expressed no such uncertainty during your earlier testimony. When I asked you if you saw the defendant during the course of your surveillance, you answered, 'I did not.' Isn't that correct?"

"Yes, but—"

"And today you're a little less certain?"

"Yeah."

"But you're not telling us that you *did* see Michael Chin on the scene before the shooting, are you?"

"No. Only that I'm not one hundred percent sure I didn't."

"Okay. I can live with that."

She bent down and flipped over to another page of her yellow pad.

She said, "Now, during the probable cause hearing you were present when the Commonwealth's other witnesses testified, isn't that right?"

"Yeah, I watched some of the testimony."

"I'm referring to the testimony of the three men who were arrested with the defendant. You were present when I examined them, were you not?"

"Yes, I was there."

"And you heard me ask each of them if they saw John at the scene of the shooting?"

"Um-hum."

"And what was their testimony, as best you can recall?"

"I object, Your Honor." DeMarco, rising halfway from his chair. "The testimony of those witnesses is what it is. There's a transcript. I don't see why we need Detective Carvalho's recollection of it."

"On the contrary, Your Honor," said Sarah. "What the detective knew about the importance of IT's testimony is highly relevant to my claim that the police did not act in good faith to preserve the informant's identity and whereabouts."

"She may have the question," said the judge. DeMarco sat down heavily.

"Detective?" she prodded. "How did the witnesses answer my question about John's presence?"

"They said they hadn't seen him there in a while."

"In fact, they said John hadn't been around for weeks, isn't that right?"

"Yes."

"And that Michael Chin was the only person dealing drugs out of the apartment on the day of the shooting?"

"Yes."

"And Michael Chin had been the only person dealing there for *weeks* prior to the shooting?"

"I think that's right."

"And all three of them testified to that effect?"

"Yes, they did."

"And you were aware that their testimony flatly contradicted the information you had been given by your own 'highly reliable' informant, isn't that right?"

"Well, I don't know about 'flatly contradicting.' It's different, anyway."

"Different? We're talking about the three eyewitnesses who claim Michael Chin ran in with the gun. And they say that Michael Chin, and Michael Chin alone, was working out of the apartment for weeks before the shooting. All three of them say they never saw the man your own informant told you was actually living in the apartment and was dealing drugs out of it just two days before the shooting. And you call it 'different'?"

"Well, it doesn't get too much more different than that," said Carvalho, surrendering. An unconvincing smile hung off his face.

"It certainly doesn't," said Sarah sharply.

She paused, leaning into her notes. Carvalho looked around the courtroom again. Matthew noticed that he did not look in the direction of Mrs. Dunleavy and her brothers-in-law.

"Detective Carvalho, do you recall having a conversation with Captain Oliver Gogarty on the night of the shooting? Who is Captain Gogarty, by the way?"

"He's the head of DCU. The Drug Control Unit."

"So he's your superior?"

"My boss, yeah."

"And you had a conversation with him that night, after the shooting?"

"He was there on the scene, so I must have talked to him. I'm sure I did."

"Didn't he tell you then that the identity of your informant would have to be disclosed?"

"Gogarty told you that?" Carvalho looked surprised.

"Please. You know how it works. I ask, you answer."

"He might have said something like that. I don't remember exactly."

"But after breaking into an empty apartment, you must

have known, did you not, that identification would likely be a major issue at trial?"

"Well, we arrested four people and found one gun. I guess I knew the case was going to come down to which one of them did the shooting, if that's what you mean."

"And despite that awareness, and despite the advice of your captain, you took no steps at that time to secure IT's availability in the likely event his identity had to be disclosed?"

"I told you. I had no reason to think he wouldn't be available."

"I take it your answer is no, you didn't take such steps." She waited for him again.

"That's right."

"In fact, didn't you go to Captain Gogarty a couple weeks later, after I filed my motion to compel disclosure of your informant's identity? And didn't you ask him for advice on how you could preserve IT's anonymity?"

"Yeah, I did," Carvalho raised his voice a little, as if suddenly recalling the injustice of it all. "He was a productive, working snitch. I didn't want him burned if I could avoid it. Plus he might end up getting himself killed."

"Killed? But didn't you testify today that IT had no problem with testifying?"

"I said he was a good snitch. I never said he had brains. Most of them didn't go to Harvard, you know."

"And IT never—by the way, what did you call him, anyway?"

"I said before. I never knew his name."

"Oh, I heard that. But what did you *call* him? You didn't go driving around Jamaica Plain calling out, 'IT! IT!' did you? Or was it, 'IT, call home!' "

There was laughter from the audience, especially in the front where the press was congregated, and a sleepy smile crept across Judge Doyle's face. He was still facing away from the witness and looking out the window. The pigeon had been joined by two others, and the three of them moved jerkily about on the stone ledge.

"Of course not," snapped Carvalho, obviously smarting

from the ridicule. "That was his code name. 'I' for informant, 'T' because he was the one after 'S.'"

"But you didn't call him that to his face, did you?"

"No."

"So what *did* you call him?"

Carvalho looked at her, clearly stumped for a moment. Then he said, "Nothing. 'My man,' sometimes. But mostly, nothing at all."

"And how did you say you got in touch with him, again?"

"Sometimes he'd call me and we'd set up a meet. Other times I'd cruise his neighborhood, looking for him. If I saw him I'd make eye contact from the car and, like, signal him." Demonstrating, Carvalho cut his eyes to one side and tipped his head slightly in the same direction. "Then he'd know to meet me in the alley back of Blackmon's Spa. He was reliable that way."

"Did you pay him for information?"

"Sure. You think these guys do it 'cause they're public spirited or something?" Carvalho was not smiling.

"How much?"

"Let's see," said Carvalho, looking up as though he were trying to read numbers off the ceiling. "On a warrant, he got a hundred bucks if we seized contraband, twenty if we came up empty. And he'd get thirty or forty dollars if we made a good bust without a warrant. There's records of all this."

"Oh, we'll get to that. How much if he made a controlled buy for you?"

Carvalho shrugged. "Twenty-five, maybe thirty bucks."

Sarah smiled. "That's a handsome little cottage industry, wouldn't you say?"

Carvalho smiled back. "I wouldn't want to have to live off it."

"You said he was a productive snitch. Just how productive was he? How often did you use him?"

"A lot."

"Can you be a little more specific? Ten times? Fifteen?"

"Maybe as many as fifteen."

"You told Mr. DeMarco that you would meet with IT at least twice, sometimes more often, each time you used him as the source of information, whether to obtain a search warrant or to make a warrantless arrest. Is that right?"

"Yes. On average, anyway."

"So if he helped you get fifteen warrants, you would have met with him at least thirty times?"

"I guess that's right."

"Over what period of time did he supply you with information?"

"The last couple of years or so."

Sarah reached down and picked up stack of papers bound together with a large spring-loaded binder clip. She looked up at the judge. "May I approach the witness, Your Honor?"

By the time Judge Doyle nodded his assent, she was already walking toward Carvalho. She handed him the packet of documents.

"Detective Carvalho, I've just handed you a series of affidavits used to obtain search warrants. The originals are on file with the clerk's office. All of them appear to bear your signature. Would you please have a look? Take your time."

DeMarco straightened up abruptly. He stared intently at Sarah as she walked back to his table and handed him a duplicate of the documents Carvalho was perusing. She caught his eye and smiled, and Matthew saw something pass between them.

"I have assembled them in reverse chronological order, Detective," she said after a few moments, while Carvalho was still thumbing through the papers. "The one on top is your affidavit in this case. The second and third are those used to get warrants in the *Lovelady* and *Rovario* cases, which you mentioned in your affidavit. The *Rovario* affidavit refers to the case for which the fourth affidavit was issued. The fourth affidavit refers to the defendant in the fifth, and the fifth refers to the sixth, and so on, all the way through the pile of affidavits. Do you see that, Detective?"

The witness was slow in responding. Then he looked up and nodded.

"You have to use words, Detective."

"Yes, I see that."

Sarah Kerlinsky leaned forward with both hands on the table. "And doesn't every one of those affidavits identify IT as the confidential source of the information?"

"Yes," said Carvalho.

"And did you sign all those affidavits?"

"It appears to be my signature, yes."

"How many cases are we talking about here—Strike that. I'll save you the trouble of counting. You've got fifty-two affidavits there, going back almost three years. That's a lot more than fifteen, isn't it?"

Judge Doyle looked alert now, the pigeons forgotten. He wheeled his chair around to scowl at Carvalho.

"Who counts?" said Carvalho, an edge in his voice now.

"I do," Sarah responded. "Because if, as you said, you met with him twice each time you needed a warrant, then we're up to at least a hundred and four meetings with him. Am I right?"

"If you say so."

"No, you say' so. I'm just doing the math. Now, search warrants weren't the only thing you used IT for. Didn't you tell us you also made warrantless drug arrests based on information IT gave you?"

"Yes, sometimes."

"Well, how often is 'sometimes'?"

"I don't remember. I told you I didn't count." Sullen now.

"Fortunately," she said, reaching forward to grasp another set of documents, "we don't have to rely on you for that. I had a subpoena served on the Drug Control Unit for copies of all reports of warrantless arrests in which IT was identified as a source of information. Do you know how many reports I received?"

DeMarco started to rise. "Your Honor, how is he supposed to know how—"

"Ms. Kerlinsky," interrupted Judge Doyle, "let's just get to it, shall we?"

"Sorry, Your Honor. Detective, departmental records indicate that you used IT to make at least thirty-eight warrantless arrests. That makes an additional seventy-six contacts with IT, bringing the total to—let's see now—one hundred seventy-two meetings."

Carvalho glared and said nothing.

"I can also tell you," Sarah continued, "that in response to the same subpoena, DCU produced records indicating that

IT made at least eight controlled drug purchases under your supervision. Presumably, these called for still more meetings with IT. Now, let's not quibble over the exact number, but you would agree with me, would you not, that you must have had at least a hundred seventy-five meetings with this man over the last three years?"

Carvalho stared at her.

"Detective?" she prompted

Carvalho lifted his hands before him like a man asked to do the impossible.

"I guess," he answered. "I must have."

"You spent a lot of time with this guy. And you don't know his name?"

"No."

"In fact, you didn't even have some sort of nickname to call him—other than 'my man.' Isn't that right?"

"Yeah."

"Did you ever know where he lives?"

"No."

"Or who he hangs out with?"

"No, I don't."

"How long he'd been in Boston?"

"No."

"Did he have brothers or sisters?"

"I don't think he ever mentioned any."

"What was his educational background?"

"I don't know. I told you, I didn't ask questions."

"Had he ever been incarcerated, to your knowledge?"

"I don't think so."

"Do you know this for a fact?"

"No."

"Did he have an arrest record?"

"Not that I'm aware of. At least I wasn't able to find his picture in any of the mug books."

"Which you only looked at *after* you learned of the court's order to produce him."

"Yeah, that's right."

"Was he a dealer?"

"I don't know."

Sarah Kerlinsky stopped and looked down at the pad in

front of her. After a moment, she said, "You told us today that you met with IT seven times since the shooting, and once just two days afterwards."

"Yeah, I did."

"And you never sought to learn his identity or where he lived, did you?"

"I told you I didn't want to—"

"That's a yes or no question, Detective Carvalho."

He paused as if to consider this.

"No," he said at last.

"Did anyone at DCU order you to get that information?"

"No. Not until April 17th, when the DA told me about the judge's order." Carvalho nodded in DeMarco's direction.

Sarah Kerlinsky looked at DeMarco, too. "And the district attorney didn't tell you to secure that information before April 17th either, did he?"

"No."

Judge Doyle shot a look at the clock. Sarah apparently noticed this, for she said, "Just a couple more questions, detective. Have you ever heard of something called 'Special Order 8577'?"

Carvalho looked puzzled. "Which one is that? We got a lot of special orders."

"I'll read you its full title: 'Special Order 8577. Subject: Procedures in the Use of Informers.' Does that ring any bells?"

"It's the department's policy for keeping track of snitches."

"So you are aware of the policy?"

Carvalho grimaced with impatience. "Yeah, I know about it, but you got to—"

"You've answered my question," Sarah cut him off. "The policy requires officers using informants to record on an index card each informant's name, address, and other background information. The informant is to be assigned a number for identification, which is to be noted on the card. And the cards are kept by police supervisors. Does all that sound familiar?"

"Yeah, that sounds about right."

"Did you ever set up such a card for IT?"

"I didn't, no."

"Did anyone else at the department enter his name on a card, to your knowledge?"

"No."

"The policy further provides that any informant trading information for money must be interviewed by a supervisor and photographed before payment is made. IT was never interviewed by one of your supervisors, was he?"

"No."

"And his photograph was never taken?"

Carvalho looked exasperated. "Look," he said, "you don't understand. You tell a snitch he's gotta meet with a captain and have his picture taken, and forget it. He's history. You know what I'm sayin' here? *Nobody* follows that policy 'cause nobody would have any snitches if they did."

"So your answer is no, you didn't have his picture taken?"

"That's right," he answered. He was angry now.

"And are you telling us you never followed departmental policy on keeping records on informants?"

"I'm telling you, nobody did," he snapped. "It was a joke cooked up by a bunch of lawyers in the legal office."

"Sort of like this hearing?" She smiled at him.

Carvalho lifted his chin defiantly and, tilting his head to one side, he opened his mouth to respond. DeMarco was on his feet shouting his objection before he could answer, but it was evident to all that Carvalho was about to snarl his agreement.

"I withdraw the question," Sarah, her voice edged with contempt. "And I'm finished with the witness."

"So am I," said Judge Doyle, his mood blackened. "I'll see counsel in chambers. Five minutes."

He had almost made his angry way out of the courtroom before the bailiff could cry, "All rise!"

Matthew watched as Carvalho wearily pulled himself out of the witness chair and walked listlessly between the two counsel tables. Then he stopped and turned toward Sarah.

"It *is* a joke, you know," he said. He spoke flatly, sullenly.

She lifted her head to look at him.

She said, "Not to Michael Chin, it's not."

She held his gaze. It was Carvalho who looked away first.

Then he pulled open the gate in the rail and walked slowly up the aisle and out of the courtroom.

Not once, Matthew noticed, did he look in the direction of Mrs. Dunleavy.

# 13

---

## Jonah's Wife

"What the fuck," asked Judge Doyle a few minutes later, when the lawyers were ushered in before him, "is going on here, Jerry?" He had his feet on his desk and a lighted cigarette in his right hand. The chief justice for administration had forbidden smoking in the courthouse, but there wasn't much he could do to enforce his fiat against judges who enjoyed life tenure.

"I'm not exactly sure, Judge," DeMarco answered. He crossed his legs and clasped his hands over his knee.

"You got a narcotics officer with a nose Karl Malden would hide under a bushel. He's got a mystery snitch who gets around like Kilroy. As far as I can tell, this IT is the guy's only snitch. Does he exist or is he just a Fig Newton of Carvalho's imagination?"

Sarah jumped in. "Nobody's suggesting that, Judge. Carvalho's shielding his snitch, probably to protect the case against my client, but that doesn't mean he never had one."

Judge Doyle eyed her suspiciously. Then a tiny smile tugged at the corners of his mouth. "I'll be goddamned," he said slowly, admiration in his voice. "You got some nerve, sister. You pushed this right to the edge, bringing in all those warrant affidavits. When you can't afford for me to find there was no snitch. But, then, Jerry can't either. Can you, Jerry?" His eyes never left Sarah's.

DeMarco looked from the judge to Sarah and then back to the judge before answering. He was missing something here. But, then, he still didn't understand why Sarah had introduced IT's fifty-two warrants in the first place. He said, "The evidence doesn't warrant that inference, Judge. Just sloppy policework. Not following procedures."

Judge Doyle snorted contemptuously. He dragged his feet off the desk and, squinting through the smoke, he leaned forward to snuff out his cigarette. "You guys are not making it easy for me. With trial two weeks away."

"Judge," said DeMarco, "these are street cops. They violated departmental policy, sure. But the policy on informants was never intended as a procedure for preserving evidence. It's only there to promote effective drug investigations. The officers ignored them because they thought they would interfere with doing their job, not because they were hiding evidence. Carvalho was ignoring them *before* the shooting ever took place. And a long time before he had reason to hide evidence in this case. I don't see how the failure to follow them here shows deliberate efforts to conceal exculpatory evidence."

The judge dismissed him with a wave of his hand and looked away. "Give me a break, Jerry. You get that much information from a person, you get it that many times, and over such an extended period, you're going to know more about him than Carvalho admits. A *lot* more. Shit, I know more about my new *barber,* and I've only been going to him for six months."

"But you don't have an understanding with your barber not to ask personal questions. And he has no interest in being closemouthed about himself."

Judge Doyle looked unconvinced. "Sure, Jerry. And Mark Fuhrman really *did* go over the wall without waiting for a warrant because he feared for O. J. Simpson's safety. You want me to look as dumb as Judge Ito?"

"Judge," said Sarah, "you're right that Detective Carvalho

is not a credible witness. The evidence here shows one of two things. Either the police are refusing to produce a witness they are capable of producing, or they knowingly avoided taking steps to preserve evidence that would have led to his identification and production. In either event, you've got deliberate misconduct."

"Or there's a third possibility," the judge added. "That the snitch never existed and Carvalho is lying to save his skin. Him and his pal Pescatore."

"Piscatello," DeMarco corrected him.

"Whatever." Judge Doyle didn't look at DeMarco. "In which case there never *was* a witness whose testimony could contradict those three cokeheads Jerry plans to parade in front of the jury."

"That's just speculation, Judge," said Sarah.

"Hey, I been around the block, sister. You think I don't know what game you're playing here? You're rolling the dice. Except it's my balls you're playing with. You brought out all that stuff about the other cases IT finked on so that I couldn't say I believed Carvalho without looking like a goddamn bozo. Christ, Jonah's *wife* wouldn't swallow that garbage. But to make it look that bad you had to push it real far. So far, in fact, that you run the risk of me gutting your defense by finding IT never existed at all. You're betting I won't do that because neither of you want me to. And that, little lady, is pretty high-stakes poker. At my expense."

Sarah stiffened visibly.

"I know, I know," Judge Doyle said, raising both hands in the air as if to ward her off. "I shouldn't call you that. Counselor, then. We don't want the Gender Bias Committee to get their knickers in a knot. But you follow my drift."

"I'm downwind of it, Judge."

They smiled tightly at each other.

DeMarco spoke up. "It should come down to prejudice, Judge. And frankly, I don't see how the defense has been prejudiced. Let her argue all this to the jury. After all, it's the prosecution that's lost the ability to cross-examine IT to challenge Carvalho's affidavit. If anything, it's me who will take it on the chin with the jury for the loss of the witness."

Sarah turned to look at him. "That leaves me with a will-o'-the-wisp on a piece of paper drafted by a lying cop. To put up against three live witnesses. And you tell me *you're* the one who's prejudiced? I don't think so, Jerry. And besides," she added as she swiveled her head back toward the judge, "I've cited a line of cases in my brief which hold that misconduct as pervasive as this does not require a showing that the defendant was prejudiced. The truth-finding process itself has been tainted beyond recall, and nothing could restore the public's confidence in the system if my motion were denied on the technical ground that there was no prejudice."

Judge Doyle laughed out loud. "You *must* be quoting the SJC from memory. Who else could say that crap with a straight face? You want to destroy faith in the system—assuming there's any *left*—you go dismiss murder charges against an accused cop killer because the cops are sitting on some junkie."

Judge Doyle wheeled his chair backwards and stood up.

He said, "But I hear you. I'll look at your cases. And yours, too, Jerry. Now, if you'll get the hell out of here, I'm gonna try to find a way out the back without tripping over all these TV people."

# 14

---◆---

# Fire in the Belly

D unston Shipley said, "It's rather peculiar, actually. There is a curious split in the comments we've received."

Matthew Boer pressed his back against the antique maple settle as he listened to Dunston Shipley summarizing his partners' comments on the quality of his work. Thrice postponed, Matthew's annual performance review had stalked him for months, lurking ominously in the dark places during the early hours when he could not sleep. Those were the times, when he lay awake at night, that he was least defended against the predations of his own ravening judgments, and his thoughts, gerbil-like in their mindless agitation, would scurry about the edges of his fearsick consciousness and gnaw at his self-esteem. Now, at nine-fifteen on a brilliant spring morning, he was about to watch four Daphnis & Clooney partners chew away at it, too.

The five of them sat in a big sunny corner office that was chockablock with early American antiques. The room was dominated by a heavy oak partner's desk, which was flanked on the left by a handmade revolving bookstand and on the right by a hard walnut couch. The pewlike settle was right in front of the desk. A Windsor rocker with a calico cushion was positioned in the corner, at the intersection of the plate-glass windows. On the wall behind the desk, a blue-and-white sampler counseled the reader in Latin not to let the bastards grind you down; its gay blue flosses were a cheerful contrast to the drab bar association plaques that hung alongside it.

The office belonged to Barbara (Don't Call Me Barb) Dwyer, the chair of the firm's Associates Committee. Pudgy, frosty-haired, and led about by a jutting, squared-off jaw that suited her bumptious manner, Barbara Dwyer sat with her hands clasped on the desk in front of her. Matthew's view of her was partially blocked by a vase filled with fresh daffodils and jonquils. The flowers served to set off the opalescent sheen of her skin.

Barbara Dwyer was a trial lawyer of legendary ferocity and sangfroid. She was especially adept at the close-quarters combat of divorce law. To Matthew, the high-backed settle had always seemed cruelly out of place in front of her desk, for no one sitting in it would ever dream of trying to warm himself before Barbara Dwyer. She was as cold and hard as a headstone, and not nearly as heartening.

Ben Fleishman sat in the rocker near the window while Shipley talked. With his right ankle crossed over his left knee, Fleishman slipped his middle finger into his dangling trouser cuff, sliding the finger back and forth as he examined the stitching. Once he looked up and winked at Matthew. Matthew instantly thought of Hannah Teitelbaum. "Men who wink," she had once told him, half in jest, "are asking you to collude in their shame." Matthew didn't know what she meant exactly, but it seemed oddly appropriate at the moment.

The speaker, Dunston Shipley, was something of a throwback, a reminder of the firm's bygone heritage as a Yankee bastion that would never have soiled its letterhead with names like Fleishman and Teitelbaum. He headed the trust and estates department—Elder Hustle, Ira called it. Short and trim, Shipley had a tidy, blunt mustache that belonged on a British colonel. He wore a blue blazer, a paisley bow tie, a button-down oxford shirt, and gray trousers that ran out of leg a full two inches above the tops of his shoes. The pant legs had puzzled Matthew the first time they met. Later it struck him they must be a nautical tic, a displaced effort to save his cuffs from the salt water that slopped over his Top-Siders on the deck of his boat. From which, apparently, he had only reluctantly disembarked.

The last member of the committee was Rowell Falk, a tall, thin man of Ichabod Crane proportions whose massive brow was dormered out above a lantern jaw. He peered out over brown-rimmed half-glasses perched on the end of his nose. Falk's angular frame was folded up on the hardwood sofa he shared with Shipley. Unlike the others, Falk looked directly at Matthew while Shipley spoke. A pleasant, even encouraging, smile accompanied his gaze. Matthew found Falk's manner strangely reassuring.

"On the one hand," Shipley was saying, "partners are singing your praises, especially about your ability to do legal analysis and writing. 'First rate,' to quote Ben here."

Matthew glanced over at Fleishman, who winked again.

"There also seems to be general agreement,' Shipley continued, "that you relate well to clients. You are very well regarded by the ones you work with, and they appear to like and trust you. These are great strengths, Matt."

Shipley looked up and smiled. Then he bent down toward the yellow pad on his lap.

"However, there may be a little trouble brewing in the area of practical skills. Very little in-court exposure for someone five years out. Some partners have the impression you are skittish about new experience. A couple report that you need to work on your deposition skills. The sense seems to be that you are a tiny bit"—Shipley twisted his mouth as he groped for the right adjective—"timid, I guess. One partner says you seem to shy away from confrontation."

Barbara Dwyer cut in. "Dunston's maybe being overly delicate here. It's the toe-to-toe stuff we're talking about. The willingness to butt heads. If you can't convince the department that you can do it, you're in the wrong line of work. This is a rough business, not the *Harvard Law Review*."

Fleishman said, "I think I can give you a useful example, Matt."

*He's going to hurt me,* thought Matthew. *He's trying to seem helpful, but he's going to hurt me.*

"I reviewed the transcript of that plumber's deposition in the *Felter* case. When it came time for you to question him, you did fine for the most part, though for some reason you felt the need to go over a lot of ground already covered by others."

*The damn crossword,* Matthew said to himself.

"But then, when Atwater started objecting and arguing with you over the relevance of your line of questioning, you let him get you off track. You seemed to get flustered and then you just dropped your tack entirely and moved on to something else. As a result, we don't have a record we can put before a judge to challenge his position that the witness should not have to answer your questions. You have to ask the questions anyway, and endure his abuse, if it comes to that. So you can build a record to show what line of inquiry Atwater is blocking. You never did that, Matt, and Atwater got away with instructing the plumber not to answer."

"Maybe," said Barbara Dwyer, "you should consider whether you have the fire in the belly to be a litigator. Some people just can't deal with the hostility. And you have to be able to mix it up in this business."

Shipley said, "In fairness to Matt, though, he hasn't had a lot of opportunities to find out if he *does* like to mix it up. Not much court time. Not even a lot of depositions."

Matthew quailed before the specter of more depositions.

Dwyer was unmollified. "It's the same thing," she said, slower now, sounding a bit exasperated. "All this *moaning* about not getting enough courtroom experience here. It's bunk. The truth is, those who want it bad enough get it. Like Rob O'Leary. When he was coming up, as a senior associate, he was in court all the time, all over the place. Suffolk, Middlesex—out in *Pittsfield,* for Christ's sake. And all the time associates were crying that they couldn't get into court. But *he* was. You know why? Because he wanted it bad enough. You gotta want it, Matt."

"I'll work in a car wash before I'll hustle like Robolawyer," said Matthew. Or wanted to, anyway. What he actually said, and with a smile, was, "I wasn't moaning, Barbara."

Fleishman said, "I'm not convinced you don't have the fire. I saw you argue that motion in front of Judge Sullivan last month. You handled questions from the bench just fine. Mind you," he smiled, taking back half of his compliment, "the judge was uncharacteristically courteous that day."

"Courteous?" said Barbara Dwyer, curious now. "Which Sullivan are we talking about here?"

"Sullivan the Lesser," said Fleishman, and they all knew he was referring to an unpleasant bully in the superior court whose wife was a highly respected judge on the appeals court. "And believe it or not, he was downright cordial."

"He must have run over a puppy on the way to work," Dwyer said sourly.

Fleishman laughed appreciatively. "All the same, Matt did just fine. So I suspect it *is* a matter of exposure. At your level, you should be *managing* cases. Maybe we ought to get you off some of the bigger cases you're on and get you some middle-sized ones, where you're running the case on a day-to-day basis. Have younger associates reporting to *you*. Be glad to feed you some of mine."

Fleishman smiled wolfishly at his invitation.

Matthew said, "I've got this new case that may get me some of that experience."

"You mean the witness in the *Chin* case?"

Matthew nodded.

Fleishman raised his mammoth eyebrows and nodded back in appreciation. "You may be right. You get in the pit with the DAs and defense lawyers like Sarah Kerlinsky and you'll find out in a hell of a hurry if you wanna be a litigator. Teitelbaum's helping you on this?"

"Yes."

Barbara Dwyer rolled her violet-lidded eyes toward the ceiling at the mention of Ira's name.

Shipley added, "Plus this fellow's your own client, right?"

"Yes, he is."

This seemed to please Shipley. He said, "It can't hurt to bring in business."

Fleishman grinned at Shipley. "Wait till your little old ladies wanting codicils to their wills start bumping into drug informants in the reception area. They're not a tony set, you know."

Shipley held his smile, but he could not hide his discomfiture at the prospect.

"Whatever the reasons," Shipley said, "your performance has got to improve in the areas we've been discussing if you are to have a future here at D and C. It's a matter of some urgency. I don't mean to sound alarming, but I would not be doing you any favors if I were not blunt about these things at this point in your career."

As if by prearrangement, Dunston Shipley and his partners maintained a brief silence to allow his summation to strike home. They needn't have worried.

Falk, who had watched Matthew throughout, now spoke for the first time. "Maybe," he said, "it's a case of right church, wrong pew."

Matthew had no idea what he was talking about. Feigning paranoid suspicion, he looked furtively over his shoulder at the back of the settle. Fleishman and Shipley laughed lightly, and Falk smiled.

"Did I forget to genuflect?" Matthew asked.

"No," said Falk, still smiling. "No homage due. I meant to be encouraging. Don't be too disheartened by negative feedback from the litigators. Consider the source."

Fleishman and Shipley laughed, as if at an old joke among friends, and Falk grinned back at them. Barbara Dwyer stared impassively at her cut flowers.

Falk continued, "Why not give some thought to trying your hand at corporate work? Your undoubted skills—analysis, writing, handling clients—are well suited to a counseling practice." Falk smoothed his silk tie out over his flat belly. "I guess it's no secret around here what I think of litigation. It's a waste of talent and money and psychic capital. A necessary evil, perhaps, but an evil nevertheless. You may find it more rewarding—and more digestible than fire, if you doubt your stomach—to work at building things instead of tearing them down."

He looked at Matthew and smiled. This seemed to be a cue for Matthew to say something.

"Interesting," he said.

But in his mind's eye Matthew could see only the racks of library shelves devoted to the claustrophobic intricacies of the Internal Revenue Code.

"To be honest," he said, "I never thought I could master enough tax law to do corporate work. Everything I do now has to be close-captioned for the tax-impaired."

Falk smiled indulgently, then waved the thought away. "I doubt that would hold you up for long. Tax is like one big crossword puzzle and I'm sure you would get into it. Give it some thought, why don't you? You could just try it on in bits, a few assignments here and there. See how it fits."

"I'll think about it," said Matthew, meaning it. "It's very interesting."

*"Interesting?"* said Teitelbaum in disbelief two hours later, when he and Matthew were having lunch. "See how it *fits?* How do you *think* it's gonna fit?"

"Like a saddle on a sow?"

"Spare me your bucolic similes," said Teitelbaum, turning his head away in mock disgust. Then he gestured toward a pizza pan of food in front of them. "Don't be shy, now. Dig in. It's delicious."

Matthew looked timorously at the little servings of curried meat that were piled like dog droppings on a round sheet of *injira*, a flatbread made, according to the menu, from an East African grain called teff. They were seated at an uncovered plastic table in a grubby Ethiopian restaurant at the foot of Beacon Hill. Wot's My Line offered, Teitelbaum had promised, first-class cuisine and Third World ambiance. A peek into the men's room suggested that the hygiene matched the ambiance.

Matthew tore off a piece of the bread and tasted it. It had the look, texture, and savor of a damp washcloth. There was no silverware in evidence, so he followed Ira's lead and used a bigger piece of bread to pick up a dollop of meat. Then he shoved everything into his mouth. He chewed slowly, letting the hot spices have their way with him. Not bad, once you got past the clamminess of the *injira*.

Teitelbaum spoke with his mouth full. "I can't see it, Matt. You'd be miserable as one of Rowell's chew toys." He pointed to the food on the table. "Jesus, this is good." He paused to chew. "Don't you think so?"

"Are you asking about the food or Falk?"

"Fuck Falk. The food, of course. Remember, man is the only species that cooks."

"It's not bad. What kind of meat do you think is in this wot?"

"Mink? Who knows? Who can tell, with a menu that has an unvarying list of 'Daily Specials of the Week'?"

Matthew laughed. "I'm getting filled up on that bread, though."

"Yeah," said Teitelbaum, deftly assembling another dank East African taco with one hand. "It takes a little while to get the hang of not eating too much of the utensils. But corporate law? Why don't you just go get a job in a *bank*, for Chrissake?"

Matthew said, "I didn't say I was going to do it. I just said I'd think about it. They're right, in a way. The litigators, I mean. I don't crave the fight like they do. Like *you* do. The other side never seems as unreasonable to me as they do to people like Fleishman."

"Or Barbara (Don't Call Me Barb) Dwyer," added Ira, grinning.

"Indeed. But we've worked together enough for you to know me. I can't work up a sense of high dudgeon just because somebody's on the other side. They always seem like they're just doing their job, doing pretty much what I'd do in the circumstances. Maybe I'm not cut out for litigation."

Teitelbaum sucked sauce off the webbing of his thumb and looked at Matthew. "Like you're stuck with an FM soul in an AM world? Look. There are only two kinds of lawyers. Those who *do* litigation and those who create it. I think it's more fun to clean up a mess than to make one. And I think you do, too. Well, I admit I've had to push you at times. Maybe you're not the most innately aggressive lawyer in the shop. And maybe you're never going to be an eat-'em-up-and-spit-'em-out thug like Dwyer." Ira smiled. "You ever notice how her adversaries are always the worst slimeballs she's ever seen? But there are lots of very effective litigators who aren't burdened with her beefy sense of entitlement and perpetual outrage. It's just a question of finding a style you're comfortable with."

"I'm not too comfortable right now," said Matthew, feeling an ungentle rumbling in his stomach. "I may be getting to the Third World part of the meal."

"You see!" exclaimed Teitelbaum, a didactic finger in the air. "You've got fire in the belly after all!"

# 15

---

# An Act of Total Cowardice

From *The Boston Globe* (June 6, 1995)

## Judge Throws Out Murder Charges in Officer's Killing

*By Eddie Felch*
*Globe Staff*

Castigating police officers for pervasive misconduct and apparent perjury, a judge yesterday dismissed first-degree murder charges against a man accused in the murder of a Boston police detective in Chinatown earlier this year.

In what legal observers characterized as an unusual step, Superior Court Judge Robert C. Doyle held a short public hearing solely for the purpose of announcing his long-awaited ruling in the emotionally charged case. Doyle told a courtroom packed with the family members of slain Detective Francis X. Dunleavy that police failure to produce a confidential informant whose testimony might clear his alleged killer, Michael Chin, "was due to deliberate and egregious inaction by the Commonwealth."

"As a consequence of the misconduct of the police officers involved, this court cannot assure that the defendant [Chin] can receive a fair trial," Doyle wrote in a 36-page ruling.

Doyle described as "utterly incredible" the testimony of two police detectives, Raymond A. Carvalho and Salvatore Piscatello, who claimed they were unable to locate the missing informant.

Doyle also chided Jeremiah DeMarco, the assistant district attorney who has been prosecuting the case. DeMarco, he said, had failed to disclose to the court that he did not know the informant's whereabouts when, at an earlier hearing, he convinced the court to defer ordering the police to reveal the informant's identity until closer to the time of trial. "Had the Commonwealth been candid with this court at that time, the witness's testimony might have been secured for trial," the judge ruled.

## DA blasts decision

Suffolk County District Attorney Jackie Crimmins said at a news conference that he will seek an immediate appeal before the Supreme Judicial Court. Flanked by members of Dunleavy's family, Crimmins characterized the ruling as the product of a judge who had no experience in the realities of police investigations. "Until we appoint judges who are sensitive to the needs of law enforcement officials, criminals will continue to snicker at such mockeries of justice," said Crimmins.

Crimmins is a candidate for the Democratic nomination for governor.

Following a meeting with the district attorney's office, Stephen Dunleavy, a brother of the slain detective, called the judge's ruling "an act of total cowardice." Struggling to retain his composure and surrounded by relatives, Stephen Dunleavy said, "We are outraged by the judge's decision." He also decried the court's "personal attack" on DeMarco, who he said retained the confidence and support of the family. Stephen Dunleavy and three of his brothers are members of the Boston Police Department.

DeMarco said he was "deeply disappointed" in the judge's ruling. "It is unfortunate that the court saw fit to discredit the testimony of veteran police officers," DeMarco said, referring to Carvalho and Piscatello. "But even if he didn't believe them, there was no reason to fault the good faith of the district attorney's office."

Defense attorney Sarah Kerlinsky said, however, that she believes the judge had little choice under established legal standards. "The officers involved engaged in the all-too-frequent practice of 'testilying,' " she said. "Given such massive misconduct, the court had no choice but to dismiss the indictment."

## Chin not to be released

Doyle ordered Chin to be released from Charles Street Jail, but stayed the order until this afternoon to allow the district attorney time to appeal to the state's highest court. The district attorney's office is expected to request at an SJC hearing today that Chin be held without bail until Doyle's decision is reviewed by the high court.

After speaking with her client, Kerlinsky said Chin "is pleased with the ruling. But he's an immigrant who's terrified and bewildered by this business. He is anxious to have this behind him."

On February 7th, Dunleavy was shot twice through the closed door of an apartment in Chinatown as he and other officers were executing a warrant to search for illegal drugs.

Chin was arrested with three other suspects in an apartment immediately below the one from which the fatal shots were fired. Prosecutors dropped charges against the other suspects, who have testified that Chin ran into the lower apartment carrying the gun which police later determined was the murder weapon.

On April 17th, Doyle granted a defense request to order the police officers to identify and produce a confidential informant whose testimony could help to clear Chin. The informant was given the code name "IT" in an affidavit prepared by Carvalho to obtain the warrant. According to the affidavit, "IT" told Carvalho he had seen a thin, 5'11" Chinese man in his late thirties named "John" selling drugs from inside the apartment.

Chin, 23, is Chinese, but he is barely five feet tall.

The informant's testimony, ruled Doyle, is the "strongest available evidence" to refute the testimony of the three witness who claim Chin ran into the lower apartment with the murder weapon.

During the brief morning hearing in Suffolk Superior Court, Doyle said, "To reach this difficult decision . . . I have had to consider the importance of the public's right to a trial and the defendant's right to a fair trial. I have come to the painful conclusion that a fair trial is not possible in this case."

# 16

---

## The Talk of Des Moines

The light had changed from red to green, but the lines of cars ahead of them at Leverett Circle did not budge. The unmarked Plymouth was stuck in the seven lanes of traffic seeking to squeeze onto the two-lane ramp that snaked its way onto the Central Artery and toward downtown Boston.

Raymond Carvalho directed two short blasts of the horn at a sleek black BMW convertible idling just in front of them. It had a vanity plate. 4IAM40. When its driver pivoted his head slightly to check out the racket in his rearview mirror, Carvalho leaned hard on the horn and kept it there. He was still honking when the driver opened his door and stepped languidly out of the car.

"Cocksucker!" Carvalho muttered as he watched the tall husky man walk serenely toward him. Tanned and fit in an expensive summer suit, the man moved nimbly, like an athlete, full of the comfortable assurance that came with his size and wealth.

"Easy, Ray," said Salvatore Piscatello, who was riding shotgun with him. "It's just a traffic jam."

The big man reached the driver's-side door of the unmarked. He leaned on the sill of the open window and bent over to look in at Carvalho, his floral tie brushing against the car's finish. He had an open, pleasant face, and the corners of his eyes crinkled with an indulgent smile as he peered in at the smaller man who glowered at him from the driver's seat.

"Hey, pal," the man said, his voice measured, without rancor or challenge. "How 'bout we change places for a while? You go wait in my car and I'll honk *your* horn."

The man's smile broadened.

"Ray," Piscatello said softly, putting a monitory hand on Carvalho's right arm.

Carvalho gave the big man a light shot to the breastbone with the back of his left hand. When the man pulled back and straightened up in surprise, Carvalho grabbed his tie and jerked it hard, smashing his face into the lintel of the car door. The man staggered backwards a couple of steps.

Carvalho sprang out of the car, deaf to Piscatello's shouts behind him. The man stood in front of him, hunched over, his hand cupped over his nose. He was bleeding now, the blood dripping down his shirt and tie. Carvalho drove the toe of his shoe hard into the man's shin. The man howled with pain as he lifted the wounded leg off the ground, his bloody nose forgotten. He stumbled backwards and fell to a sitting position in the street. Looking up, he winced and raised his hands to cover his face when he saw Carvalho cock his fist.

Carvalho felt Piscatello's meaty arms lock his own from behind. He went through the motions of trying to shrug him off, but Carvalho could feel the rage leave him as he struggled against Piscatello's grip.

"Ray, Ray," Piscatello said softly. "That's enough."

"Cocksucker," said Carvalho, hissing at the crumpled man on the pavement below him. "Let's run the fucker in."

"No, Ray! That's enough. Jesus, look around you."

Carvalho looked around, breathing hard. Cars continued to insinuate their way toward the entrance ramp, most of the drivers keeping eyes front, resolutely ignoring the sitting man they had to drive around. A white-haired woman in the passenger seat of a brown Volvo stared at Carvalho in horror.

She was holding a road map. The Volvo had Iowa plates. *Wait'll they hear about this in Des Moines,* he thought.

He let Piscatello shove him back into the driver's seat. After Piscatello got in, Carvalho put the car in gear and bullied his way around the BMW. Just before turning right to ascend the ramp, he caught a glimpse of the big man in the rearview mirror. He was hobbling slowly to his car while the traffic slid by him on both sides.

"Jesus Christ, Ray," said Piscatello.

"Cocksucker," said Carvalho, looking straight ahead. "Everybody's gotta have an attitude. Let's go get a drink."

# 17

## The Slide

Sarah Kerlinsky had a drink, too, but she was celebrating. It was a glass of St. Emilion from the expensive bottle Maury had whipped out with a flourish when she walked in the door. The girls were grinning at her from either side of him.

"Hooray for Mommy!" he called, beaming.

"Hooray!" echoed the girls.

Sarah burst out laughing. She moshed them all together in her arms. "Oh, thank you," she said. "What a wonderful surprise!"

"Congratulations, Sarah," said Maury. "It sounds like a real coup."

"We'll see," she said, her caution a reflex. "If it stands up." But she could already feel the tension beginning to wash out of her. She breathed deep and let her shoulders sag. Accepting the glass of wine, she smiled. "But it *is* good news, isn't it?"

"It sure is," he agreed. "So we're having a little victory supper—right, girls?" He looked around at his confederates.

"Yeah," said Rebecca, who was wearing a smudged yellow apron. "We're gonna barbecue hot dogs. Daddy says I can put them on the fire."

"Wow!" Sarah widened her eyes.

"Grilled eggplant sandwiches for us oldsters," Maury reassured her.

Sarah took it all in. "I have," she said, "the *best* family in the whole world."

When the call came she was sitting at the kitchen table admiring the artwork Leah had brought home from school. The smell of burning charcoal floated in from the deck, where she could see Maury and Rebecca leaning over the grill to turn the wieners. "Not too close," he warned, his left arm keeping her back.

Sarah plucked the phone off the wall and tucked it under her ear as she took the next picture Leah handed her. "Hello," she said.

When her caller started talking, she dropped the drawing and clutched the phone with both hands. It took her so much by surprise that she listened longer than she should have. Long enough, apparently, for Maury to notice her silence and catch the change in her expression, for when she hung up he was staring at her through the screen door, the grilling tongs hanging down along his right leg. She met his gaze and rolled her eyes toward the ceiling. As a show of bravery, it was transparently hollow.

"Who was it?" he asked.

"He didn't exactly introduce himself," she said dryly.

"Anonymous? What did he want?" Concern collected in the lines around his eyes.

"To vent his spleen, I guess. And to scare the hell out of me."

"It looks like he succeeded," said Maury. He slid open the screen door and stepped into the kitchen. "You look positively gray."

She shook her head once, dismissively. "It was just some kook who's unhappy with the way the legal system works—and with my role in it, apparently. It's nothing to worry about."

She said this for her own sake as much as his. Because she was more disturbed than she felt she could let on. The voice had been poisonous and crude, but she had received obscene phone calls before. This one was more upsetting somehow. She had been more than a faceless quailing female to her caller, and he was not just someone who got off on frightening women. It was . . . more personal. Yes, that was it. It was her own actions that had set him off. And that made her feel more of a target.

"Did he threaten you?"

"Well, he didn't promise me some civic award, if that's what you mean."

"No. I meant did he make any threats."

"I guess so. But really, Maury, it's nothing to get worked up about. You get an unpopular ruling in a highly visible case, you expect crap like that."

He wouldn't let it go. "Sarah, you don't know anything about this guy. You should call the police or something."

"The police?" She sounded incredulous. "Come on, Maury. What are they gonna do? I'm not exactly on their A-list right now. Believe me, knowing I'm safe and snug would not give them a warm and fuzzy feeling. For all I know, that *was* a cop."

And then there it was again: he looked away and disengaged. She felt a flash of irritation.

"Don't *do* that, Maury," she said, angry now.

He looked back at her, miffed too. "Do what?"

"That little slide of yours. You always do that when you get mad. Instead of staying in there and working it out."

He looked away, as if in exasperation. "So what do you *want* me to do?"

"Tell me what's going *on* in there. It's not just about me not wanting to call the police, I know that. There's something on the tip of your tongue and you just slide off. Say it."

Leah watched them both while her parents looked at one another in silence for a moment. He seemed to make up his mind. "You always have to be right," he said at last.

"Too bad," she said, giving no quarter. "I can't help that."

He watched her motionlessly.

She added, softer now, "I had that problem with a friend in law school. She was always right and it was hard for me.

I had to learn to live with it. It wasn't easy, but I got through it."

She didn't say he would have to as well, but it was there in front of them. She could tell he was hurt. Then he broke off and slid away again. She let him go.

"Daddy!" called Rebecca from the deck. "Come quick! The hot dogs are on fire."

"Coming!" said Maury. Turning away from Sarah, he brushed his hand over Leah's hair on the way to the door. Lured by the prospect of incinerating wieners, Leah followed him outside. He slid the door shut behind them.

Through the screen Sarah watched her family huddle around the Weber kettle.

# 18

---

# A Single Voice

## MEMORANDUM

*Privileged and Confidential*

---

TO:     Matthew Boer

FROM:   Isaac Rosenthal
        Managing Partner

RE:     *Commonwealth v. Chin*
        Matter No. 18236-111

DATE:   June 22, 1995

   The Management Committee has reviewed your confidential memorandum on the new matter referred to above and has approved your proposal for processing it so as to maintain confidentiality within D&C. The cash retainer in the amount of $5,000 has been deposited to an individual client trust account that is identifiable only by the matter number.

Given the public interest in the case, intense scrutiny may be directed at the firm if this matter becomes public. In that event, it is imperative that we be prepared for press queries and coordinate our responses to them. I ask that you notify me personally if, and as soon as, you should hear that your client has been taken into police custody. Then we should meet to discuss how to ensure that D&C may speak with a single voice.

Thank you for your cooperation.

cc: Management Committee

    Rowell Falk
    Benjamin Fleishman
    Petina Stong
    Lindsay Wolsey

# 19

## Johnny Appleseed

Captain Oliver Gogarty, chief of the Drug Control Unit, led the way into his squad room. Behind him trooped Jeremiah DeMarco, Kieran Joyce, and a grave young man who looked familiar somehow.

Gogarty was thin and rangy, with steel-gray hair, a pronounced and bobbing goiter, and rimless glasses. He looked like a bookish man, a schoolteacher woefully out of his depth in a police station. At the front of the room he perched one bony hip on an unoccupied steel desk and looked at his detectives.

"OK," he said, his voice a reedy squawk. "Pipe down. We got company."

Gogarty waited again, then said, "Most of you know Jerry DeMarco here. He's been handling the *Chin* case. Jerry wanted to have a word with you about the case. And about Frannie."

Gogarty turned toward his guests.

"Jerry?" he said. Then he took two steps toward the detectives and took a seat with his men.

DeMarco stepped forward and looked out at the faces of

the fifteen or twenty detectives in the room. Carvalho and Piscatello were not among them.

DeMarco said, "I'm sure I don't have to tell you what's happened to the case against Michael Chin. There isn't one. The court threw it out.

"If you've followed the story in the press, you also know that we went before the single justice yesterday and managed to convince him not to release Chin until our appeal is heard. And you know we plan to bring an appeal.

"But what the media has not told you is anything about our chances of winning the appeal. Well, let me make it easy for you. They suck."

He let his vulgarity sink in.

"Judge Doyle's decision is based on his assessment of the credibility of the witnesses who testified, namely Ray and Sal. You need to understand something about appellate judges. No matter how disposed they might be to want to see this case get tried, the SJC is not going to tell a sitting judge he should have believed a witness he says he didn't believe. They're not gonna do that. So all that leaves for us, on appeal, is to claim that the case should go to a jury even if Ray and Sal lied. Even if, to put it the way the SJC will see it, the police are deliberately hiding a witness whose testimony is critical to Chin's defense. And for our side, that's a crap argument. We're gonna give it our best, but I gotta tell you, straight up, I don't think it's gonna fly. We're gonna lose the appeal. And the guy who gunned down Fran Dunleavy is gonna dodge the big one."

DeMarco paused. The room was dead quiet, then an air conditioner kicked in, its motor lugging under the load. He resumed.

"Michael Chin did it, all right. You know that. I know that. Christ, the judge even knows that. His prints are on the gun, his confederates have fingered him, he's confessed it to a cellmate. So he's the one. But he's still gonna walk unless you guys can help us.

"We need the witness.

"I know you've been looking for him ever since Ollie ordered you to find him a couple months ago. And I don't know if this IT character really exists or not. Maybe Ray's been telling the truth all along. Hell, this guy could be the Johnny Appleseed of informants, for all I know. He sure gets around enough. But frankly I don't give a damn anymore. Whether it was IT or ET or AT&T, *somebody* supplied the information—and damn good information, as it turned out—that led to that warrant. The one Frannie was trying to execute when he died. I gotta have him. 'Cause without him this case is gonna stay in the toilet."

DeMarco looked over at Gogarty, who stared blankly back at him. Then DeMarco turned back to the squad.

"Listen, my old man was a cop. So I understand, you know what I'm saying? I know about Cinderellas. And I know nobody wants to hurt Ray. He's one of your own. So is Sal. Nobody wants to expose anybody to harm from outsiders. I understand this.

"But damn it, Frannie's one of your own too. Somebody's got to stick up for him. And for his wife and kids. You gotta weigh that. Please. Don't let's get so caught up in the code of the streets, or whatever you want to call it, that we can't see through to what's really important here. 'Cause we've gotta be able to explain what we do to Doreen. And Frannie's kids. And to his brothers, four of whom are cops, too. Like Steve Dunleavy here."

DeMarco turned to the intense young man who had accompanied him into the room.

DeMarco said, "Steve, this is Frannie's squad."

Stephen Dunleavy nodded a stiff greeting to the men in the room.

DeMarco walked across the room to a flip chart mounted on an easel next to a bulletin board. He picked up a magic marker and wrote a seven-digit number on the chart. The only sound in the room was the squeak of the marker. He turned back to the detectives.

"This is my number," he said. "Please, if you know anything—anything at *all*—about the source of the information that went into Ray's affidavit, call me. Anonymously, if you prefer. The number is my direct line; no switchboard operator to ask your name. Just call. We can't do it without your help. Don't let Frannie's killer dance on out of here."

There wasn't a sound in the room.

# 20

---

# If Your Phone Don't Ring, You'll Know It's Me

Matthew Boer was headed down the hall to get his first corporate assignment from Falk when Sally called him back.

"Matt!" she called. "Do you want to talk to somebody named Danny?"

"Sure." Matthew turned back and walked toward her.

Arms akimbo and gum in her mouth, Sally faced him in the center of hallway. A pretty if anorexic-looking young woman with frosted blond hair spun into a curly heap on top of her head, Sally Cassidy had been Matthew's secretary for more than two years. He shared her with Ellen Stritch, the lawyer whose office backed on to his. Sally was a cracker-jack and a godsend, in Matthew's view. To say she needed little supervision was a grotesque understatement, for she knew far more about the mechanics of the court system than Matthew. In exchange for her guidance, Matthew had only to endure her irascible temper and listen sympathetically to her soap opera of a love life.

When he reached her he could see she was a little put out.

She said, "He wouldn't give me his last name. He said you'd know who he was."

Matthew smiled, placating her. "He's right. Thank you, Sally."

"Well, it's rude," said Sally, and she flounced back to her cubicle.

Matthew closed the door of his office and picked up his phone.

"Danny?" he said as he eased into his chair.

"Hey, Matt," said the excited voice. "It's over! It's all done, right?"

"For now," Matthew said. "The case has been dismissed, but there'll be an appeal. It's good news, though."

"You think the DA will win the appeal?"

"I think he's facing long odds," said Matthew, parroting the assessment he had heard earlier that morning from Teitelbaum. "The SJC is unlikely to reverse."

"This is good," said Danny. "Very good. So, Matt, you think you should give back my money?"

Matthew laughed out loud. "If you want, Danny. But I don't think you're out of the woods yet."

There was a brief silence on the line.

Danny said, "I don't understand."

"Well, the judge's dismissal is going to have the effect of turning up the heat on the police. Those cops are not gonna want to see a cop killer go scot-free. There will be tremendous pressure to come up with the informant. They could crack. Maybe even Carvalho himself. So it may not be over yet, Danny."

Danny was quiet again.

"So what do we do now, Matt?" he said at last.

"Same thing, Danny. Same plan. Just lay low and call me if there's trouble."

"I hope I don't call you," said Danny.

Then he hung up.

# 21

---◆---

## No Names

The late afternoon heat was downright wilting inside the phone booth on East Berkeley Street. Even with the door wide open the man could feel the sweat popping out of him. *Gotta be the last phone booth in the city,* he thought. The receiver was hot to the touch, and it seemed to blister his ear as he punched in the number on the slip of paper he held between his thumb and the receiver. While waiting for an answer, he got as much of his body out of the booth as the cord would allow. He looked up East Berkeley Street in the direction of the police station. There was no one in sight. The booth made a crackling noise, as if the Plexiglas were buckling from the heat. Seeking comfort, or perhaps to relieve his tension, the man rolled his shoulders like a cat.

The man could hear the phone ringing on the other end again, then a soft click as it was answered.

"DeMarco."

The man froze for a moment, saying nothing. He stepped back into the booth and shut himself in with the heat.

"Hello?" said DeMarco, sounding busy and irritable. "Who is this?"

The man cleared his throat.

"Uh, no names," he said. "You said no names."

This time it was DeMarco who paused, but not for long.

"That's right," he said gently. "If that's the way you want it, no names. Have you got something for me?"

The man let out a sigh.

"Yeah. That snitch. The one you're looking for."

Another pause. DeMarco filled in the silence.

"You mean IT?"

"Nah. Not IT. The snitch wasn't Ray's. He was Frannie's. Ray just did the warrant. But Ray can't tell you that."

Again, a pause.

DeMarco said, "I understand. Do you know who the snitch is?"

"Yeah. He's a Chinese guy. Lives in an apartment over on Harrison. Frannie picked him up on a holding charge back in, like, November or December. Booked him, then didn't show up for arraignment and the charges were dropped. Frannie said he turned him. He told Frannie he had the word on a big delivery."

"I need a name," said DeMarco softly. "You got a name?"

The man expelled his breath again, as if giving himself time to make up his mind.

"Yeah," he said at last. "I got a name. Danny Li."

"Can you spell the name?"

"D-A-N-N—"

"Just the last name will do." DeMarco sounded exasperated.

"L-I."

"Thank you," DeMarco said. "Believe me, I know what—"

But the line was dead.

Martin Kelleher quietly replaced the receiver. He opened the door and stepped out of the booth, plucking at the back of his shirt where the sweat had pasted it to his back. Then he walked back down East Berkeley toward the station. He stayed in the shade wherever possible.

# 22

---

## One Asshole at a Time

"Dr. Trubs," said Salvatore Piscatello as he slid onto the barstool, "gimme what's good for what ails me. A Rolling Rock and one of your prefab pizzas."

Raymond Carvalho joined him on the adjacent stool. He ordered a double Jameson.

"Doctor," snorted Trubs contemptuously. "You know the difference between a doctor and a bartender?" He stripped the plastic off a Tombstone frozen pizza and shoved it into the microwave.

"What's that, Trubs?" asked Piscatello.

"A doctor," said Trubs, poking at the timer pads on the microwave, "only has to look at one asshole at a time."

"Good one, Trubs."

The whiskey worked wonders. The first hit made Carvalho's stomach muscles sag at last, and his brain kicked into gear. The truth was, he always did his best thinking after a couple whiskeys. To clean the carbon out of his nervous system. That was when things would snap into sharp focus, like when the optometrist snicked in the perfect test lens during an eye exam.

The microwave beeped and Trubs slid the pizza in front of Piscatello.

While Piscatello ate, Carvalho thought. It was plain that Judge Doyle thought he was calling his bluff. The judge figured that he either had no IT to produce or, if he did, he was deliberately withholding information on how to get hold of him. So the judge had turned up the heat, knowing the pressure from DeMarco and the department and Frannie's family would be intense. He was betting Carvalho would crumple and come clean.

Well, fuck him. Carvalho had no snitch to produce and he was not about to trigger perjury charges by admitting the affidavit and all of his testimony were false. That would wipe out more than fourteen years on the force and probably land him in the house of corrections. Ex-cops did not fare well in jails. He wasn't about to buy into that neighborhood, Frannie or no Frannie. Doreen or no Doreen.

Right now, there was no way they could touch him. IT might be pretty implausible, but he doubted they could even get an indictment for perjury with what they had so far. As long as he and Piscatello hung tough. Of himself he had no doubts and he planned to stick close to Piscatello.

There was only one person he had to worry about.

Frannie's snitch.

If they found him, and if he blabbed that he was the source and that he had passed along to Frannie, not Carvalho, the information that made its way into Carvalho's affidavit, things might take a nasty turn for the worse.

But how could they find the snitch? He had heard about DeMarco's pitch for anonymous calls, but who could come forward? Nobody. Frannie was well known as a keeper of secrets, and he was dead. He hadn't even confided in Carvalho, his partner. Who did that leave? Nobody.

As he was raising his glass for another sip, Carvalho froze. Fear clutched at his stomach muscles again. Why *didn't* he know who Frannie's snitch was? He was likely someone they had busted and turned. Carvalho would have been in on it. Unless . . .

Carvalho turned to Piscatello, who was still tucked into his pizza.

Carvalho said, "I just thought of something. Wait here till I get back, OK?"

"Where you going?" asked Piscatello. He had tomato sauce on his cheek.

"To the station for a minute. Just don't leave here till I get back. Finish your pizza."

Twenty minutes later Carvalho had Dunleavy's folder of arrest reports open on his desk. He went back four months before the shooting, ignoring all the reports that listed himself as an officer assisting in the arrest. That left him with quite a few candidates, thanks to his own rather shabby record of absenteeism. The legacy of his hangovers, as Kieran Joyce had pointedly reminded him. He paged carefully through the arrest reports in which he himself made no appearance.

And there it was. The only Chinese-sounding name in the lot. Danny Li. Possession of heroin. November 29, 1994. Officer assisting arrest, Det. Martin Kelleher.

Carvalho picked up the phone and called the County Cork.

"Trubs?" he said. "It's Ray. Put Sal on, will you?"

*Fuck me,* he thought. *Should have figured it out months ago.* How long would it take DeMarco? But, then, why should he? DeMarco was looking for one of Carvalho's snitches, not Frannie's.

"So whadja do, Ray?" he heard Piscatello ask. "Put out an APB on that poor asshole in the Beemer?"

"I got him, Sal."

"Got who?"

"Frannie's guy. I got our snitch."

"Son of a bitch," said Piscatello, almost reverently.

# 23

## Megaphone

Once his caller had hung up, Jeremiah DeMarco quickly made three calls of his own. The first one, after breaching Lorraine's perimeter defenses, interrupted a meeting between Jackie Crimmins and Patrick Noonan, his campaign manager.

"Jeremiah," said Jackie. "To what do I owe this interruption?" He did not sound nearly as displeased as Lorraine had predicted. But then, it was late enough in the afternoon for the Irish whiskey.

"You owe it to one Danny Li," said DeMarco, bursting with the good tidings. "He's our snitch. I just got an anonymous call."

"Now *that's* news that's worth being interrupted for," said Jackie. "So IT exists after all. What else do you know about him?"

"Not much, except that he lives in the Harrison Street project."

"He's a Chinaman?" Jackie sounded surprised.

"Makes sense, doesn't it? As long as you don't feel compelled to give him credit for the other fifty affidavits."

"Have you picked him up yet?"

"No. That's what I wanted to talk to you about. I don't think we should use the department on this. You might as well use a megaphone. I want your OK to bring in the state troopers to pick him up."

"The staties? Yes, that's smart thinking, Jeremiah. Hold on a second. I'll give you Walter Hurley's direct number. Tell him I asked for this personally. He'll take care of it."

"I'm also going to need authority to rent a hotel room to hole this guy up in. We can't exactly stick him in the Charles Street jail."

"You've got it. And Jeremiah?"

"Yes?"

"Good work. Making that pitch to the officers, I mean. That's damn good work."

"Thanks, Jackie. Now let me see if I can bring him in."

DeMarco's second call was to Walter Hurley, the state police commissioner. The third was to his secretary, asking her to pull the jacket on Danny Li. Just to make sure he'd be ready to roll, he wanted to get started on the draft of a motion for reconsideration. To put before Judge Doyle.

# 24

## The Wrong Idea

Matthew Boer carefully laid the blade of his chef's knife across the lighted burner and lit another one under the heavy saucepan. He dribbled olive oil on top of the pat of butter in the pan. When the knife was hot, he turned off the burner and set the knife on the cutting board.

"What if you forget your knife on the fire?" asked Laura. "Wouldn't that ruin its temper or something?"

"Not to mention what it would do to mine," said Matthew.

Laura was sitting on a stool beside the counter, a glass of red wine in her hand. She wore jeans and a yellow T-shirt that promised "Reasonable Doubt for a Reasonable Price" on behalf of a criminal defense firm on Commercial Wharf. Outside, the fresh June rain that blurred Matthew's kitchen window had shooed away the scorching heat of the past week.

Matthew unwrapped a disk of *pancetta* as thick as his thumb and slipped it free of its casing and onto the cutting board. He balanced the heavy round of bacon on its edge and cut down through its circumference, slicing it into two thinner disks. The bacon sizzled softly as the hot knife glided through it. Then he piled one slab on top of the other and diced them both into small cubes. Picking up the cutting board, he turned back to the cookstove and swept the bacon into the foaming fat in the saucepan. The hiss in the pan soon modulated to a snapping sound, and Matthew turned down the gas under the pan.

He was chopping a red onion when Laura spoke again.

"Where," she asked, "would a kid from Sleepy Eye, Minnesota, learn how to make—uh, what was the name of that sauce?"

"*Amatriciana*. It's named after a town near Rome. And you're right. I didn't learn how to make it in Sleepy Eye. I don't think there was a single Italian family in the town. I picked it up from my ex-wife. I think of the sauce as my share of the divorce settlement."

"What was it like?" she asked a moment later.

"My marriage or the divorce?" Matthew said, feeling a little defensive. In the almost three months they had been dating, Laura had never voiced any curiosity about his ex-wife.

Laura took a beat before answering. "Neither," she answered, looking away. "I meant growing up in something called Sleepy Eye, Minnesota."

"Well, on Saturday nights we used to hang around the stoplight."

Matthew wondered if she had intended the more intimate question she now disclaimed. Had his reaction shunted her onto a safer track?

Laura grinned. "Isn't Minnesota one of those progressive states in the middle somewhere? All tundra and liberal politics?"

"Not the little farm towns out on the plain. Sleepy Eye voted two-to-one for Alf Landon." Talking out of the side of his mouth, he used his Groucho Marx voice. "The town was so conservative . . ." He fluttered his fingers around an imaginary cigar and waggled his eyebrows to cue his audience.

Laura made a megaphone of her hand and pretended to shout. "How conservative was it?"

"The Unitarians burned a question mark on my lawn."

Laura laughed out loud.

"Hey, it was a bummer," Matthew added. "Everybody knew the tastiest church suppers were the ones at Our Lady of Intellectual Solace."

Matthew dumped a big can of imported tomatoes into his ricer and cranked the handle vigorously until everything but the seeds and a few bits of peel had passed through the mesh into the mixing bowl beneath. He disassembled the ricer and rinsed it out in the sink. Then he checked the saucepan. After giving it a shake, he leaned his hip against the stove and, stirring the bacon with a wooden paddle, he looked at Laura. She was sipping her wine, her soft gray eyes on his. A fine-looking woman, he said to himself.

"Sleepy Eye has about thirty-five hundred souls. Mostly Scandinavians and Germans and Dutchmen. There was one Jewish family—he was a lawyer, wouldn't you know. And a few Irish families. Some French that migrated down from Saskatchewan. Mexican laborers in the summer. If you didn't farm you worked at businesses that catered to farmers. A lot of corn and soybeans and hogs and dairy cattle. Once you get away from the Minnesota River valley, the land is flat like Kansas. You could look forever down the federal highway, and in the summer the heat rising off the blacktop would make this shimmering mirage that stayed ahead of you no matter how fast you drove. And believe me, you wanted to drive fast."

"Are the winters as bad as they say?"

"What do you mean?" he asked innocently. Laura rolled her eyes.

He fished out a few browned chunks of *pancetta* and checked them for crispness. Just right. Most of the fat had been rendered. Using a slotted spoon he scooped the bacon out of the pan and spread the bits to dry on a paper towel. Then he added the onion to the saucepan, gave it a shake, and turned up the heat a little.

"Everybody knows about the winters," he continued as he stirred the onion. "What they don't tell you about are the summers. They're beastly. You know, weather extremes in the middle of the continent and all that. Plus incredible humidity."

"As bad as the East Coast?" As a native, Laura needed convincing.

"Oh, much worse. It's got ten thousand lakes, remember? Where do you think the moisture goes? That's why there are so many mosquitoes—as big as gophers. It's a decent place except for that godforsaken climate. Spring is nice, mind you—both days of it. And talk about your crisp autumns . . ."

"Is that why you left?"

Matthew was stumped for a minute. "No," he said at last. "I'm not sure why I left."

He directed his attention to his sauce. The onions seemed ready. He poured in the strained tomatoes and added salt and a few twists of the pepper mill. Then he crushed a dried red pepper between his thumb and fingers and brushed the flakes and seeds off his hands over the pot. He stirred the pot.

"Don't even *think* of touching me with that hand till you wash it."

Matthew smiled. "To tell you the truth, I never thought of myself as having *left* Minnesota. In the sense of making a conscious decision to leave the place, I mean. I just sort of went other places because there was some attraction there. Like heading east for graduate school. Then back, this time to Northfield to teach. And to Boston for law school. Even when I decided to come to work at Daphnis and Clooney, I never said to myself, 'You're not going back.' It still seems like home. You know what I mean?"

"Not really. When I was growing up, there was never any doubt that I was leaving Paramus, New Jersey." Laura curled her lip in disdain. "First chance I got."

Matthew grinned at her. "Who could blame you?"

"Indeed."

She seemed almost morose for a moment, as if the vista of the endless strip mall that passed for her hometown were spread out before her. She poured herself another glass of wine while Matthew busied himself with filling a large stockpot with water for the pasta and turning on the gas under it. He pulled a box of penne out of the cupboard and set it on the counter next to the stove.

"How long till we eat?" asked Laura. "I'm ravenous."

"Half an hour."

He opened the refrigerator and took out a wedge of fresh *pecorino* wrapped in white butcher's paper. After stripping off the paper, he grated a rounded bowlful of the cheese. He used the pads of his fingers to pick up a few shreds that had missed the bowl and put them in his mouth. It was while he was savoring the sharp tang of the sheep's cheese that his curiosity finally got the better of him.

"So tell me something," he said, his back to her as he carried the bowl of cheese to the table in the breakfast nook. "Were you really wondering about life in Minnesota? Or did you start out asking me about my marriage and then back off?"

He turned around and they looked at each other. He could tell she was making up her mind. Then she smiled and dipped her head to one side as if to signal surrender.

"Guilty," she said, compressing her lips into a tight half smile and raising both hands in the air, the wineglass tipping precariously to one side. "I was afraid you might get the wrong idea or something."

They smiled at each other, not sure what to say.

Then Laura said, "So did you?"

Matthew narrowed his eyes in puzzlement. "Did I what?"

"Get the wrong idea?"

"No. I was just surprised. We never talked about it before." Then he frowned and cocked his head to one side. "Wait a minute. What wrong idea?"

She actually blushed.

"Well," she said, "you might think I was, like, getting serious or something."

"Would that be the wrong idea?" he asked, smiling slyly.

"To me or to you?" she asked. Tossing it back at him.

They looked at one another and smiled. With a start Matthew suddenly realized she was scared, and he immediately felt frightened himself. And then, without any conscious deliberation, he risked an honest answer.

"Not to me," he said, letting his smile fall away.

"Me either," said Laura.

Soon they were grinning at each other like monkeys and, in a brief silence broken only by the soft rain, everything between them changed.

Finally, Laura unwound a finger from the stem of her wineglass and pointed at the stove. "Your sauce is boiling." She arched an eyebrow.

Matthew didn't respond at first. Then he reached out and brushed the side of her face with the back of his hand. "Tell me about it," he said.

They both laughed.

"Delicious," Laura pronounced a little later, her mouth full of the spicy pasta. Matthew was still filling their salad bowls. "My compliments to your ex-wife."

"I'll see she gets them. Bread?"

"Uhm," she said, reaching for the loaf.

They ate in silence for a while. A comfortable silence.

"I had my first experience as a corporate lawyer today," Matthew said as he filled his plate with a second helping of pasta. He sprinkled more of the *pecorino* on top and idly mixed it in with his fork.

"For Falk?" asked Laura, her mouth full of bread. "Is he any more pleasant when he isn't viewing you as a litigator?"

"So far. He's an interesting guy. How many lawyers do you know who would frame a certificate from Outward Bound and hang it in their office?"

"Outward Bound?"

"Yeah. It's right there next to the picture of him with some high-tech maven whose initial public offering went through the ceiling. Apparently, the Outward Bound folks dropped him on an uninhabited island off the coast of Maine with a box of matches and a pocket knife. Left him all alone for five days. You know what Ira said when he heard about it?"

"I've given up trying to guess what Ira might say."

" 'The poor island!' "

Laura laughed. "I take it he survived all right."

"Hard to imagine, isn't it," Matthew said. "Falk always struck me as the kind of guy who'd put shoe trees in his sneakers. Assuming he ever wore any. When the boat arrived to pick him up, he had all the wildlife lined up doing legal research for him. Then, when he got back, he bought the island."

She laughed.

"No, really. He bought the whole goddamn thing and built

a cabin on it. He browbeat some real estate associate into handling the purchase. Falk says he goes up there every chance he gets. Which isn't as often as he'd like because his wife isn't into outdoor plumbing."

"Who could blame her? So what's he got you doing? Due diligence? Drafting employee stock option plans?" Mischief in her eyes. She was teasing him.

"Nothing so glamorous," Matthew said dryly. "Two things, really. One is negotiating a noncompete agreement with an executive who's leaving one of Falk's computer companies."

"My," she said, a half smile on her face.

He ignored her. "The other case is really more like litigation. Falk has an arbitration hearing coming up in California in a couple weeks, and he wants me to see if I can settle it. The client is a computer hardware sales rep who got terminated by some outfit in Silicon Valley. They make computer boards. Our guy had an exclusive contract that entitles him to commissions on all sales from the New England area—that's his territory—for ninety days after termination. They claim that's not what the contract means."

"Sounds gripping," Laura said sourly.

Matthew grinned. "Not as sexy as arguing over working drawings for hanging ceilings?" he asked, referring to the one that fell on Felter.

"At least there's an injury in it somewhere. Something human, you know."

"Not once the lawyers get there." Matthew picked up the empty plates and headed for the sink. "You ready for dessert?"

The phone rang.

"Can you get that, Laura?" asked Matthew. He was rinsing the plates.

"Hello," she said. She listened for a bit. Then she covered the mouthpiece and looked up at Matthew. "It's somebody named Danny. Sounds a bit wound up. You want it?"

"Oh, shit."

Matthew dried his hands and took the phone from Laura.

# 25

---

# No Wonder

Danny Li had been arrested on Friday evening by two state troopers in plainclothes. Each of them grabbing an arm, they took him coming out of his Harrison Street apartment building and hustled him, uncuffed and alone, into the back seat of a waiting car. It was a new Crown Victoria, big and blue and shiny as it idled next to a Chinatown hydrant. It was unmarked, but any observant passerby would have made it for a police car.

Weaving through the light late-evening traffic, the Ford climbed onto the Massachusetts Turnpike and sped west. The troopers rode in silence. When they left the city limits and entered Newton, they seemed to sense the mounting terror of their charge in the back seat. The trooper riding shotgun, a tall man with a handlebar mustache, turned toward Danny.

"We're taking you to a hotel in Needham," the trooper said, referring to a suburb west of Boston. "The city's not safe for you right now. The DA wants to have a few words with you, that's all."

"I don't want to talk to the DA," said Danny. "I want my lawyer."

The trooper turned toward the driver. "You hear that, Earle? 'My lawyer.' Mr. Li's got himself a lawyer already."

Earle was a short fat man in a baseball cap. He said nothing.

The tall trooper turned back to Danny. "We can't do nothin' about that. You'll have to talk to DeMarco. The DA."

Earle turned on his right blinker and moved the Ford into the exit lane that would take them southbound on Route 128, the inner beltway that girdled greater Boston. Danny was quiet for the rest of the trip, which lasted only a few more exits. Then the troopers got off Route 128 and turned almost immediately into the entrance to the Needham Sheraton.

The hotel was a brightly lighted tower of medium height that had been plunked inconsiderately among the squat, sprawling commercial buildings that were splayed out between the beltway and the Needham-Dedham border. Notwithstanding its festive lighting and grand curving driveway, the hotel looked forlornly out of place in its tawdry suburban setting.

The troopers drove around to the back of the building and parked. Danny was whisked through an unlit entrance, down a carpeted hall, and finally into what turned out to be a small suite, with a bedroom and a cramped sitting room. He was still getting his bearings when Earle spoke for the first time.

"No minibar," he said. "The cheap fucks."

Earle walked to the television and picked up the remote. Then he slumped heavily into a Naugahyde chair and clicked on the television. He started surfing.

The tall trooper looked at Danny and spread his arms in invitation. "Home sweet home," he said. "You might as well get used to it. There's nothing gonna happen till morning anyway. DeMarco's not gonna blow *his* Friday night to come all the way out here. I mean, he ain't a lawyer for nothing. Right, Earle?"

Earle grunted. He seemed to have settled on *Homicide*.

Danny said, "I want to call my lawyer."

The tall trooper shook his head sadly. "There it is again. 'My lawyer.' Does Herman Vu have a stable of shysters on call for you guys or what?"

"I don't know Herman Vu," said Danny. "And I'm not going to say anything without my lawyer."

"Hear that, Earle? Guy knows his rights." To Danny he said, "Look, I told you. You gotta take that up with De-Marco. Meanwhile, relax, for cripe's sake. Nobody's charging you with anything and nobody wants your confession. So what do you need a lawyer for? We're not even gonna ask you any questions. In fact, we'd prefer it if you'd, like, just shut up. You know what I'm saying?"

Danny did not respond.

Earle said, "No HBO either." He had tired of *Homicide* and was running through the channels again.

The tall trooper said to Danny, "Why don't you go have a lie-down in the bedroom. Like I said, it's gonna be a while."

Danny said, "Can I call my girlfriend?"

The trooper rolled his eyes and sighed in exasperation.

Danny pressed. "I should be back now. She will worry."

The trooper considered this. "What do you think, Earle?" he asked. "Should we let him call his little China doll and set her mind at ease?"

"No details," said Earle, after a moment.

"Right," said the tall trooper. "Keep it bare bones. Don't tell her where you are or who you're with or nothin'. And no talk about lawyers. You got that?"

Danny nodded.

"Okay. There's the phone. Be quick about it."

Danny went to the small desk by the window and picked up the phone. He peered at the instructions on a decal glued to the console next to the buttons.

"You gotta dial nine first," said the tall trooper.

"Have you told them anything?" Matthew Boer asked Danny twenty-four hours later, when the call came in. Laura had taken over cleaning up the kitchen and Matthew was sitting on the stool she had occupied when he was cooking.

"No. But he says he will do the drug charges again if I don't. Can they do that? My—" Danny stopped, then lowered his voice. "My friend said they were dismissed."

"Your friend? You mean Dunleavy?"

"Yes. Can they?"

"Well," said Matthew, guessing, "if the charges were dismissed because the arresting officer failed to appear, the dismissal would probably be without prejudice. So they could reinstate the charges. I think. But they're the least of your problems."

"I want to get out of here, Matt. I tell him I will not talk to him without my lawyer and he tells me, 'You don't have to talk. You just have to listen.' Then he threatens me."

"Who does? Who's been talking to you, Danny?"

"The DA. DeMarco. He says the court will make me tell. He—"

Suddenly, Danny was gone. Matthew could hear muffled voices on the line, but nothing he could decipher. Matthew's heart began to beat wildly. Then someone else was on the line.

"Who is this?" said a peremptory voice.

"Matthew Boer. I represent Mr. Li. Who is *this*?"

"Never heard of you. What firm are you with?"

Matthew realized he was about to get run over by the sheer aggression of the guy. He took a measured breath and said. "You haven't answered my question. Who are you—and what are you doing, busting in on my conversation with my client?"

The voice paused, but only briefly. "This is Jerry De-Marco. I'm the first assistant in the Suffolk County district attorney's office. And Mr. Li has been picked up as a material witness in a criminal case."

"You've got no right to hold him. Release him now or I'll get a writ for his release from Judge Doyle."

*That's more like it,* Matthew thought, with satisfaction. A little fire in the belly.

"Ah," DeMarco said, a smile in his voice, "I'm glad to hear you mention the good judge. It means we're both thinking of the same case. And *that* means I do indeed have the right guy."

Matthew closed his eyes. *Fuck me,* he thought. And Ira off in the Berkshires somewhere until Monday.

"You still can't hold him."

"The hell I can't. He's a material witness in a capital murder case. He's refusing to cooperate. He'd disappear if I released him. Plus, he'd be in grave danger if I dumped him back on the street."

"He's in 'grave danger' only if you publicize his identity. Anyway, that's his business, not yours. You can't force your protection on him."

"Oh," said DeMarco, "did I forget to mention? There's an outstanding possession beef against him. I can hold him on that as well."

"Those charges were dismissed," said Matthew.

"I can always recharge him," said DeMarco.

"The arresting officer is dead. You've got no case."

"Ah, but he had a fellow officer who assisted him in the arrest. I'm confident he'll want to do everything he can to secure Mr. Li's testimony for the trial of Francis Dunleavy's killer. Don't you think so?"

"We'll have to see what the judge says about that," Matthew said lamely.

DeMarco laughed. "Come on," he said. "Tell me, which firm are you with?"

"Daphnis and Clooney," said Matthew. "And he's entitled to a bail hearing."

DeMarco paused.

"No wonder," he said at last.

# 26

---

# The High-Priced Spread

As instructed, at nine-thirty on Monday morning Matthew notified Ike Rosenthal, via voice mail, that his client had been taken into custody. Then he gathered up the motion papers he had drafted the afternoon before and hurried to Pemberton Square. Passing through the security check at the courthouse, he asked the two security guards for directions to the lockup.

The two guards looked him over. They both wore dark-blue polyester blazers with imitation brass buttons.

"You a lawyer?" asked one of them, a fine-featured black man with bad, crenelated teeth. He was carrying a metal detector.

"Yes."

"And you don't know where the lockup is?"

Matthew smiled wanly and shook his head.

"I'm glad you're not *my* lawyer," the guard said, and both of them laughed. Matthew smiled along with them.

Fifteen minutes later, having filed his motion papers with the clerk's office, he was standing before a court officer in the lockup. A small, featureless man in his middle thirties, the officer was seated behind a desk that blocked access to the holding cells some ten feet beyond him. A name tag pinned to the breast pocket of his neatly pressed shirt identified him as Officer Bevilacqua. Talk and shouts emanating from the holding cells kept the noise levels disturbingly high.

"I'm here to see a client you have in custody," said Matthew.

"What?" said the court officer, cupping his left hand behind his ear. "You're who?"

"My name is Matthew Boer," he said, almost shouting now. "I'm a lawyer. I want to see my client. Name is Danny Li. He's being held as a material witness."

"Try the morgue!" said a voice from the holding cell. This prompted raucous laughter from the other prisoners.

Officer Bevilacqua let his hand drop from his ear and looked evenly at Matthew. Then he picked up a clipboard from the desk and signaled Matthew by tipping his head sharply in the direction of the door. Matthew followed him through it and back out into the hallway. The court officer closed the door behind them, muffling the din from the holding cells.

"You shouldn't talk about material witnesses in the holding area," said Bevilacqua sternly. "Especially by name. Word travels fast in there. You wanna make trouble for him?"

"No, I'm sorry," said Matthew, ashamed of himself. "I just want to talk to my client."

Bevilacqua looked at him for a moment, disdain pulling at the corners of his mouth. "What's the name again?" he asked. He raised the clipboard.

"Danny Li."

"Nope," he said after turning back the pages on his clipboard. "I don't got him."

Matthew's shoulders sagged and he looked away. He could feel the pressure knotting up in him. "Where else could they be holding him?" he asked. "Jerry DeMarco had him arrested and they tell me I have a bail hearing at ten-thirty."

Officer Bevilacqua widened his eyes slightly. "This is the snitch DeMarco's been looking for?" His put-upon pedagogue's manner had deserted him.

Unsure how to respond without giving away too much, Matthew paused before saying, "I don't know about that. All I know is DeMarco has my client and there's a hearing. Where would he be?"

"You got me. All I can tell you is I don't have him. But if this *is* the snitch, DeMarco's probably holing him up in his office somewhere."

"Thanks," said Matthew, starting up the hall. Then he stopped and looked back at Officer Bevilacqua. "Can you tell me how to get to the DA's office?"

Like the black security guard before him, Officer Bevilacqua seemed to size him up and find him wanting. "Try the sixth floor," he said. Then he shook his head and went back into the lockup.

But at the district attorney's office, Matthew was told that First Assistant DeMarco had just left for court. Matthew checked his watch. It was ten-twenty. He tore off in the direction of the elevators. By the time the courthouse's antiquated elevators deigned to appear and he had made his way to Judge Doyle's courtroom, the judge was already striding toward the bench. DeMarco was standing behind one counsel table, Sarah Kerlinsky behind the other. The spectators' seating area was empty. And there, standing in the jury box between two court officers, stood Danny Li.

The bailiff told them they could be seated, but DeMarco remained standing.

"What have we got here, Mr. DeMarco?" asked Judge Doyle, reaching down to take Matthew's papers from the clerk. "I have a jury to charge at eleven and I don't want them to start without me."

"This is not my motion, Your Honor," said DeMarco. "The occasion is a bail request for a material witness."

Judge Doyle put on his reading glasses and looked at the papers. He frowned. "In the *Chin* case? I thought that was on appeal."

"I filed a motion for reconsideration last Friday, Your Honor. I have reason to believe that this witness is the informant we've all been wrangling over. His discovery forms one of the grounds for my motion."

Judge Doyle grinned. "I don't know whether I'm more

surprised or pleased, Mr. DeMarco. Who's bringing the bail motion?" He riffled through Matthew's papers looking for the signature page.

"I am, Your Honor," said Matthew as he pushed open the gate to enter the well of the courtroom. DeMarco and Kerlinsky turned to watch him. DeMarco smiled stiffly and nodded as Matthew passed him on his way to the lectern in front of the clerk's desk.

Judge Doyle looked down at him as he held the papers. "And you would be . . . ?"

"Matthew Boer, Your Honor. From Daphnis and Clooney."

"My, my," said the judge, beaming. "The high-priced spread. We aren't often graced by such finery over here on the criminal side. To what do we owe this unwonted pleasure?"

*Oh, Jesus,* thought Matthew. He decided it was best to plunge right in.

"To Mr. DeMarco's decision to walk all over my client's constitutional rights."

DeMarco sprang to his feet, but Judge Doyle raised his right hand and silenced him before he could get a word out.

"Mr. Blower, we prefer to leave personalities out of things here. If you've got an argument that your client should be released on bail, please make it. I'll draw my own conclusions about the conduct of the district attorney."

"Certainly, your honor. And it's Boer. B-O-E-R."

Judge Doyle acknowledged the correction with a nod.

"Your Honor," Matthew continued, "my client—he's identified only as John Doe in the papers—is not a defendant in this case. There are no criminal charges pending against him. There was no subpoena issued for his testimony. He was not in hiding or making an effort to flee the court's jurisdiction when Mr. DeMarco's men descended on him. Notwithstanding this, he was arrested outside his residence on Friday evening and has been held against his will since then in some hotel outside Boston. There the district attorney threatened to resuscitate charges that were dismissed last year if my client did not agree to tell him what he wanted to hear. No one read him his *Miranda* rights. He was not brought

before a magistrate where the issue of his immediate release
might be raised. He was denied his right to confer with counsel for over twenty-four hours. Even then, he was vouchsafed
nothing more than a single, short telephone call to me on
Saturday night—a consultation that was cut off by the district
attorney as soon as he mentioned Mr. DeMarco's name."

"You Honor," said DeMarco, still on his feet.

"In a moment, Mr. DeMarco," said the judge without looking at him. "Let him say his piece."

"In fact, Your Honor," said Matthew, "to this moment I
have not had an opportunity to meet with my client. He has
been denied process in—"

"Let me cut to the chase here," Judge Doyle interrupted,
countermanding his own directive. He skimmed through the
papers. "You want bail for your client. You want Mr.
DeMarco here to leave him alone. (Wouldn't we all.) And
you want an opportunity to confer with your client. Have I
got all that straight?"

"Yes, Your Honor. I think—"

"Let's take it one piece at a time. Does the Commonwealth
object to bail?"

DeMarco stood up again, his hands pinching his waist.

"Yes, Your Honor. Following Your Honor's order of dismissal, I made a plea to members of the Drug Control Unit
of the Police Department for someone to come forward—
anonymously, if necessary—with information about the
missing informant."

"If you'd done that months ago," Judge Doyle said dryly,
"we might be past all this."

"Perhaps," said DeMarco. "Though I doubt it. The police
may have needed Your Honor's order dismissing the indictment to bring home the seriousness of my request."

Christ, thought Matthew. The suck-up was actually com-
plimenting the judge for ruling against him.

"At any rate," DeMarco continued, "I received an anonymous call on Thursday afternoon from a police officer—at
least I assume that's who it was, given what he knew. He
named Mr. Boer's client as the source for the information
that went into Detective Carvalho's affidavit. He told me
where the witness lived and that he had been charged with

a drug offense. The caller also informed me that the information was passed not to Carvalho, but to Detective Dunleavy. I then arranged for his—"

"Wait a minute," Judge Doyle snapped. "To Dunleavy? Then he's not the elusive IT? Is that what you're telling me?"

"I don't know how to answer that at this point, Your Honor. If my anonymous caller has his facts straight, there certainly appear to be some discrepancies in Detective Carvalho's testimony. But the witness has not cooperated with the investigation. He has said absolutely nothing in response to my questions. I have offered to kill the prospect of any charges being brought against him. I have offered him immunity and personal security in a safe house at a comfortable distance from Boston until after the trial—as well as assistance in relocating afterwards, if he so desires. He has expressed a total unwillingness to cooperate with my office or the court. I have every reason to believe he may disappear if released on bail. And even if he sticks around, I don't have to remind Your Honor of the serious dangers he faces on the street. He should be held without bail—not in jail, mind you, but in a safe house—until trial. Failing that, he should be kept in custody at *least* until Ms. Kerlinsky and I have had an opportunity to examine him under oath."

"OK," said Judge Doyle, cutting him off. "Mr. Boer, strut your stuff." He leaned back in his chair.

Matthew winced. "Your Honor," he said, "there is very little risk that my client will flee the jurisdiction. Bear in mind that he was never under any obligation to come forward with information. Nor was there any obligation to answer Mr. DeMarco's questions during his illegal confinement—questions posed while he was denied an opportunity to seek advice of counsel. He did what every citizen has a right to do: to stand on his rights under the Fifth Amendment.

"My client doesn't want the Commonwealth's protection, Your Honor. He could not be more adamant on that point. Please bear in mind, Your Honor, that he comes from a tightly knit immigrant culture that is traditionally suspicious of all political authority. He is terrified of the police and even more so at the prospect of being held in custody. However benignly *we* might perceive Mr. DeMarco's intentions and arrangements for his comfort, my client has a far greater fear of the state and the police than he does of remaining at large among his own people. Nor am I aware of any legal obligation for a witness to accept protection.

"I repeat: The risk that he might flee the jurisdiction is infinitesimal. He is not a junkie. He is no derelict. He is a stable, responsible member of the Chinese community. He has a steady job as the manager of a restaurant in Chinatown, and he has lived more than three years in his apartment at twenty-one Harrison Street. He has no—"

"This is outrageous, Your Honor!" DeMarco was on his feet and shouting now.

Matthew turned to look back at him in confusion.

DeMarco continued. "He's disclosing identifying information in open court! I ask that the record be impounded immediately!"

Judge Doyle was also angry. "The record will be impounded," he said sharply. "And Mr. Boer, try to stay off the tops of your own client's toes, will you?"

Matthew's ears burned.

"I beg your pardon, Your Honor," he squawked, his mouth dry. "The courtroom was empty. I assumed this proceeding was in camera."

The judge ignored him as he purposefully swept his gaze across the courtroom. "All counsel and court personnel are ordered to say nothing—I repeat, *nothing*—about what you hear today, and to take every possible measure to maintain the confidentiality of the witness. If I see any of this in the *Herald* or the *Globe* tomorrow morning, there will be hell to pay. Is that clear to everyone?"

The universal nods of assent suggested it was.

"Now, Mr. Boer," he said ominously to Matthew, "do you have anything further to add?"

"I think that will do it, Your Honor."

"I should hope so. But before we all go off on a wild-goose chase here, tell me this. Is your client this IT or not?"

Matthew froze, fear coursing through him like electrical current. He breathed deeply and said, "With all respect, Your Honor, I can't answer that question without revealing client confidences. I ask you not to press it."

The courtroom fell silent. Judge Doyle glared at him over his half-glasses, his eyes narrowing as his anger mounted visibly. It occurred to Matthew that his client might get released while he himself spent the night in jail.

"If I may, Your Honor?"

The voice belonged to Sarah Kerlinsky, who spoke for the first time. Judge Doyle cranked his head gravely in her direction and showed her a frown of annoyance.

"A suggestion, Your Honor," Sarah went on, undeterred. "I think there is a way to resolve this without getting into a confrontation over the scope of the attorney-client privilege."

The judge was silent, marmoreal, as he looked at her. Sarah seemed to take it as leave to proceed.

"It is not Mr. Boer's testimony but the witness's that everyone wants. I have grave doubts that this is the IT about whom Detective Carvalho testified so glowingly. He's probably just some low-level snitch the Commonwealth wants to fob off on us to convince Your Honor to reinstate the indictment. Or the SJC, if you don't go along. But whoever he is, let us find out. Order the witness to appear for the taking of his deposition, at which time Mr. DeMarco and I can put our questions to him."

"How do we know he'll answer our questions?" DeMarco interjected. "He's shown no willingness to cooperate so far."

Matthew, who had regained some of his composure, jumped in. "Your Honor, that means nothing. My client has been under no obligation to answer anybody's questions to this point."

Judge Doyle looked down at Matthew again. "Are you telling me he's willing to testify at a deposition?"

Recalling Danny's earlier resolve to say nothing at all, Matthew felt trapped again. "As I said earlier, Your Honor, I have not had an opportunity to confer with my client since his arrest. But given the district attorney's threats to revive old drug charges, I would have to discuss his rights under the Fifth Amendment."

DeMarco spoke up again. "Your Honor, the Commonwealth will agree not to bring any drug charges if the witness cooperates by giving testimony."

As DeMarco sat down, a young man entered the court-room from the rear and walked up the aisle.

"All right," said the judge, as he watched the intruder lean over the rail and whisper into DeMarco's ear. "I'm going to order the witness to appear to have his deposition taken at Attorney Kerlinsky's office next Tuesday morning, a week from tomorrow. That should give you two"—he nodded toward DeMarco and Matthew—"time to work out the terms on which he will testify. And I am—what is it *now*, Mr. DeMarco?" The judge's snappishness was triggered by DeMarco's standing up again.

"I'm sorry to interrupt, Your Honor," said DeMarco, "but I've just received some disturbing news. A court officer in the lockup has notified my office that Mr. Boer showed up there this morning demanding to see his client. Apparently, Mr. Boer identified the witness by name—quite loudly, I'm told—and described him as a material witness, all within earshot of prisoners in the holding cells. The court officer called my office out of concern for the safety of the witness. Under the circumstances, I—"

"What am I to do with you, Mr. Boer?" Judge Doyle asked, a look of disgust on his face. "You come in here pleading for your client's release, and for his right to refuse police protection, while you yourself seem to be doing the most to expose him to further danger."

Stunned, Matthew said, "I apologize, Your Honor. I did not know where Mr. DeMarco was holding my client. I assumed it would be in the lockup. It was so noisy in there it was necessary to speak loudly to be heard. I did not think I—"

"I *guess* you didn't think," Judge Doyle said savagely. He seemed to consider for a moment, and then he turned toward the jury box and looked at Danny. "Officers, please bring the witness to the bench. To the sidebar." He waggled his fingers in an impatient come-hither gesture.

They did as they were told. As he neared the bench, Danny shot a glance in Matthew's direction. He looked terrified.

They stopped at the left side of the bench.

Judge Doyle leaned over in Danny's direction. He spoke softly and Matthew had to strain to hear everything he said.

"I'm sorry for this mess you find yourself in, but I'm afraid you're going to have to put up with us a while longer. Right now, I just need to ask you a couple of questions. OK?"

Danny nodded.

"Is your English good?"

"Yes, sir," said Danny, his voice surprisingly clear and loud in the almost empty courtroom.

"Have you been following what's been going on here pretty well?"

"I think so."

"You've listened to me give your counsel a pretty hard time this morning. And serious questions have been raised about whether his continued representation is in your best interests. Do you understand what I'm saying?"

"You want to know if I still want him for my lawyer?"

Judge Doyle smiled. "Right on the money. If you wish to be represented by someone more experienced in criminal proceedings, I'm sure we can find you someone."

"No," said Danny. "Matt is my lawyer. I don't want a stranger."

"Well, we might be able to find someone who shares your ethnic heritage."

"No." Danny seemed, if anything, firmer in his resolve. "I know Matt."

"All right. And is it true that you refuse to accept police protection?"

"Yes."

"Despite the risks that you might face on the street?" Judge Doyle glanced meaningfully at Matthew.

"I want to go home."

"You understand that I am ordering you to appear to answer questions from Mr. DeMarco and Ms. Kerlinsky. Will you obey my order to show up for your deposition next week?"

"Yes, but I have nothing to say. I don't—"

"Well, we'll have to cross that bridge when we come to it. I'm sure Mr. Boer will explain your options and obligations in that regard. Right now I want you to tell me you will show up as ordered. Will you do that?"

"Yes, I will come."

Judge Doyle rolled his chair back to the center of the bench and faced the lawyers in front of him.

"Mr. Boer," he said, "if your client had not expressed such a strong preference for your continued representation, I'd be inclined to strike your appearance. What troubles me is that you have made statements inappropriate to safeguard the identity of your client. First in the lockup and then in open court before me. But as I said, the witness wants you."

Judge Doyle's disappointment in Danny's judgment was evident.

"Who am I," he went on, "to interfere with his right to counsel of his choosing? But I can't advise you strongly enough to seek direction from someone more experienced in criminal matters. Do I make myself clear?"

"Absolutely, Your Honor," said Matthew.

"All right, then. The witness's deposition will take place next Tuesday, as I said earlier. Bail is set at five hundred dollars." He turned back to Danny. "Can you make bail?"

Danny said, "Yes, my girlfriend can—"

"I will call her immediately, Your Honor," said Matthew.

"Whatever," said the judge, looking down at the clerk now. "The witness is further ordered to inform Mr. DeMarco before leaving Suffolk County for any reason. And the district attorney and his agents will leave the witness alone. Is there anything else?"

There wasn't, and Judge Doyle stood up.

"All rise!" cried the bailiff. The judge disappeared behind the curtain. Matthew smiled at Danny—reassuringly, he hoped—as the court officers led him away. Then he turned to leave, almost bumping into DeMarco, who stood athwart the opening between the two counsel tables.

"Is Ira Teitelbaum still at your firm?" DeMarco asked brusquely. His head was thrown back and his chest seemed to jut out at Matthew.

"Yes, he is," said Matthew.

"I suggest you have a long talk with him or someone equally experienced before you show up for the deposition."

When it became apparent that Matthew was not going to respond, DeMarco turned on his heel and left. Matthew let out a long breath as the courtroom doors swung shut behind him.

"A rough morning?"

It was Sarah Kerlinsky, whose presence he had forgotten for the moment. He turned to her, expecting more derision, but her smile seemed concerned, even kindly. Her skin crinkled about bright brown eyes that peered through oval, gold-rimmed glasses.

"You didn't do nearly as bad as those two let on," she said. "Think about it. Despite all the abuse, you got everything you asked for. Your client is free and Jerry has to stay away from him. That's why Jerry's being such a jerk. He's got to flex his arrogance, even when he loses. And all that business about endangering your client is just a lot of hot air."

"The judge doesn't seem to think so."

Sarah's smile widened into a grin. "Oh, he was waiting for something like that. In case you didn't notice, he hates big law firms—especially when he thinks they're slumming by showing up in one of his criminal cases. Trust me, he'd have found something else to hit you with if you hadn't handed him a convenient club."

Matthew grinned at this. They were walking toward the elevators now.

"Well, I owe you a debt of thanks," he said. "For speaking up when you did. I thought sure he was going to find me in contempt for not answering his question about IT. You got him right off my case."

"Sometimes," she said, "you have to pivot to the side a little and let them bull on through. Especially with macho types like Doyle and DeMarco. It's cleaner that way."

She pushed the down button for the elevator.

"So," she said softly, changing the subject, "what's he going to say?"

"Nothing," said Matthew. "Nothing at all, if he has his way."

"He won't, you know. Have his way, I mean. They'll get an immunity order if they have to and then they'll put him in jail until he agrees to answer Jerry's questions. You better prepare him for that."

"I've tried, believe me. And he's terrified of being in jail. It's a hell of a mess."

"I can see that," she said, impatiently punching the button several times to summon the tardy elevator. "It's a tough spot to be in. Tell him to bring a toothbrush."

Then, looking up at him with a smile, she added, "Tell me this much, will you? Do I want him to testify?"

Matthew considered this for a moment. Of course not, he thought. Danny could destroy the fiction that there ever was a five-foot-eleven Chinese dealer working out of the apartment. And that might demolish her main line of defense. But how much did he dare tell her? Or would it be better to have her on his side?

"No," he said at last, just ahead of the muffled metallic chime that announced the elevator's arrival. "You don't want him to testify."

"Thanks," she said, and the two of them squeezed into the crowded elevator. They spoke no more as the doors closed behind them.

# 27

## A Target-Rich Environment

Raymond Carvalho stood at the very prow of the boat. In his right hand he held a plastic cup filled with lukewarm beer. The fingers of his other hand were interlaced with Donna's. In fact, landlubber that she was, Donna had him by both hands, her left clutching his arm tightly as the blunt prow bludgeoned its way through the light chop. The brandy-colored river water spumed up and sprayed them lightly, making Donna flinch and grip his arm painfully, but Carvalho didn't mind.

At Carvalho's suggestion, she had called in sick and they had boarded the *Charles II* for a lap around the Charles River Basin. The canvas-canopied tourist boat took on passengers from a small paddleboat marina that had been dug out at the foot of Cambridge Side Galleria, a new urban mall across the river from the Boston Science Museum. Laden with tourists and shoppers, the boat had chugged out of the newly cut Lechmere Channel and churned its way diagonally across the Charles toward the Esplanade on the Boston side of the river. Then the ride smoothed out.

A fresh breeze rose off the water. Cumulus clouds pil-

lowed up over the rooftops of Back Bay and slid lazily like
stately giant swans across a blue sky. Carvalho took a deep
breath and then exhaled noisily, his lips blowing. He could
feel the city's toxins leaching out of him and his stomach
muscles slackening their grip at last. Donna sensed his release. It was odd, the way she seemed to know things about
him.

"It's beautiful, isn't it," she said, resting the side of her
face against his shoulder.

"Beats the hell out of East Berkeley Street," he said. He
had a sip of beer and felt an unaccustomed revulsion at the
taste. He poured the rest over the side.

Turned out to be something of a surprise, did Donna
Something (for so he still called her, even after learning her
name was Righetti—no relation to the former Yankee ace).
That business about not remembering whose bed he was in
should have ended it before it began, and, Jesus wept, he
must have been snot-slinging drunk when they met the night
before. But they hit it off. A hygienist for a dentist in Sharon,
she was warm and understanding, eager in the sack, always
up for a good time. Of course, the drive to Easton was a
bitch, but it was a lot more inviting than the prospect of his
empty apartment. And so far they hadn't been together long
enough for her, like Rosa and all the women after her, to
start resenting that he was a cop.

They were quiet for several minutes. The "captain" of the
boat, a fuzzy-cheeked college student who'd landed a cushy
summer job, was describing the buildings and landmarks that
rolled by along the Boston shoreline. If Carvalho worked it
just right, he could shut out the voice completely and watch
the city drifting backwards, towed out toward the harbor and
the open sea. Which would be fine with him, thank you very
much.

He said, "My old man used to go on about boats all the
time."

"Was he a fisherman?"

"Nah. He loaded trucks at Polaroid in east Cambridge.
Beat his fucking brains out for nickels and dimes all his life,
and he hated it. But he always talked about the dory and the
sea and how *his* old man was a real Portuguese 'cause he

was a fisherman and all. The closest my old man got to being a fisherman was making his own *bacalhau*. That's salt cod."

"A dory. Is that a boat?" She sounded dreamy, far away.

"Yeah, it's a kind of one-man rowboat they would take out. To go after cod, mostly. Dangerous as hell."

"More than being a policeman?" She smiled.

He gave a snort. "Who knows? He used to take me to see my grandfather, you know. Down to New Bedford. Scrawny little old guy with a face like a walnut. Squinted a lot. He came direct from the Azores and still had the accent. He smelled of fish. Every time I saw him, he stunk like fish. It was all over his pickup and even his house. My old man smelled it too, you could tell. And he'd be bummed out all the way home. So I knew even then he was full of shit."

"Your father?"

"Yes. He didn't regret 'giving up the sea.' He never had it to give up. He just hated his miserable life and then he'd get to thinking the 'old life' was the way to go. Till he made one of those trips to New Bedford and the smell of fish would stink up his make-believe."

"So you knew you didn't want to be a fisherman."

"Oh, I never had any doubts on that score. What I learned was I didn't want to live like my old man either. I didn't know what that meant for me till I got out of the army and got a chance to go with the department. It was a way out, you know what I mean?"

"Oh, yes," she said with conviction. "I know what you mean."

"It was a damn good life for a long time, the department."

"Was? It's not good anymore?"

"Ah, who knows?" he said, and she let it drop.

They were silent again. The boat glided past the huge structure that housed the Boston University law school, a misshapen tower of precast concrete that surged far above all its neighbors. It was a bleak edifice, all cement-gray except for inexplicable bits of colored piping on recessed panels that ran vertically up the end walls.

After passing under the BU bridge, the boat made a slow loop and began the return trip alongside the Cambridge shore.

"So," said Donna, "what do you want to do when we get back?"

Carvalho smiled. "Slip into something more comfortable," he said. "Like you."

She laughed happily. "Oh, I know *that*," she said. "I meant besides."

"Get some salt cod?"

"Ugh!" she said, screwing up her face.

He laughed, she laughed with him, and his beeper went off.

He looked down and tipped the pager away from his body so he could read the phone number displayed on it.

"It's Sal," he said, his voice dripping disappointment. "I gotta call him as soon as we get back."

He could feel the pressure building again. It was as if he had never left the shore.

"Mr. Boer?" said the voice on the phone.

"Yes?"

"Hi. This is Eddie Felch with the *Globe*. I was hoping you might be able to confirm a story we plan to run tomorrow morning."

Christ, that was fast, thought Matthew. It was less than twenty-four hours since he and Sarah had walked out of Judge Doyle's courtroom, and already the press was on to something. Was this his fault?

"I doubt if I can help you," he said. Doubtfully.

"I understand your predicament," said Felch, smoothly. "Please, just listen and see if you can't keep me from screwing it up too bad. OK?"

"Well, I don't—"

"Thanks. I see from the docket in the *Chin* case that you entered an appearance yesterday. On behalf of someone identified as John Doe, who is not named as a defendant. A witness, I presume. You filed a motion to get him released on bail, which was allowed. And you filed some supporting papers, all of which, like the record of the hearing itself, have been impounded. Have I got all that straight so far?"

Matthew paused before replying. "All except that business

about my client being a witness," he said. "I can't comment on that."

"Aw, come on, Mr. Boer," Felch said. His tone was convivial, understanding, the mild exasperation of one trying to convince a friend to venture beyond his routine morning pastry. "What else could he be? The case was dismissed because there was no witness. The DA moves to reconsider on Friday, hinting darkly that he has important new evidence. What else could he be signaling but the discovery of a witness? And then *you* show up to bail a John Doe who was arrested Friday night. What do you expect me to infer?"

"Whatever you like," Matthew chuckled. "I'm just not going to confirm it. Judge Doyle has issued a gag order in the case and I'm not about to violate it. *That* you can quote."

" 'Nuff said. I understand. Can I at least get a little background here? On you, I mean. Daphnis and Clooney is not exactly a hotbed of criminal lawyers, now, is it?"

Matthew laughed. "No, it's not," he said "And neither am I. A criminal defense lawyer, that is."

"So how come you're involved in this?"

"I can't tell you that. Sorry."

"Well, give me a little about your background, then. I gotta fill with something."

Matthew gave him the highlights of his resume and described the nature of his practice at the firm, such as it was. As he talked, he could hear Felch's fingers working away at the keyboard of his computer. They spent four or five minutes on this flattering topic, with Felch asking fluff questions, before the reporter abruptly shifted gears.

"One last question," he said, with the tone of one about to ring off. "Courthouse rumor has it that your client is Chinese. Is that true?"

Matthew froze. For too long. Just as he was about to protest that he could not comment on the rumors, Felch said, "Thank you, Counselor. Your silence speaks volumes."

And then he was gone.

Like everything else that had happened since Danny's call on Saturday night, the conversation had spun out of control. After the hearing, Matthew had managed to reach Julie all right, and she had shown up at the clerk's office in less than twenty minutes. Producing five hundred dollars—in cash, of course—she posted Danny's bail. Matthew bought the three of them coffee and sandwiches from the deli in Two Center Plaza. They sat at one of the metal tables bunched together outside in Pemberton Square and ate under the noonday sun. Danny seemed relieved, jubilant even, to be out at last, and he was voluble in expressing his gratitude for the good work Matthew had done in obtaining his release. Matthew smiled bleakly as he listened to his happy client.

After giving Danny time to enjoy himself, Matthew sought to bring him back to earth. He asked Julie to leave the two of them alone for a few minutes. She exchanged a few words with Danny, in Chinese, and took her leave.

"He's a good judge for me, right, Matt?" Danny asked as he and Matthew watched Julie cross the square and ascend the stairs that would take her to Tremont Street. Her long black hair flowed in her wake.

"That remains to be seen," said Matthew. "All that neighborly concern he showed you today will evaporate pretty fast if you don't answer DeMarco's questions next week. He'll toss you right back in jail. And I mean jail this time, not some comfortable hotel with personal bodyguards."

Danny's face clouded and he said nothing as he flicked a glance at Matthew and then looked away.

Matthew plowed on. "And he'll keep you there till you agree to answer the questions. So you need to weigh your options here."

"I can't go to jail, Matt. If I am in jail, they will find out who I am."

"I suspect you're right. You may want to reconsider DeMarco's offer of protection and relocation."

"No." Danny shook his head.

"I don't see a Plan C here, Danny. You may have to pick one of them."

After reflecting a moment, Danny turned to look at Matthew. "What if they can't find me?" he asked. "You know, I disappear for a while? How long will they wait?" Once again, Danny wasn't looking at him, his eyes sweeping the square and then climbing the facade of the old courthouse. "The trial will be over sometime."

Matthew shook his head. "You're under a court order to appear on Tuesday. I can't advise you to disobey that order. And besides, not showing up would be disastrous. You keep telling me you don't want certain people to know who you are. Well, what do you think will happen when you don't show? I'll tell you. DeMarco will have the police combing the city to find you. And how can they find you except by circulating enough information about you to identify you? Then the people you're so scared of are sure to figure out who you are, and you'll end up in the same boat you'd be in if you had testified—but without DeMarco's help and protection. I'm not sure you've got much of a choice here, Danny."

Danny's gaze continued to rake the granite pediments and pilasters of the old courthouse. "I need time to think," he said at last.

Matthew stood up and shoved his chair back under the table. "You do that, Danny. Meanwhile, I'll do some checking to see if I can find some other way out. Give me a call tomorrow, OK?"

Danny nodded but said nothing.

Matthew walked back to the Trifle Tower.

As he approached his office, Sally informed him that Ike Rosenthal wanted to see him as soon as he got in. Matthew told her to call him and tell him he was on his way. Then he trudged back up the hall and went down the library staircase.

The managing partner of Daphnis & Clooney was ensconced in the southeast corner of the thirty-eighth floor, where his half-round desk was turned to face two glass walls that afforded a magnificent view of Boston Harbor. Out on the harbor an enormous freighter was washed in the crisp light of the late New England summer as it glided away toward the open sea. A telescope was set up on a tripod near the juncture of the glass walls. One of the inside walls was completely taken up by a single painting, a life-sized rendering by Gorman of an Indian woman in soft reds and greens. Family pictures, happy faces caught in vacation poses at Cape Cod or the Vineyard, cluttered the other wall. And in the middle of the room, Buddha-like, sat Ira Teitelbaum with his beatific smile.

Ike Rosenthal rose and shook hands with Matthew across the desk. He was a small man, almost completely bald on top but with a heavy beard that needed shaving twice a day. He wore a floral tie with a handsome if ill-fitting beige suit of lightweight linen. Matthew only knew him well enough to say hello to, a prim, cordial lawyer who enjoyed a city-wide reputation as a shrewd deal maker and an unrivaled master of the sundry arcana of Massachusetts real estate law. Now in his fourth year as managing partner, he had also proven himself as an effective businessman and administrator.

"I hear you had a little excitement while I was away," said Ira, his smile broadening, if that was possible, into an almost needling grin.

"That's a bit of an understatement," said Matthew.

There was a rap at the door and Ben Fleishman entered the room.

"Hello, all," he said. "Sorry I'm late."

Rosenthal said, "We're just getting started, Ben. I wanted the four of us to get together on this so we'd have a common strategy. Especially with the press interest likely to be generated."

Rosenthal sat back down. Matthew and Fleishman took seats on either side of Ira.

Rosenthal said, "Matt, why don't you start by telling us what's happened since Friday?"

Matthew took them through the events of the past forty-eight hours. He slid over the shaky bits of his own performance, saving them for Ira's ears alone. He finished up by recounting his promise to research ways to keep Danny from having to testify.

As if to confirm Sarah Kerlinsky's assessment, Rosenthal appeared to be quite pleased with the results of the hearing.

"We seem pretty much on top of things so far," he said. "I admit this isn't exactly my métier"—Rosenthal smiled at this thought—"but it sounds like you achieved about as much as you could have hoped. I doubt you're going to find much wiggle room for your client, though."

"That's what I've told him," said Matthew. "Though I think it's a good sign that defense counsel's interests seem to coincide with ours."

"Sarah Kerlinsky?" said Ira. "Don't look for her to do you any more favors, Matt. She was helpful, sure, but that woman could follow you into a revolving door and still come out first. Notice how she jollied out of you the critical information she had to have. That your client's testimony is bad news for her."

"But that means we both have an interest in keeping Danny from telling what he knows," Matthew protested.

"Your mutual interests are not *that* congruent. She doesn't want him to talk, sure, but beyond that, all bets are off. Be careful."

"Well, I'm going to leave the courtroom strategy to you guys," said Rosenthal, cutting off this line of discussion and taking charge of the meeting again. "The only case I ever took to court was an uncontested divorce—and I lost." He chuckled to himself. "My principal concern," he added, turning serious, "is how to handle the media. What are your thoughts on that?"

Matthew was puzzled. "Hasn't Judge Doyle taken care of that for us?" he asked. "He issued a gag order."

"Yes and no," said Fleishman. "There's still enough on the public record to generate legitimate inquiry—and for us to respond in a professional fashion. The firm will not be damaged by a little public recognition of our role—by that, I mean Matt's role—in such a high-visibility case. So I think we should play the media a bit ourselves."

Rosenthal made a sour face. "I don't like it," he said. "It goes against my grain. And how do we make sure everyone is on the same wavelength on this? I can tell you from bitter experience, managing a bunch of lawyers is like herding cats." He seemed to reflect gloomily on the painful wisdom of his remark.

"Makes for a lot of cross-sterilization, I admit," said Fleishman with a grin. "But I think it's pretty simple. We just send a memo around telling everyone—and I mean everyone—to refer all inquiries to a single person. And that person is the only one who talks to the press."

"And who's the press contact?" asked Rosenthal.

"Why, Matt, of course." Fleishman looked over at Matthew and grinned.

Matthew was flabbergasted.

"It's a target-rich environment, Matt," said Ira. "This way we'd be limiting the number of targets to one." Ira smiled.

Fleishman shot an annoyed glance at Ira.

"After all, it's his case, and his client," Fleishman continued, gradually turning back toward Rosenthal. "He's senior enough to handle it. And he's obviously been doing a top-notch job on a very delicate matter so far."

*Thank God, Judge Doyle impounded the record of that hearing,* thought Matthew. He'd handled that "delicate matter" with the deftness of a palsied mohel.

Sort of the way he handled Felch's phone call the next day.


Raymond Carvalho called Piscatello from a pay phone off the food court at Cambridge Side Galleria. As he listened to them calling out Piscatello's name in the squad room, he watched Donna's slim figure gliding toward the ladies' room. *Sal,* he said to himself, *don't fuck up my afternoon.*

"Piscatello."

"Sal, it's me. What's up?"

"Ray, Jesus. It's about time. Where you been?"

"At sea."

"Huh?"

"Just tell me what's going on, OK?"

"It's all over the department, Ray. DeMarco and a couple staties picked up a snitch Friday night. Held him over the weekend. He got bailed out yesterday. Nobody knows his name so I don't know if he's our guy or not. But word is he's a Chinaman."

"Ah, Jesus!" Carvalho slapped the concrete-block wall hard with the flat of his hand. It hurt. He closed his eyes and tried to think.

After a moment Piscatello said, "You still there, Ray?"

"Yeah, I'm here. If it *is* him, that would explain why he never came home over the weekend."

"We missed our chance when he slipped away Thursday night. Ray, what do we do now?"

Carvalho could hear the fear in Piscatello's voice. He decided to ignore the question.

"I don't get it," Carvalho said. "How would DeMarco know to look at Dunleavy's busts?"

"I don't think that's how he got the name. They say he got an anonymous tip from somebody in the department."

"But who?" Carvalho said, calmer now and thinking. "Nobody knew who he was except Frannie. So who could tip?"

"That don't matter now, Ray. What matters is where we go from here."

"OK, OK. You keep an eye on his place for now, and I'll spell you tonight. The guy shows up, we'll find out what's going on."

"I suppose you're right, Ray," said Piscatello, without much conviction.

"We'll get him, Sal," said Carvalho. "The sun don't shine on the same dog's ass every day."

Carvalho's right hand clung to the receiver for several moments after hanging up. Something was wrong here. Something didn't figure. And the answer was just out of his reach. He could feel it.

Matthew Boer was at his desk by eight-fifteen the next morning. He had awakened with dread and waited anxiously through the gathering dawn for the sound of the *Boston Globe* hitting the screen door. Blessedly, when it arrived, Eddie Felch's story on the "new mystery witness" in the *Chin* case contained no intimation that he was Chinese. For that gratuitous bit of luck—or journalistic reserve, if that's what it was—he was deeply grateful. For a while there with this case, he had felt as if everything he touched had come apart in his fingers like rotting fabric. Now, at last, he could exert himself on more familiar ground, investigating the substantive legal issues that might bear on Danny's options. He would spend most of the day researching whether he could demand an immunity order before Danny could be forced to testify. Even if the issue was a loser in the end, it might buy

Danny some time. He grabbed a couple of yellow legal pads to take with him to the library.

The phone rang. He hoped it would be Laura. She was still sleeping when he had left his apartment.

It was Laura. He shut the door and sat on the desk.

"How come you didn't wake me, you bastard?" she demanded.

Matthew smiled. "So you could growl at me for waking you? Some choice. I'll pass, thanks. I'd rather be at a distance when you start your morning witch-hunt for unbelievers."

He could hear her yawn. "Ha, ha," she said. "I wanted to be there when you read your press notices. Are you famous yet?"

"Not as much as I feared. Felch didn't use the business about Danny being Chinese. Maybe he thought he needed stronger confirmation."

"Doesn't sound like Eddie," she said. "It's not like he'd be risking a libel suit if he reported that 'reliable sources inside the courthouse' told him the witness is Chinese. I suspect he's being nice to you. Why burn his source?"

"You mean so I'll be grateful and pliable the next time he calls me for information?"

"Something like that."

"Oh, great. Just what I need. A little low-level extortion thrown into the mix. Why did I ever talk to him in the first place?"

"Oh, Matt. You talked to him because your bosses told you to handle press inquiries. And like most lawyers, you're flattered by calls from the press and arrogant enough to think you're smarter than journalists. You didn't expect him to know his own business as well as you do. Next time you'll know better. And hey, I hear Fleishman thinks you can handle the pressure." Matthew had told her about the meeting in Rosenthal's office. "The way you dodged those big ol' bears at the bail hearing. Big smoke."

"Oh, right. I figure the only reason they didn't catch me was because they slipped in my shit."

Laura laughed. "My hero," she said. "Listen, I gotta go. See you tonight? My place?"

Matthew agreed and hung up. What a turnaround since dawn. When he was listening for the paperboy.

The phone rang again and he picked it up.

"What did you forget?" he asked with a smile, but it wasn't Laura.

"I forget nothing," said a harsh voice. "And neither will you. This is Jerry DeMarco," the voice added, unnecessarily. "And I intend to ruin your fucking day."

Matthew was taken aback, his pulse rate jumping as he girded himself for a round of unpleasantness.

"What can I do for you, Jerry?" he asked, his tone as neutral as he could make it.

"Oh, you've done enough, Boer. And not just for me. I'm calling about your client."

Matthew felt his annoyance overtaking his fear. "Jerry, I don't have to listen to this. Is there some reason I shouldn't hang up right now?"

"You want a reason, asshole? I'll give you a reason. It's your client."

"What about him?"

"He's dead."

"What?" Intonation and volume drained from his voice like color from a face.

"That's right, Counselor. Dead. And it was real ugly, too. Looks like he was beaten to death. A storekeeper found him early this morning, dumped in an alley in the South End."

Matthew said nothing. He stood immobile with the phone to his ear.

"Don't have much to say now, do you, hotshot? All your good work for naught. Just like mine."

"Jesus," Matthew whispered at last.

"Hey, I'd tell you to have a nice day, but it sounds like you got other plans. Enjoy."

DeMarco hung up.

Shaking, Matthew set the receiver down on the desk. He leaned down on the desk with both hands. He listened to the blood roaring in his skull like the sound of surf in a conch shell.

Then he bawled like a beaten child.

# II

---◆---

# SECRETS

### DR 4-101. Preservation of Confidences and Secrets of a Client

**(B)** ... [A] lawyer shall not knowingly:

**(1)** Reveal a confidence or secret of his client.

**(2)** Use a confidence or secret of his client to the disadvantage of the client.

—American Bar Association
**Code of Professional Responsibility**

---◆---

# 28

# The Ermine

Audrey had been out the morning he saw the ermine. She took off by herself, to go cross-country skiing over the new snow. He watched her from the bay window at the back of the big kitchen as she worked her way along the fence line that led up the hill to the woodlot. By the time she disappeared into the trees, he could not discern her shape at all, only the cobalt blue of her down parka and the bright spot of red that was her stocking cap.

He was grateful for the solitude. Walking to the old cast-iron cookstove, he laid another length of stove wood on top of the coals in the firebox. Then he poured himself a fresh cup of coffee. On the return trip to the window, he paused to stoop over the CD player. He chose a recording of the *Coronation* concerto, slipped it into the machine, and pushed the play button. Then he settled into the rocker and sipped his coffee.

He had been up for more than two hours already, plowing steadily through the poetry of George Herbert in preparation for the class he was to teach next semester. The start of the spring term was more than a week away, but he still had a lot of material to cover before then. The Mozart was a sorbet, he told himself, something to cleanse the palate between rich courses of seventeenth-century sacred verse. The piano solo washed over him, its glittering arpeggios cascading through the room while the orchestra waited breathlessly to reenter. Looking out at the new snow polished by the sunlight, he watched as coruscating crystals eddied and swirled above a snowdrift in the corner where the woodshed met the farmhouse just outside the window. A declivity like the trough of a wave had been scooped out of the leeward slope of the snowdrift.

They had rented this five-acre rump of a farmstead, he and Audrey, a year and a half ago, when he first took the teaching job. It was their first place together as a married couple, and he still loved it, even though everything else about the move seemed headed downhill. The teaching had palled, which surprised him, but he was clearly failing to impart his passion for Renaissance poetry to the grim sons and daughters of farmers, driven children for whom the college was but a forced march en route to the suburbs of midwestern cities. And the head of his department, a withered parsnip of a woman who was grotesquely miscast as a Walt Whitman scholar, seemed to have taken a dislike to him. He could read the writing on the wall.

Even more surprising was the change in his relationship with Audrey. They had lived together for more than two years before marrying, but from the time they moved into the farmhouse she had grown increasingly distant. She rapidly acquired an active distaste for her own job, which was teaching social studies at an underfunded regional high school. It was work she judged (rightly, he suspected) much more demanding and even less rewarding than his own, and she nursed an imperfectly concealed disdain for his grumbling about the soft indignities of academic life. Sex had become an infrequent and highly complicated transaction, as their relationship tangled into a hard knot of anger and withering isolation. As with his job, he had the feeling they were just waiting for it all to end.

It was the tip of the tail he noticed first—a twitch of black against a field of glistening whiteness. The ermine had paused, its back humped, at the very crest of the snowdrift. It could not have been more than eight inches long from nose to tail. Its eyes, feral obsidian beads sunk in the white fur, seemed fixed on his, and the two of them sat eerily still, only three feet of space and a pane of glass separating them. For a moment, he experienced a total suspension of conscious thought, sensing only a quivering thread of connection between them as the sleek white creature twitched a whisker and waited, timelessly alert.

Then a dark shadow stained the snow and, with shocking swiftness, the black figure of a great wolfish dog leapt to the top of the snowdrift. The ermine was gone by the time the dog landed. The dog pumped his hind legs wildly for traction as the snow gave way beneath his flailing haunches. Then he bounded off in pursuit of his vanished quarry. Snow disturbed by the leaping floated and spun above the flattened snowdrift. Two small clods of snow, kicked up by the dog's feet, slid down the windowpane.

Lying in his bed almost nine years later, Matthew Boer experienced anew the sense of disquiet and foreboding that had come over him after the dog had disappeared. Oddly, the incident seemed even more disturbing in retrospect, but he could not put his finger on what made it so.

He was able, however, to put his finger on the telephone, which had rudely routed his thoughts. Striving to keep the sleep out of his voice, he brought the receiver to his ear and said hello. He stiffened when he recognized Laura's voice.

"Matt? I tried you at work. They said you weren't in yet. It's after eleven. Are you okay?"

"Yes, I'm okay. I'm just sleeping in, that's all."

"Sleeping in." It was an irritated echo, not a question.

He sat up, plumping a pillow and wedging it behind his back. "Yeah. I was remembering this ermine I saw when I was living on the farm outside of Northfield. A neighbor's dog chased it away."

"An ermine? You mean, like a weasel?" She sounded annoyed.

Matthew winced. "I guess. Though the memory loses some of its resonance when you call it a weasel. You see, it was perched on top of this perfect, unspoiled snowdrift and—"

"Listen," she cut in, "I don't know from weasels. I'm from Jersey, remember? What I *do* know is you have to pull yourself together. From everything you tell me about your job, you should not be 'sleeping in' and daydreaming about white weasels."

Matthew despaired of explaining the experience and the dread with which it seemed freighted now. "I guess you had to be there," he said.

"What's going on, Matt?" she asked, concern overtaking her irritation. "You have to snap out of this. OK, you screwed up. It happens. But you've got to get on with your life. And your career."

Matthew felt a tiny needle of anger.

"Career," he said acidly. "What career? I tell you, the Trifle Tower is Entropy Acres as far as I'm concerned. I haven't been given any work in weeks that wasn't just research. Except for Ira, of course—and Falk, who still feeds me corporate work. But to the litigators, I'm dead meat. Yesterday Fleishman even threw me off the *Felter* case."

"He did?" Laura sounded surprised. "Because of Danny?"

"Oh, no," said Matthew bitterly. "He's much too slick for that. He comes on all supportive about that. 'A genuine tragedy.' 'Could have happened to anybody under the circumstances.' No, he said I had a conflict of interest. You know why?"

"I haven't a clue."

"Because of you."

"Me!"

"Yeah. I'm sleeping with the enemy. Technically, you know, we're adversaries, because of the contribution claims."

Contribution was a claim brought by a defendant in a negligence action accusing a third party, usually a codefendant, of being jointly responsible for the plaintiff's injuries. Their clients had sued each other for contribution in the *Felter* case.

"Mind you," Matthew continued, "he's not accusing me of spilling client secrets across the pillow. Nothing so crass from a gentleman like Fleishman. No, it's 'the appearance of impropriety.' What would it look like to the client?"

"He's claiming he just found out about us?" Laura was incredulous. "It's not like we've been slinking around in secret. I mean, you brought me to your firm's annual dinner."

"Ah, it's just bullshit. Lo Fat is one of the firm's major clients, and Fleishman doesn't want him to discover his hotel is being represented by the guy who's responsible for the notorious murder of a Chinese witness. With all the splash in the press, who could blame him?"

"*You* could. Goddamn it, Matt. What's wrong with you?"

"What do you want me to do, Laura? It's *his* client."

"Well, for starters you could get pissed off. Jesus, you make me want to give you a *shake* or something. If this is the sensitive male of the nineties, count me out. Making a hobby of your feelings. Swilling around in them. You think life is something that happens to you. Don't be so fucking passive. *Do* something!"

"Like what?" Matthew asked. He reflected sourly that this was just like her. But, then, it was Laura's feisty saltiness that had attracted him in the first place. When one of her avuncular superiors took her aside and suggested she might find it easier to get ahead at her firm if she "acted more ladylike," her response—"Why don't you suck my dick?"—had settled *that* issue for good and made her reputation as a tough cookie. Even the goggle-eyed partner who was the butt of her remark told the story admiringly. Matthew doubted, however, that it would work for him.

"Anything," she said. "Go to the department chair and tell him you want meatier assignments. Tell them you want to know where you stand."

"I know where I *stand*, Laura. I'm a pariah. And the department head is Fleishman, after all. Look at it from their perspective. A firm client gets murdered and it's my fault. The record of the hearing—no need to impound it now—has the judge castigating me for loose lips and incompetence. DeMarco blasts me on television. The press is all over it. And the Board of Bar Overseers wants to discipline me for fucking it up. *You* be the client: would you want me representing you?"

Laura did not answer.

"So," Matthew continued, "I'm not sure where I go from here. But I think I should be looking for a new job."

"It'll blow over, Matt," said Laura, softer now. "You'll see."

Her sudden tenderness brought him close to tears. He waited until the moment passed.

"It's not going to blow over," he said, his voice husky, barely more than whisper. "Not inside. You know what's the worst of it? It's not that sad look on his face when I left him sitting there in Pemberton Square, worrying about going to jail. When he looked so trapped. No, it's remembering how he was just before that, bouncing around and happy to be free, babbling on about what a fantastic job I did for him. I tell you, it makes me just cringe every time I think of it. What a feckless fucking bumbler I was!"

"You're not a bumbler. Stop gnawing your liver. You just got in over your head in a case you weren't prepared to handle, and at a time when you had no one around to help you."

"You mean because Ira was out of town when Danny got arrested? No. That doesn't cut it. I could have called someone else. Like Fleishman. Or anybody else with experience in criminal law. But I didn't. And you know why? Because I wanted to show them. I wanted to prove I was up to it. They had their doubts and I was going to put them to rest. So I go riding off alone to Suffolk Superior to break lances with DeMarco. Jesus, Laura, I could live with the incompetence. It's the fucking grandiosity that sickens me."

"So you're human," said Laura. "You'll get over it. And, hey, I still love you."

Matthew was silent.

"Did you get that, fella?" Laura demanded, her tone lighter.

"Yes," said Matthew. "I love you, too. I'm just stuck in this trough right now. Maybe I'll dig myself out of it, but it's going to take a while. I can't explain."

Laura laughed briefly. "You don't have to *explain* it, lover. Just get through it."

"But I don't think I will until I do understand it."

"That's bullshit. You and Ira, you know, you always think

you have to figure everything out before you can absorb it. Sometimes it just doesn't figure out."

"Maybe so. But it's like I wanted to find something out about myself when I went into Doyle's courtroom. You know what I mean? Like, what's really *in* there, in me. Well, I found out way more than I wanted to know. It's like this huge hand grabbing me by the back of the neck and pushing my face down and a voice says, 'You wanted to look, asshole? Well, *look!*' " Matthew paused. "Is this making any sense at all?"

Laura exhaled audibly. "I'm not sure," she said. "Just don't try to tell me it has anything to do with white weasels, okay?"

Matthew actually laughed.

"It probably does, on some level," he said, feeling some relief.

"You goddamn English majors," said Laura.

# 29

## Can You Say "Indictment"?

There wasn't room enough in Kieran Joyce's office for everyone to sit, but Captain Oliver Gogarty said he didn't mind standing. Joyce leaned back in his chair, stolidly chewing gum, his hands clasped behind his head. Jeremiah DeMarco sat directly across the desk from him. He was holding a Styrofoam cup filled with coffee. Raymond Carvalho and Salvatore Piscatello occupied the other two chairs in front of Joyce's desk. Gogarty chose to stand behind them, his left arm drooped over a gray filing cabinet near the door. Only Joyce could catch his eye without turning around to look at him.

Carvalho took Gogarty's position as a bad sign. Had his boss decided to leave them out there on their own? He hoped Piscatello hadn't picked up on this. As the prospect of Michael Chin's release grew more likely, it was evident to Carvalho that Piscatello felt guilty whenever his thoughts turned to Frannie and Doreen. Worse, Piscatello was scared of getting caught. Immediately after the hearing he had voiced his surprise at the number of times IT had been used. All of which meant that Carvalho had his hands full as it was, just seeing to it that Piscatello stayed with the program. Any hint that Gogarty might be about to cut them loose could unnerve him completely.

"So," said Joyce.

He snapped his gum, waiting as he panned across the faces in front of him. When no one responded immediately, he said, "It's your show, Jerry." Though he addressed DeMarco, it was Carvalho whose eyes he met. With his hands shoved into his pockets, Carvalho held his gaze.

DeMarco pushed his chair back a little and pivoted to his left so he could take in Carvalho and Piscatello as well as Joyce.

"Well," said DeMarco, "I know I'm beginning to sound like a broken record here, but I'm gonna try again. Michael Chin is about to walk."

"Not too good, though," said Joyce with a smirk. "I hear somebody at the jail used him to swab the shower walls."

DeMarco shot Joyce a look of pained disappointment. "He was beat up pretty badly and he's got witnesses who say the guards started it. But that's not exactly good news for anybody, Kieran."

"Sometimes you gotta take your satisfaction where you can, Jerry," said Joyce, his smirk tighter.

"There may not be much satisfaction there. Sarah Kerlinsky's got a pretty good claim for violation of his civil rights. And if the murder charges ever do go to trial—that's a big if—she'll have yet another incident to show that people in uniform were out to get him. Would you find satisfaction in watching him walk if he's also carrying a check for six figures from the Commonwealth?"

"Long as it's with a limp," said Carvalho.

Joyce and Piscatello laughed. DeMarco glared at Carvalho.

"Look," said DeMarco, "maybe I'm wasting my time, I don't know. But I tell you, he is truly gonna walk if I don't get some help from you guys."

"What do you want from me, Jerry?" asked Carvalho. "I tried to find your witness. I struck out. I got up there and let Kerlinsky take her shots at me. The judge didn't see it our way. What's left to do?"

"You know what's left, Ray. You come clean."

The room was silent as Carvalho narrowed his eyes.

DeMarco pushed on. "There was no IT. Well, maybe there was two or three years ago, but for a long time he's been nothing more than a convenient tag to slap on the latest rumor, whenever you needed a warrant. Your story about him being responsible for over fifty warrants is so incredible it's a joke. I know that. You know that. Even Judge Doyle knows that. And, Sal, you know that, too."

DeMarco had pinned his gaze on Piscatello when he addressed him. Piscatello looked away.

DeMarco continued. "So let's stop kidding each other. Someone in the department tells me Danny Li was the source for the information for the bust. That he was Frannie's snitch, not Ray's. This jibes with Frannie's collar records, which indicate he arrested Danny and then let the charges die. The timing of the arrest is about right. And why else would someone feel the need to kill Danny the day after he's released? So I figure my departmental tipster has it right."

"You heard from this 'tipster' lately?" asked Carvalho.

"No. I figure the murder scared him off."

Joyce said, "Maybe you can get Judge Doyle to order the department to produce him for you."

"Very droll," said DeMarco, shaking his head. "Maybe I *am* wasting my time with you guys. But you know what? The AG isn't. His boys have asked for a transcript of your testimony about that bogus 'search' you guys staged for Judge Doyle's benefit." He paused and caught Piscatello's eye again before adding, "Both of yours. Given what transparent hokum your testimony was, they'll descend on the department with subpoenas for records of all the payments made to your fictitious snitch. They're gonna want to know where the money really went. And the intimate details of your 'search'—where you went and who you talked to. In the process, they'll take a real hard look at all that fake overtime you guys put in trying to find the elusive IT." Then, speaking slowly, as if to a child, he asked, "Can you say 'indictment'?"

Carvalho caught a glimpse of Piscatello, who looked stricken.

"Horseshit," said Carvalho, jumping in quickly. "IT exists.

And he disappeared. The only guy who says otherwise is some crank caller you can't find. You're blowing smoke here, Jerry."

"Am I? Are you that sure, Ray? Tell me, what do you do when they call you before the grand jury? You know you lose your job if you take the Fifth—which is what any good defense lawyer is going to advise you to do. I tell you, if Chin walks this way, somebody's gonna take the fall. I'm betting it's the two of you. Of course, I don't have as much to bet as you guys. Nobody's gonna be trying to put *my* ass in jail. Or take away my pension. So think about it *real* hard before you dismiss it as horseshit, is all I'm saying."

Joyce said, "Strikes me that's the scenario that would play out if they *do* come clean. Assuming, of course," he added with a half smile and a nod to Carvalho, "they aren't already telling the truth."

"Maybe. Maybe not," said DeMarco. "Maybe, if I tell him I need his help, the AG will deal on this. You guys go in and set the record straight before Judge Doyle. Tell him there never was an IT. That Danny Li was the real source for the information. You tell him how you couldn't live with yourselves knowing Frannie's murderer got off because you got a little overzealous in trying to do your job. That would give me a good shot at getting the indictment reinstated against Chin. And the AG cuts you some slack for doing the right thing in the end. Say the word, and I'll go see him."

"You representing my men now, Jerry?" The question came from Gogarty. Carvalho smiled to himself. Maybe Gogarty was solid after all.

DeMarco spun his head around to look at Gogarty, who was smiling faintly. DeMarco smiled back at him and stood up.

"No, of course not, Ollie. You got union lawyers. Check it out with them."

DeMarco stepped around Carvalho's chair and dropped his cup in Joyce's wastebasket. Then he picked up his briefcase and opened the office door. He looked back at Carvalho and Piscatello.

"But I wouldn't wait too long, guys," he said with his hand on the doorknob. "The more momentum the AG's investigation builds up, the less likely they are to make a deal. I hope I hear from you soon."

When he had left, Gogarty stepped forward and took the chair DeMarco had vacated.

Gogarty said, "He's right about one thing. You take the Fifth and you're gone. It's right there in the contract."

"Jesus," said Piscatello. He squeezed the right side of his forehead with his thumb and two fingers, pincerlike.

"We got nothing to worry about, Sal," said Carvalho. "We don't need the Fifth."

Gogarty said, "Like the fella says, 'Maybe. Maybe not.' It's real easy to get tripped up on the details. I was you, I'd talk it over with the lawyer."

"Jesus," said Piscatello.

"Jesus," said Carvalho, when he and Piscatello were alone in the squad room a few minutes later. "Buck up, Sal. DeMarco's got dick. The AG's got less. We're clear as long as we hang tough."

Piscatello said nothing. His brow corrugated with worry, he sat behind his desk with his fingers laced over his bulging belly. Carvalho sat in front of the desk, one wooden chair under him and another holding up his feet, which were crossed at the ankles. Both detectives had coffee mugs half full of Seagram's from Carvalho's drawer. Carvalho swallowed another slug of rye.

Carvalho filled the silence. "Nobody can say we didn't hunt for the guy. How they gonna prove we *didn't* go to all those places looking for him, like we said? I tell you, we got nothing to worry about."

"DeMarco's right about all those affidavits, though," said Piscatello, looking up at Carvalho. "It's pretty hard to swallow the idea that one snitch got around that much, all over the fucking city."

Carvalho pulled his feet off the other chair and sat up straight. "All right," he said. "Let me make this real easy for you, OK, Sal? Try it this way. You didn't know how much I used the snitch. You understand? You tell 'em you were as surprised as anybody after the hearing when you found out how many warrants I used him for. Tell 'em you're as suspicious as they are about the affidavit. But you didn't know that when we were looking for him. You had no reason to think he didn't exist. That way you're totally safe, 'cause nobody can prove we faked the search."

"You mean hang you out to dry just to save my skin? You think I'd do that?" Piscatello looked offended.

"I'm *begging* you to, Sal. If that will make it easier for you. All they got is suspicion anyway. Based on the long odds against there being such a world-class snitch as IT. But they're still just suspicions, even if you say you're suspicious, too. Shit, they don't have enough for an indictment, let alone a conviction. Unless"—he waited briefly for Piscatello to catch his eye—"unless one of us caves."

Piscatello looked away. And with a jolt of fear, Carvalho understood.

"Jesus," he said. "It's not the AG. That's not what's bothering you. It's Doreen, isn't it?"

Piscatello snapped his eyes back to Carvalho's.

Carvalho shook his head. "Ah, Sal. She's not—"

"It's not Doreen," Piscatello interrupted. "It's Frannie. Christ, Ray, I thought we were just going through the motions so nobody got hurt when this thing went to trial. I never thought they'd spring the asshole. Frannie was my friend, too, you know. It would eat me up to know that bastard skipped because of me."

"Not because of you, Sal. Me. If he walks it's my fault. Remember, search or no search, I had no snitch to produce, and Doyle would have thrown out the case whether you helped me or not. You just came to the aid of a fellow cop in a jam."

"He still walks," said Piscatello. Then he leaned forward, staring intently at Carvalho. "But what if DeMarco's right, Ray? What if the AG agrees to butt out if we come clean? And Doyle reinstates the charges. Maybe we nail the guy."

"That's a pipe dream, Sal," Carvalho said harshly. "For one thing, the AG isn't just gonna pat us on the back for coming forward like good Cub Scouts. Bless me, Father, for I have sinned? No way. He'd want a plea to some lesser charge, and then it's 'bye-bye job.' And pension. Explain that to your wife and kids.

"And," Carvalho added, "Chin *still* walks. Think about it, Sal. What have we got for DeMarco? Two cops who already lied under oath telling the jury not to worry about what IT might tell them because the real snitch was some Chinaman. Who, by the way, can't back us up 'cause he's dead. Conveniently murdered right after he was identified. How do you think that plays for the jury? You think the trial wouldn't be a cakewalk for Kerlinsky?"

"I don't know," said Piscatello, looking confused now. "I'm no lawyer. At least it'd be a shot."

"A long one, Sal. Very long. But not as long as your wife's face when you tell her you're gonna have to look for another job. Like driving a fuckin' forklift or something. And that might be *after* we end up doing a little time in the house of corrections. Me personally, I don't look forward to the all-male company, you know?"

Piscatello looked as if he wanted to cry. "I don't know, Ray. You were always the smart one, you know? I just went along with you and Frannie. You were the guy could figure out what would work in court and all. All I ever wanted was just to do my job. Do my job, maybe have a few pops after work, then go home to the wife and kids." He paused. "Ah, Ray," he added. "What a mess."

"You said it," said Carvalho.

*You don't know the half of it,* thought Carvalho. He looked down at his hands and rubbed his fingers lightly over the scabs on three of his knuckles. He was swamped with self-loathing.

"Jesus," said Piscatello.

# 30

## There Are No Atheists

There were already two phone messages waiting for him when Matthew Boer reached his office at eight-forty. The one from Fleishman he turned facedown and did his best to put out of his mind. The other was from a California lawyer named Shadwell, who represented the computer manufacturer that was shafting Falk's sales rep. With the scheduled arbitration hearing now less than a week away, Matthew and Shadwell had been exchanging settlement numbers over the past few days, the gap between them closing in tiny, agonized increments. Matthew hoped it would settle, and quickly, as he had loads of work ahead of him to prepare Falk for the arbitration. He dialed the number on the pink slip.

"Tom Shadwell."

"Good morning, Tom. It's Matt Boer returning your call."

"Morning, Matt. I was sitting here banging out a brief for our arbitration and I thought I should bring you up to date."

"You make any progress with your client?"

"As a matter of fact I have, though I must tell you, it's like pulling teeth. I think I've reached the bottom of the barrel here, Matt. If this won't do it, I'm afraid it's going to have to be up to the arbitrator."

"You may be right," Matthew said. "So what's the number?"

"I think I can get you one-forty," said Shadwell. "And like I said, that's pushing it."

Matthew straightened up sharply. An offer of $140,000! Their last offer, two days ago, had been $115,000, and Falk had leaned hard on the client to take it. The client insisted (foolishly, in Matthew's opinion) that his claim was worth a quarter of a million. Later that evening, however, after Matthew had gone over the weaknesses of his case, the client had finally given him authority to settle as low as $130,000, a number Falk believed downright foolhardy. And now to have an offer of $140,000!

Suddenly, a calm descended over him, and he smiled to himself. He drew a deep breath and expelled it audibly, for Shadwell's benefit.

"That won't do it, Tom," he said. "I'll pass it on to the client to see if he'll change his mind, but I don't think he will."

"Well, you gotta do what you gotta do, Matt," said Shadwell, "but you're making a huge mistake." Shadwell's tone conveyed an urbane pity for the unworldliness of his adversary. "Meanwhile, I'm going to have to insist on those sales records I requested in my letter last week."

Matthew smiled to himself. "You'll get them. And I'll get back to you if my client has a change of heart."

After hanging up, Matthew sat quietly and inventoried his feelings. He felt a sense of satisfaction, yes, even gratification, but he couldn't say how much of it was just dumb luck. He was most struck, however, with what he did *not* feel. There was no fear. Every other negotiation, even before reaching its critical stage, had left him edgy, taut as a bowstring, always dreading something—that his sallies were unreasonable, the client would get screwed, the other lawyer would play him for a patsy. Something. But not this time. Why? Because he had read the situation correctly? He felt confident he had, but there was more to it than that. He was sure of it.

Ten minutes later he found Rowell Falk in his office on the floor below, where he was feathering out the prose of one of his acolytes at a long maple table across the room from his desk. Falk was renowned for his elegant draftsmanship, and the associates who serviced him (they teemed about him in Malthusian repletion) had to be able to write well. They got paper-trained early or were bluntly asked to move on.

Matthew peered through the sidelight as he rapped on the office door. Falk looked up and waved him in. Matthew closed the door behind him.

Falk was in his shirtsleeves, wearing maroon suspenders and a matching tie over a blue dress shirt. He glided his chair over to his desk and punched a few keys on his personal computer. A confusing succession of stock quotes, graphs, and pie charts materialized, then dissolved, on the screen as Falk frowned at it. Then he wheeled his chair around to face Matthew squarely, smiling languidly as he rocked backwards.

"You have to follow the market, Matthew," he said, as if anticipating the question Matthew was asking himself but had no intention of voicing.

"I've got all I can do to keep up with what appears in the papers," Matthew said. Scuttling to avoid another paean to Microsoft, he added, "I thought you'd like to know that I just got off the phone with Shadwell. They're up to one-forty." Matthew worked hard to contain his smile.

Falk raised his eyebrows. And smiled.

"Not bad, Matthew," he said slowly. "Not bad at all. Our friend is going to snicker at me for wanting him to take the one-fifteen."

"I rejected it," said Matthew.

Falk's expression did not falter.

"You rejected it," he echoed vacantly.

"Yes. They'll come up."

Falk's countenance darkened into a glower. When he spoke it was with a tone Matthew knew well. That trademark tone he took with an associate who had missed something, like adverse tax consequences or a flank bared to legal assault from some obvious quarter.

"You've figured that out, have you?" he asked. "Even though the offer was within the range your client instructed you to accept."

"Oh, I called him," said Matthew, brightly. "He agreed with me. We called Shadwell right back and demanded one eighty-five. Because they'll come up."

Falk paused momentarily. "I see," he said icily. "And would it be presumptuous of me to ask how you divined that?"

"Because," Matthew said, looking at his watch, "it's only six o'clock in California. And it was five-thirty when Shadwell called me. He's in his office, in a sweat over this arbitration, and he couldn't wait to get the deal done. They'll come up. Shadwell has the authority to come up."

Matthew grinned. And then, slowly, Falk did, too.

"You know," he said, "you may be right."

As if in confirmation, the phone beeped. Falk reached behind him to pick it up. He listened for a moment.

"This is Falk," he said, his eyes flicking up to meet Matthew's. "Oh, hello, Tom." Falk glanced at Matthew again and mugged a look of mock surprise. "No, Matthew's right here. He had your call forwarded to my office. Hold on a second, I'll put you on the speaker." He pushed a button on the console and replaced the receiver.

"Do I still have you, Tom?"

"I think so. Good morning, Rowell," said Shadwell. On the speakerphone his voice sounded as if it were coming out of a drainpipe. "And hello again, Matt."

"That was quick, Tom," said Matthew. "What's the news?"

"My client will go one-sixty-five. No more. Final offer. Take it or leave it."

"Done," said Matthew. "Send us a check and a form of release for his signature and we'll take care of it."

"Pleasure doing business with you. And, Matt?"

"Yes?"

"Next time don't bust my chops. Bye, Rowell."

Falk reached over and pushed the disconnect. Then he turned back to Matthew, who felt jubilant.

Falk was no longer smiling.

"Don't you *ever* pull a stunt like that again."

"Like what?" asked Matthew, flabbergasted.

"Going off on your own."

"I wasn't off on my own, Rowell. I cleared it with the client."

"You didn't clear it with *me*," said Falk, leaning forward now.

"I didn't clear it with you because you told me to settle the goddamn case, that's why." Matthew's own anger caught him by surprise.

"Yes, I did," said Falk. "But within the parameters we had discussed. Parameters that were, as you knew, already dangerously broad, in my judgment. You should have come to me first, before exposing the client by venturing outside them."

There was a rushing noise in Matthew's ears, and he heard his own voice as if it were furred about, like Shadwell's, with an electronic hum. "You mean," he said harshly, "like I did with Danny Li?"

Falk stopped, his eyes locked on Matthew's. In the brief silence Matthew felt his heart knocking against his ribs, but it was anger that drove it, not fear. Then Falk sat back again. When he spoke, his voice was softer, neutral.

"No, Matthew, I did not mean to allude to that. I'm sorry if I gave that impression."

"It would almost be a relief if you had," said Matthew, looking away now. "At least someone would have said it out loud. Nobody, *nobody* ever talks about it. Except Fleishman, and then only to say it was *not* the reason he wanted me off the *Felter* case."

Falk paused again. He pulled his glasses off and held them by the temples.

"Listen, Matthew. I know my management style is a bit, well, crisp."

Matthew stared back at him. Crisp? The only question, Ira had once told him, an associate should ever ask when Falk called you to his office was whether he wanted you there before or after he hung up.

"You know what they say, don't you?" said Matthew. "There are no atheists in Falk's office."

Falk gave a snort of appreciation.

"Cute," he said dryly. "But just because I'm hard to please doesn't mean I don't care. I'm sure you're carrying a lot of guilt over what happened. That's natural. But most of it is unnecessary. I consider what happened to Danny to be a failure of the firm, not of you personally. It was an institutional shortcoming. We did not have the right support structure in place. And, by the way, nothing you've shown me suggests that you possess any serious deficiency as a lawyer. The noncomp agreement you drafted last week was more than adequate, and you've done fine work in settling this arbitration. First rate, even—if we put to one side that you left me out of the loop at the end."

"Frankly," said Matthew, "I didn't tell you because I was afraid you'd make him take the one-forty. So maybe I *was* off the reservation."

Falk laughed out loud.

"Matthew," he said, "don't ever let them tell you you don't have fire in the belly. They're full of baloney."

# 31

## The Angel of Death

Ira Teitelbaum agreed.

"See!" he said gleefully a half hour later when Matthew described what had happened with Shadwell and Falk. "I told you you were a litigator. And let's not overlook how you put the spurs to the great Rowell himself. I tell you, Matt, you're in the right business. Oh, shit."

Cream cheese had slid off his pumpernickel bagel and onto his tie. Setting the bagel down on top of the brief he had been reading, Ira pushed his chair back in disgust. He lifted his tie with one hand and used the other to dab at it with a napkin.

"Shit," he said again, resignation in his voice as he examined the smeared silk. "This happens all the time."

"Why don't you tuck it in your shirt when you eat?" asked Matthew.

"I mean to. I keep forgetting. Hannah says if I ever got snowed in, I could last for six weeks just sucking my ties."

"It's funny," said Matthew, changing the subject. "I think I actually like Falk. Today, anyway. He says he wants me to work with him on an article he's writing. He could have blown me off for doing an end run around him like that. And he didn't have to say what he did about Danny."

His tie forgotten, Ira picked up his bagel again. It left a grease stain on the brief.

"You mean that little *nostra culpa*?" he asked. "I suppose you're right. I never said he was a *bad* guy. Just an asshole when he doesn't get his way. But don't give up on litigation yet, ok? Falk will get back to treating you like shit soon enough, and Fleishman will come around. You'll see."

Matthew's spirits sagged at the mention of Fleishman. For a moment there he had almost forgotten what he and Fleishman had discussed shortly after the meeting with Falk.

"I need to ask you about that, too," said Matthew.

"Fleishman? You mean you didn't come just to crow about all that swag you're hauling back from California?"

"No. Come on, Ira. This is serious."

"Jeez," said Ira. He raised his hands in front of his face as if to ward off a blow. "I'm sorry. Did I miss one of your mood swings? What is this? Are you getting hot flashes or something?"

"You're right," Matthew conceded. "I'm touchy. Fleishman called me about the investigation at the Board of Bar Overseers. Bar counsel wants me to agree to accept a public reprimand. Ben doesn't come right out and say so, but I have the feeling he thinks I should take it."

The Board of Bar Overseers was the agency created by the Supreme Judicial Court to police the conduct of lawyers, and its bar counsel was responsible for investigating and prosecuting charges of unethical conduct against a lawyer.

"Public?" Ira stiffened as he raised his voice. His eyes narrowed to slits and he listened intently, the bagel in his right hand forgotten.

"Ben says there'll be a public hearing if I don't agree," Matthew continued, "and that a hearing might be more harrowing than taking a formal reprimand. What do you think, Ira? Jesus, I don't want to rehash all that business at a hearing."

Ira was quiet and Matthew could tell he was angry. He dropped the bagel in a wastebasket behind his desk and then looked up at Matthew. When he spoke, his voice was shorn of its usual banter.

"This is what I think. When you came to me with that first 'greetings' letter from the board, I told you to go to Fleishman. He's the man, after all, and the board is made up of big muck-a-mucks like him, so I figure you want someone who can schmooze with the schmoozoisie. But public discipline? I don't see it.

"Look, they only hand out four kinds of discipline to lawyers: disbarment, suspension, public reprimand, and admonition. Admonition is private; no one knows about it. Now, from what I understand, they don't disbar or suspend you unless you steal money or lie big-time, like in open court. Or get convicted of some felony. That means a public reprimand is your downside, the absolute *worst* you could get. And what can they say you did wrong? Handled a case you weren't ready for. Unintentionally divulged client secrets. That's it. Nothing willful or underhanded. You made a mistake—one with drastic consequences maybe, but a mistake nevertheless. That sounds like the stuff of private discipline to me. I don't see the board giving you a public reprimand."

Matthew considered this. "All you're telling me," he said, "is that I'd probably win if I went to hearing. But like I said, I don't think I could go through one. Maybe they know that."

Ira shook his head. "Sure. That's what they're hoping. But they also have to know they can't win at hearing. You'd end up with an admonition."

"Maybe they don't care," said Matthew. "Don't forget about all the publicity."

Ira smiled. "My favorite was the headline in the *Herald*. SNAGGED SNITCH SNUFFED. Classy."

Matthew winced. "Jesus, don't remind me. But maybe the publicity means the prosecutor *has* to try for more. Like the Kennedy-Smith rape trial. The DA must have known it was a loser, and if the defendant wasn't a Kennedy they'd have buried it. But how could he ever explain to the media why he didn't try the case?"

"You mean," asked Ira, "there are some you gotta lose?"

"Something like that."

"Maybe. But I don't think this is one of them. Lawyers

may think of bar counsel as the angel of death, but she answers to the Supreme Judicial Court, not the public. She doesn't have to stand for election like a district attorney. So she cares what the bar, and the court, think of her. If you ask me, she won't want a public hearing either, 'cause she'll look punitive and vindictive going so heavy after an honest lawyer who made honest mistakes. I think they'll cave if you stand your ground."

"What if you're wrong?"

"Hey," said Ira, "scared money can't win. Ask your pal Shadwell. But you've got nothing to worry about yet. If they haven't caved by the day the hearing opens, *then* you can tell them you'll take the public reprimand. What have you got to lose by hanging tough for a while? Like I said, it's not as if they could ever get anything *more* than public reprimand."

"That makes sense," said Matthew. "But why do you think Fleishman doesn't see it that way?"

Ira looked angry again. "I don't know. 'Cause there's another reason you can't take the deal. Nobody from D and C has ever been disciplined by the Board of Bar Overseers. I can't *imagine* the firm would let you stay on if you got a public reprimand. And word of the reprimand would—how should I put this?—sharply depress the market for your services elsewhere. That makes it a no-brainer. You can't afford a public reprimand."

"You know," said Matthew morosely, "most of the time I could give a shit about that."

"Right now you may think like that. Six months down the road you might see things very differently."

"It's not like I'm burning any bridges—assuming there are any still standing."

Ira smiled. "Well, don't leave them unguarded, either."

"You think this is Fleishman's way of easing me out?"

Ira thought for a while. Then he said, "No, I don't think so. Not consciously, anyway. You know, maybe *he* doesn't want a public hearing. He can't be eager to put the firm back in all that negative limelight. Just because he's so smart doesn't mean his judgment is immune to such concerns."

"Great," said Matthew sourly.

"Hey," said Ira, "you can still cut a deal. Look what you did with that Shadwell."

# 32

---

# A Prophylactic

DAPHNIS & CLOONEY IS OBSERVING CASUAL DAY ON FRIDAYS, declared a tastefully printed notice in the reception area. PLEASE FEEL FREE TO JOIN US.

Matthew looked up from the notice and caught the eye of the receptionist, who seemed to be struggling to contain her mirth. A dazzlingly beautiful young woman named Celeste, she was chastely imprisoned within the gleaming mahogany pen of a circular reception desk.

"Are they afraid, if we don't warn them, that the clients will think we just decided to dress like pigs?" she asked.

Matthew laughed. He wondered how many hours of lawyer time had been burned up deciding on the wording, not to mention the wisdom, of the notice. Shaking an admonishing finger at her, he asked sternly, "Are your toes decent?"

Celeste giggled, her eyes as big and brown as chestnuts. She opened her mouth to answer, but all Matthew heard was a discreet beeping noise. Celeste twisted her smile into a rueful moue and pushed a button on the console in front of her. "Good morning, Daphnis and Clooney," she warbled.

Open-toed shoes, like jeans, sneakers, and floral tops

(whatever *they* were), had been expressly excluded from the definition of "appropriate casual attire" in a Management Committee memo that finally permitted, on an experimental basis, casual dress on Fridays in the summer. The memo's dress code had unleashed such howling derision throughout the firm that it was immediately withdrawn and a special committee was formed to reconsider the matter. The century-old unwritten dress code for law firms (dress like an under-taker) had managed to stave off ridicule for so long precisely because no one had tried to codify it. Matthew found it especially delicious that the Management Committee's taxonomic vigor had been set off by a decision, however halfhearted, to loosen things up.

He watched Celeste juggle a flurry of incoming calls for the next few minutes. The mouthpiece that arched out from her headset bobbed a cruel two inches away from her plump lips. Finally, there was a lull and Celeste leaned back in her chair.

"Whew!" she said. "Now where were we? Oh, yes."

She swung her chair ninety degrees to her left and raised her outstretched legs so that Matthew could see her black pumps. Her toes were covered.

"You see?" she said, twisting her head back to look at him. "Decent."

"Indeed," said Matthew, admiring her legs.

"So are your Dockers," she said, spinning her chair back to its original position. Looking down at the little piles of pink slips on the desk in front of her, she added, "No messages, Matt."

"Thanks, Celeste. Keep out the wogs."

"Huh?" She frowned.

"Hold down the fort, I mean. And enjoy Casual Day."

"You, too!" she called as he headed up the hall.

But the air-conditioning in his office was too frigid to be dressed, as he was, in short sleeves. He rubbed his arms to warm himself.

His desk was piled with photocopies of appellate decisions and law review articles and the notes he had taken while reading them. Matthew had been flattered that Falk, who took such pride in his own reputation for legal writing, had asked

Matthew to write an article with him. And as a coauthor, not as a research flunky whose recompense would be confined to a grateful footnote. Who would have suspected someone with a practice like Falk's to have an interest in criminal law? But there he was, full of ideas and spewing arguments on when an identification at a police lineup was too suggestive to be admitted without violating the Massachusetts constitution. The topic was new and rough sledding to Matthew as well, but he kept reminding himself how much more agreeable it was than reviewing and sorting those cartons of documents in the *Felter* case. Matthew hoped to have a first draft for Falk's review in another week.

There was a soft rap on Matthew's door, so soft it took him a moment to identify it as a knock. He looked over his shoulder and spotted a brunette head peeking timidly into his office from around the corner.

"Oh, hello, Ellen," he said. "I wasn't sure I heard a knock."

"Hi, Matt. Can I talk to you for a minute?"

"Sure." Matthew dropped his pen and swung his chair around to face her. She quietly closed the door and took a seat. She was clutching a sheet of paper in one hand.

Ellen Stritch was a tiny, mousy young woman with whom Matthew shared a secretary and adjoining offices. As always (even on Casual Day!), she wore a dark suit and a scarf knotted into a clownishly big bow tie over a white blouse. Her outsized tie colluded with horn-rimmed photogrades that were much too large for her face in making her head look even smaller than it was. Only three years out of law school, Ellen still worked tirelessly and without complaint at every task assigned her. She seemed to have invested all her emotional capital in the firm's overwrought self-image as a consistory of humane, public-spirited professionals, and she voiced openly her concern for its morale and financial success. She had team spirit.

In other words, a vicious case of Stockholm Syndrome. Most associates seemed to fall into it during the first year or two—unless, like Robolawyer, they immediately went over to the other side as collaborators. But Ellen still showed no signs of remission. Matthew fully expected they would find her curled up in a fetal position under her desk one morning. Or giving dramatic readings from the Boston Building Code to the tourists in Quincy Marketplace.

"I'm sorry to interrupt you," she said. She had a husky voice that cracked a lot without ever sounding sexy. She seemed nervous.

"It's nothing," he reassured her, smiling.

"I don't know if this is something I should bother you with or not. But I thought maybe you might know something about it."

She paused.

"Yes?" said Matthew, encouraging her.

"Well, as you know, Ben Fleishman asked me to take over your spot on the *Felter* case."

This was news to Matthew. He knew he was off it, *that* was painfully clear, and he recalled noticing that the cartons of documents had disappeared from his office. But he had not known who succeeded him.

"You have my condolences," he said with a smile.

A flicker of confusion clouded Ellen's brown eyes. Then, satisfied he wasn't serious, she flashed a bleak smile and went on.

"Well, I've spent the last few days preparing to make the document production and I came across this, like, weird thing. I don't know what to make of it."

"Weird," said Matthew, blankly.

"It's—well, maybe I should just let you take a look."

Matthew took the document she held out before her. It was a single sheet of paper, letter-sized white bond. An original, not a photocopy. In the top left corner were the holes left by a missing staple. Typed across the top, in capitals and underlined, were the words "SCHEDULE OF BENEFICIARIES." And below that caption, about a quarter of the way down the page, was a single name. Otherwise the page was blank.

The name was Danny Li.

Matthew turned the page over. Nothing on the back. Disturbed at the mention of the name in such an alien context, he looked up at Ellen, who was watching him closely.

"I don't understand," he said. "What is it? Where did you find it?"

"It's a schedule of beneficiaries, presumably for a nominee realty trust. I found it in one of the files we got from Lo Fat on the development of the hotel. It was in a folder full of extra copies of trust and partnership documents."

"A realty trust? What realty trust?" He pointed to the staple holes. "And what was it attached to?"

Ellen shrugged. "I don't know. I found it loose like that. Nothing else in the files refers to Danny Li. And I've been through them all now, cataloged them and everything. I thought *you* might know."

Matthew shook his head, handing the page back to her. "No," he said. "Danny never told me anything about this. I mean, the Hotel Adams? That's way out of his league, you know what I mean?"

Ellen stared at the document.

"Are there other loose schedules like this?" Matthew asked. He was intrigued.

"No. I mean, there are other schedules of beneficiaries, but it's clear what trusts they relate to. They're always bundled together, like. And this is the only schedule that lists an actual human being as a beneficiary. All the other beneficiaries are entities—other trusts, a corporation, sometimes a partnership. But no people. So this one stuck out for that reason as well as—well, you know, because of the name."

"You're right," said Matthew. "It's very curious. Maybe it would help if I took a look myself. There could be something in the files I'd recognize that would make sense of all this."

Ellen Stritch looked startled by his suggestion. He could feel her pulling away. Get thee behind me.

"You better ask Ben, Matt," she said, shaking her head slightly. "He told me we're supposed to maintain a Chinese wall to screen you from this case. All the documents have to be kept in a dedicated workroom, one of those across from the Dead Partner's Office. You've got a conflict of interest, he says. In fact, I wasn't even sure I should raise this with you, but I can't see how it can have any relation to Felter's tort case and it was, as you say, curious."

Ellen smiled shyly, inviting reassurance. Matthew was suddenly very curious himself, and involving Fleishman would surely block any further inquiry.

"I'd have done the same thing, Ellen. Like you said, it's weird. And you're right about keeping me out of this." He swung his feet up to rest on his desk and leaned back, speaking the classic body English of command, avuncular superior to aspiring underling. "In fact, now that you bring up the conflict business, you might not want to mention to Ben that we talked about this. He might throw one of those celebrated tantrums at both of us. You know how fastidious he is about matters of legal ethics."

Actually, Matthew had no idea how Fleishman felt about such matters, but he doubted Ellen did either. Her eyes skittered in sudden fright like a rabbit on a freeway.

"Yes, you're right," she said, sounding grateful. "Thanks. It's just one of those screwy things, that's all. Thanks for listening."

Matthew gave her a self-deprecating sideways nod as she stood up.

"And, Matt," she said with her hand on the door, "I'm sorry about what happened. It must be really awful."

"Thank you, Ellen," he said, "I appreciate it."

When he heard the door click shut, Matthew took a deep breath and expelled it slowly. His thoughts were racing. What did all this mean? Danny and the Hotel Adams! It made no sense. He tried to think through what he had just learned.

A nominee trust. It was a popular vehicle for holding title to real estate. For two reasons. For one, it was possible to transfer interests in the property without actually having to draw up and record a new deed, or even, as would be the case of a corporation, transferring shares of stock. The beneficiaries—the *real* owners—simply sold pieces of paper entitling the buyer to a proportion of the beneficial interests— say, a twenty-five-percent share of the trust's property—and this would be reflected on the trust's schedule of beneficiaries. Thus, developers liked nominee trusts because it was so easy to sell pieces of the deal without a lot of legal rigmarole.

But that was just convenience. Of even greater attraction was the cloak of secrecy a nominee trust cast over the actual ownership of property. Title to a piece of property was listed not in the name of the beneficiaries but of the trustee—usually the developer himself or his lawyer or maybe a corporation created just for that purpose. A straw, in other words. And since the schedule of beneficiaries did not need to be included among the documents filed with the registry of deeds, only the owners knew who they were.

But what did that tell him? That Danny was listed as the sole beneficiary of some real estate trust. That the mystery trust might have something to do with the Hotel Adams, since the schedule was found in a file of documents relating to the development and ownership of the hotel. Maybe. But how? And why? How could a small-time hustler like Danny be playing with such heavy hitters? And why hide Danny's interest through a nominee trust?

*Irons. I got irons,* Danny had said. Was this what he was talking about?

What Matthew found even more of a mystery was why he cared. Whatever Danny's relationship to the Hotel Adams or Lo Fat, it had nothing to do with his own clumsy lurches on Danny's behalf. And it wasn't as if Danny had left any heirs, so far as he knew, who would be pleased to discover that the deceased might have left them a piece, however minuscule, of a fancy downtown hotel complex.

But Matthew could not suppress his curiosity. He wanted to know what part Danny played in all this. And in order to find out, he needed to take a look at the documents Ellen had cataloged. Ellen knew nothing about Danny. Matthew, however, might be able to pick something up in them that would afford a clue to Danny's role.

Fleishman had ordered a Chinese wall. Was it overkill? Matthew supposed it made sense. He was conflicted out of representing Lo Fat and the hotel because of his relationship with Laura. So the firm erects an imaginary divide, known as a Chinese wall, between him and other lawyers working on the *Felter* case. They are instructed not to discuss the case with him. The client's files are segregated and kept away from him. Once stacked idly in Matthew's office and neglected for weeks, those cartons were now tucked carefully away in an airless workroom two floors away. All to reassure the client (and, if necessary, the court) that Matthew would have no future access to client confidences, secrets someone might claim he could have blurted to Laura in the throes of sexual passion. A prophylactic measure, as courts described it. (Laura would *love* that.) Yes, he had to admit it made sense.

Except for one thing.

No one had bothered to tell Matthew.

Matthew wanted a peek at those files.

# 33

---

# Don't Leave Home Without It

Matthew stopped off at reception on his way back from lunch and asked Celeste if she could reserve conference room 37H for the late afternoon. To his surprise, the room was available immediately. Usually, even in late summer, with so many lawyers away and vacant courtrooms stultifying in the August heat, 37H was harder to book than a table at Aporia. Maybe luck was breaking his way.

Matthew hurried to his office and started packing. He scooped up the materials for the article he had been working on when Ellen had dropped her teaser that morning. After stuffing them all into a huge briefcase known as a litigation bag, he picked it up and lugged it to the elevator.

He rode down two floors, then trudged through Trusts and Estates on his way to the southwest corner of the Trifle Tower's rectangle. There, occupying space that in any rational pecking order would have been a corner office allotted to a senior partner with a lot of clout, was conference room 37H.

Actually, 37H had once been an office. Its last inhabitant had been Brison Tucket, a handsome old WASP with a magnificent head of white hair who had run Trusts and Estates for two decades. Tucket had died there—died in the saddle, so to speak. His secretary had found him, eyes open and sitting straight up in his chair with a Mont Blanc pen in his hand and an estate tax return on the desk in front of him. Only the odd tilt of his head suggested there was anything amiss. When they took him away, the EMTs had to break two of his fingers to release his grip on the pen.

The office had remained undisturbed for months after Tucket's death. At first, it was cordoned off like a crime scene, and people lowered their voices as they hurried past it—some with a frisson of wonder at such unflinching devotion, others imagining that the stench of death lingered about the space. There were partners who might have vied for the right to succeed to the office, but, curiously, no one had. Perhaps it seemed too tacky. Or maybe some did demand it and the Management Committee found it too tendentious to choose among the claims of rival pretenders to apostolic succession. But however it was decided, a conference table and chairs and photographs of the firm's founding partners were moved into the space, and the office had remained a conference room for more than four years. A coveted conference room. One with a view. It was known as the Dead Partner's Office.

The story was told of how Ira Teitelbaum and a junior associate had once shown a new client around the firm after hours. Ira suggested they show him the spangled skyline along Fort Point Channel from the Dead Partner's Office, and on the way down the hall the associate explained how it had come by its peculiar name. He then pushed open the door and stepped back to allow the client to take in the view. The client's gaze, however, never reached the plate glass but fell instead on the conference table, where a half-clad lawyer was vigorously buffing the mahogany with the backside of a naked young woman. Ira quickly pulled the door shut as the client gaped.

"What the hell was that?" the client asked, rather pointlessly under the circumstances.

"That," said Ira, "was the live partner."

Dead or alive, it provided good cover, thought Matthew,

as he laid out on that same table the papers he had brought
with him. To anyone who saw him there, it would be evident
that he wanted to get some work done away from the telephone, and no one would wonder why he had chosen the
most attractive conference room to do it in. Even Ellen
Stritch seemed unsurprised to see him there as she trooped
by on her way to the *Felter* workroom. The workroom was
located at the end of a short corridor almost directly across
from 37H. All Matthew had to do was make himself look
busy until everyone left. Then he could slip across the hall
and have his way with Ellen's documents.

Matthew picked at the work in front of him in desultory
fashion, doing his best to fill the hours until the floor emptied
out. He considered, then rejected, the idea of telling Ira about
Danny's mysterious appearance in Lo Fat's files. He had
nothing whatsoever to go on, and broaching it to Ira would
put his friend in an awkward position. Ira was a partner in
the firm, after all, and he could hardly encourage Matthew's
plans to rifle through the files of a client when he was supposed to be screened off from the case. He went through a
similar mental exercise about Laura, and chose not to com-
promise her either, given her ongoing participation in the
*Felter* case.

He was just going to have to scale the Chinese wall all by
himself.

He waited until almost nine-thirty, after the cleaning crew
had made their nightly rounds. Then, carrying a yellow pad
with him, he stepped out of the Dead Partner's Office and
peered up and down the hardwood hallway. He saw and heard
nothing. He hurried diagonally across the hall and slipped into
the narrow corridor that led to Ellen's workroom.

Most of the firm's lighting had been shut off, so the corridor was lit only by the reflected light from the main hallway. Matthew looked about for the light switch, but before
he could find it he abandoned the idea. No point drawing
attention to himself. He continued up the corridor in the
semidarkness.

There were two other workrooms along the corridor, but
both of them were empty and dark. The one he had watched

Ellen enter was at the very end, on the right. Matthew stopped in front of the door, glanced quickly over his shoulder, and grasped the doorknob.

It was locked.

Shit! He hadn't thought of that. He should have, of course. If you want people to believe you're serious about segregating a client's files, you lock them up.

Matthew stared at the lock in the half-light. The keyhole was in the doorknob itself. So it wasn't a dead bolt. Maybe he could open it by easing a credit card into the slot and sliding the catch back into the lock. Hey, it worked in the movies.

He set the legal pad on the floor and reached into his pocket for his wallet. He took out his American Express card.

Suddenly he heard the sound of a door closing. He froze. The sound had come from somewhere near his end of the floor. He heard footsteps. The sound of rubber soles on the hardwood floor. *Scrinch. Scrinch.* Growing louder.

They were coming in his direction.

Matthew pulled himself as flat as he could into the doorway and waited. He watched the lighted segment of the main hallway that was visible at the other end of the narrow corridor. A figure moved across it, then disappeared. A man, he could tell that much, but he could not identify him from the brief glimpse afforded him. The sound of the footfalls diminished and silence finally regained its hold.

Then light in the main hallway went out and Matthew was plunged into near-total darkness. The only remaining light was a mere glimmer from the Dead Partner's Office, just around the corner.

Matthew took a deep breath and let it out. This was crazy. If the man had looked up the corridor he would have seen him. Matthew could think of nothing that would explain his presence here, at this time of night. And how did he know somebody else wasn't still around? *I should get the fuck out of here right now,* he told himself.

But he didn't.

He felt the embossed printing on the credit card between his thumb and fingers, and he knew he was going to try.

He groped around the knob in the darkness and felt the

strip of wooden molding that covered the seam between the door and the jamb. When he pressed against the door, pushing it away from the molding as far as it would go, his fingers felt the gap between the door and the molding widen just a little. Good. The door had been installed with generous tolerances.

Applying continuous pressure against the door by leaning his left shoulder into it, he slipped his AmEx card into the gap and bent the card enough to force it into the seam between the edge of the door and the jamb itself. The fit was tight, but by working the card back and forth, he was able to move it down slowly, feeling for the catch where it should fit into its slot in the jamb. The card fetched up against something hard. He knew it was the catch.

But the catch wouldn't budge. He wriggled harder. Nothing.

Matthew let go of the card and shook his right hand, which ached from writer's cramp. After a brief rest he tried pushing the card farther into the seam until less than an inch of plastic protruded, but this only reduced his leverage. The catch still wouldn't move.

Then he discovered he couldn't move the card either. He worked at it for a while, but a mounting panic overtook him as he realized he could not get the card out of the seam.

*Oh, great,* he thought. *How am I ever going to explain what my credit card is doing wedged in a locked door?* He struggled for several more minutes, but all in vain. He realized the card was not going to move.

Matthew turned around and leaned his back against the door. He closed his eyes and slid to the floor. Wrapping his arms around his knees, he pulled them to his chin. He sought to control his breathing, which was coming in short, scared gasps.

After two or three minutes, he grew calmer. He knew what to do. He got up and returned to the conference room. He checked his watch. It was ten-twenty. He picked up the phone and dialed.

"Hello."

"Hi, it's me," he said.

"Hi, it's me," Laura echoed. "I thought you were gonna be at the office half the night."

"I'm still here. I need your help on something."

"Wow! You think I can handle it?"

"Please, Laura. This is serious."

And he told her. Everything. When he finished, she was quiet for a time.

"Did I ever tell you you're out of your mind?" she said at last.

"Many times. You were right."

"So," she said, "what do you want me to do? Come over there with a hairpin?"

"No. A pair of pliers. So I can get my credit card out of the doorjamb."

"Now? Does it have to be tonight?"

"Yes. There's no telling who might find it before I get back in the morning. Besides, I wouldn't be able to sleep a wink, knowing it's sticking out of the door like that."

"Okay. Pliers."

He met her outside the main entrance to the Trifle Tower twenty minutes later. She waited in the car while he went back up to the thirty-seventh floor and wrenched his misshapen American Express card out of the door. Then she drove him back to her place in the South End.

"I still don't get it," she said when she was driving down Tremont Street. "What exactly were you trying to do?"

Relaxing at last, Matthew spotted two winos arguing in the doorway of the Wang Center. "I told you," he said. "I wanted to have a look at the real estate documents."

"Oh, that I got. I mean with the credit card. What was that supposed to accomplish?"

"I was trying to feel my way to the slot in the dark but I couldn't get there."

She started to laugh. "Maybe you should have put some hair around it, lover."

Matthew closed his eyes and let her laughter wash over him. He couldn't help smiling.

# 34

---

## The Fetch-up

Raymond Carvalho kept his knee pressed tight against the middle drawer of his desk. At times he applied so much pressure to the joint he was sure the metal pull would leave a red wale on the flesh. But he did not let up. The dull pain in his knee contained him, kept him focused. It kept his knee from shaking. Kept the drawer shut and the whiskey where it belonged.

The squad room was downright pacific this morning. There were no manacled arrestees on the premises, the shrill human refuse from the previous night's sweeps having been cleared out hours earlier. Only the faint smell of their fear and stale sweat lingered after them. Officers occupied only two of the desks. One detective had a pencil between his teeth like a pirate's dagger as he poked at an electric typewriter that hummed ominously back at him. The other was talking softly into the phone. Probably to his girlfriend. Or his bookie. *I should get in this early more often,* Carvalho told himself.

Carvalho lit a cigarette and slipped the lighter back in his jacket pocket. Piscatello wasn't in yet. Late. *A meeting with the lawyer and Gogarty about the attorney general's investigation and Piscatello's late.* He took a deep drag and thought about the bottle in the drawer.

The AG didn't bother him. He was nothing, a pesky fly at the supper table. Nothing more. He would never get anywhere with what he had. In fact, Carvalho could have put him out of mind completely if it weren't for the lost time. *That's* what was eating him up. Maybe he could talk about it with Donna. Should he? He didn't know.

There were footsteps in the hallway and Martin Kelleher filled the open doorway. Surprised, Kelleher broke stride when he spotted Carvalho, then wandered off to his right, keeping his distance as he walked to his own desk at the far end of the squad room. He sat down at once and buried himself in the papers in front of him. Nothing but a stack of red hair was visible above an opened file folder.

Kelleher was avoiding him, all right. And Carvalho knew why. It hadn't taken long to fill in the missing piece that had nagged at him when he first heard of DeMarco's anonymous call. Given how tight-lipped Frannie had been about his snitch, Carvalho had been sure he was the only one who could have known to look for the snitch among Frannie's busts instead of his own. He and Piscatello. But he had overlooked Kelleher's role in Danny Li's original bust. It was right there on the arrest report, and he had missed it. As the officer assisting in the arrest, Kelleher would have known, or could easily have deduced, that the missing snitch was the Chinaman they had busted.

Carvalho's lips went white with fury as he relived the rage that had coursed through him when he figured out that Kelleher had to be the caller. There was the snitch, fresh out of jail and destined to have his testimony squeezed out of him like K-Y jelly so Carvalho could get screwed up the ass. And where was the guy who dropped dime on him—on all of them? Off somewhere slurping carrot juice or some such horsepiss and congratulating himself on playing the solid citizen. Only Piscatello's brawny intervention had kept him from hunting him down right then and ripping the hide off his sorry ass. Later, Piscatello had promised, later. Not now.

*Not now either,* Carvalho thought bitterly as he watched

Kelleher struggle to look busy under his blistering stare. *Later, pal.* He'd set him straight.

As if he could read his mind, Kelleher got up and hurried from the room. Carvalho's fury gradually subsided and he slipped back into the turbulent vortex of dread that had gripped him before Kelleher appeared. His thoughts darted at once to the middle drawer, and he kneed the handle again.

*You're a piece of shit,* said the voice. Out of nowhere, just like that. *A piece of shit.* And he knew the voice was right. Again, as he had daily over the past weeks, he dredged the narrow channel of his memory for the time he had lost out of that Tuesday night. The night the snitch was killed. Piscatello had calmed him down about Kelleher and brought him another double. He remembered watching the light from the wall sconce over the booth shimmer like a harvest moon in the pale whiskey. As he sipped, his thoughts had skittered from Kelleher to Danny to Donna, then to DeMarco and back to Danny and to the need to find a way out of this sucking spiral. He remembered when Piscatello went home, leaving him alone in the booth.

But after that, nothing. Zilch. Nothing until he woke up in his own bed at eleven-thirty the next morning. His first, dopey sensation was of his sweated shirt clinging to him like shrink wrap. When he pulled the fabric away from his skin, it stung as chest hair plastered to the cotton came away with it. Sitting up in panic, he saw the blood, nearly dry now, spattered in crusty gouts all over his shirt and hands and smeared on the sheets. He lurched into the bathroom to wash himself off, only to confront in the mirror the harrowing spectacle of his own face spotted by more flecks of dried blood. None of it was his, he soon determined, except for the light bleeding that still oozed from his scuffed knuckles. And there was the searing pain in the swollen middle knuckle of his right hand. It felt as if he had broken a bone or something, but on what? Or whom?

It wasn't until he was cleaned up and on the road to the station an hour later that he heard the news story on the radio. A murder in the South End. As-yet-unconfirmed reports that the victim was a confidential informant released on bail two days earlier. Beaten to death. Carvalho felt the air being sucked out of the car, and he almost plowed into a minivan as he yanked the Plymouth onto the shoulder and brought it to a shuddering stop. He shut off the engine and gripped the steering wheel with both hands, hearing nothing over the roaring in his own ears. He stared at his skinned and swollen knuckles.

Then he was sick, heaving the meager contents of his stomach out the car door he just managed to get open in time. When the contractions stopped, he sat up slowly, wiped his chin on his sleeve, and closed his eyes. His abdominal muscles were still sore from the retching and his breath was coming in short, tortured gasps.

That was when the voice started in earnest. *You're a piece of shit. A little turd.* God knows, it was not an unfamiliar refrain, but it had taken on a new, more insidious resonance now.

Carvalho was jolted out of his rancid reverie by the phone on his desk. His cigarette had accumulated an inch of ash. He stubbed it out with one hand and picked up the phone with the other.

"You better get down here, Ray." It was Joyce. "It never rains but it pours."

"Sal's late. I'm still waiting for him."

"No he ain't, Ray. That's what I'm tryin' to tell ya. He's not coming. His new lawyer's here instead."

Carvalho heard a humming noise again. It did not emanate from the typewriter.

"What are you talking about?" he asked. As if he didn't know.

"I'm talking shit, Ray. Forget the fan. It's all over the walls. You understand me? Sal has his own lawyer and he's been to the AG. Smoot's waiting for you. Get your ass up here."

Joyce rang off.

Carvalho hung up. Then, slowly, he moved his knee and pulled open the middle drawer. The half-empty fifth rolled to the front of the drawer, the rye sloshing around in the bottle. Light from the fluorescent overheads glinted off the glass. He looked at it for a long time.

No. Some vestigial instinct for self-preservation asserted

itself, and he slid the drawer shut. He pushed himself to his feet and headed for Joyce's office. The knee hurt enough to make him limp going down the stairs.

There were four of them in Joyce's office. Joyce himself and Gogarty, of course, and Warren Smoot, the lawyer from the patrolmen's union who represented Carvalho and Piscatello. Or had until Sal went out and hired the new guy. The new guy looked familiar, a slight, tidy man in his late fifties, with thin gray hair parted on the left and then swept straight back. Despite the muggy August weather, he wore a heavy gray suit complete with vest and watch chain. He was seated alongside Joyce's desk, facing the chairs in front of it like Joyce himself.

With an embarrassed half-smile, Smoot lifted his hands and eyebrows in a propitiating gesture. *What can I say?* Smoot was a big, shambling galoot with no hair, purse lips, and an expressive face. He was coatless, his rep tie was fastened with a knot the size and shape of a duck egg, and his collar tabs curled upward like the toes of an elf. *My lawyer,* Carvalho thought desolately.

As usual, Joyce led off. "Ray, this is Nachman Weiss. He's been retained by Sal in this business about the snitch."

Weiss flicked his eyes briefly in Carvalho's direction, but otherwise did not acknowledge his presence. No rising, no hand offered. Just a glance.

"Miami Weiss?" Carvalho sounded incredulous. Weiss narrowed his eyes at this but did not respond. Carvalho remembered him now. A spiteful little player in the Boston Municipal Court, where his abrasive manner pissed off DAs and judges alike on behalf of benighted petty criminals who mistook nasty for tough. His clients generally got hammered. *Slick move, Sal.*

"Mr. Weiss has just told us that Sal went to the AG, Ray," Joyce continued. "And then to Jerry DeMarco." He paused to allow Carvalho to absorb the import of this. "I'm sure you can guess what he told them."

Carvalho forced himself to look coldly from Joyce to Weiss, then to Smoot. "When did all this happen?" he asked.

"Yesterday," said Weiss. He compressed his lips, forcing

them down at the corners like a bulldog's. "Once I had informed Mr. Smoot here that he no longer represented Mr. Piscatello, I contacted the attorney general's office. As I am sure you can understand, I thought it best that my client be the first to go on record as eager to make things right." This last was said with ill-disguised relish, a vengeful jab at the man who had used his sobriquet.

"Jesus Christ," said Carvalho. There was acid in his voice as he turned toward Smoot. "He tells my lawyer yesterday, and I have to hear him spring it on me like this? Who the fuck's side are you on, Smoot?"

Smoot looked dumbstruck, his eyes widening.

"Didn't it ever occur to you," Carvalho continued, "to tip me off that something like this was gonna happen?"

Smoot opened his mouth uncertainly. He was not an articulate man at the best of times. What was it Joyce had said about Smoot? If you played charades with him you could let him use words and it wouldn't help. Before Smoot could stumble on something to say, Weiss jumped in.

"I instructed Mr. Smoot to keep the fact of my representation confidential. He gave me the courtesy of keeping my confidence."

"Courtesy! What do you assholes think this is? Some fucking smoker at the Knights of Columbus? And you're not supposed to tell who stuck around for the stag films?"

"Sal was my client, too, Ray," Smoot managed at last. His voice was big and rumbling, but there was no authority in it.

"Not once Miami here called you, he wasn't. You shoulda called me, Warren. Some fuckin' lawyer." Carvalho shook his head in disgust.

They were all quiet for a time. Then Carvalho looked hard at Weiss.

"So what did you get from the AG? He agree to break it down to some misdemeanor? For Sal, I mean?"

Carvalho could tell Weiss was deciding whether to answer the question. He must have figured the AG would tell them anyway, so he said, "No, and it's a she. Dorothy McGuire's in charge of this. She said she wouldn't talk to any of us until after we had set the record straight before Judge Doyle.

No promises. I talked to my client and we went to DeMarco late yesterday afternoon."

Carvalho laughed, a few staccato bursts of incredulity.

"You mean you got *nothing?* Not a fucking *thing?* Jesus Christ, Miami." He looked away, shaking his head again. "How much did Sal pay you for that nifty bit of footwork? Couldn't you at least come away with a handful of magic beans?"

"They will remember who came to them first," said Weiss. He sounded petulant, dogged. Less sure of himself. "And DeMarco says he will do all he can."

"Oh, I bet he will," said Carvalho, smiling now.

"I think we're getting off the track here, Ray," said Gogarty. "It's done. It's out there. You gotta reassess your position. Maybe you want to go have a word in private with Warren here."

Carvalho snorted derisively. "With able counsel?" He gave his unhappy lawyer a sour glare. Then he looked over at Gogarty.

"No, boss," Carvalho continued. "I can read the finger-painting on the shithouse wall. If Sal says there was no search for the snitch, there was no search. I can't exactly claim he's lying, can I? And there was no snitch. What other move have I got but to go down the chute with Sal? Christ Almighty, Sal"—he was talking to himself now—"you shoulda told me. Now we're headed for one hell of a fetch-up."

"Maybe not, Ray," said Joyce. "Coming clean is bound to cut you some slack."

"Like what?" asked Carvalho. "Five Hail Marys and an act of contrition?"

He laughed harshly and turned to walk out the office door.

"Where are you going?" asked Smoot.

"To take a piss, Warren. You wanna come and help? The doctor said I shouldn't lift anything heavy. You look like you'd be up to *that,* at least."

Carvalho headed for the stairs, leaving the four of them sitting in silence.

# 35

---◆---

## The Key

Matthew and Ira walked out of Torts, a spiffy new deli that had established a tenuous foothold in the no-man's-land between Downtown Crossing and the Combat Zone. They walked back up Washington Street toward Downtown Crossing. There Washington cut off the westward advance of Summer Street, the last two blocks of which had been closed to traffic to create a pedestrian mall separating Filene's and Macy's. With the heat of the noonday sun plastering their shirts to their backs, both men carried their suit jackets over their shoulders.

Ira slowed down as they reached the top of Summer Street and ruefully ogled the food vendors' carts that congregated there. Strips of steak for burritos sizzled over charcoal across the street from Andean immigrants who were assembling a Peruvian pork sandwich under the watchful eye of a hungry stockbroker. Umbrellas shaded barrows that trumpeted pretzels, Argentine barbecue, fried dough, lemonade, egg rolls, shish kabobs, and hot Italian sausages with onions and peppers. The melding of odors was intoxicating, and Matthew felt hungry all over again.

"I knew we should have eaten here," Ira said. "How come every time I let you talk me into going to some mainstream place, we end up regretting it?"

"Torts was supposed to be okay," said Matthew. The longest line was for the burritos, ten or fifteen people deep. Office workers milled all around them, standing, sitting on benches and brickwork and curbsides, eating and talking.

"The place was well named," said Ira. "Did you ever figure out how to tell the difference between the lettuce and the alleged roast chicken in that sandwich?"

"The thick stuff was the lettuce."

Ira laughed. "I'll bet the meat was greener," he added. "And don't forget those lovely truck-ripened tomatoes. And on top of everything, I have to pay for *your* lunch too."

"I'm sorry. I forgot my AmEx card had expired."

In the thick foot traffic Matthew stopped to let southbound pedestrians pass. When he did, a young Asian woman banged into him.

"Sorry," he said. She looked up at him blankly for a second and then passed on before he recognized her.

"Julie?" he called after her receding figure.

She stopped and looked back over her shoulder. It was Julie, all right. Matthew hadn't seen her since the day he last saw Danny, when she had walked away from them in Pemberton Square after Danny's release on bail. She wore black dungarees and a rose sweatshirt.

No flicker of recognition ruffled Julie's vacant expression. She blinked back at him in the dazzling sunlight.

"Julie, it's me, Matt Boer. Remember?"

Slowly, she nodded.

"How are you?" Matthew asked, stepping toward her. "I would have called you if I'd known how to reach you. I'm very sorry about what happened."

Julie gave him a tiny smile of acknowledgment. "I'm okay," she said.

Matthew turned to Ira and said, "You go ahead. I'll see you at the office later."

Ira waggled his fingers at him and headed down the Summer Street mall. Matthew looked back at Julie. She was snuffling, he noticed, and her attention seemed to have been dislodged, but she regained her focus when he addressed her again.

"Are you sure you're all right? Can I buy you a cup of coffee or something? Tea, maybe?"

Julie took her time processing his request before slowly shaking her head with another slight smile.

Matthew took her arm and gently walked her a few steps out of the flow of pedestrians and into the shelter of the doorway to a Foot Locker. He looked at her with concern.

"Are you sick? You look like you have a cold."

"Yes," she said after a moment, "I'm sick. The flu. But I will be OK."

Matthew's sudden understanding took him by surprise, and he blurted out without thinking, "It was you, wasn't it?"

She looked up at him, uncomprehending.

"It was you Danny was buying dope for," he said. "Wasn't it?"

Julie paused, then smiled wryly. She put her head down and started to walk away. Matthew stepped in front of her.

"I *knew* Danny wasn't into drugs. Especially heroin. He was just too active, too much the eager wheeler-dealer."

"Please," she said. "I must go."

"Just two minutes," Matthew insisted. "I need to know something. OK?"

She looked up at him, expressionless, waiting. Then the tiny smile again.

"Do you know anything about a real estate deal Danny might have been involved in? And about his relationship with Lo Fat?"

Her expression did not change. "I know nothing of these things. Now, I go, please."

"Please. You must know *something*. It may have something to do with why he died."

For the first time Julie's face was suffused with animation and she held his eye.

"I *know* why he die," she said sharply. Matthew braced himself, but she shifted focus. "Danny never talk about business with me," she continued, looking down. "He ask me to leave when he talk business."

So he did, Matthew remembered. He tried another tack.

"Did he ever tell you he was afraid of somebody?"

She paused again, as if deciding whether to answer. Then she said, "Only at the end, when he said people follow him."

"Who?"

She shook her head. "I don't know." Then she looked away and said forcefully, "I go now."

As she walked away, Matthew was immobilized. He stared at the Nikes and Adidas in the window and tried to make sense of what she had just told him. She was almost out of sight before it hit him.

Danny had been killed on Tuesday, less than thirty-six hours after he posted bail.

*When was there any time for somebody to be following him?*

He wheeled around and started running after her.

"Julie! Wait!"

When he caught up with her and grabbed her arm, he had to use both hands to stop her. Even then she did not turn around, but steadily leaned forward to pull her arm away from his grasp.

"Just one more question, Julie. I promise. Please."

Gradually he felt her arm muscles slacken, and she turned her head back toward him. She did not look at him, her face sagging like a sulking teenager's.

"You said he was being followed. When was that?"

Julie looked at him, seeming confused. He tried again.

"Danny was killed the second night after he got out of jail. Was it the night before he was killed, the Monday?"

Her expression did not change.

*"Think,"* he pleaded. "When did he tell you he was being followed? Was it before or after he was picked up by the police?"

Julie's confusion seemed to break up like cloud cover as comprehension finally took hold.

"Before," she said firmly. "The night before police come. Danny was very scared."

Her dark brown eyes filled with tears, and Matthew suddenly glimpsed a tiny piece of her great loss. His own sorrow welled up within him and left him groping for composure. The grief hit him like a physical blow, and he realized that this was the first time he had felt Danny's death as a personal loss. The pain before, he realized, was a self-pitying indulgence compared to the real anguish she displayed. Now, seeing hers, he was swept away by the raw force of his own sorrow. The discovery plunged him into shimmering bewilderment, and for a few seconds he was lost to his surroundings. *I need to sit down,* he thought.

She tugged her arm free of his grip and broke the spell. "I'm sorry," he said, his voice sounding foreign, not like his own at all. "Please believe me, Julie. I did everything I knew how to do to help Danny. Listen"—he took a business card from his wallet and handed it to her—"if there's ever anything I can do to help you, please just call. Anything at all. OK?"

As she looked down at the card in her hand, Matthew smelled again the steam from Danny's fish soup in the Cao Palace as he accepted the same card and a similar offer. Centuries ago.

When she looked up at him again, he asked, "What are you doing with yourself? Are you working?"

"Yes," she said. "I still work at Nankin. Like before. I am OK."

He watched her walk away down Washington Street toward the Combat Zone and Chinatown. A small sad figure, tiny steps. Doomed.

And then, out of nowhere, he was shot through with quivering excitement. There was something else he was feeling, too, and it took him a while to identify it. It was elation.

Someone had been looking for Danny before he was arrested. Before, that is, Matthew had an opportunity to fuck up.

Now he *had* to take a look at Lo Fat's files.

This time he had a key.

It was quite simple, actually. The next day was Thursday, when the firm served its weekly catered lunch for lawyers. The free lunch was a team-building ritual Ellen Stritch seldom missed. At exactly twelve noon, he strode into her office and asked if he could have a look at her personal edition of the Massachusetts statutes. Ellen smiled and nodded toward the multivolume set of blue softcover books on her credenza. He was still perusing one of them five minutes later when she rose and pulled on her dark suit jacket.

"Are you going down for lunch?" she asked.

"Jeez," said Matthew. He made a show of pulling back his cuff and checking his watch. "Is it noon already? No, I'll catch a sandwich later. I don't want to lose my train of thought."

"Feel free," she said, and she walked out the door.

Matthew waited, the volume open in his hand, for two or three minutes to make sure she did not return for something. Like her purse. He could see it on the floor underneath her desk. He reached over and picked it up by the strap. He unsnapped one of its flaps and began groping among its contents.

It was the only loose key he saw. He didn't dare try it out in broad daylight; he'd just have to hope he had the right one. He slipped it into his pocket, replaced the purse, and hurried out of the office and down the hall to the elevators. He rode all the way down to the ground floor and then walked across the main lobby to the escalator that descended to the Red Line subway station. At the bottom of the escalator he took a right in the direction of the trains and stepped up to a locksmith's kiosk that was nestled between Heels While You Wait and a Dunkin' Donuts concession.

Ten minutes later he was back in his office, with Ellen's key safely restored to her purse and the duplicate in his pocket. Later that afternoon, he returned to the Dead Partner's Office to resume his vigil.

This time he waited until after ten, and he made a full circuit through the thirty-seventh floor to make sure no one was still hanging around. Then he walked right up to the workroom and tried the key.

It worked.

# 36

## The Dinner Theater of the Soul

You couldn't tell if you didn't know him, but Ira Teitelbaum was upset. With his back to Matthew, his massive bulk blocked the view of the gas range, where he was heating dried chilies in a smoking skillet. The peppers hissed on the cast iron as he pressed down on them with a spatula. Ira flipped the blistered chilies over and turned around to face Matthew.

"So," he said. "Let's just be clear on what's happened here. You didn't want to burden me with this before you went and did it because you figured I'd stop you. Right?"

"Right," Matthew admitted. "Wouldn't you have?"

"You betcha. But now that you've had your look at the files, it's OK to tell me. Because I wouldn't rat out a friend to Fleishman?"

"I hope not," Matthew said, with an ingratiating half-smile.

"You're presuming an awful lot on our friendship."

"Not *too* much, I hope."

"Don't patronize me, Matt." Ira turned around and ministered to his peppers for a few minutes.

Matthew looked over and grimaced at Laura, who was sitting across the table from him. Hannah sat next to her. They were all in the cluttered kitchen of the Teitelbaums' condominium in the fashionable Fisher Hill neighborhood of Brookline. It was Friday evening, the day after Matthew's successful foray into Ellen Stritch's workroom. He was just starting to tell them all what he had found in the files.

"It's done, Ira," Hannah said. "Even if it was a mistake, it's not like some major crime."

Ira spun around angrily.

"It's not *done,* Hannah. Jesus Christ! Someone who's technically my employee has just told me he broke into a locked room so he could take a look at a client's confidential files. Files that were locked up, mind you, specifically to keep *him* from seeing them—for fear he'd share what's in them with Laura. Which, I gather, he's already done. And he thinks I'm supposed to keep it to myself. No, Hannah. It's not *done* by a long shot."

He glared at Matthew, still holding the spatula. The peppers hissed behind him.

This was worse than Matthew had expected.

"You sound like one of your peppers, Ira," said Hannah. "They're burning, by the way."

Ira lurched back to the stove and hurriedly scooped out the chilies and slid them onto a plate.

"Shit," he said dejectedly. "They *are* burned." He picked up the plate and dumped the peppers in the sink. Pointing his spatula at Matthew, he said, "You can diddle my law firm, but don't fuck with my chilies!"

Matthew smiled, relaxing a little.

"I'm sorry, Ira. You're right. I shouldn't have done it and I shouldn't have involved you in it."

"Shit," said Ira, poking the blackened peppers into the disposal. Disgusted, he dropped the spatula in the sink. "So much for enchiladas."

"Let's order pizza," said Hannah.

"If it would help," said Laura, "I could ask to be taken off the *Felter* case, too. Once I tell them about Matt and me and how he's been screened off, they'll probably agree. They won't want to be one-upped by Daphnis and Clooney in the let's-be-ethical department. And that way, at least, what Matt's told me couldn't hurt your client."

Laura caught Matthew's wondering eye and smiled at him. "The case is getting wicked boring anyway," she said.

"It still sucks," said Ira. He seemed to be sulking.

"You're right, Ira," said Matthew. "It's very messy and it would be embarrassing as hell if it got out. But the client hasn't been harmed and if Laura withdraws, there's no potential for future harm either."

Ira was silent. Hannah stood up and walked over to the wall phone.

"What kind of pizza?" she asked, the receiver in her hand.

"Sausage and mushrooms," said Ira. "And peppers," he added gloomily. "Don't forget the goddamn peppers."

·  And Matthew knew it was all right.

"But put all that other stuff aside," Matthew explained over pizza half an hour later. "Who cares what entity holds title to the land or got the construction loan? What really matters is who gets the money. Right?"

No one said anything. He took a sip of beer and went on. "From what I can tell, the entity that gets the stream of income generated by Adams Place is a limited partnership called Beach Limited Partners IV. It's entitled to all the rents earned from the tenants, less what Lo Fat's management company takes for running the property. Beach then turns around and makes payments on the mortgage. What's left after that is net profit, to be distributed to the Beach partners. And who are they?

"Well, the only general partner is a corporation called Pagoda Development, which is Lo Fat's development company. Pagoda was set up long before the hotel project, and Lo Fat has probably used it before."

"As the general partner of Beach Limited Partners I, II, and III?" suggested Laura.

"Most likely. For previous projects, anyway. Now, Beach has four limited partners. One of them is New England Mutual Insurance Company, which was the takeout lender."

"What's a takeout lender?" asked Hannah.

"It's a bank that gives you the borrowed cash in those

little white cardboard boxes you get in Chinese restaurants," said Laura.

She and Hannah laughed, but Matthew ignored them. "It's the bank that supplies the permanent financing when the project is completed. So called because it pays off, or takes out, the previous lender who provided the construction loan. The takeout lender is like the bank that holds the mortgage on your house. Sometimes it's offered an equity position in the project—a little piece of the deal on top of the interest it earns on the mortgage loan. To sweeten the deal for the lender. So New England Mutual takes a limited partnership interest. Nothing unusual about that.

"Nor is there anything noteworthy about the second limited partner. Adams Hoteliers, Inc. It owns and manages the hotel itself. Adams is a wholly owned subsidiary of the Randolph hotel chain. Big national outfit. The hotel is the anchor tenant for Adams Place. Like New England Mutual, it bargained for a piece of the action when it signed the lease."

Matthew glanced over at Ira, who was being uncharacteristically silent during all this. His head was down and he was pushing a pizza crust around his plate with a fork.

"The other two limited partners are realty trusts. One of them, the Bursting Rapture Realty Trust, holds just a tiny share of the partnership interests. One and a half percent. Judging by the name, its beneficiaries are probably some of the Chinatown businessmen who went into the deal with Lo Fat."

"Probably?" It was the first time Ira had weighed in. He did not look up from his plate.

"There are no schedules of beneficiaries for either of the two realty trusts," Matthew explained. "So we don't really know. All I know for sure is that the trustee of Bursting Rapture is something called"—Matthew consulted his notes— "the Hesperidee Corporation. Whatever *that* is. But like I said, this one has a teeny share."

"Why do I get the sense you're building us up for the fourth one?" Laura asked.

"Ah," said Matthew, smiling. "That's the limited partner that got my attention. The Twenty-seven Fayette Realty Trust. Established in 1991. It owns a fat eleven percent of

Beach. The trust documents identify its trustee as Sinon, Inc. Sinon's mailing address, according to the trust instrument, is forty-five Milk Street, in Boston. Suite seven-fifty."

"I know that building," said Laura, straightening up. "I've taken depositions there. It's mostly filled with office suites for lawyers."

Matthew nodded. "You're right. I walked over there this afternoon. And suite seven-fifty *is* a law office." He flipped through the notes on his yellow pad. "Hanrahan, Gordon, Morrissey and Palmer. They probably drafted the realty trust documents. Ever hear of it?"

Laura shook her head. So did Ira.

Matthew decided to air his hunch. "I believe," he announced as unportentiously as he could, "that the loose schedule of beneficiaries Ellen showed me goes to Twenty-seven Fayette. I think Danny was its named beneficiary."

Ira snorted his incredulity. "How did you figure that out?" he asked. "By matching up the staple holes?" He had raised his head and was looking at Matthew now.

"Nothing so scientific," Matthew answered, ignoring the scornful tone. "I just put some things together. One, Danny told me he couldn't go into witness protection because he had something cooking. Irons in the fire, he said. Participation in the hotel project would be a pretty hot iron.

"Two, it wasn't just that he was scared of being identified as a snitch. He was, of course, and for good reason. But he *was* a snitch, after all, and he didn't have to be. When Dunleavy busted him for buying dope, he could have contested it. Or even take the hit. You were the prosecutor, Ira. What's the worst he would have gotten for a first-offense possession?"

Matthew looked at Ira and raised his eyebrows to coax an answer out of him.

"Short probation," Ira shrugged. "Unsupervised."

"That's what I figured. And I asked him about it. He just clammed up on me. Now, considering how difficult it must have been for Danny to turn snitch—given his heritage, his personal temperament, and his distrust of cops—why did he do it? Because there was something even more threatening about a drug conviction than being a snitch. What could that be? I think he was afraid somebody would think he was a druggie."

"Like who?" asked Laura.

"His momma," suggested Ira.

"Like someone he was in business with," said Matthew. "Someone who might view him as an unreliable junkie. That might cool those irons. And depending on what the irons were, it might put Danny in danger. Better, then, to be a secret snitch than to carry a public conviction as a heroin user."

Matthew paused to finish his beer.

"This is pretty thin stuff," said Ira. "You better have more than that."

"Three," Matthew continued. "When he was in the middle of the restaurant case, Danny refused to answer questions at his deposition about whether he owned interests in real estate. He was quite explicit about his fear. He was afraid he'd get killed. Remember?"

Ira nodded.

"Well, that suggests there may have been something a little less than legal going on, don't you think?"

Staring back impassively, Ira didn't answer.

"Consider, too, that the hotel was built by then and, in fact, this realty trust had already been set up when Danny came to us for help in the lawsuit over the Lotus Blossom. What would happen if the people he was doing real estate business with thought they were dealing with a junkie? They'd be afraid he couldn't be trusted to keep secrets anymore—precisely what Danny feared if he testified about his real estate dealings at that deposition three years ago."

Ira was shaking his head in dismay.

"One more thing," said Matthew. "Number four. It's the name. The Twenty-seven Fayette Realty Trust. Danny's restaurant was located at twenty-seven Fayette Street in Waltham. Is that just a coincidence?"

He had Ira's full attention now.

"So add it up," Matthew continued. "Danny had some real estate dealings three years ago. He was too scared to talk about them. He's so scared of a drug conviction he turns snitch. He's got 'irons' so attractive he won't run away even if his life is in danger. His name pops up on a loose schedule of beneficiaries in files belonging to the hotel developer. And there just happens to be a realty trust, missing its schedule of beneficiaries, whose name is the same as the address of Danny's restaurant. What does it all suggest to you?"

Hannah frowned. "Are you telling us that Danny Li owned eleven percent of Adams Place?" she asked, incredulous.

"No," said Matthew.

"He was a straw," said Ira, softly now.

"A cutout," said Laura.

"He held it for someone else," Ira explained.

"Someone," added Matthew, "it was very dangerous to do business with."

"Like Herman Vu," said Laura.

"Could be," said Matthew.

"Herman who?" said Hannah.

"Herman Vu," said Laura. "He's a gangster. The head of the Tung On, an organized crime outfit that runs Chinatown. Bad, bad people."

Ira pushed his chair back from the table.

"So what?" he asked. "Where does all this take you? I mean, you're not intending to represent Danny's estate in collecting his eleven percent of the profits, are you?"

Matthew admitted he was not.

Ira said, "Everybody's been assuming all along that Carvalho and company were breaking into one of Vu's retail outlets when Dunleavy got shot. Odds are Vu ordered Danny killed once he learned Danny had sent the cops knocking. So he already had a motive to kill him. All your fascinating research has raised is the possibility that Vu may have had yet *another* reason to want him killed."

"Which was . . . ?" asked Hannah, frowning.

"Because he was a snitch," said Matthew. "And a snitch is not the sort of person who could be trusted to keep secret the fact that Vu owned a piece of Adams Place."

"Which brings me back to my original question," said Ira, his eyes hard on Matthew's. "*So what?* You think it lets you off the hook for screwing up? Aren't you still the reason Vu or whoever discovered Danny's identity? Does this get you over the guilty funk you've been in from all this? This black dinner theater of the soul you've been putting on for us?"

"Ira, stop it," said Hannah. "Matt's had—"

"No," Ira insisted, raising his voice. "I'm *not* stopping. I admit it was a hard thing, a horrible thing to have to go through. And I've listened to it and lent a sympathetic ear. Christ, we *all* have. But enough is enough. Now you tell me you've violated I don't know how many ethics rules—certainly more serious stuff than what the Board of Bar Overseers is looking into now. And to what end? You're rooting around in a kind of onanistic fervor, just to build out of Tinkertoys an intricate theory to establish what is—*at best*—an additional motive for the prime suspect to murder Danny."

Ira stopped and the four of them were silent. Ira still seemed angry. Hannah looked embarrassed. Laura, Matthew sensed, probably agreed with Ira.

"And what a theory!" Ira went on. "For crying out loud, didn't you ever hear of Occam's razor? When forced to choose between two theories to explain a given set of phenomena, always prefer the simpler. Buddy, you've opted for the complicated one. In fact, 'complicated' doesn't touch it. It's a Rube Goldberg contraption. The squirrel knocks the nut in the cup, which goes down and trips the lever that sets all the little wheels turning . . ." Ira moved his hands in intersecting circles as his voice trailed off.

"My theory may not be as simple as kill-the-snitch, but it holds up, Ira. Admit it. It explains phenomena that don't fit any other plausible theory."

Ira shook his head.

"Most importantly," added Matthew, "you have completely ignored one bit of data that puts everything up for grabs. It also 'lets me off the hook,' as you like to put it."

"What 'piece of data'?"

"Julie said somebody was following Danny on Thursday, the night before he was arrested. If she's right—and she sounded *very* sure—then it's likely somebody was on to Danny before I even showed up on the scene. So how, I ask you, did they find out he was the snitch?"

Ira was silent for a while. When he finally responded, his voice was lower, his tone less assured.

"There are lots of possibilities. Julie's pretty fucked up

and probably can't be relied on to read a clock, let alone remember what happened just before the bottom fell out of everything she knew. Danny himself was pretty jumpy about the whole business. He might have imagined he was being followed. Christ, maybe somebody just wanted to mug him. You don't *know*."

"You're right about that," said Matthew. "I don't know. But I know enough to suspect that somebody discovered— before I screwed up—that Danny was DeMarco's missing snitch, and they went and killed him or tipped off the people who did. And then I've got all this odd business about Danny having some connection to Lo Fat and the Adams Place project. How can I *not* look into it?"

"You're gonna track down Danny's killer?" Ira was grinning now.

"No. You're right. It's not that I'm gonna be able to 'catch' the murderer. You don't 'catch' people like Herman Vu. I just want to know about Danny. I want to know what happened."

"Where do you start?" Laura asked.

"With those who had access to the knowledge that Danny was the snitch. The cops. The DA's office. The Management Committee. Me. You. Did I leave anybody out?"

Ira just shook his head.

# 37

---

## Concentrating Fog

Thanks to a tip from the clerk, Sarah learned almost immediately that Judge Doyle had entered an order allowing the Commonwealth's motion to reinstate the indictment against Michael Chin. Rather than wait a day or two for mail delivery, she made her way across Boston Common and over to the clerk's office to pick up a copy. McFeeterson offered his condolences, but she knew his heart was with DeMarco on this one.

The order itself was worse than anticlimactic. It was a whimpering disappointment. The weasel hadn't even bothered to file a memorandum explaining his decision. There was just a handwritten notation scrawled along the lefthand margin of DeMarco's motion. *The Commonwealth having demonstrated its inability to comply with the order to produce the subject witness, the motion to reinistate indictment is ALLOWED. Doyle, J.* No discussion of the perjury by Carvalho and Piscatello. No mention of Danny Li's death. Not even a finding whether Li was in fact the informant whose information led to the warrant. If nothing else, the lack of findings gave her another arrow for her quiver on appeal, should she need it.

As she thought about it, she took heart from the absence of any finding on the question whether IT existed or not. It bolstered her belief that Doyle would allow her to argue that he did exist and that the police were hiding him. She smiled grimly to herself as she thought of the contortions DeMarco would have to go through to prove a negative—that there was no IT—and do it through the testimony of an admitted perjurer like Carvalho. She also took a certain sardonic satisfaction from the specter raised by the other fifty-one warrants for which IT had supplied probable cause. Crimmins would soon be sputtering as dozens of convicted drug dealers were sprung from prison when their convictions were set aside because of police misconduct. Should do wonders for his campaign.

While she was here, she figured she might as well use the court library to do some of the research she had been putting off. She was unlikely to get another chance soon, for she was about to be immersed in trial preparation again. Leaving McFeeterson's lair, she crossed Pemberton Square and made for the courthouse annex, an ugly gray tower erected in the thirties. She squeezed into a crowded elevator and pushed the button for the twelfth floor.

The elevator made its slow ascent, with stops at every floor. With the flow of people in and out at each stop, she found herself maneuvered to the rear of the car. As a result, when the doors opened for the sixth floor, she was not immediately visible from outside the elevator. It would have been almost impossible, however, for Sarah not to notice the cameras and news crews huddled in the hallway before the doors of the district attorney's office. Several passengers leaned out to see what was going on, and Sarah herself caught a glimpse of Jackie's crewcut in the crowd of reporters.

The elevator doors finally closed and the car shuddered into motion, rising to the seventh floor. Two passengers got off and, on impulse, Sarah joined them. She stopped for a moment, wondering what she was doing, and then hurried down the stairway.

When she got to the sixth floor again, she eased open the

stairway door and peeked out into the hall. It was still mobbed with people and she was able to slip out the door and hang back against the end wall where she could observe the proceedings.

Jackie Crimmins was still regaling the reporters who had gathered in the hallway. Some shouted questions over raised notepads; others craned forward with outstretched microphones. Jackie had the big grin on, which suited the occasion, but the face of DeMarco, who towered over him, was dour.

Jackie raised both hands for quiet and got it. The big grin was still there, poised confidently above a brilliant blue tie with geometric figures like glittering shards of stained glass. A fluorescent tube in one of the wall sconces was flickering.

"Ladies and gentlemen, please," said Jackie indulgently. "I've made my statement. Justice will be done in the murder of Detective Francis Dunleavy. I don't have much to add. As I said, the man responsible for this welcome turn of events is my first assistant, Jeremiah DeMarco. He'll fill you in on the details and answer any questions you may have."

DeMarco put on a smile and stepped forward, flinching a little as microphones were thrust at him. Standing beside Jackie, who radiated self-assurance in this environment, DeMarco looked skittish and stiff. He cleared his throat.

"As Jackie told you," he began in his rolling baritone, "Judge Doyle has allowed our motion to reinstate the murder charges. You may recall that those charges were dismissed when police officers failed to produce a confidential informant whose testimony the court believed would be helpful to the defense. We in the district attorney's office suspected that the officers' reluctance to cooperate stemmed from fears that the informant's testimony might uncover irregularities in the search warrant. We issued pleas to members of the Police Department for help, for anonymous tips as to the identity or whereabouts of the missing informant."

"Are we talking 'irregularities' here—or perjury?" The question was put by a young blonde Sarah recognized immediately as a reporter with the Channel 6 evening news. She had always seemed sophisticated and dominating on the screen, but Sarah was struck now by how tiny she was in person. Mousy, even.

"Well, it's not my place to comment on that," DeMarco responded. "That's for another day. Suffice it to say, the officers had reason to be concerned. Fortunately, our pleas bore fruit, and I received an anonymous call from someone in the Department. I was told the informant was a young man named Danny Li, who had been working with Detective Dunleavy. Mr. Li was immediately taken into protective custody. Unfortunately, he insisted on being released and, over our objections, he was. As we all know, the young man was brutally murdered less than two days later.

"Frankly, I thought our chances of getting the case revived were next to none at that point. But I underestimated the esprit de corps that animates the police officers who serve this city. Rather than see a killer go untried for the murder of a fellow officer, two detectives from the Drug Control Unit came forward and volunteered new information. Critical information. Exposing themselves to great personal risk, both officers recanted testimony given in pretrial proceedings. They have filed sworn statements supporting our efforts to get the court to reinstate the charges."

"They knew the color of their duty," Jackie added, nodding resolutely, and Sarah almost laughed out loud.

DeMarco continued. "Detective Carvalho has acknowledged that the informant he used to get the search warrant, identified as 'IT' in his affidavit, was a fiction, a composite of several informants he had used in the past to obtain search warrants. The actual source of the information that led to the warrant, he revealed, was an informant who worked with Dunleavy. Carvalho never met the informant. Instead, Dunleavy told Carvalho what his source had told him and asked Carvalho to obtain the warrant. Carvalho then plugged that information into his affidavit, attributing the information to his own fictional informant. When the court later demanded that he produce him, Detective Carvalho was afraid to disclose that he had made false statements to obtain the search warrant. To hide that fact, he fabricated a search for the nonexistent informant. Detective Piscatello assisted him in faking that search.

"With help from Carvalho and Piscatello, we were able to convince Judge Doyle that we have produced IT—or at least the person who provided the information Carvalho attributed to his fictitious IT. Mr. Li's death is tragic—believe me, we would have liked to have his testimony to clear away some of the confusion generated by Carvalho's affidavit. But his 'unavailability,' if you will forgive me for using the chilly language of the law governing these circumstances, cannot be laid at the door of the police or the Commonwealth. Trials go forward all the time after witnesses die. It will be for a jury to decide whether the Commonwealth's witnesses are telling the truth or whether Mr. Li's statements, as embedded in Carvalho's affidavit, suffice to cast a reasonable doubt as to Michael Chin's guilt. The trial is set to begin three weeks from tomorrow. Now, your questions."

"Does Ms. Kerlinsky agree that Danny Li is IT—or whatever?"

"Of course not," said DeMarco, smiling. "She believes the police cooked all this up after Li was murdered. I find that *extremely* difficult to believe. Why would they risk admitting they lied under oath only to compound their lies with further perjury? And they offered their testimony with no promises of immunity from our office or from the attorney general. But, then, Ms. Kerlinsky has other fish to fry."

Jackie, his index finger in the air, joined the fray. "Don't pay too much attention to what comes out of the business end of that lady's mouth. Criminal defense, after all, is the art of concentrating fog."

Sarah could resist no longer. Stepping forward, she watched the surprise blossom in DeMarco's face when he saw her there. Jackie looked unruffled, delighted even.

"Ms. Kerlinsky!" he shouted. "And just in time to see that our report is balanced. Tell us, have we left anything out?"

Sarah smiled as she stepped up beside him, joining him in front of the cameras and microphones.

"I must confess I'm a little confused by all that praise for lying policemen," she said as she shook his hand. "But you did neglect to mention one teeny little thing."

She paused long enough to force him to ask. "And what would that be, now?"

"That despite Mr. DeMarco's claims, Judge Doyle did *not* find that IT does not exist. That will be a question for the jury—and a very difficult one for the prosecution, I might add. But I have a question for *you*, Jackie."

Jackie widened his eyes comically and mugged for the reporters. "Watch out it's not leading," he admonished with a grin.

Smiling tightly, she ignored his manner. "If you believe IT does not exist, can you assure us that the Commonwealth—in the interest of justice, of course—will not oppose all the motions for new trial that will surely be brought by the victims of Detective Carvalho's fifty-one *other* false affidavits? Leading, I presume, to the release of dozens of wrongfully imprisoned drug dealers?"

Jackie's big grin remained in place but it wasn't as animated as it was before. He lost no time in responding. "Case by case, Sarah," he said. "We'll have to take each of them on a case-by-case basis."

For a moment the two of them smiled wordlessly at one another in front of the cameras.

"Mr. Crimmins?" It was the woman from Channel 6 again. What was her name? "Eddie Felch has reported in the *Globe* on rumors that large quantities of drugs may have disappeared from the Tyler Street apartment at the time of the raid. Are you investigating whether police officers might have seized and then hijacked the drugs?"

"More fog," said Jackie, his smile turning sardonic. "But then, that's Eddie's stock in trade. There is not one scintilla of evidence to suggest any such thing."

"Wasn't an empty suitcase retrieved from the apartment?"

DeMarco stepped in. "An attaché case, yes. That item shows up on the police inventory taken after the raid. But it's hardly remarkable, under the circumstances. We are not looking for some phantom bag of cocaine."

"Mr. Crimmins! Mr. Crimmins!"

"Yes, Bill."

"How do you see your chances of getting a conviction now? Wouldn't you agree that the prosecution's case is weaker after all this?"

Jackie's big grin was back in all its splendor. "It's a hell of a lot stronger than it was yesterday."

Sarah couldn't argue with him on that one.

# 38

## Different Strengths

Digging into the implications of what he had found in Lo Fat's files had fattened up Matthew's folder on the *Chin* case, but it had also taken a toll on his work at the firm. To make amends, he came in early. He first went through the mail that had piled up undisturbed over the past few days. He sorted pretrial motions and discovery requests into a single pile for later action. Junk mail from stockbrokers joined advertisements for educational seminars in his trash basket. He hurried through interoffice memos relating to firm administration. He was paging impatiently through the previous week's new case report when Ira bulked large in his office doorway.

"You hear the news?" asked Ira. His spilling belly had turned his belt over, exposing the white fabric that lined the waistband of his trousers.

"What news?" Matthew asked, his eyes flicking up at Ira, then back to the page he was reading.

"Judge Doyle has reinstated the charges against Chin. It goes to trial in three weeks."

"Yeah, I heard." Matthew had reached the section that

described changes to prior new case reports. He frowned.

Ira said, "For somebody who's so bent on catching a murderer, you're pretty blasé about it all."

"I don't care who killed Dunleavy. I just want to know who killed Danny. Say, what's this all about?"

He handed the new case report to Ira, who took it and sat down heavily in a chair in front of the desk.

"What?" he asked, flipping to the first page of the memo to get his bearings, then back to the page Matthew had indicated.

"The second-to-last entry on the page. The one that says the originating attorney is being changed on a case opened two weeks ago. Did you notice it?"

"You know I never read this shit," said Ira, handing it back to Matthew.

"An OA credit claimed by Robolawyer was taken away from him and given to Barbara Dwyer."

"Good for her," said Ira with a grin, warming as usual to any bad news about Robolawyer. "You got a problem with it?"

"No," said Matthew. "I just don't understand it. How could there be any confusion over who's responsible for originating a case? A client calls O'Leary to hire him on a new case and it's his OA, right?"

"Oh, no. It's not that simple. A lot of associates make the same mistake. You think the OA credit is for bringing in the *case*. Not so. It's for bringing the client, and once a client, always a client. What this means is that the client first came to the firm through Don't Call Me Barb. So she was down as OA for the initial case. Apparently, the client called back years later and asked for Robolawyer. But that doesn't make him the OA all of a sudden. Barb *always* gets the OA credit, even if the client despises her and the only reason he came back was because he loves the work Robolawyer did for him. I like to think of it as oligopoly with a human face. Breaks your heart, though, doesn't it—to see Robolawyer lose the credit?" Ira was grinning again.

Matthew was still frowning. "Then I'm still confused. You mean I had no right to claim OA credit for Danny when I opened the new file on the *Chin* case? The OA should have been whoever was OA on the first case—the restaurant case?"

Ira smiled indulgently. "You named yourself OA?"

"Yes. Didn't you notice? It was right above where you were listed as RA."

"I told you. I don't read this crap. But you're right. You shouldn't have been the OA."

"Then how come nobody complained? Like Barbara did, when she saw Robolawyer's entry in the new case report?"

"Have you forgotten?" Ira asked, tilting his head to one side. "Hel-lo in there. Try to keep up with me on this, OK? *We kept Danny's name a secret, remember?* If the real OA didn't know the client's name, how could he complain that you were ripping off the credit?"

Matthew bit his lower lip. "He couldn't, you're right." He paused for a moment, looking down at the new case report. "Unless"—Matthew looked up at Ira—"unless he was on the Management Committee and got my memo supplying the name."

"Jesus," said Ira, exasperation in his voice. "Does everything come back to Danny?"

Matthew was not deterred. "I'm not a hundred percent sure, but I think the original OA was Fleishman, and *he* got my memo. He would have known who Danny was. Why didn't he complain?"

"Well, that I can't answer. Fleishman is a bear on these things. He's not the type to let the credit slip by him. Are you sure he was the guy?"

"No. But he was the guy who put me on the Lotus Blossom case in the first place."

"He's also the department chair, so that means fuck all. He's *supposed* to assign lawyers to cases. Get on the network and let's run it."

Matthew nodded and turned to his computer. He clicked on the icon (an admonishing forefinger) for accessing the conflicts data base. He entered Danny's name and waited. The response was quick and unequivocal.

"I was right," Matthew said. "It *was* Fleishman."

Matthew turned back to Ira and looked him hard in the eye.

"What?" Ira demanded.

"I was just thinking. About this October afternoon when I was twelve, maybe thirteen. I was out walking through cutover corn rows and I came to a pasture with a new barbedwire stock fence around it. I sat down next to the fence and leaned my cheek against one of the new fenceposts. I remember the cedar felt cool on my skin and out of the corner of my eye I could see the shiny staple that held the wire to the post."

"How idyllic," said Ira dryly.

Matthew ignored him. "Anyway, I reached up and grabbed the top wire and, like, twanged it. When it's a new fence, they're stretched as tight as piano strings. It didn't make much of a noise, but there was this *thrum* that passed from the post to my cheek and then spread right up my skull. You know what I'm saying?"

Ira shook his head. "Not a goddamn clue."

"Well, I just got the same feeling."

"Because you learned Fleishman was Danny's OA?"

"No. Because he didn't bitch," Matthew said. "Why didn't he claim the credit?"

"Who knows? Maybe he didn't notice it. Or he forgot he was the OA. It's not like he made a stack of money on the first case. Shit, maybe he was trying to help you out by letting you take credit for bringing in business."

It was Matthew's turn to cock his head skeptically and lower his eyebrows at Ira.

"OK." Ira conceded, raising his hands. "An unlikely motivation. Ben Fleishman is not a candidate for instant conversion to mensch. But don't make too much of it. There really *are* such things as coincidences, you know."

"I just want to make sure I haven't missed any dots that need connecting," said Matthew.

"Not everything is connected. I mean, *dignity* and *diarrhea* both begin with *d* but believe me, they have nothing else in common. So don't go off half-cocked, OK?"

"I'm not about to," said Matthew. "I'm just wondering if I should load up."

Ira got up. "You know," he said, "you were a lot more fun before all this."

"Everything was more fun 'before all this.' And I haven't told you what I found when I looked up the firm of Hanrahan, Gordon, Morrissey and Palmer in *Martindale Hubbell*."

*Martindale Hubbell* was the leading national law list, an encyclopedia of lawyers broken down by state. It supplied short professional biographies and descriptions of practice areas for lawyers and their law firms.

Ira, looking bemused, said nothing. He rested his hands on the back of the chair.

"The Morrissey in the firm name is one James E. Morrissey, who describes himself as concentrating his practice in civil and criminal trial work. He also happens to be representing the three men who were arrested with Michael Chin after Dunleavy's murder. Doesn't it strike you as a little odd that the law firm that acts as a mail drop for Danny's trust should show up representing three defendants in a murder case where Danny is a key witness? Or is it just that *Morrissey* and *Michael* both begin with *m*?"

"Jimmy Morrissey?" Ira asked, wonderingly.

"You *know* him? I thought you never heard of him."

"I just didn't recognize his firm. But Jimmy? Oh, yes. I know Jimmy Morrissey. From way back."

Ira sat down again, his smile back in place.

"Well," said Matthew, "why do you suppose—"

"Jimmy Morrissey," Ira butted in. "There's a piece of work. When Jimmy was starting out he was a court lizard. He used to pay the clerks in the criminal session to page him every twenty minutes. That way the crowd—mostly defendants and their families—came away thinking he must be the busiest lawyer in the courthouse. He's been a ham-and-egger all his life, but he's also a cagey, devious son of a bitch who can pick you clean if you're not on your toes. A damn good man with a jury."

Ira laughed. "One time somebody asked him how he managed to fill his eyes with tears every time he addressed a jury. He said he would just reach up and pull one of those little hairs out of his nose."

Matthew laughed as Ira demonstrated the procedure. "Come on," Matthew said. "I read a bail motion he filed early on in the *Chin* case. The man can't write an English sentence."

"Oh, I'm sure you won't catch him snapping off any Ciceronian periods. Writing is not his métier. The guy doesn't come to life on paper. But then, I'll bet no one ever had to cut the word 'jejune' out of one of his briefs—unlike a former academic we all know."

"Touché," Matthew said with a smile, feeling the hit.

"There's a place in the profession for the Jimmy Morrisseys of the world," Ira continued, his rabbi's finger wagging again. "Sure, he'd never make it past the door at a tony joint like D and C. But it takes all kinds. Remember the goat fucker."

Matthew shook his head as if to clear it. "Excuse me?"

"I didn't tell you about the goat fucker?"

Matthew gave him a half-smile as he shook his head. Obviously, Ira was about to correct the omission.

"Well," said Ira, settling in and lacing his fingers over his massive stomach. "Guy gets arrested for copulating with a goat. He goes to the family lawyer. The lawyer says, 'Whoa, boy, this is too big for me. You need a criminal lawyer.' Guy says, 'Who do you recommend?' So the lawyer thinks about this for a minute and says, 'Well, there's two guys in town who are pretty good, but they have different strengths and weaknesses. One of 'em is great at picking juries but is a bust at cross-examination. The other is savage on cross but he could give a shit about who's on the jury. Which one do you think you want?'

"So the guy thinks it over and he decides to go with the one who picks juries. The case goes to trial and, sure enough, the lawyer spends six days picking a jury. He goes over *every*thing. Then the prosecutor opens by putting this cop on the stand. 'Officer,' he says, 'tell the jury what you saw on the morning of October 12th.' And the cop says, 'I was driving down Route Thirty-three and looked out my window and I saw the defendant there copulating with a goat.'

"The prosecutor sits down and the defense lawyer stands up. 'Now, Officer,' he says, 'what did you see *after* you saw my client copulating with a goat?'

"The cop says, 'I saw the goat turn around and clean him

up with his tongue.' There are gasps in the courtroom and the defendant covers his face with his hands.

"And just then juror number four turns to juror number five and whispers, 'He's right. A good one'll do that.' "

After he had stopped laughing, Matthew said, "So OK, different strengths. And Morrissey's are with juries?"

"Also, he's shrewd and court-smart. And often, as I said, just a teeny bit devious." He paused, frowning. "Jimmy represents the three witnesses?"

Matthew dug into his *Chin* file and handed Ira the docket sheet.

The docket sheet was a chronological log of every event that occurred in a case and every document filed in it. Counsel for the parties were listed at the top of the sheet. Jeremiah DeMarco for the Commonwealth. James E. Morrissey was named as counsel for defendants Dai Cheng, Michael Chin, Lai Huong, and Warren Liu, but a series of *x*'s had been typed through Michael Chin's name. Sarah Kerlinsky's name, as counsel for Chin, appeared just below Morrissey's.

A check of the earliest calendar entries on the docket sheet, going back to mid-February, confirmed the obvious. Morrissey had originally appeared for all four defendants at the bail hearing. Kerlinsky entered her appearance on Chin's behalf a few days later, leaving Morrissey to represent only the other three. The principal witnesses for the prosecution.

"What do you think?" Matthew asked.

"Hmm," said Ira. "Nothing out of the ordinary, really. Morrissey has them all until it becomes apparent three of them can cut themselves a deal by turning on the fourth. Classic conflict of interest. So he withdraws from representing Chin and Sarah replaces him."

"That's what I figured," said Matthew. "But who hired Sarah? I mean, I can understand how a ham-and-egger like Morrissey would be taking appointed cases, but would somebody of Sarah Kerlinsky's caliber?"

"Are you kidding? Of course she would. She probably fell all over herself trying to get appointed to handle *this* case. I don't see your point."

"If you're right, I guess I don't have one," said Matthew.

"I just was wondering who was paying for the representation here."

Ira didn't seem to be listening. He was carefully running his finger down the list of entries on the docket sheet, a puzzled look on his face.

"They're not there," he said at last, quietly.

"What's not there?"

"The affidavits of indigency. There aren't any. None of the defendants filed one."

"Which means . . . ?" Matthew was confused.

"Which means," Ira said, raising his voice a bit, "that they did not get assigned counsel. You don't get a public defender unless you sign an affidavit of indigency. *Then* they'll assign counsel."

"You mean they're not indigent?"

"I don't know about that. But I do know the state is not paying for Kerlinsky and Morrissey's services. Somebody private is paying their bills."

Matthew got it immediately. "Somebody like Herman Vu," he said.

"That would make sense, I guess. Assuming their drug operation was one of his, he would likely pay for their lawyers. It's an employee benefit. Free legal care."

"And," said Matthew, "the first guy he sent them was Morrissey, the guy who's connected to Adams Place and Danny's trust. If his firm was the mail drop, they probably drafted the trust documents as well."

"That would make sense, too," Ira agreed. "*Assuming* you're right about Danny's connection to the trust and to Vu."

"Surely, Ira, this *strengthens* that assumption. The coincidences are starting to pile up too high to be dismissed as, well, coincidences."

"Maybe," said Ira, scratching the back of his neck and looking out Matthew's window. "Maybe. It would explain why Vu might think to go to Morrissey. But it doesn't explain how Sarah get in this?"

"Well, like you say, she's good. And once it was clear that the other three were going to accuse Chin, Vu would need to get him somebody good."

"But that's just the point," said Ira. "Why would Vu *let* three members of his gang point the finger at a fourth? Can't be good for the morale of the troops—not to mention Chin's. Think about it. What options are open to Chin if he gets convicted—except talk to the DA about Vu and his operations? So if you're Vu, why pay for separate lawyers? In fact, why not just tell them all to shut up and stick with Morrissey? Why bring Sarah into this at all?"

Matthew didn't know. But he was willing to bet Morrissey did.

# 39

---•---

# The Ham-and-Egger

Nassur Tosuni," said the clerk in the crowded courtroom, "you are charged with assaulting a police officer and resisting arrest. How do you—"

"Shut up, fucking poofter. That is answer," said the prisoner, who was standing in the jury box. "You fucking poofter, thank you." He was thin and shirtless, and bald except for the swatches of tightly curled black hair gathered around the ears. His dark eyes, deep sunk into cheeks pocked like raw tripe, blazed and darted about the courtroom.

"You just keep quiet," said the judge, a white-haired man with a puffy face Matthew had never seen before. "We'll hear from you in a moment."

"Fuck you in a moment. All right, poofter? All right, I fuck you. That is answer."

"The police report indicates that you—"

"Fuck cops. Fuck the Irish, all right?"

"If you don't shut up I'm—"

"Fuck judge, too."

"Ida," the judge said wearily to the clerk, "please tell me

this gentleman is represented by counsel." He removed his reading glasses and looked about the room.

"I have just been given that honor, Your Honor," said a plump young woman in braids who hurried from the right side to the center of the court. "Mr. Tosuni appears to be indigent, Your Honor, and I have been assigned to represent him—for his arraignment at least."

"Fuck lawyer too. This is not true. That is answer."

The judge put his glasses back on. "Do we assume this is a plea of not guilty?"

"Yes," said the woman. "That seems a safe assumption."

"I fuck you, answer you, stuff you, poofter. Is that enough for you answer?"

"That is not ans—no answer," said the judge, "but I will construe it generously as a plea of not guilty. The prisoner is bound over for trial. Has the Commonwealth been so imprudent as to waive bail?"

"No, Your Honor," said an assistant district attorney still in his twenties. "In view of the violence involved, and the fact that Mr., ah, Mr. Tosuni refuses to give a current address, the Commonwealth requests bail in the amount of twenty-five thousand dollars, twenty-five hundred cash."

"What has your client to say about that?" the judge asked the woman standing before him.

"I hesitate to ask him."

"Fuck you."

"Do you wish to ask for bail?" the judge said to the prisoner.

"You ask bail yourself, poofter. Now ask me."

"I don't have to ask."

"Fuck the bail. Fuck America."

"I take it, then, you don't wish to seek bail."

"Stuff that."

"No application for bail. The accused is remanded to custody while awaiting trial."

"Fucking bastard, poofter, Irish potato fart."

"Thank you for shopping at the BMC."

As the prisoner was led away to the lockup by two burly bailiffs, the decibel level in the tiny courtroom rose perceptibly. Chairs creaked, papers shuffled, throats cleared, handcuffs clicked. The young lawyers involved in his arraignment whispered and laughed quietly to one another as they walked over to the right side of the courtroom.

Sitting on a bench along the side wall, Matthew craned his neck to look for Jimmy Morrissey. He hoped he would be able to identify him. A spacey receptionist at the offices of Hanrahan, Gordon, Morrissey & Palmer who called herself Taffy had suggested he might find Morrissey in the Boston Municipal Court, where he had an arraignment that morning. Armed with Taffy's description ("a short chubby guy with, like, gray curls?"), Matthew scanned the room for the lawyer.

There. In the second row. Morrissey was lurching to his feet as the judge retired for a midmorning recess. Then he sat back down, lowering his head to read something on his lap.

Matthew stood aside for the departing lawyers and spectators, then made his way to Morrissey's left side. He was still groping for a conversational icebreaker when the man looked up at him, a questioning look on his face.

"Can I help you with something?" he asked. His voice was raspy, a spring-tooth harrow pulled across blacktop. The reading material in his lap, Matthew noticed, was a copy of *Sports Illustrated*. On the page Green Bay Packers were piled like split stove wood left to dry in the sun.

"Uh, yes," said Matthew. "Are you James Morrissey?"

"Bull's-eye," the man said, smiling. "You got him. Call me Jimmy."

The man offering his hand had a round, red face and bushy hair, most of it gray. Roly-poly, you'd call him. His features and figure spoke of dissipation until you reached his eyes, which were clean, clear blue, and very alert.

Matthew shook the hand Morrissey offered. Opting for the direct approach, he said, "I wasn't sure you'd see me if I called for an appointment. So I waited until I figured you'd be in court and I called your office and asked where to find you. Taffy sent me here."

Morrissey's smile remained in place.

"My name is Matt Boer. I had the misfortune of representing Danny Li in the *Chin* case."

Morrissey blinked and said nothing for a moment. Then he dropped Matthew's hand and said, "You were probably right. I don't think you'd have gotten an appointment."

"I was hoping I could have just a few minutes to talk about Danny." Matthew took a beat and held Morrissey's eye. "As you can imagine, it's been a rough couple of months."

He watched Morrissey size him up before responding.

"I don't know what I can tell you," he said at last. "But, hey, I know what it's like to lose a client like that. Though I expect it's not as rare in my practice as it is yours. Let's see if we can find us a table."

Morrissey got up and gestured to Matthew to follow him. They left the room by the back door and Morrissey led him down the hallway to the marble-railed gallery above a grand atrium below them. Between the balustrade and the wall, nestled among the pillars, were several wooden consultation tables and chairs. Most of them were occupied by lawyers and clients, but Morrissey found an empty one in the corner farthest away from the courtroom they had left. He took a seat, propped his elbow on the table, and rested his chin in the heel of his hand, his fingers drumming on his cheek. He waited.

Morrissey's blue eyes glittered at him, and Matthew wondered for a second what he was doing here. *To test my hunch,* he reminded himself. See if he could pick up something, anything that might reassure him that he was on the right track. He got right to it.

"You represented three of the people arrested in the Chinatown raid. Well, all four of them at first, till Chin got his own counsel. I assume you learned you had a conflict of interest and spun Chin off to Sarah Kerlinsky."

Apparently declining to treat this as a question, Morrissey gave nothing away. He just stared intently at Matthew.

"Your clients did not file affidavits of indigency. Neither did Chin. So that means you're both getting paid privately." Matthew shifted in the chair. "Which is to be expected in these kind of cases, I suppose—where someone higher up in the enterprise has to take care of the rank and file. I don't expect you to confirm this. I understand your position. I just mention it because it lays down a line—a money line—

running from somebody to you, and from that same somebody to Sarah. Because how could Chin manage to get his defense funded by somebody different from the somebody who's funding the defense of the other three? So I figure we're talking about the same Somebody. How'm I doing?"

Morrissey remained motionless, the whisper of smile on his face. Matthew pushed on.

"Let me see if I can lay down another money line for you to consider. You have a more direct connection to Danny Li. Your office is the address of record for something called the Twenty-seven Fayette Realty Trust, an entity that gets eleven percent of the profits from the Hotel Adams."

Morrissey's expression did not change and his vivid blue eyes remained on Matthew's, but Matthew noticed his nostrils contract when the names were mentioned.

Matthew continued. "This information comes from Lo Fat, a name I'm sure you know well. He's a client of my firm, but I'm not telling you anything you don't already know. It turns out Lo Fat has a schedule of beneficiaries for an unnamed real estate trust which lists Danny as the sole beneficiary. Since I know Danny owned a restaurant on twenty-seven Fayette Street in Waltham at the time the trust was declared, I figure he's the beneficiary of the trust of that name. You see anything wrong with my logic here?"

Morrissey was grinning now. He pulled his feet up on the table and leaned back until his chair butted up against the railing.

"So I got another money line," Matthew said. "Profits from Lo Fat's hotel come to the trust via its mail drop, which is your office. Now, I know Danny doesn't have the kind of—what should I call it? *heft?*—to be getting such a big chunk of a major development. So it stands to reason the money makes its way out of your hands, through Danny, to somebody else."

Matthew leaned forward in his chair and spoke distinctly. "Isn't it possible, just possible, that the somebody on the receiving end of the money line leading *out* of your office is the same somebody on the giving end of the money line that runs *in* here to pay your legal fees in the *Chin* case? And

Sarah's too, by the way. What do you think, Jimmy? Am I all wet here?"

Matthew sat back and watched Morrissey, whose grin remained stolidly in place.

And Morrissey said nothing at all. He just waited.

Finally, Matthew broke into his own grin. "You've given me as much of an answer as I could have hoped for. You haven't denied it or expressed shock or incredulity—or thrown me out. I gotta think I'm on the right track, Jimmy."

Morrissey slid his feet off the desk and sat up straight, his forearms flat on the desk. Matthew watched his smile harden as he prepared to speak, the pleasantness gone now.

"You think I'm some kind of meatball, don't you? Some storefront bozo who picks up a buck anywhere he can."

"Not at all," said Matthew. "My friend Ira Teitelbaum tells me you're one hell of a lawyer."

"Just sleazy? Is that it?"

"I didn't even say that. Just because you agree to serve as a mail drop doesn't mean you're dirty. Could be an innocent service to a client."

Morrissey lifted both hands in supplication. "Then what do you want of me?"

"I just wanted confirmation that the somebody at the end of the two money lines was one and the same person. You gave me that."

"I gave you nothing. And you don't want to know what you want to know. You with me here?"

Matthew frowned. "I'm not sure I am."

Voices were raised in anger at a table further up the rail, but Morrissey paid them no mind. His smile was gone now. "I mean, this shit you're playing with is shit you oughta leave alone. You talk about logic. Well, use it. What's the upside of using any of this speculation you've cooked up here? There isn't one. Think about it. It's a lose/lose proposition. If it's not true, you end up smearing a lot of decent people with good reputations. Like Lo Fat. Or me and Sarah. And whoever else you got in mind. No upside there. All downside, like libel suits and shit.

"And if it *is* true? Even worse. Because if the kind of somebody you're hinting at is in the picture, he's not going to stand by and watch some fancy-firm putz jeopardize a lot of delicate and intricate business arrangements. You with me?"

Matthew nodded. "You mean it could be dangerous."

"I mean you don't want to know the answers to your questions. You feel bad about Danny? OK. I've been there. Do your mourning. Beat your breast. Get on with other things. Trust me, you don't need this shit."

"Maybe I owe it to Danny," Matthew said stubbornly.

"You owe Danny *nothing*. Like I said, you don't want to know what you want to know. Bury it. That's my advice."

Matthew stood up. "I thank you for talking to me. And for the advice."

Morrissey stood up, too. "Take it," he said.

And Morrissey left.

Matthew leaned over the railing, staring vacantly at the caryatids that supported the gallery.

# 40

## Lying Is Impossible

Sarah Kerlinsky's conference room also did duty as library and workroom. She was using it in the latter capacity today, she and her intern, a co-op student named Jeannette from the New England School of Law. They were preparing for trial in the matter of *Commonwealth v. Michael Chin*.

It was almost one o'clock in the afternoon and Sarah yawned, rubbing her eyes. They were red and sore. Neither woman had had much sleep over the past week, and they expected to carry on at this pace until the trial began—and ended.

Sarah was working on blocking out the likely course of her cross-examination of the prosecution's witnesses—anticipating responses and tying questions to trial exhibits. Jeannette manned the computer, assembling and organizing material for insertion in the trial notebook, a three-ring binder in which Sarah hoped to have everything she would need for the trial right at her fingertips.

She heard voices in the front of the suite, then approaching footsteps. Maury materialized in the open doorway with a smile on his face.

"Hi," he said. "Hello, Jeannette."

"Hi," Sarah replied, immediately feeling edgy and pressed for time.

"You had lunch?" he asked. "I thought maybe—"

"I was just gonna get us something," said Jeannette, logging off the computer even as she got to her feet. "What can I bring you, Maury?"

"Anything," he answered. "Something with tuna."

"Sarah?"

"A Greek salad."

Maury took a chair at the table. Looking back to watch the door close behind Jeannette, he grinned. "She didn't lose any time getting out of here. You must have her well trained."

Sarah laid her pen on the pad in front of her and sat back. She pinched her waist and rolled her shoulders to relieve the stiffness. "She probably didn't want to feel like a third wheel. You're not exactly a regular around here." Her remark had a put-upon edge to it that she regretted at once, and she sought to blunt it by smiling warmly at her husband.

"Well," said Maury, "I don't get to see you much when you go into hibernation like this. Not without the girls, anyway. So I thought, why not drop in for lunch?"

She felt a tug of affection. "I'm glad you did, Maury. Though I'm afraid I won't be very good company. I get my head in all this"—she gestured vaguely toward the papers and law books heaped on the table—"and it's hard to just shut it off."

He shrugged. "So don't. Tell me about it."

"The case?" she asked.

"Sure," he said, scooting the chair closer to the table and settling himself comfortably. "What's the hard part?"

Sarah's smile twisted wryly. "The hardest part is not making too much of a pig of myself. Over all the lies I have to work with. The testimony—that already given as well as what's likely to come—is so full of lies I'm afraid they'll hate *me* for rubbing everybody's nose in it. That they'll balk at accepting the enormity of it. Suppose they say the cops couldn't really have been *that* bad?"

"They. You mean the jury? That they won't accept that the cops could be lying so much?"

"Something like that. I mean, some of the lies are admitted, recanted. But maybe they'll reach a bottom, a point where a jury will refuse to believe they could be lying anymore."

She stopped herself. "This is gibberish. I *have* been living with this crud too long. I'm starting to mindfuck myself. OK, keep it simple. The cops lied before and I should be able to make people doubt they're telling the truth now."

"Lying is impossible," Maury said quietly.

She frowned, eyeing him sharply. "What?"

"Gregory Bateson," he explained. "A famous observation from one of the giants in *my* field."

"I thought he was a shrink. Didn't he write about schizophrenia, like R. D. Laing?"

"Yes," Maury replied, "but he was an anthropologist first. He was married to Margaret Mead for a while."

"I guess I knew that," she admitted. "But so what? I don't get it."

"Bateson's point was that, no matter how easily the conscious mind may be fooled by a lie, the organism as a whole picks up more data. And it knows, at some level, when it's being lied to. In fact, that precept is the basis for his theory of schizophrenia. A child hears 'I love you' from a parent whose conduct conveys a conflicting message. The child processes the real truth subliminally, and the madness comes from the contortions he goes through trying to reconcile the two realities."

Sarah tilted her head to one side. "So you're telling me the jury always knows when a witness is lying." She did not sound convinced.

"At some level, yes. That's the theory, anyway."

"Well, not in my business," she retorted, her tone gone dismissive. "I see them swallow lies all the time."

"My point," he stressed, "is that instead of being deceived, they deceive themselves."

"What am I supposed to do with *that*?" she demanded, more irritably than she intended. "All your theory does—"

"*Bateson's* theory," he reminded her.

"Whatever—all it does is shift the site of deception from the witness to the juror. The deception is still there, and if it holds long enough, Michael Chin can get tagged for murder."

He looked disappointed. "Aw, Sarah. I'm just making conversation. I'm not trying to give you pointers on how to expose witnesses."

"You seem to think they're already exposed."

Maury shook his head. He looked away, scanning the wall of books to his left. She knew him, that look of mild irritation and disconnection. He was hurt, sliding again. She regretted getting on him like that.

"I'm sorry, Maury. I warned you I was all wrapped up in this stuff. I've got a man's life at stake in a week, and knowing that tends to muck up my social graces. What few I have," she added with a smile.

He smiled back at her. "I'm sure you'll get him off." He paused briefly, then asked, "Is he innocent?"

She was taken aback. "Of course he is."

"No. I don't mean innocent as in 'innocent until proven guilty.' Like all your clients. I mean, did he do it? Shoot that cop?"

Sarah was suddenly furious. "What kind of a bullshit question is that?"

"I don't think it's so bullshit. It's pretty straightforward."

"There's nothing 'straightforward' about it," she said harshly. "It implies a judgment—that you doubt everything I stand for. My whole profession. As if there would be something wrong with defending him if he wasn't 'innocent' enough for you."

He shook his head again. "You're wrong, Sarah. I'm not questioning what you do for a living. I think it's quite noble and necessary. I just want to know what you think happened."

"It was more than that," she insisted. And she was damned if she'd tell him what she knew.

"No," he said, emphatically. "You're wrong."

Neither of them said anything for the next few angry moments. Maury's gaze seemed to be focused on a spot midway between them. It was he who resumed first, his tone more measured.

"You remember a couple months ago, when you asked me to tell you what was going on in my head when I got pissed at you about that anonymous phone call? And I said what I said, about you having to be right all the time?"

She nodded, remembering.

"You told me, 'Too bad.' That I would just have to get used to living with somebody who's right all the time. Remember that?"

She relented. "I was kind of hard, wasn't I?"

"No," he said. "That wasn't it. You were *wrong*. That wasn't what I meant at all."

Sarah was bewildered. "Then why didn't you tell me that?"

"Because," he plodded on, "you immediately leapt to the conclusion that it was *my* problem. You went off about some friend of yours who was cursed with being right too often. And I just thought, the hell with it, you were doing it again. So I just let you go on about it. But Sarah, I wasn't saying you *were* right all the time. I was saying you had to *be* right all the time, and that you don't quit till people let you be right. You're like a dog with a bone. Even when you're wrong—like now."

She looked down, saying nothing. She had the eerie sensation of seeing a side of herself only others saw. Like walking past one of those triple mirrors in a clothing store and catching a glimpse of yourself from an angle not otherwise observable. She didn't like it.

Maury tilted to one side far enough so he could look up and catch her eye. "You really *don't* have to be right all the time, Sarah. I'm sure it's a great asset in your profession, but it's kind of rough on the home life, if you know what I mean."

She met his smile with a weak one of her own.

"It would help," she said, "if you'd stay *in* there instead of just shutting down like that. If you don't tell me straight out what's going on, how am I supposed to know?"

Maury's eyes crinkled in mischief. "At some level, the organism knows."

He started laughing and she threw her ballpoint at him.

He raised his arm and the pen bounced off it and onto the floor.

They were both still laughing when Jeannette arrived with the sandwiches.

# 41

---

## Skydragon

Matthew and Laura climbed the long, shabbily carpeted stairway to the Skydragon, a second-story restaurant that fronted right on Beach Street, the main drag of Chinatown. At the top of the stairs they found themselves in an open foyer, with a long bar to the right and an immense dining room fanning out in front of them. Although it was almost nine-thirty, the room was still about half full, its evening clientele a mixture of Asians and Caucasians.

A young Asian woman in a white blouse and black slacks greeted them.

"Two?" she asked.

"We're looking for a friend who should already be here," said Laura, craning her neck as she scanned the dining room. "There," she said, spotting her quarry. "That's our friend over there. Thank you."

The young woman smiled and stepped aside. Matthew trailed after Laura as she spun her way among the big round tables and headed toward the back of the room. She waved to a slight man who sat at a small square table shoved up against the wall about fifteen feet from the kitchen doors. The man smiled and waved back at her.

"He must be a cherished patron to get such a choice table," Matthew grumbled. "So close to the kitchen and all."

"Shut up, she explained," said Laura.

"I know, I know. He's making sure we have privacy."

By the time they reached the table the man was standing to greet them. He gave Laura a hug, then gripped both her shoulders as he looked her over. "Laura, sweetness. *God,* we miss you! How could you go native like that?"

"I got tired of the hustle, Eddie," she said, smiling warmly. "Here, let me introduce you guys. Matt Boer. Eddie Felch."

"I guess we sorta met already, didn't we, big fella?" said Felch, through a mocking smileful of yellow teeth. Recalling warily his telephone conversation with the reporter the day after Danny's release from jail, Matthew nodded and said nothing as they shook hands.

Eddie Felch's features were clustered together in a clump around his nose, leaving his dark eyes a little too close together and crowding the bridge of his nose. This imparted a feral quality, which was exacerbated by the quick movements of his gimlet eyes. He wore jeans and running shoes and a pale-blue denim workshirt with a black-and-white polka-dot tie that dangled loosely from the open collar.

The three of them sat down. Felch retrieved a burning cigarette from an ashtray and puffed on it. He addressed Laura through the smoke.

"So tell me the truth. You don't miss the *Ledger*?"

"Come on, Eddie. *Nobody* misses the *Ledger*. The real question is do I miss the game."

"And?"

"A little, once in a great while. When I remember what it was like when things were popping. But generally? I'm pretty content with my choice."

"Hmmm," said Felch, theatrically touching a pensive finger to his lips. "You think I should consider a career change?"

Laura laughed. "I don't think so, Eddie. The tedium would get to you. At least you get to do a story and move on. Lawyers never finish the story, and they only move on when the client loses interest or runs out of money. I'm sure you'd loathe it."

"You're probably right." Felch sighed and dragged on his cigarette. He had the odd habit of holding his cigarette out in front of his chest, with his elbow raised off the table and tucked into his side. The effect was oddly effeminate for a man of his macho manners, and it caused him to look out through a scrim of smoke at his table companions. "So what's up, sweetness? You didn't set this up just so I could meet the legal beagle here, did you?"

Felch cut his eyes in Matthew's direction as he finished. Matthew did not respond. The hostess arrived with menus and a stainless-steel teapot.

"Actually," said Laura, pouring herself a cup of tea, "it was the legal beagle who wanted to meet *you*." She leaned forward and spoke in a stage whisper. "I think he wants to pump you for information." She poured for the two men.

"Now *that's* a switch," said Felch as he watched Matthew, sardonic mischief in his voice. "Have you got something to swap?"

"You mean like last time?" Matthew cracked a half-smile as he watched the reporter stub out his cigarette.

"You're not sore at me about that business we had, are you?"

"No," said Matthew. "In fact, I should probably thank you for not embarrassing me. You could have implied I had confirmed that my client was Chinese. Not that it matters anymore."

Felch said, "There was no reason to go into the ethnicity of the witness if I couldn't produce the name. And put yourself at ease. It took no great leap of imagination to guess that the witness had to be Chinese—once you discarded the notion that this IT was the snitch."

"Well, I'm grateful anyway."

"But enough about you," said Felch. "What do you want from me? The skinny on Vu and the Tung On, I hear. I repeat: do you have anything to trade?"

"Maybe I do. But you can't use it—at least not yet. If ever."

"Gee, what a deal." Felch's voice was flat.

"I don't have enough yet to offer you more than that. But if it pans out, it could mean a story on Vu's involvement in the development of Adams Place."

Laura flashed a puzzled glance at Matthew. Felch said nothing for a time. Then he said, "Oh, what a surprise. I could die from a surprise like that. Listen, I beat that nag to death years ago and never got through the horseshit."

"Couldn't connect him to the money?"

"No, as a matter of fact." Felch seemed a little surprised. "You got ideas about that?"

"I don't know how the money went in, but I think I can put you on to how it got back out to Vu."

"Well," Felch grinned, "never kick a dead gift horse in the mouth when it's down. That's my motto. So tell me."

Matthew held his gaze and said nothing. Again Felch paused, as if sizing up his interlocutor.

"OK," Felch said. "In your own sweet time. It's not like you're asking me to give away any trade secrets here, right? What is it you want to know?"

"It's like Laura said. I want to know about Vu and the Tung On. Everything."

The waitress arrived and, since Felch had chosen the restaurant, they let him order. Then he lit another cigarette, took a deep drag, and dangled it in front of him. He squinted through the smoke as he talked.

Historically, he explained, organized crime in Chinese communities had been monopolized by the Cantonese tongs, which were broken into individual criminal societies called triads. The Tung On was the triad that ran the show in Boston. The TOs, as they were known on the street, participated with other major triads in an international umbrella organization calling itself the 14K.

In the eighties the FBI trailed Herman Vu to Hong Kong, where he attended a big conference of the 14K with chiefs of other triads. Like the Ghost Shadows out of New York. And the Kung Lok triad from Toronto. The feds got excited, calling it the Asian Appalachia, after the famous Mafia gathering that put La Cosa Nostra on the map in 1957. In Hong Kong Vu and the others carved up territories and agreed to render assistance to one another. They sealed their pact by "burning the yellow paper"—a ritual symbolizing brother-hood and the start of a new business venture.

"I guess," said Felch, "it makes as much sense as pricking your finger or whatever it is the guineas do."

The gathering in Hong Kong was of major significance for Herman Vu, for it marked the formal recognition of his accession to power in Chinatown, the fruits of several years of clawing and murdering his way to the undisputed leadership of the Tung On.

The parallels to the Mafia were intriguing, Felch explained, but they didn't really go very far. The triads were much older, going back to the seventeenth century, and were likely to outlive the Cosa Nostra. Linguistic and cultural barriers remained much higher for the Chinese than the Italians, who had become pretty much assimilated now.

"Look at the North End," Felch said. "There are as many yuppies living there as Italians these days. Nobody would say that about Chinatown. They remain a very insulated bunch."

The insularity of the community added another layer of protection for the Tung On. The TOs relied on intimidation, of course. Two years earlier someone had fired shots in broad daylight on a market day in the middle of Beach Street. Somebody just sending a loud message, Felch explained. Although the police arrived on the scene while the cordite was still watering eyes, they could not find a single person who even heard the shots, let alone saw something.

"I talk, I die," Matthew muttered to himself.

"What?"

"Nothing. I'm sorry. Please go on."

Even without intimidation, the TOs were pretty secure. They catered to a very popular vice among the Chinese—gambling—and as a community they were averse to looking outside for help. What's more, the TOs fed predominantly on their own people, which meant there were not many outsiders with beefs against them. All of which made them very hard to infiltrate. The DEA in particular had found it well-nigh impossible to crack it. The Tung On was a tight group in a tight community.

"They're mostly involved in gambling?" asked Laura.

"It's their lifeblood," said Felch. "Especially mah-jongg. And pi-gow, whatever that is. The games have long cultural roots and are very popular. Big shots and dishwashers belly up side by side to play at the social clubs. If you could read Cantonese, you'd see schedules posted everywhere in Chinatown, on lampposts and store windows. In fact, on your way out tonight, you take a look out the big window across from you as you head down the stairs. You'll be able to see right into the second-story windows across the street. That's the Son Van Social Club, which is full of mah-jongg players at the moment. There must be a dozen similar establishments in this little neighborhood."

"But that's not their only business," prodded Matthew.

"No, indeed. Protection is a biggie, too. There isn't a Chinese business in town that doesn't pay tribute to avoid unpleasantness. The TOs take up a big collection during the Lion's Dance at New Year's, but there are weekly protection payments, too. They even shake down the pimps from the Combat Zone next door.

Matthew recalled the chrysanthemums at the Lotus Blossom.

"And let's not forget drugs," Felch added. "They've been importing and distributing heroin from Asia's Golden Triangle for the last two decades."

"And now cocaine," said Matthew.

"Ah, yes," said Felch with a grin. "At last we come to your friend Danny. Coke is a new product to keep up with the times. You don't want to lose market share, you gotta offer a complete product line. The Asian community isn't as monolithic as it was when Vu came to power in the early '80s. Now you got Vietnamese gangs and gangs from Fiji trying to horn in, with new products and services. Now, Vu is a master at juggling the various ethnic groups—including the wiseguys—without too much public unpleasantness. But the pressure toward disintegration is there. Once Vu is gone, you may see open warfare in Chinatown."

"You make him sound like Marshal Tito," suggested Matthew lightly. "Holding Yugoslavia together."

Felch pursed his lips and nodded seriously. "Why not? In New York there was a lot of fatal gunplay in a Chinatown restaurant a couple years ago. Our little Chinatown is down-right placid compared to stuff like that. But when Vu's gone? All I know for sure is there will be another influx of Chinese immigrants—legal and otherwise—as we near mid-1997, when the British cede control of Hong Kong to mainland China. And even after that, since a lot of them go to Toronto or Montreal first, thanks to Canada's easier immigration laws. But there will be a serious shakeout, that's all I know."

Matthew changed the subject. "What do you know about Vu's involvement in the development of Adams Place?"

Felch stubbed out his cigarette. "Yes. Well, a few years back I heard lots of rumors about him pumping cash into the deal when the developer—I forget his name—was short of cash."

"Lo Fat."

"That's the guy. The unofficial mayor of Chinatown, they call him, and he'll tell you to your face there is no such thing as the Tung On. I tell you, tofu wouldn't melt in his mouth. But the word on the street was he was short and Vu helped him out. Suddenly he had cash. But I could never trace the money. Can you?"

"Maybe. Can we agree you won't print any of this unless I give you the go-ahead?"

"It's off the record," said Felch, nodding vigorously.

Laura said, "More than off the record, Eddie. He means not even without attribution. No stories based on information from 'confidential sources.' We're talking deep background here, right?"

"Absolutely."

There was laughter from a big table behind Felch's back. Matthew glanced at the table, at which seven or eight Asian men sat, smoking and drinking tea. As if to shut out the merriment, Felch leaned toward him.

"How," Felch almost whispered, "did the money come out? If you can demonstrate that, no one would care how it went in."

Matthew looked at him for a moment, entertaining second thoughts, then decided to take the plunge. He told the reporter what he knew about the real estate trusts that held interests in the development. He described the 27 Fayette

Trust and his belief that its beneficiary would turn out to be
a cutout for Vu. He did not mention Danny's role in any of
it.

Felch interrupted him. "This isn't anything new, you
know. The trust and its place in the chain of ownership I
discovered years ago by digging through records in the Registry of Deeds."

"Did you notice that the address listed for the trust is the
same as Jimmy Morrissey's law firm? The same Jimmy Morrissey who's one of the defense lawyers in the *Chin* case?
Right there you've got a connection between a Chinatown-
based real estate project and a Chinatown drug bust. A tenuous one, I concede, but a connection all the same."

Felch turned to Laura. "Is this how he practices law?
Building cases on will-o'-the-wisps?"

Laura shrugged noncommittally, but Matthew could tell
from the tightness of her lips against her teeth that she was
angry. He pushed on.

"When you learn the identity of the beneficiary of the trust,
you will be convinced. I can't tell you who that person is
yet. Lawyer rules, you know. But I *can* tell you that the name
will get your attention. And that you will agree that the name
is the right one."

Felch smiled. "That must mean the name isn't Herman
Vu."

Matthew smiled back. "You're right. The name is his cutout. And once you know it, you will find a whole new vista
of investigation before you. But I can't tell you any more
right now."

Felch was silent for a time, a newly lighted cigarette suspended in front of him.

"Daphnis and Clooney," he said at last. "Of course. You
guys represented Lo Fat."

"Still do," said Matthew. "All the more reason for you to
sit on everything I've told you."

"Everything you've told me—which ain't much—is available from the public record."

"I guess that's right. But you said you wouldn't use it. If
I'm to have any chance of providing you with more infor-

mation—information that's *not* public—you gotta sit on what I've given you so far. OK?"

Felch puffed deeply on his cigarette and expelled the smoke through his nostrils as he spoke. "OK. You got a deal. You haven't given me enough for a story anyway. Let me ask you something else. About your deceased client."

"I can't tell you much," said Matthew, leaning back in his chair to make room for the waitress, who appeared with steaming platters of food. "Even if he's dead, what he told me is still privileged."

"You gotta be kidding."

"That's the law."

Felch shook his head. "Lawyers. Go figure. Well, then. Without stepping on the toes of your blessed privilege, can you tell me anything more about the cops ripping off a cache of cocaine after Dunleavy got shot?"

"Huh?"

"Dope. Cops. You know? There are rumors all over the place that a shitload of cocaine disappeared from the premises after the cops showed up. Wasn't that why the cops were there in the first place? What happened to it?"

"I never heard this before."

Felch turned to Laura for help again. "Is he being cute or is he really this slow?"

"Oh, he can be cute sometimes," said Laura, cutting a withering glare in Matthew's direction. "It can be hard to tell when he is."

The anger in her voice might have been lost on Felch, but Matthew heard it.

"Come on, Matt," said Felch. "Where you been? Your client was the snitch who put Carvalho and Company onto the bust. He must have told them they were gonna hit pay-dirt."

"No," said Matthew. "I mean, I can't tell you what Danny told me, but I don't want to mislead you. I know nothing about large quantities of drugs on the premises."

Laura spoke up. "Eddie, are you telling us the cops stole drugs?"

"What is this? Am I mumbling or something? I'm telling you what I hear. There was a big drop at Tyler Street, but when the bust was over, the cops came up with nothing more than a little retail inventory and an empty attaché case. The word is the cops scooped the lion's share."

"That doesn't make a lot of sense," said Laura. "Think about it. An officer is lying there bleeding to death. There's chaos everywhere. And you think the cops got it together enough to make off with the drugs?"

"Chaos," said Felch, "is opportunity. In all the confusion, it wouldn't take a lot of sangfroid for a couple of cops to see to it an attaché case got emptied before it got inventoried. It was Carvalho who signed the inventory."

"That's pretty cynical," Matthew said.

"Hey, I'm just reporting what I hear. And I hear that's what Vu thinks, too. And what makes it so cynical? We're talking about a couple of cops who fabricated the grounds for a search warrant based on rumors from some small-time dealer. Then they went and perjured themselves to hide it. Is it such a big jump from that to glomming product?"

"Well, for one thing, Danny was no dealer," Matthew said, as he started eating. "He was a restaurateur."

"Oh, right," Felch said, obviously amused. "I suppose he read about the Tyler Street operation in the *Steam Table Weekly*."

"If you're a businessman in Chinatown, you hear things. That doesn't make him a dealer."

"Christ, Herman *Vu* is a restaurateur. He owns this place."

"Then why don't you ask *him* your questions?" Matthew was annoyed, but he wasn't sure if he was feeling protective of Danny or smothering his own niggling doubts.

"Why don't you ask him yourself," said Felch. "He's sitting at the table behind me."

Matthew shot a glance at the big table over Felch's shoulder.

Felch grabbed Matthew's wrist. "Easy, now! Don't be too obvious, OK? Laura said you guys wanted info on Vu and his organization. I figured I'd bring the mountain to Mohammed. This restaurant is where he holds court. He's the one in the yellow windbreaker."

Matthew picked him out among the men at the table. Herman Vu was younger than he expected. He seemed to be in his early forties, a normal-looking man without distinguishing features. He wore large glasses with clear plastic frames and his black hair was lightly dusted with gray. He sat, silent and unsmiling, among his more animated table companions. Matthew wasn't sure exactly what he had expected, a more sinister presence perhaps, but this man, in khakis and a Curry College sweatshirt, could have passed for one of the small merchants he had seen hawking vegetables from open crates in front of the stores on Beach Street.

"Looks like a suburbanite, doesn't he?" asked Felch, as if reading his thoughts. "That's because he is. Lives in Milton. Drives a minivan. On the books, he owns a couple restaurants, including this one. But that's the guy."

As Matthew watched, a young man approached the table and bent over to whisper to Vu. Vu cocked his head to one side as his listened, then turned his head slightly and stared at Matthew. So did the young man. The tiniest of smiles traversed Vu's features, and Matthew was suddenly stricken by certainty.

*He knows who I am.*

Morrissey?

Matthew felt chilled, transfixed by the man's gaze. There was nothing particularly striking about his eyes. They were not flat or dead or empty, like the eyes of psychopathic villains in popular novels. Vu's were ordinary; brown and alert, nothing more. And somehow that made them seem more frightening.

Then Vu said something to the young man, and the young man turned away and left the restaurant without another word. Vu broke eye contact and directed his attention to something said by the man sitting to his right. He did not look over at Matthew again.

"Eat up," said Felch as he dumped rice on his plate.

But Matthew had little appetite. When, a little later, he and Laura walked out of the dining room, he paused at the top of the stairs and peered into the windows of the Son Van Social Club across the street. As Felch had promised, the place was full, though the glimpse afforded did not enable him to identify their activities as gambling.

He started down the stairs and reached for Laura's hand. She angrily pulled away from his touch.

"Asshole," she said bitterly.

"What?" As if he didn't know. "I told him nothing that wasn't on the public record. Nothing he couldn't learn from a trip to the registry."

"Bullshit." She stepped through the door he held for her and strode out into Beach Street. "If you hadn't told him what you found in Lo Fat's files, he wouldn't even know to *look* in the registry."

Matthew considered this for a moment. "I guess that's right," he said, hurrying after her as she crossed Beach and headed east up the other side of the street. "But I was careful not to give him anything that's not available from public records. Plus I got him to promise not to act on it until and unless I give him the go-ahead. Don't you think he'll keep his promise?"

"Of course he'll keep his promise. Eddie takes care of his sources. You don't shit where you eat."

"Then what's the big deal?"

Laura stopped to face him, looking hard into his eyes. "The big deal. First, public or not, you revealed information you learned from the confidential files of a client, Lo Fat. Second, I watched you propitiate Ira's justified anger by assuring him Lo Fat could not be harmed by your having ransacked his files. It looks to me like you're doing all you can to harm him. And third—and most galling of all, *lover*—I withdrew from the fucking case so Ira could take some comfort in your assurances. Those assurances turned out to be pretty hollow. What a sap I was."

She started walking again and Matthew caught up with her in front of the pagoda arch that spanned Beach Street at the entrance to Chinatown. He grabbed her sleeve and she stopped, turning to face him again.

"Laura, you're right. I'm sorry. You said you got out of the case because it was boring, for Christ's sake."

Laura looked away in disgust. "Boy, are you dumb sometimes." She spun her gaze back at him. "I did it for *you*, asshole. So that you wouldn't spoil your relationship with

Ira over what I *thought* was a onetime lapse. I didn't know it was just your opening move."

Her voice trembled and Matthew saw the pain in her eyes.

"I'm sorry," he said softly. "I did not mean to hurt you. I just wanted to set things up with Eddie. If things work out I won't be telling him anything else about what I found in the files anyway."

Laura looked both bewildered and annoyed. "What are you *talking* about?"

"Eddie Felch is like a gun and I'm loading him up, is all. I don't expect I'll have to pull the trigger. I just want to point him at people."

"Can we, like, talk English here?"

"I have a plan. Sort of a plan, anyway. It's still taking shape. But to make it work, I have to be credible if I threaten to take the story to the press."

"A plan to do what?"

"To expose the guy who tipped Vu that my client was Danny."

Laura stared at him.

He didn't tell her about what he believed had just passed between Vu and him. He saw no point in frightening her— if she believed him. And that was a big if at the moment.

She walked off without him.

# 42

---•---

# The Wolf

•

He was already there when Raymond Carvalho sat up in bed with a start. The old man was squatting like a yogi on top of the radiator, his skinny silhouette backlit by the moonlight that streamed in through the bedroom window. Carvalho stared at him in horror, but the old man just snickered through his nose at his discomfiture.

"I was wondering when you'd wake up," he said, his chill voice an almost inaudible hiss but still utterly clear. "Dead to the world, you were."

The old man puffed on the stub of a reeking cigar and chuckled malevolently through a caul of purple smoke. He was ancient, a tiny brown-skinned man with mottled flesh stretched tight over an almost hairless skull like the hull of a coconut. He had pointy features to go with his worn pointy cowboy boots. Cross-legged, he held one of the curling toes in his lap as he rocked himself gently from side to side on the radiator. Even in the near darkness, Carvalho could pick up the cyanotic blue of his eyes.

"What's the matter?" the man leered at him. "Cat got your tongue? You, who's always so quick with the mouth?"

"Who are you?" Carvalho managed at last. "What do you want?"

The old man expelled another wheezing snicker. He stopped rocking. "How soon they forget! Or try to, anyway. But I'm still here, Raymond. What are we gonna do about that, huh?"

"What are you talking about?" Carvalho felt cold, chilled even, but he was afraid to gather the covers around himself. It seemed critical that he remain absolutely motionless.

"You're a piece of shit, Raymond! You know that. I know that. In fact, I'm here *because* you and I know that. So let's keep our cards right here on the table, OK?"

The old man took another drag and, showing visible pleasure, released a stream of dense cigar smoke toward the ceiling. He tapped the stogie against one of the radiator's cast-iron fins and knocked ash onto the floor.

"You'd like to forget that, wouldn't you, Raymond? You think if you don't look you won't see it, but that just means you only see it when you don't expect to. You with me here, shitheel?"

Bewildered, Carvalho shook his head. The old man seemed to find this gratifying.

"We're talking about the gobbet here, Raymond. Remember? That indigestible bite-sized mushy little stinking chunk of sour crap? The real you, pal. You can pretend you don't see it because it gets swept along in the slurry of all that other slop that you *think* is you. But you and me, buddy, we know the truth. We can see it. For us, it's like the sewer pipes are made of clear plastic and we can watch the turd get sucked along through them even if other people can't. You know what I'm talking about now, Raymond?"

Carvalho stared bleakly. The old man blinked, his irises a bruised purple, and watched him intently.

"The turd is growing, Raymond. It's filling out like a stripling. Putting on weight. Doing push-ups to build up its strength and endurance. You catch my drift here?"

Carvalho was trembling now but said nothing.

The old man ground out his cigar on the sole of his boot and dropped the remains on the floor. Carvalho heard a soft groan beside him. He flicked a panicked glance at Donna, lying next to him, and watched as she rolled away from him to face the wall. He turned back to the old man, who was smiling again. The old man nodded in the direction of Donna's sleeping form.

"Took another hostage, did you, Raymond? You worried I might wake the little lady? Not to worry. This is just between us boys."

A harsh laugh erupted from the old man, then disintegrated into a rheumy cough before dying away as a wheeze. "But enough horsing around, Raymond. What am I doing here? Haven't you figured it out, Raymond? Because you and I will be seeing a lot more of each other from now on. Like I said, the gobbet is swelling. Billowing. Burgeoning. Ballooning. Blowing itself up. And Raymond? I'M TALKING TO YOU, RAYMOND!" The old man's shout rang off the bedroom walls.

"Yes?" Carvalho said when he found his voice.

"Pretty soon that's all there'll be. All gobbet. Just pure shit. And you and me, we'll be together always."

"No," said Carvalho hoarsely. He tried to move but found he could only flail his arms. "No."

The old man cackled gleefully. Then he lifted the bedroom window effortlessly and crawled onto the sill. Looking back, he wiggled his eyebrows at Carvalho as if commending a crude joke and silently let himself tumble off the ledge into the darkness. Carvalho was left alone with the chilled moonlight and the stink of the old man's cigar.

"No," Carvalho whispered, wildly flinging his arms about in an effort to move, but he still could not budge his lower body.

"Ray? Ray!"

"No."

"Ray!" It was Donna, who was sitting up and staring at him, concern in her eyes. "What are you doing?"

He shook his head violently and looked around the room. By the light of the moon he could see that the window was closed now. He heard a click as Donna turned on the bedside lamp. Panic seized him again when he saw the ashes strewn across the floor on his side of the bed. But there were no cigar butts, just an overturned ashtray. He must have knocked it off his nightstand when struggling to move. He took a deep breath and looked over at Donna.

"Bad dream?" she asked with a smile.

"It wasn't a dream. At least, I don't think it was. Jesus, it was awful!"

"What was so awful?"

Carvalho made a shrugging gesture with his hands. "I don't know what to tell you. I mean, it was just this little old man sitting by the window, telling me what a piece of shit I am. Then he dropped out the window. I don't know what made it so scary. I don't even know if it was real."

"Well, I doubt it was real. The window's latched and it's four stories down. It had to be a dream."

Carvalho shook his head slowly. "I don't know. It was too real."

He reached over and plucked a cigarette from the pack on his nightstand and lit it. Donna pulled her head back out of the way as he exhaled his first drag.

Donna laid her hand on his arm. "You look terrified. Maybe it's because you're nervous about the trial."

"Christ," he said glumly. "Thanks for reminding me." He could feel his thoughts lurch from his night terror to the garish courtroom where they would lay him open like a bluefish. "I'm not looking forward to it, that's for sure."

"In a few days it'll be all over, Ray."

"I don't think so. The AG's holding fire and nobody knows what Internal Affairs will do with all this. It's a long way from over."

Donna was silent, stroking his arm.

"I go over it and over it in my head," he continued, "and I can't figure out how to play it. All the angles, I mean."

She pulled the covers more closely around her. "You don't have to play the angles, Ray. Just tell them the truth. Isn't that what you've done already?"

"The truth." Carvalho said with a grimace. He dragged deeply on his cigarette. "I don't think I even know how to do that anymore. People ask me questions, nothing questions, and I never give a straight answer. You know, questions like do I like Twinkies or *NYPD Blue*? And quicker than I can open my mouth I'm figuring out what answer to give them.

I don't even *wonder* if it's the fucking 'truth' or not. It never occurs to me. The wheels are turning and I'm calculating what they wanna hear or what I want from them. You know what I mean?"

Donna bit her lip. "I'm not quite sure. You mean it's about wanting people to like you? People pleasing?" She smiled at him. " 'Cause you always seem like you could care less."

"Nah, it's more than that." He looked gloomily out the moonlit window. "Like, there's this time when I was still married and I was watching a ball game or something and Rosa asked me if I put out the trash. It was supposed to be my job, putting out the trash. But I didn't. So she shouts to me from the other end of the house, did I take out the trash. I get up and pull the bag out of the can in the kitchen and throw it into the garage. I don't put it in the garbage can or anything. I just toss the bag in the garage and shut the door and go back to the tube. Then I told her I took out the trash. And in my mind, you know, I figured I had. But I hadn't. *That* was the 'truth.' But it wasn't until years later that I saw that."

Donna was frowning now. "OK, maybe you made mistakes. We all do. But you're not, like, a dishonest person or anything."

He turned to look at her. "You don't get it. I'm telling you, sometimes I don't know if I'm lying when I do it. I have to figure it out afterwards. You call that honest?"

Donna shifted her ground. "Maybe you're trying to do too much here. Forget about the truth. It makes you sound like a father confessor. All you have to do in court is tell them what happened."

"I can't even do that. I can't tell them everything that happened."

Donna's face assumed a puzzled expression. "I thought you already did. Or that Sal will if you don't. I don't see the problem."

"The problem—well, there's two problems. There's some stuff I can't tell them, stuff that has nothing to do with making up all that crap to get the warrant. Stuff that might get me in deeper shit than perjury."

Donna was silent. He could tell she was deliberately refraining from asking. He didn't want to tell her either.

"Is Sal in it, too—this other stuff?" she asked at last.

"Pretty much."

Donna was quiet again. Then she said, "You mentioned two problems. If that's problem number one, what's number two?"

Carvalho said, "Some of it I don't remember."

"Nobody expects you to remember everything."

"No," he said, his voice low. "You don't understand. I got no memory of some things. Zippo."

"Are you talking about the blackouts?"

Carvalho snapped his head around to stare at her.

"Don't look so surprised, Ray. You told me, remember? The day after we met and you couldn't remember who I was?" She smiled. "Or did you black *that* out, too?"

"No, I remember."

"Well, are you telling me you're not worried about them? They'd worry *me*."

"No," Carvalho said. "They worry me, too."

"It doesn't mean you're crazy or anything. It's not even all that weird. My first husband used to get them. The doctor said some people just get them when they drink. I guess it's pretty normal."

Carvalho considered what she said, then shook his head. "It's not just having dead spots," he said. "I had 'em for years and they never really bothered me. Not much, anyway. There's just this *one*. Where I don't know what happened."

"Which one?"

Carvalho slid past her question. "You ever see that movie *Wolf*? You know the one. Where Jack Nicholson gets bit by this wolf? It gives him all these superpowers, like a strong sense of smell, and he can, like, hear people whisper way across the room. Plus he stops being a wimp and starts getting in everybody's face, kicking ass, you know?"

"Like a wolf?" Donna was smiling.

"Yeah. Like a fucking wolf. The only trouble is he gets up one morning and finds a couple of bloody fingers in his coat pocket."

"Yucko. I'm glad I didn't see it."

"But wait. The thing is he can't remember what he did the

night before. No memory at all. He knows *something's* wrong. And then he hears about some girl he knows getting killed, her throat gets tore out or something, and he thinks it musta been him. So he starts chaining himself to the radiator at night."

"Was it him? Who killed the girl, I mean?"

"No. But that's not the point."

"What *is* the point?"

"The point," Carvalho said, "is I got a night like that, too. No memory. And some bad shit happened. Really bad." Carvalho paused. He didn't look at her. "What if it was me?" he asked.

Donna stared at him. "You find any fingers?" She showed a smile but it was unconvincing.

"Not quite," he said. "But close."

She was quiet again, then asked, "Do you wanna tell me? What you're afraid might have happened, I mean?"

"No," he said at once. "At least, I don't think so. Not yet anyway."

"No wonder you have nightmares." She lay back down.

Carvalho snorted. He stubbed out his cigarette.

"So what's the wolf, Ray? What bit you?"

Carvalho just shook his head, feigning confusion, but in his heart he knew what bit him.

# 43

## An Evasive Answer

With his office door shut, Matthew forced himself to look over the comments Rowell Falk had made on the first draft of the article they were writing together. Falk hadn't even asked for a draft. Calling upon his technical fluency, he had directly accessed a soft copy of Matthew's draft through the firm's computer network and printed out a draft for himself. It was characteristic of him to bull his way into a work in progress before an associate had put it into a form he deemed fit for presentation to a senior partner.

All the same, Matthew was astonished to discover how few comments there actually were. Either he was on the right track or Falk's understanding of criminal constitutional law was as superficial as he felt his own to be. And Falk, he knew, was superficial about nothing.

Matthew smiled at the specific revisions his boss had made. Some were nits, and some obviously expressed his notorious crotchets, but all, Matthew had to admit, were improvements. Aside from a general crack that most of his prose was "untranslated from the original academic," Falk seemed genuinely pleased with Matthew's efforts.

Despite this, however, Matthew found it hard to concentrate. Too much was going on that he had not absorbed. Laura was still angry with him about the business with Felch. She found his "plan" to use Felch next to ridiculous, and he had to admit to himself it wasn't much of a plan so far. Just a sense of direction, really. He hadn't even told her who the likely target of his suspicions was. So he couldn't blame her. He certainly had nothing to take to Felch, given the state of the evidence on which he was building his suspicions. And when he thought of broaching them to Ira, he felt the prickle of an anticipatory squirm at the derision he would most certainly endure.

Maybe if he tried to lay it out on paper? Yes. It might help to see it written down in black and white.

He set the draft article aside and positioned a clean yellow pad on the desk in front of him. Facing the blank page he fibrillated his pen between the rows of his teeth and considered where to start.

There was a sharp rap on the door. It swung open immediately and Ben Fleishman slipped smoothly into the room, his hand on the door handle. Fleishman arched his shaggy eyebrows inquisitively.

"We need to chat," Fleishman said softly. He quietly pushed the door shut behind him without looking, then folded his long frame into a chair in front of Matthew's desk.

It was a conversational prologue that normally would have set his feelers to quivering with apprehension, but Matthew felt unaccountably calm. He said nothing as Fleishman gave him a controlled half-smile.

"Matt," Fleishman said, "we need to get off the pot on this business with the Board of Bar Overseers."

Matthew eyed him levelly. "I didn't know we were on it."

"Well, we've been sitting here with bar counsel's offer to settle things with a public reprimand. She called me this morning to find out where we stand."

Matthew frowned. "I thought I was pretty clear about where I stand. Or sit."

Fleishman took a beat. Then he said, "The last I remember, you wanted to let them stew about it for a while. I think they're running out of patience, Matt. They're about to file a petition for discipline."

"I won't take a public reprimand," Matthew said, the words tumbling out of him. "I don't deserve it. Plus, I've done the research on the sanctions given out in similar situations, and I don't think they can get public discipline anyway. There's a good chance I'll get no discipline at all. So why should I settle for public discipline?"

Fleishman narrowed his eyes. "In how many of these cases you studied did the client end up dead?"

The comment would have crushed him earlier, but Matthew felt only fury now. Even so, he had to stifle an almost overwhelming urge to tell him—to shout out, in fact—that it might not have been his fault. But he did not mention his talk with Julie and how someone else had been looking for Danny before his arrest. He said nothing at all.

"Anyway," Fleishman continued, "that's your call. If you've got the stomach for a public hearing, at which all the gory details will be aired all over again, you're probably right to reject the deal. Are you sure that's what you want?"

"Why do I even have to decide that now? I got nothing to lose by letting them go ahead and file charges. It's just another warning shot, to scare me into caving in. But maybe, if my research is right, *they'll* fold when we get closer to the hearing date."

"That's going to take some pretty steady nerves, Matt. The charges will be public, and that could make it unpleasant— even if you win in the end."

"I've been through something of an annealing process lately," said Matthew dryly. "But I want to know something, Ben. I know you think I should take this deal but I—"

"Wait a minute, Matt," Fleishman said firmly, interrupting him. "I'm not trying to push you in any direction. I just want to explain the downside of all your options."

"But you *haven't*!" Matthew said, raising his voice as he struggled to contain his agitation. "You haven't told me the downside of taking a public reprimand."

Fleishman frowned. "Isn't that obvious?"

"No, it is not." Matthew had spoken himself into boldness.

"What about my career after a public reprimand? Like, would I be finished at D and C if that happened?"

Fleishman started to open his mouth, then shut it. "I'm not sure I can answer that, Matt."

"Why not? Or am I toast here anyway?"

"That's not my decision. You know the firm has a process that—"

"Oh, horseshit, Ben. You're the chairman of the department and the firm's star trial lawyer. Nobody brings in more business than you do, except maybe Falk. If you wanted it, it would be your decision."

Fleishman's nostrils quivered with suppressed anger. When he spoke his enunciation was crisp, almost staccato. "Let's get something clear. This is not a discussion about your partnership prospects. That's a decision for which the firm has a carefully designed deliberative process. Even before this unfortunate business with Danny, you were aware that you needed to overcome certain, well, *obstacles* if you were to have a future at D and C. I did not come in here to discuss whether the firm will make you a partner."

"I'm not asking you to do that. I just want to know what impact a public reprimand would have on my prospects. Isn't that a piece of data I should take into account in making this decision?"

"And I'm telling you I don't know the answer to your question. No one's ever had to face it here before."

"Maybe it doesn't matter. I mean, is all this your way of telling me the decision's already been made to dump me?"

Fleishman gave a sigh of exasperation and looked away. "No," he said when he turned back to look at Matthew. "Nobody's scheming to 'dump' you. I'm trying to get you to think of me as your legal counsel for a moment, not as your superior. You must focus on the bar discipline case."

"Well, I'm focused," said Matthew. "Give her an evasive answer. Tell her to go fuck herself."

Fleishman blinked, then grinned at him. "OK, Matt. I'll give them the word, though you'll forgive me if I'm a little less, uh, demotic. And by the way?"

Fleishman was standing now, his hands on the back of the chair.

"What?"

"How come you didn't show us this side before? What took you so long?"

*It has something to do with getting the holy shit kicked out of you,* he thought. But he only shrugged. He nodded as Fleishman took his leave, shutting the door behind him.

Matthew struggled to quell the riot of his feelings by taking deep breaths. He turned over in his mind the bits of his conversation with Fleishman as he tried to make sense of his roiling thoughts. He eventually succeeded in pulling a false calm over them. Willy-nilly, he found himself mulling over his vague suspicions once again.

Except they were stronger now. Nothing remotely conclusive, of course, but it just felt right. If Danny's murder was related to his holding a share of the profits of One Adams Place—in other words, if Danny was *not* killed because of Matthew's mistakes in Judge Doyle's courtroom—who else could be responsible for the leak? Everything seemed to point in one direction.

At Ben Fleishman.

He picked up his pen again and focused on the blank yellow pad. He would detail the evidence that pointed to Fleishman as the man who fingered Danny. On the first line he wrote, *Knew Danny's identity.*

As a member of the Management Committee, Fleishman was one of a tiny group of people who knew the identity of Matthew's client. Aside from the committee and Ira and Laura, no one else knew that Matthew's client was Danny. Fleishman knew. He had access.

Of course, others also had access elsewhere. Or might have gained access. The DA certainly knew, but what motive could DeMarco or others in the office have to expose their own witness? And why arrest him and go through the charade of opposing his release if they planned to leak the name? Furthermore, Danny had told them nothing, so they could not have known whether his testimony would have been helpful or harmful if he had lived to testify. Perhaps, if DeMarco thought his case was a sure loser, Danny's death would give him an unassailable excuse for losing it. But was that enough of a motive to collude in his murder? No. The leak couldn't have come from the DA.

The police? If there was an anonymous tip from inside the department, there might be others who knew or could ferret out the snitch's identity. For that matter, Carvalho and Piscatello probably knew all along. But if they did, why wait until his arrest? It wasn't as if Danny had been in hiding before then. They could have killed him anytime before then—before he might have implicated them in perjury and the falsification of a search warrant. But they waited. Why?

Or did they? Julie said Danny was being followed before he was arrested. Maybe it was the cops. Maybe they had decided to kill him but DeMarco's troopers scooped him up before they had the chance to get the job done. But that didn't make sense either. The only reason for Carvalho and Piscatello to kill Danny in the first place was to conceal their perjury. Why, then, would they come forward and admit the perjury *after* he was dead—when the risk of exposure had died with him? The most reasonable explanation was the one they gave: that they believed Chin was Dunleavy's killer and they didn't want Chin to get off scot-free. Carvalho and Piscatello just didn't make sense.

He supposed he shouldn't overlook the possibility that Vu's own network might have detected Danny's identity all by itself. Or Lo Fat himself. (And who, Matthew thought wryly, wouldn't savor the prospect of a killer with a name like Lo Fat.) But there was no evidence to suggest that had happened. If anything, the timing of Danny's murder—just two days after his release—suggested it was connected with his arrest.

Who did that leave? Dunleavy's family perhaps? Especially his brothers? As policemen they, too, might have had access to information from which they could deduce Danny's identity. They certainly had a motive: the fear that Danny's testimony might undermine the prosecution of the man they passionately believed had slain their brother. But they, like DeMarco, couldn't know whether Danny's testimony would help or harm the prosecution. Their participation seemed too farfetched.

No. He still felt an inner conviction that Danny's death

sprang from his connection to Adams Place, not to Dunleavy's murder or the world of drug dealing. He returned to his yellow pad. And Ben Fleishman.

Item two: *Didn't squawk about OA credit.*

Matthew dug into the file and extracted the photocopy he had received earlier in the week. After he and Ira had consulted the computer to establish that Fleishman was Danny's OA, Matthew had sought hard-copy confirmation from Central Files, which forwarded a copy of the index card for the Lotus Blossom case. The photocopy reproduced the two sides of the five-by-seven card. He examined the typewritten data appearing on the face of the card for what must have been the fifth or sixth time.

```
LI, DANNY                    No. 13287-101
21 Harrison Street           Dept.: Litigation
Apt. 413
Boston, MA 02116             Opened: 3/8/92
(617) 555-8721 (H)
(617) 555-9834 (W)


Mai Sum v. Danny Li, et al.
Civil Action No. 92-1354 (Middlesex Sup.)


         OA: BF
         RA: BF
```

The back of the card listed the names and addresses of other parties involved in the case: Mai Sum as an adverse party, the other co-owners as fellow clients of the firm, and the Lotus Blossom, Inc., as an interested party.

The card confirmed that Ben Fleishman was the originating attorney for the first case involving Danny, the dispute over ownership of the Lotus Blossom restaurant. That meant he was entitled to the OA credit on the new case Matthew opened, which translated into an extra share of the fees earned on the case. Yet when Matthew erroneously named himself as OA, Fleishman did not complain. Even Ira admitted it was not like Fleishman to miss a detail of financial significance like that. Matthew did not believe he had overlooked it. So why hadn't Fleishman squawked?

Matthew could think of only one reason. Fleishman did not want to draw attention to his association with Danny. As Lo Fat's lawyer, Fleishman would know about Danny's connection to the hotel project—and maybe even Vu's status as a silent partner. After all, wasn't it Fleishman who had told him in the very beginning that Danny was a referral from Lo Fat?

Then Fleishman saw Matthew's memo naming Danny as the missing witness in a notorious murder case. Bells must have gone off for him when he saw the memo, and the urge to warn Lo Fat that he had a drug informant as a business partner must have been more than he could resist. Did Fleishman suspect what would happen to Danny? Matthew didn't know. Maybe Fleishman knew Lo Fat would pass it on to Vu. Or maybe he thought Lo Fat would just find a way to ease Danny out of the ownership picture, like replacing him with another straw beneficiary. In any event, Fleishman would not want anyone to know that he had leaked the information. He couldn't cover his tracks completely because the firm's records named him as the original OA, but he could at least make sure he did nothing to call attention to himself. So he made no objection to Matthew's claim to be OA.

Matthew scribbled on his pad again.

*He set me up to be the goat.*

After Matthew had procured Danny's release on bail, the prudent course would have been to duck all queries from the media. That had been Ike Rosenthal's initial instinct, and he had been right. The firm should have avoided the press entirely and declined comment when it could not. It was Fleishman who insisted they trade on the notoriety of the case to cultivate favorable publicity for the firm. And it was Fleishman who suggested that Matthew be the one to field inquiries. Like a lamb to the wolves. Or a goat.

Matthew grimly recalled Ira's jibe about how Fleishman's

plan would narrow the number of targets to one—and the look of annoyance Fleishman gave him at the time. Fleishman must have known that Matthew, who was inexperienced in such matters, would be in over his head. And that he might give away more than he should. Then, if Matthew screwed it up and something happened to Danny, accusing fingers would point at Matthew, not Fleishman. In fact, Matthew did get snookered, in his very first conversation with Eddie Felch. It was only fortuitous that Felch chose not to print what he had gleaned from the conversation.

And how did Fleishman respond when Danny got killed? *He booted me off the Felter case.*

Why? Matthew had assumed it was because he didn't want his Chinese client to be embarrassed by an association with him, especially after the public lambasting he took from Judge Doyle and DeMarco. But if Fleishman was the one who had leaked Danny's identity, he would have had an even better reason to want him off the case: he did not want Matthew to discover Danny's involvement in the hotel project. That discovery might engender the very suspicions Matthew was now entertaining.

Someone (Fleishman? Lo Fat?) had obviously picked through Lo Fat's files in an effort to remove all traces of Danny's role, but you could never be sure you had pulled everything. Fleishman needed to cut off Matthew's access to the files entirely. So he seized on Matthew's relationship with Laura as an excuse to dump him from the case. A conflict of interest.

It was kind of ironic, when you thought about it. It was Fleishman, not Matthew, who had the telling conflict of interest. As a member of the firm, Fleishman had an ethical obligation to maintain Danny's most vital secret—his identity. Yet he also had a competing obligation zealously to protect another client, Lo Fat, who would have been anxious to learn that Danny, his business partner in a secret and probably illegal transaction, happened to be a police informant and, so far as Ben knew, a drug addict to boot. But, ethically, Fleishman could not tell him. It was a classic conflict. No matter what he did, one of the clients could be injured. Matthew wondered if Fleishman had ever thought of it that way.

In any event, he pulled Matthew off the case. And, just to be safe, he set up a Chinese wall to put the files completely out of his reach. Under lock and key. Without even advising Matthew of the fact.

As it turned out, Fleishman's fears had been well grounded. Despite all his precautions, someone overlooked that innocuous-looking schedule of beneficiaries that Ellen Stritch unearthed from a folder of extra copies. She had brought it to Matthew. And that had set Matthew off on the hunt to learn Danny's role in the project.

And now?

*He's trying to maneuver me out of D and C.*

Matthew underlined the sentence as he thought back over his talk with Fleishman a few minutes earlier. Fleishman's equivocations left him convinced that Ira was right: a public reprimand by the Board of Bar Overseers would finish him at the firm. Yet Fleishman clearly wanted him—was pressing him even, he could feel it—to take the reprimand. *He wants me out,* he thought. *Out of harm's way.*

Matthew picked up the pad and leaned back in his chair as he looked over what he had written.

It was even worse in black and white. He was right not to present his theory to Ira. It was pathetic. A chain of tenuous inferences linked by speculation. And conditioned on two premises he could not prove: that Danny held an interest in One Adams Place (probable) and that he was killed because of it (pure supposition, supported only by Julie's recollection and powered by his own guilt-driven wish that it be so).

Yet something even more vital was missing from the "evidence" he had cataloged. Beneath his list Matthew wrote, *MOTIVE?* In block capitals, pressing hard with the felt pen. The word seemed to stare back at him accusingly. A credible motive, if he had one, might soak into the fissures of his theory and bind its friable fragments into a solid structure. But Matthew could discern no motive. Certainly nothing strong enough to drive Fleishman to act as an accomplice to murder. Or even, to put the best possible gloss on his actions, to jeopardize Danny's safety by warning Lo Fat about him.

But nothing came to mind. He could think of no reason why Benjamin Fleishman, a secure and respected professional in (as Ira liked to put it) the filet mignon of his career, should want to soil his hands by revealing Danny's identity. No doubt he and Lo Fat went back a long way and a certain fraternity of interest must have developed between them, but Matthew could not imagine an interest sufficient to drive someone like Fleishman to finger Danny.

It just didn't make sense.

Matthew circled the word and laid his pen down on the pad.

He needed a motive.

What he got, however, was a phone call. It was Central Files.

"Mr. Boer?" The voice was sharp, to the point. The Venerable Beadle.

"Yes, Mrs. Beadle," he said.

"Last week I sent you some conflicts material on a case and you called back with a request for a copy of the original new case form," she reminded him. "It was *Mai Sum v. Danny Li, et al.* Matter number—"

"Yes," Matthew interrupted her. "I remember."

"Well," she said, and she hesitated, her tone taking on a timbre that was uncharacteristically tentative. "I don't seem to have it. The new case form, I mean. It's gone."

"Gone?"

"Yes. It's missing from the file drawer. I can't understand how this could have happened." She seemed genuinely disturbed by the break in her records.

"Is there only one copy kept? I mean, you don't keep another copy somewhere?"

"No. The information is entered immediately into the data bank and then incorporated into the weekly new case report for distribution to all lawyers, but no one keeps copies of those. We don't either."

Matthew was frowning now. "So no one has an original record of the opening of the case?"

"Well, I suppose Mr. Fleishman might have kept his copy of the report when he filed it. You could ask him for a copy. And a copy would also have gone to the department chair."

Yeah, right. Same guy. Fleishman was also the chairman of the litigation department.

"But," Mrs. Beadle continued, "the data is still good. For conflicts-checking purposes, I am confident you may rely on the computer data and the index cards I sent you last week. The information on them was taken directly from the new case form when it was first received."

There was a pause, and Matthew realized that Mrs. Beadle—Mrs. Beadle!—was seeking assurance. He supplied it.

"I'm sure I can," he said.

It was an evasive answer.

# 44

---

# Courtroom 506

As she had during the first four days of trial, Sarah Kerlinsky made sure she was the first person to enter Courtroom 506. The fifth day in the trial of Michael Chin for the murder of Francis Dunleavy was not scheduled to start until nine-thirty, but Sarah (after inquiring knowledgeably about the family of the officer stationed at the courthouse doors) had gained admission before the building was open for business. By the time she made her way to the battered oak defense table, the one closest to the jury box, resumption of the festivities was still more than an hour away.

Sarah dropped her burden on the table and lowered herself into the straight-backed wooden chair. She laid her hands, palms down, on the worn surface of the table and looked around her. Like returning, she thought, to the comfortable old parlor of a favorite aunt.

Nothing had changed, of course. Little natural light penetrated the grimy glass in the big mullioned windows to her left. The carpet, some dark beige color originally, was as depressing as ever, and the bruised wooden furniture—desks, chairs, benches like pews—were mute testimony to the state's curious indifference to its once magnificent court-houses. Well, maybe not so curious, she thought. There weren't many votes in boosting appropriations for courthouse maintenance.

The only object in the room that radiated something of the ritual majesty she had once ascribed to the administration of justice was the judge's bench itself. It was fifteen feet long, an elevated console like a burnished mahogany bar, soon to be lit discreetly by the two green-shaded gooseneck lamps deployed on its surface. There was a shelf full of tawny law books behind it—purely for show, of course—while drooping American and Massachusetts flags flanked the judge's chair like fagged-out sentries.

Just in front of the bench but still above floor level were the clerk's table and, to the judge's right, the stenographer's station. The witness stand, a small dais surmounted by a wooden chair indistinguishable from the one Sarah sat in, was tucked into the corner off to the judge's right, equidistant from the stenographer and the jury box.

Just the way it should be, Sarah thought. Once again, she was struck by the diminutive scale of the courtroom. Given the momentous stakes of a murder trial, and the rocking, sometimes ferocious drama that accompanied it, she was always taken aback by the puny stage on which the shabby pageantry of American justice was played out. It reminded her of that replica of the *Mayflower*—so absurdly tiny and claustrophobic it was almost impossible to imagine it bob-bing its way across the turbulent Atlantic, packed with so many people and so much hope and terror and history. Court-room 506 seemed just like that.

With a logic she didn't begin to understand, her thoughts sidled from those frightened seafarers to her own family. She had spent a precious hour with the girls the night before, but she had neglected them terribly over the past two weeks. It was always like this when she was on trial—she knew that and so did they—but it gnawed at her anyway. Rebecca had been tearful and clingy when she left, and it was all she could do to get a good-bye out of Leah over the drone of the video that held her captive. It was, she admitted, no way to raise a family. Yet she could not imagine a life for herself that did not involve doing pitched battle with bullying men between dreary, piss-yellow walls like these. Maybe, when it was all over, she could use part of the hefty fee she was earning to take the girls someplace special. Sedona, maybe. Or Santa Fe.

But damn it, it *was* going well. The testimony of the three men arrested with Michael had been far from devastating, thanks in large measure to their poor command of English. On cross-examination she had succeeded in bringing out the lurid details of their criminal records, DeMarco's promises not to prosecute, and the contradictions that riddled their testimony. She had also elicited their acknowledgment that John, the mystery man IT had described as dealing out of the apartment, did in fact exist.

Michael's cellmate, to whom he was supposed to have bragged about doing the shooting, had proven himself to be grubby and pathetic, a transparent fraud. She had only to make the jury take a good look at Michael—tiny, terrified, and possessing little English—to drive home how preposterous it was that he would have made such a boast to the hulking Hispanic thug on the stand.

The forensic evidence she had treated dismissively. She didn't really have a quarrel with the ballistics. Let them have the gun as the murder weapon; the only way to tie it to Michael was through Jerry's unsavory witnesses. And she had wrung a useful concession out of that technician from the state lab. When he tried to pooh-pooh the negative results of Michael's gunpowder residue test after his arrest, she'd made him look like a vacillating fool by rubbing his face in his own testimony from prior cases in which he had championed the reliability of the test. As a result, she felt convinced, the jury had not missed the significance of the department's failure to detect traces of gunpowder on Michael's hands.

Today they would return to the wonderland of IT and Danny Li. To Raymond Carvalho and his sidekicks. Not to mention Danny's girlfriend, Julie Soo, who Jerry hoped would shore up his claim that IT never existed. After that, Jerry would rest. And she would, too, without putting on a defense. She would not put Michael on the stand.

She started to unpack her litigation bag, carefully opening the three-ring trial notebook she and her intern had prepared. Then she set up her laptop, plugging the AC adapter into the extension cord that had been duct-taped to the carpet beneath the table. A recent acquisition paid for out of her retainer, the computer gave her "real-time" access to what the stenographer keyed in, allowing Sarah to view on the screen the transcript of a witness's testimony almost as it was spoken. When she had the computer up, she turned back to the three-ring binder for a last run through her cross.

Forty minutes later the rear doors opened and Philip O'Gara, the bailiff, entered. A slight, birdlike young man in thick glasses, he had often prompted Sarah to wonder how he could ever quell a physical disturbance in the courtroom. Sarah was still greeting him when she noticed that Matthew Boer had followed him in. Matthew hung back, smiling uncomfortably from the first pew beyond the rail, until O'Gara moved off to go about his chores.

Sarah smiled back at Matthew. "Good morning," she said. She heard a click and one of the gooseneck lamps spilled creamy light across the bench.

"I hope I'm not intruding. I wanted to be sure to get a good seat."

"Not at all, Matt," she said. "I hadn't noticed you here before. Have you been watching the whole time?"

"No," he said. "I just wanted to see the part about Danny. Right now, the rest of it seems a bit—I guess you could say *remote*." He smiled shyly.

Sarah smiled back and bit her tongue. He looked different somehow, and it took her a moment to identify the change. It was his eyes. They had seemed frightened when she last saw him, while they waited for the elevator after Danny's bail hearing. Now they looked positively haunted, cradled by dark half-moons. *His client's death must be eating him up,* she thought, and her heart went out to him.

"I'm sorry for what happened," she said. "You took a lot of undeserved abuse for the job you did."

"Thank you," he said, his lips pulled back tight against his lips. "As a matter of fact, I wanted to talk to you about that business. About some odd things I've stumbled across." He smiled again, adding, "When you get some time."

"No. Not now, Matt. After the trial. I've got nothing for you now."

He looked puzzled and she wanted to help, to tell him what she knew. It would give him some relief, she knew, but this was not the time—if ever. Right now, she had Michael to worry about.

"We'll have lunch," she said. "I promise. Right after I get my NG."

Matthew's smile broadened a bit. "What if it's not an acquittal?"

"It will be." She was not smiling.

Then she deftly extricated herself from the conversation and returned to her work. She had barely picked up where she had left off when the doors burst open again and Jerry DeMarco strode in. He was trailed, as he had been since the trial started, by a coterie of reporters. Sarah closed the binder and sat back to wait for the show to begin.

"Julie Soo," she answered.

"And where do you reside?"

"At twenty-one Harrison Street."

Jerry DeMarco smiled brightly at her from the lectern set up just in front of the counsel tables. "That sounds like a familiar address," he said, looking over at the jury. "Danny Li also lived at that address, did he not?"

"Yes," said Julie. Her eyes, unwavering, stayed level with his. "Danny and I lived together. He was my boyfriend."

"I'm sorry for your loss," DeMarco said gently.

*Smarmy,* thought Matthew. But it was Julie who held his attention. From the moment she walked to the witness stand, he couldn't get over the change in her. She was wearing makeup now, and a crisp white blouse above a pleated black skirt. She appeared fresh and alert. Very present. No snuffling, no runny nose. Had they put her through rehab or what?

"Do you work, Ms. Soo?"

"Of course," said Julie, her eyes narrowing slightly. "I work at the Nankin."

"That's the big restaurant at the foot of Beach Street? Near the arch?"

"Yes. I am a hostess."

DeMarco shoved his left hand in his jacket pocket, his thumb protruding. "Ms. Soo, I'm afraid I have to ask you a few questions about Danny. OK?"

"Yes." She pulled herself into a more erect position, cocking her head slightly to her right. She looked very alert.

"Did Danny ever discuss his dealings with the police?"

Sarah was on her feet. "Your Honor, I'm going to have to object to any hearsay about what Danny may have told her."

DeMarco said, "Your Honor, I—"

"Overruled," Judge Doyle interrupted.

DeMarco looked back at his witness. "Ms. Soo?"

"Yes, he did."

"Tell the jury what you know."

Julie paused a moment before proceeding. Then she took them briskly through the story of Danny's arrest by a policeman he called Fran. And how he had been pressured into supplying information in exchange for dismissal of the charges. Sarah raised more hearsay objections, but Judge Doyle consistently overruled them. DeMarco then had Julie describe two meetings she had observed between Danny and Dunleavy, including one in which the detective had been introduced to her. Both meetings—she recalled the dates with precision—took place during the week before the shooting.

But, again, it wasn't the substance of her testimony that held Matthew's interest. He was transfixed by her new manner. Most curious of all, there was none of the stumbling diction and pidgin English he recalled hearing her use. Her English was better than Danny's had been. What was going on here?

DeMarco asked, "What kind of information did the police want, did Danny say?"

Sarah didn't bother to stand up this time. "I reiterate my objection, Your Honor."

"Noted and overruled," said Judge Doyle.

"What kind of information?" DeMarco prodded.

"About drugs."

"To your knowledge, did Danny have access to that kind of information?"

For the first time Julie cast her eyes down toward the floor. "Yes," she said quietly.

DeMarco looked in the direction of the jury, then back at the witness. "I'm sorry we had to put you through all this painful business again. To remind you of it all."

*Covering his ass with the jury,* thought Matthew.

"Everything reminds me," she said, looking up sharply, bitterness in her voice. "The apartment, Chinatown, everything." She seemed suddenly to be on the verge of losing her composure.

"I'm sure," DeMarco said soothingly. "Thank you. That's all I have for now, Your Honor."

Sarah stood up and walked slowly to the lectern as DeMarco beat a hasty retreat to his own seat. She laid her notebook on the lectern and raised her eyes to look at the witness.

"What will you do now, Ms. Soo?" she asked softly. "You sound as if the city is full of painful memories."

*Starting compassionately,* thought Matthew. Where DeMarco left off.

"It is. When this is finished, I will go to Montreal. My sister lives there."

"I can understand why you might feel that way. So let's see if we can get through this quickly. Now, you mentioned you saw Danny with Detective Dunleavy on two occasions before he was killed. Was any other policeman besides Dunleavy present at these meetings?"

"No."

"Did Danny ever mention meeting with other policemen?"

Julie paused again. "Ever?" she asked.

It was Sarah's turn to pause. Then she said, "Well, let's start with the two weeks preceding the murder."

"Which murder?" Julie asked, with stark directness.

"I'm sorry. I meant Detective Dunleavy's murder."

"No. He didn't mention other policemen then."

A silence took possession of the courtroom. Matthew

could almost hear Sarah thinking furiously as she pondered whether to ask the next question.

She risked it. "What about *after* Dunleavy's murder?" she asked.

"Well, I—I'm not sure. I mean, Danny wasn't sure."

"Yes?" Sarah urged.

"One night Danny told me some men were following him."

"When was this?" Sarah glanced quickly over her right shoulder at DeMarco, as if anticipating an objection, but he remained motionless, staring straight ahead at the witness.

"The night before they took him away." Her voice trailed off in a diminuendo, forcing everyone to crane forward to hear her. "He sneaked out the back door of a restaurant and got away from them. I asked him who they were, but he said he didn't know for sure. He said he thought they might be policemen."

There was still no objection from DeMarco, and Matthew noticed that even Judge Doyle was eyeing the prosecutor quizzically.

Sarah proceeded. "And the next day he was killed?"

"No," said Julie, shaking her head. "It wasn't the night before he was killed. I didn't mean that. It was the night before they arrested him."

Silence descended once again, but not for long.

DeMarco finally heaved himself to his feet. "I really should object to this line of questioning," he said mildly. "It's all secondhand speculation."

"I was wondering when you'd get around to it," said the judge. "Your objection is sustained." He turned toward the jury box. "The jury are instructed to disregard all testimony relating to Mr. Li's unsubstantiated suspicions about being followed. Especially as to the identity of those he might have thought were pursuing him. There is no foundation, only speculation, for those suspicions." He eyed Sarah. "Does the defense have any further questions of this witness?"

"I'm finished, Your Honor."

"Did Frannie tell you why he couldn't get the warrant himself?"

"Not in so many words," Raymond Carvalho answered. "He just said he didn't want to go out again. I got the impression he wanted to stay home." He didn't elaborate. *No point,* Carvalho thought, *making the widow look like a nag.*

DeMarco clasped the lectern with both hands and tilted his body forward a little. "What did you do next?"

"I took the stuff he gave me—'cause I wrote it down during the call—and used it to write up the affidavit. I just plugged it into my standard search warrant affidavit. And we got to Hal—that's Hal Moylan, the clerk-magistrate—and he issued the warrant that afternoon."

"And you named IT as the source for the information?"

"Yes."

"As you had done many times before?"

Carvalho shifted his rear end in the chair. Fifteen minutes on the stand and he felt stiff already. "That's right," he said.

"In pretrial proceedings before this court you defended the truth of the allegations made in your affidavit, didn't you?"

"Yes, I did. I was scared, I guess. I mean, I'd made a false affidavit and I figured I'd be in the deep stuff if I admitted to it."

"And what did you do when the judge here ordered you to produce your informant?"

"Well, I couldn't produce somebody who didn't exist. So I pretended to look for him."

"For IT."

"Yeah. Me and Sal. Detective Piscatello, I mean."

"Detective Carvalho, does IT exist?"

"No, sir, he does not."

"Did you know the identity of Detective Dunleavy's informant, the real snitch?"

"When I did the affidavit? No, sir, I did not."

"Well, when *did* you learn that his informant was Danny Li?"

"Objection," said Sarah, without lifting her head from her note-taking.

"Sustained," said Judge Doyle.

DeMarco said, "Let me rephrase the question. When did you come to believe that Danny Li was the source of the information you received from Frannie?"

"It was after the judge dismissed the case."

"This case, you mean? The indictment against Michael Chin?"

"Yes. That's when I figured it out, like I told you. From checking Frannie's arrest files."

"What, if anything, did you do with that information?"

"What do you mean? Do what?"

DeMarco was frowning at him now. "Please, Detective. Piscatello testified on this subject while you were sequestered. The jury has already heard his version of what the two of you did with the information. So let me ask the question once again. What did you do when you discovered Danny's identity?"

There it was. Problem number one, right out there. *Thanks for the warning, Sal,* he thought bitterly.

"I went looking for him. Sal and I both did."

"Did you find him?"

"Yeah, that was easy. We just hung out around his apartment. But we never actually got to talk to him. We saw him once, but he lost us. He was scared, I guess."

"When was that—that you saw him, I mean?"

"It was Thursday, the night before your guys picked him up. That was the only time I saw him."

"Why were you looking for him? Had you decided, finally, to bring him in?"

"No, sir. Not then. I wish I could say that, but it's not true."

"Then what was your objective?"

"My objective, to be honest with you, was to cover my butt. I wanted to convince him to keep his mouth shut. Maybe get out of town for a while."

"How did you propose to accomplish that—to convince him?"

"To scare him, I guess." Carvalho looked down at his feet as he spoke.

DeMarco leaned forward again and twisted his head toward the jury, all of whom were peering intently at Carvalho. "You knew at the time, did you not, that if Danny was not located, the murder case against Michael Chin, the man you were convinced had killed your partner, might never go to trial?"

Carvalho didn't answer for a moment. Then he raised his head and looked in the direction of the jury. "I did. I'm not proud of it, but at the time I was more interested in saving my own bacon than doing right by Frannie."

DeMarco allowed this to hang in the air for a while before asking, "So what changed your mind? Why come forward now?"

"Well, after we heard the snitch was dead, Sal and me, we just started talking about how rotten it was. Him"—he motioned toward Michael Chin, sitting at the table next to Sarah—"just walking away after doing Frannie. Sal, especially, was pretty tore up about Doreen and how she must be feeling, and I figured—"

"That's Doreen Dunleavy, Frannie's wife?" DeMarco turned back toward the rail and heads spun to take in the stolid woman who watched the proceedings from the first row.

"Yeah. Sal would talk about her and how rough it was for her. And then, me, I'd get to thinking about Frannie and all, how—he was more than just a partner, you know. He was my best friend. And here I am, helping his killer get off so I wouldn't have to take my lumps."

Sarah said, "Objection."

Judge Doyle was slow in responding. "Overruled," he said. "I'm sure the jury members appreciate that they, not the witness, will determine whether the defendant slew Detective Dunleavy."

"OK," said Carvalho, looking up at the judge. "But I know what I know. The fact is, I figured I couldn't live with myself if I didn't come forward and tell the truth."

"Now, Detective, you face possible criminal charges yourself for your conduct in this proceeding, isn't that right?"

"That's what they tell me."

"Has anyone made any promises regarding those charges in exchange for your testimony here today?"

"No, sir."

"No offers of immunity or reduced charges—nothing like that?"

"Zilch. In fact, I was told no one would even talk about my, uh, fate till this is all over."

" 'This' being the trial of Michael Chin?"

"Right."

"So as far as your future is concerned, nothing depends on the results of this trial?"

Sarah's weary objection was immediately sustained.

"Let me put it this way," said Carvalho. "Lying is what got me in trouble and the only thing that can help me out now is telling the truth."

"Your witness," said DeMarco.

Sarah was quick to begin her cross. "The truth, Detective?" she asked while still on her way to the lectern. Her voice was soft, dripping disappointment. "Let's take a look at how you've championed the 'truth' in this case. Before today, at least, wouldn't it be fair to say you've had little more than a nodding acquaintance with the truth?"

"Uh, Your Honor—" DeMarco began.

"Forget it," Judge Doyle snapped at him.

"I'd have to admit that's a pretty fair statement," said Carvalho. "Like I said, it's not something I'm very proud of."

"I suppose we should be grateful for that, at least," Sarah responded. "You told us IT was your snitch, but now you tell us that was a lie. Right?"

"Yes."

"A lie made under oath."

"Yes."

"And when you said IT existed, that was a lie?"

"Yes, it was."

"But now you're telling the truth."

"That's right. He never existed."

"So you say. Now, how much of the information you put into IT's mouth was true?"

Carvalho wrinkled his brows uncertainly. "I'm not sure what you mean?"

"Well, you want us to believe that IT never existed. That the real source for your information was Detective Dunleavy, who you believe got it from Danny Li. Did you invent the information itself or just the source for the information?"

"Just the source. Like I said, the information I put in

there—in the affidavit—was true. I mean, it was what Frannie told me."

"And that would include your description of John, the dealer who lived and distributed drugs out of the apartment?"

"Yes, that's how Frannie described him."

"So you're not suggesting that John never existed, are you?"

"No. He existed. Frannie told me about him."

"But you don't know where John is, am I right?"

"That's right."

"And you had no reason to believe, when you applied for the warrant, that Frannie's snitch was wrong about John living and working out of the apartment, did you?"

"No, I did not."

"In fact, it would be fair to say, would it not, that you expected to find him there when you raided the apartment?"

"Yes, we expected to find him there."

Sarah consulted her notes silently for a time, allowing the significance of this to tell on the jury. Then she lifted her head and addressed Carvalho again.

"Now, back to the business of the affidavit. You've testified that you and Detective Piscatello concocted a sham search to find IT after Judge Doyle ordered you to produce him. Do I have that right?"

"Yes."

"And you both lied, under oath, to Judge Doyle right here in this very courtroom, about that 'search'?" She spread her arms to sweep her surroundings into the ambit of her question.

"Yes, we did."

"By the way, the two of you put in for and were paid overtime for your heroic efforts to find IT, didn't you?"

"Yes."

"Now, as I understand your testimony, you found a way to divine that somebody named Danny Li might be a problem for you."

"I figured out he had to be Frannie's snitch."

"So you say." Sarah sounded far from convinced. "But we can agree, can we not, that you saw him as someone whose testimony might harm you?"

"Yes, ma'am. You could say that."

"What were you planning to do when you caught up with him?"

"Like I said, I just wanted to scare him off. To keep him out of it."

"Oh, we heard that," she said, her right arm hanging over the lectern as she watched the jury now. "I mean, what exactly were you going to *do?*"

Carvalho frowned. "I don't follow," he said.

"Well, *how* did you expect to scare him off? Threaten to beat him up?"

"No," Carvalho said angrily. "I don't operate that way." And shooting a glance at the jury, he regretted it immediately. Most of them stared stonily back at him and one member, a middle-aged white woman, looked away in unmistakable disgust.

"Don't you, now?" Sarah asked, taunting him, but she didn't pursue it. "What else did you have to scare him with?"

"He was a snitch and a junkie. All it would take was a couple cops at his door."

"But threatening to do what? Harass him? To use your position as a police officer to make his life more miserable?"

Carvalho froze for a time, uncertain how to respond. Then he said, "You wouldn't have to say anything like that. Just show up and give him the word."

"You know, Detective," Sarah said, "I don't doubt that for a minute."

She stood there with her hands on her hips like one of the tough nuns he remembered from Saint Anthony's, and the hush that followed her remark was excruciating. It was eventually broken by the sound of DeMarco's pen hitting the floor. As he bent over to pick it up, Carvalho saw Sarah catch the judge's eye as they exchanged fleeting smiles at De-Marco's efforts to distract the jury.

"So let's take stock here," she said, ticking each item off on her fingers. "We got lies. Perjury. Fraudulent overtime claims. Intimidating witnesses. Abuse of power. That's not a pretty picture, is it, sir?"

Carvalho looked straight back at her. "No, it isn't," he acknowledged.

"And yet you want us to believe that you were finally stricken by a bad conscience. That you came forward with the 'truth' at last, to tell us about Danny's role—but only *after* his murder, when he wasn't around to contradict you. Have I got that straight, Officer?"

"Objection," said DeMarco, sounding disgusted.

"Save it for argument, Ms. Kerlinsky," said Judge Doyle. He examined his watch. "It's crowding four. Are you almost finished or should we stop for the day?"

"Just a few more, Your Honor." She turned back to Carvalho. "On the night Detective Dunleavy was killed, there were four of you who participated in the raid, is that right?"

"Yes."

"And you and Dunleavy and Piscatello were all positioned outside the door to the third-floor apartment from which the shots were fired. Wasn't that your testimony?"

"Yes," Carvalho said wearily. "And Kelleher was out in the alley covering the fire escape."

"Good. We can skip my next question. But explain something to me, will you? Doesn't that mean there was no one watching the door to the *second*-floor apartment where you found the gun and the four men you arrested, including the defendant, Michael Chin?"

"I said earlier, we didn't know about the second-floor apartment."

"I didn't ask you if you knew about the apartment. I asked if there was anybody stationed in front of its door. So let me ask again. Was there?"

"No."

"So there was nothing to stop the people in the second-floor apartment from just sashaying right out the door and disappearing?"

"Except they didn't. They were all there waiting for us when we came down the fire escape."

"But you don't know that, do you?"

"Yes, I do. I was there when they were arrested."

"No. I mean you would have no way of knowing if anyone had walked out that door before you got there, would you?"

Carvalho shrugged. "No, I guess I wouldn't. But why—"

"Thank you, Detective," she said, moving on briskly.

"You've answered my question. By the way, were you aware that Detective Kelleher testified this morning?"

"Marty?" Carvalho was surprised.

"That's the fellow. Detective Kelleher told us about a meeting that took place in a restaurant called"—she peered down at her notes—"the Blue Diner just before the raid in which Detective Dunleavy was killed. Do you recall attending such a meeting?"

Carvalho shrugged. "I was there. I don't know if you could call it a meeting."

"Well, Detective Kelleher described it as a last-minute planning session for the raid. And that you were in charge. Does that sound right to you?"

"I guess so. I was the senior officer."

"Isn't it true, Detective, that you told the other officers at that meeting that you expected to seize a very large quantity of drugs in the Tyler Street raid?"

"I probably said something like that, yeah."

"Enough, you said, to convince the people you arrested to turn on those higher up on the food chain?"

"That was my hope, yes. Based on the information I had."

"What information?"

"From Frannie. Which he got from his snitch."

"But you did not report such a seizure, did you?"

"We didn't get a big haul, no. We got about what you'd expect in a small retail operation like that."

"But what about the big shipment you told Kelleher about?"

"It often happens that way. You gotta remember: snitches are like used-car salesmen. They're always promising more than they can deliver. That's how they keep your interest."

"Do you recall telling Detective Kelleher and the others, that night in the diner, that you were awaiting word that a major delivery had been made at the location you planned to raid?"

"Yeah. Something like that. We were hoping for a big drop. But—"

She cut him off. "And isn't it true that you received an electronic page when you were at the Blue Diner?"

"I remember Frannie did. He went and called some guy."

"And Frannie reported what?"

"I don't remember what he said. The drift was everything was go."

" 'Everything' being the raid?"

"Yes."

"And wasn't the phone call the 'word' you said you were waiting for?"

"Yeah."

"That the 'big drop,' as you called it, had been made?"

"That's what I thought, yeah."

"And you were so excited by this news, you left immediately for Chinatown."

"Sure."

"But in fact the big drop had *not* been made, is that what you're telling us?"

"Well, we didn't find a suitcase full of dope, if that's what you mean."

"But you did find such a case, did you not?"

Carvalho cocked his head warily to one side. "I don't remember anything like that."

"Would you like to see the inventory you prepared after the raid? Because you described just such a case." She brandished a sheet of paper in her hand. "Would that refresh your recollection?"

"You talking about the briefcase? Yeah, I remember that. It's not what I'd call a suitcase. We found one in the apartment. It was empty."

"Who assisted you in doing your inventory of the apartment?"

"Assisted me? Nobody. It's a one-man job."

"So no one else was present when you took possession of the case?"

"What are you talkin' about? There was a roomful of guys there. An officer was down. You could hardly turn around in there."

"And everyone was very busy?"

"Yeah, they were. All over the place."

"Did you open it there, with the others around you?"

"No. I couldn't. It was locked. I needed a hammer and chisel to get it open when I got back to the station."

"Who transported the briefcase to police headquarters?"

"I did."

"Alone?"

"No. Sal was with me."

"Was he with you when you opened it?"

"I don't remember." Carvalho pulled up short. "What are you inferring? That I ripped off some dope?" He could hear his voice rising with his anger.

"The jury does the inferring, Detective. I just ask questions. Now, Detective Kelleher wasn't present during the inventory, was he?"

"No," he said scornfully. "For all I know he was still out in the alley waiting to see if anybody came out the back."

Sarah went right after his sarcasm. "You and Martin Kelleher are not exactly on the best of terms, are you, Detective?"

"Not exactly."

"You haven't worked together in some time, have you?"

"No. He seems to be avoiding me lately, which is fine with me."

"Is that because you deduced that he was the anonymous caller who gave up Danny's name?"

Carvalho said nothing.

"Oh, come on, Detective," said Sarah. "Don't look so surprised. It was right there on the arrest report. Once you picked out Danny's name from Dunleavy's arrest files, you couldn't miss Kelleher's name there, too. As the officer assisting in Danny's arrest. That made it highly probable that Kelleher made the call. Am I right?"

Carvalho stared at her. "Yes," he said.

"There's no big secret here," she went on. "Kelleher admitted as much on the stand this morning. How did you feel when you figured out he had tipped the DA's office?"

"I wasn't happy."

"Now, *there's* an understatement! Isn't it true that you went after him and assaulted him?"

Carvalho stared at her again. "What?" he said softly.

"Beat him so savagely, in fact, that he missed work for four days? But, of course, you don't 'operate that way,' do you, Detective?"

Sarah waited, motionless, as he grappled for composure.

"I don't remember doing that," he said finally, tentatively.

"You don't *remember*," she repeated, the pitch of her voice rising to track her incredulity. "So if Martin Kelleher testified that you beat him up, he was lying?"

"I don't know. When was this?"

Sarah rolled her eyes to the ceiling. "When?" she asked mockingly. "You want to know when? What is this, you can't keep your beatings straight?"

Almost oblivious to his surroundings now, Carvalho's right hand was shaking as he glared ferociously at her, his eyes fired with need. "WHEN?" he demanded.

His sudden intensity was so startling Sarah seemed at a loss herself for a moment. So much so, that she answered his question. "The very night Danny Li was murdered. Does that help fix the time for you?"

Carvalho took a few seconds to process what she said. Then his shoulders sagged visibly as he felt the tension seep out of him.

"No," he said hoarsely, as he looked down. "I mean, I don't know. I have no memory."

"You don't recall assaulting Martin Kelleher?" Sarah demanded.

Carvalho lifted his head. "No. I get blackouts sometimes. That's why I needed to know when it was. Hey, don't get me wrong. It coulda been me. I was ripped. But I don't remember. I don't remember anything about that night."

His questioner seemed to consider this, then asked, "So you have no reason to dispute Detective Kelleher's testimony about the beating?"

"No, I don't. If he said it happened, it probably did." He was sitting back in the chair now, looking almost relaxed.

"But you do recall being angry with him for coming forward with what he believed was the truth, don't you?"

"Yes, I was angry."

"And that was because he was interfering with your efforts to hide the truth about your use of informants?"

"Yes."

"I have nothing further, Your Honor," Sarah said, as she gathered up her papers from the lectern.

Judge Doyle used his index finger to pull his reading glasses down toward the end of his nose. He peered over them at DeMarco. "Anything further from the Commonwealth?"

"Very briefly, Your Honor," DeMarco responded as he stood up. He did not return to the lectern. "Detective Carvalho, what was the truth you were so angry at Martin Kelleher for revealing?"

Carvalho frowned as he answered. "That Danny Li was the snitch."

"And why didn't you want him to tell me that Danny Li was the snitch?"

"Because it would mean that IT didn't exit—and I'd be in trouble. Because of my testimony."

"Thank you, Detective." DeMarco nodded almost imperceptibly to his witness and smiled. Then he sat down.

A moment later Carvalho left the courtroom and headed for open spaces. He brushed rudely past two importunate reporters, ignoring their bleating questions about his testimony. He was still waiting for one of the building's capricious elevators to appear when the noise level behind him suddenly rose several decibels. Adjournment had followed hard on the heels of his own departure, and the courtroom doors had burst open to spill the crowd. He did not relish a ride with tittering spectators whispering about him. Abandoning the elevators, he sheared off toward the stairs on his right.

He bounced briskly down two flights, then, leaving the stairwell, made his way through the long third-floor hallway that connected the annex to the old courthouse. When he came to the end of the hallway, he could see down into the spacious atrium of the grand old courthouse. Turning right, he strode along the marble balustrade that girdled the atrium and descended another set of stairs at the rear of the building. The stairs emptied him on to the tessellated floor of the atrium, where he faced the main exits to Pemberton Square, but he turned to his right and slipped out the small rear entrance reserved for court personnel. He found himself standing at the curb of Somerset Street.

After the fluorescent gloom of the courthouse, the light

was clean and exhilarating, the outline of objects etched with a stark clarity he had known only on clear autumn days in New England. Carvalho stood stock-still and drank in the fresh air. The wind wrapped his go-to-court tie back around his neck and whipped it over his shoulder. He paid it no mind. Breathing deeply, he turned his head to the right and watched the approaching traffic as it climbed Beacon Hill.

To onlookers who had witnessed his public humiliation on the stand, he might have appeared grim and stoic. But they would be wrong. That was not how he felt at all. He knew his credibility was in tatters and that his own future was even bleaker now than it had been before his trial testimony. Given the conduct he had admitted today, he harbored little hope that the AG would not indict him. Yet for the moment he felt free. Loose, even.

He looked up at the remote blue of the sky and smiled. He thought about his encounter with the terrifying little old man in his bedroom and his conversation with Donna afterwards. He wished she were with him now. At last he could account for those severed fingers that had harrowed his soul for weeks. Problem number two was gone.

The blood had belonged to Kelleher, not Danny.

A dazzle of color winked at him from the right and like a magpie he flicked an eye toward its source. A gleaming sportscar—Italian, crimson, its top defiantly down in the late September afternoon—accelerated fluidly before topping the hill in front of him. It came to a halt behind the line of cars waiting to enter Beacon Street. The driver looked to be about forty, a tall, balding man wearing wire-rimmed glasses. His striped dress shirt was open at the collar and his tie, like Carvalho's, was swept over his clavicle. A large black dog, mostly Labrador and shepherd, sat up pertly in the passenger seat and stared straight ahead with an aura of fixed purpose.

Catching Carvalho's eye, the driver suddenly grinned at him.

"Slipped out early," the man said. Carvalho could not tell from his tone whether it was a question, an explanation, or a sly boast. Carvalho grinned back at him, the two of them in cahoots against a world of laughable obligations and absurd consequences.

Then the line of traffic moved on, dragging the sportscar with it. As the convertible pulled away, the breeze tousled the thick mane of fur around the dog's neck, giving the animal a hunching, wolfish bearing.

Carvalho stepped lightly into the empty street. He suppressed an urge to skip.

# 45

---

# Psychodicy

Matthew Boer, on the other hand, did not feel the least bit like skipping. He felt more confused than ever after the trial recessed.

Carvalho's testimony had left him unsettled. The policeman's shock, when confronted with his attack on Kelleher, had seemed genuine enough, and Matthew presumed his rage would have spent itself in the effort. He thought it highly unlikely the detective would then have gone on to beat Danny to death the same night.

It was also clear that Carvalho had been able to figure out Danny's identity on his own. This strengthened his belief that the leak needn't have come from his own blunders in front of Judge Doyle. At the same time, however, it opened the door to other scenarios for the leak beyond his own fragile suspicions about Fleishman—suspicions that still foundered for lack of motive. And on an entirely unrelated front, he remained completely bewildered by Julie's spectacular metamorphosis.

Yet, he had other obligations. The next morning he was clutching the latest iteration of the draft law review article and heading for Rowell Falk's office. Coming to a stop in front of the closed door, he rocked his head to the right and peeked in through the glass sidelight.

Falk was not alone. He was talking to a small man whose back was to Matthew. The man was short and slim, with close-cropped hair and pink, boyish ears that stuck out a little more than they should. Unlike Falk, he still had his suit jacket on.

A client. Matthew was about to move away, but Falk spotted him and beckoned him inside. Good. He'd be able to drop off the draft and get out. Matthew opened the door and eased inside. Falk's guest twisted his head around and eyed him pleasantly.

It was Jackie Crimmins. He looked as trim and natty as ever, wearing a dark blue tie that depicted colorful, rough-hewn timbers falling in three dimensions all down its silken surface. The fluidity with which the two men switched their attention to Matthew suggested they had not been deeply engaged.

"Come in, Matthew," said Falk. "I'd like you to meet Jackie Crimmins." He turned toward the district attorney, who had risen from his chair. "Matthew Boer is one of our senior associates—one of our brightest, I might add. I've been doing my best to lure him away from those conquistadors in the litigation department."

"Good to meet you, Matthew," said Crimmins, shaking his hand. The man gave off a personal warmth and intensity that took Matthew by surprise. He had a lalapalooza of a smile that scintillated at Matthew as they looked at one another. He also had the politician's gift for bestowing the conviction that you were only person around who mattered to him. A major asset, no doubt, for working a room.

"Matthew comes to us from an academic background," said Falk. "He used to be an English professor."

"Did you now?" said Jackie, still smiling as he rocked back on his heels, his hands in his jacket pockets.

"Only an instructor, actually," Matthew corrected.

"Well, you're a fortunate man, Matthew. I see too many young lawyers who come to the bar trained in nothing but business and politics and smitten with a fervent desire to make a bit of the ready. There's no depth, you know. No foundation. You made sure you got that."

There was a seductive music to Jackie's voice. It danced up and down in pitch as he talked. Matthew found himself hanging on his words, more so in personal conversation, it struck him, than when he had heard the man speak publicly.

"I can't speak for the depth," said Matthew, "but Rowell can attest that I don't have much of a head for business. Or politics."

"Matthew's the one," said Falk, with an avuncular smile, "who's been helping me with that law review article I mentioned. And doing a first-rate job of seeing to it that I don't get in over *my* depth."

"Oh, Rowell," Jackie sighed with mock exasperation, looking toward Matthew as if it fell to the two of them to collude in shoring up Falk's self-esteem—a notion Matthew found ludicrous. "You've got more breadth *and* depth than any of those second-guessers on the Supreme Judicial Court."

Falk's flinch at this compliment was almost imperceptible, but Matthew caught it. Falk looked down and fiddled with something on his desk, as if stricken by an uncharacteristic spasm of modesty. Reflexively coming to his aid, Matthew said, "As a matter of fact, that's what brings me here. I've incorporated your changes into the draft and I wanted to discuss it with you."

Falk seemed grateful for the change of subject. "I hope you didn't spend all day on it."

"No," said Matthew. "Most of yesterday I blew off. I went to watch the *Chin* trial."

He couldn't help himself. He could not have retraced the thought process by which he had come to inject that freighted topic into their conversation, though he could feel an element of defiance driving him. He kept his eye on Jackie. He didn't know whether Jackie, like DeMarco, blamed him for Danny's death, but he didn't feel like treading water in small talk if there was a tug of recrimination in the undertow. If there was, Jackie didn't give it away, for he looked blandly back at Matthew.

"I trust," he said, "that all went well for the Commonwealth?"

"Well, Sarah Kerlinsky gave Carvalho a pretty good working over. He had a hard time explaining why he went looking for Danny Li."

"I don't think," he heard Falk interject with a tinge of annoyance, "that Jackie is aware that you represented Danny in this matter."

From his look of surprise, Matthew felt certain Jackie was hearing this for the first time. Jackie said nothing for a moment as he examined him intently. Matthew managed to maintain eye contact.

"In that case," Jackie said finally, "I should probably apologize on behalf of my office for my assistant's ill-considered comments. Jeremiah DeMarco is a passionate advocate—it's what makes him an effective prosecutor—but sometimes his passion gets the better of him. I'd wager he ground a quarter of an inch off his teeth over that business with the informant. But, really, there was no call to single you out like that."

"Somebody," said Matthew, as innocently as he could muster, "should tell that to bar counsel."

Jackie frowned. "The Board of Bar Overseers?"

"They've taken a morbid interest in it, yes."

Jackie gave a little snort. "They should have better things to do."

"And so should we," said Falk, obviously displeased with this topic as well. He addressed Matthew. "Why don't you leave the draft with me and I'll review it and get back to you?"

Matthew handed him the folder. He started to take his leave. "Mr. Crimmins, it's been—"

"Were you present," Jackie interrupted him, "when I showed up for that little breakfast shindig Rowell put together?"

"Yes," Matthew said, his smile genuine. "I quite enjoyed it."

"Enough to get you on board?" Jackie asked, and Matthew could feel the wattage of his charm being cranked up a notch. "My administration will need bright young men."

Again, Matthew was taken aback by his directness. He

returned it. "To be honest with you, I don't know. I mean, you'll probably be the nominee, so I'll vote for you. But I confess I have some problems."

Jackie smiled. "You mean my breakfast oratory didn't convince you?"

"As far as it went," Matthew responded. "It's what you *didn't* discuss that bothers me."

"Such as?" Jackie cocked his head, as if anticipating fun.

"Your enthusiasm for the death penalty. I'm afraid we part company there."

Jackie clasped his jaw in the webbing of his left hand and idly rubbed his cheek. He stared vacantly for a moment at a point somewhere over Matthew's left shoulder. It was a contemplative pose.

"You know," he said softly, snapping his gaze back at Matthew, "there is a branch of theology that seeks to reconcile the existence of evil with an all-good and omnipotent God. It's called theodicy. You're familiar with the concept?"

Matthew nodded.

"Well," Jackie continued, "it's a paradox that has troubled some of our most powerful intellects. And not just theologians. I think of Camus in *The Plague* and Elie Wiesel. Norman Mailer. And Ingmar Bergman. Now," he smiled, his teasing glance lighting briefly on each of his listeners, "to those of us who are communicants in the One True Faith, there is no heart-wrenching struggle to resolve this paradox. It is embraced as one of the sacred and insoluble mysteries of the Faith, so we manage to muddle through without the need to psychoanalyze the Holy Spirit. Are you with me so far?"

"Yes," said Matthew. "I had my religious instruction."

"Catholic?" Jackie raised his eyebrows.

Matthew smiled his assent. "Well, I'm between religions at the moment. Think of me as a lapsed agnostic."

Jackie laughed. "Didn't I say you had a good foundation? Anyway, we know what evil is and where it comes from." He raised a forefinger and shook it at him playfully. "But your secular humanist, now, he has a terrible time finding a place for evil. Good, he can find in the human heart, and he believes it would carry the day if only social conditions permitted. But evil? No, sir. That isn't exactly in his intellectual wheelhouse. Weeping Jesus, the contortions they go through to discount the existence of evil in human affairs!"

Jackie looked pleased with himself. Matthew smiled encouragingly.

"So," Jackie continued, "instead of an honest coming to grips with the problems posed by theodicy, what we get today is something you might call *psychodicy.* It's the effort to explain evil as the manifestation of some psychological deficit. You hear it all the time, in differing guises. Psychopathology caused by severe childhood trauma. Dissociative thinking. Diminished capacity. Post-traumatic stress syndrome. Fugue states, for the love of Mike. It's pathetic."

"But nobody wins on an insanity defense these days," Matthew objected.

Jackie held his hand up as if stopping traffic and shook his head slowly. "Please, Matthew. Understand me. I'm not talking about the insanity defense here. You're right; that's so narrow it's seldom even an issue, let alone a successful defense. No, I'm talking about the way we're being conditioned to distance ourselves from the reality of the brute evil I see run through my office on a daily basis. Psychodicy is more insidious than that. It chips away at our capacity to judge the evildoer because we're always looking for a way to explain how he got that way. And that weakens the force of the judgment. Now, I *know* evil exists. It's as real as what hangs from a meat hook." He smiled at Matthew. "And I think you know that, too, thanks to that excellent foundation of yours. Evil is a choice, not a social by-product. It must be rooted out and destroyed. It must be crushed."

The office suddenly seemed too small for the three of them, and an oppressive silence filled the remaining space. Then Matthew said, "But even your religion has a place for redemption."

"Ah, but that's for the next world, Matthew," Jackie rejoined in a bright tone that suggested Matthew knew better. "In this one, you pay your debts. You settle accounts."

"Well, I'm sorry, Mr. Crimmins; I don't share your certainty. About either world. I guess my 'foundation' is more porous than yours."

"I doubt that, Matthew."

"Well," said Matthew, "to be honest I doubt you have much of an acquaintance with doubt. But, you know, my problem with capital punishment isn't nearly so rational. It just sickens me. I get this image of a couple of guards pulling a terrified and sniveling man out of a cell and dragging him off someplace to be killed. And I start to tremble. I want to throw up. I don't want anything to do with it."

Jackie was still and unsmiling for a moment as he held Matthew's eye. Then he broke the mood with the big grin.

"In that case, Matthew, I'm forced to retreat to my fall-back position. And it's a doozie. Are you ready?" He cocked his head again, full of mischief. "Those bozos in the State House will never pass it! The Speaker, you know, is a rabid opponent. He may be wit-free, but he's got the power to keep it from coming to a vote—and the votes to kill it if it ever did. So, you see, it's a nonissue."

Matthew chuckled uncertainly. He didn't know whether to be charmed by his candor or offended by his cynicism. He said, "Nevertheless, you've made quite a campaign issue out of your 'nonissue.' What do you call that? Polidicy?"

Jackie gave a comic shrug, his eyes open wide. "I call it using your capital while it has value." He looked over at Falk and, spinning the first two fingers of his right hand windmill-style, asked, "What was that line from Robert Frost you were quoting me earlier? Something about selling a horse?"

Falk furrowed his brow briefly, then smiled when he placed the allusion. "It was from 'The Ingenuities of Debt,' " he said. He recited:

"Take care to sell your horse before he dies,
 The art of life is passing losses on."

"Exactly," said Jackie. And they all laughed.

Jackie hunched his shoulders and raised his hands, fingers splayed. "Now, gentlemen, you must excuse me. I have to confer with my handlers on how to cope with all those sound-bite-mongers in the media."

He thrust his out hand. "Matthew, I hope you'll give our

little talk some thought. You intrigue me greatly."

"And you flatter me," Matthew rejoined, shaking his hand.

"I'll walk you out, Jackie," said Falk. "Have a seat, Matt. I'll just be a moment."

But Matthew remained standing. He wandered around the office examining the plaques and photographs on the walls. Once again he lingered before the one of Falk waving from a skiff near the dock on his island off the coast of Maine. Perhaps it was because he came from the landlocked Midwest, but he still couldn't get used to the idea that someone could actually own an island. In the Atlantic, no less.

His eye fell to the bookshelf behind the writing table. Spotting a dog-eared copy of Frost's collected poems, he smiled to himself. He eased it off the shelf and opened it to the table of contents. He found the listing for "The Ingenuities of Debt" and flipped to the page indicated. He didn't get far. It had been years since he'd read poetry with any rigor, and he found his attention drifting after a few lines.

He thought back over Jackie's odd disquisition on capital punishment. It came off as a set piece, like part of an address to the Catholic Lawyers Guild or something. He found it disturbing in a way, yet he also felt drawn to the man. With the pages of the open volume pressed against his chest, he was still sifting through his confused feelings about Jackie when he heard a voice from the doorway.

"Are you checking 'Stopping by Woods on a Snowy Evening'?"

Matthew, who hadn't heard Falk return, jumped when he heard his voice. He snapped the book shut.

"If so," Falk said with a knowing smile, "you'll discover that only parts of it can be sung to 'Hernando's Hideaway.' "

Matthew forced a laugh. "I'd forgotten all about that. Maybe I need to read Frost a little more deeply."

Falk extended his right hand. "Be my guest. He rewards the effort. Take it with you, if you like."

"I might just do that." Matthew closed the book and ran his palm over the front cover.

Falk took his place behind his desk. "You know, Matthew, I don't know which one of you charmed the other more, you or Jackie. You made quite an impression."

"He's quite a character, all right. I'm not sure what to think of that little conspectus on the death penalty."

"It was a bit—uh—" Falk twisted the corners of his mouth as he groped for the mot juste.

"Jesuit?" Matthew offered.

Falk considered this. "Maybe," he said. "I wouldn't know. Perhaps I'll leave it to you two coreligionists."

"Well, that's what it reminded me of, anyway," Matthew said. "It was a little chilling, actually. I'm always awed and even frightened by so much certainty."

"But he's right about one thing: It's all just smoke. There's little likelihood we'll have the death penalty in Massachusetts in the foreseeable future—no matter who's elected governor. I wouldn't support him if I thought otherwise. But that issue aside, he'll make a cracking good governor."

Falk settled into his chair and picked up the folder Matthew had handed him. "Now, about that draft." He opened the folder and started reading Matthew's cover memo.

Matthew sat down. It had always driven him crazy, this sitting around while senior lawyers read in front of him. It was almost as bad as listening to them take phone calls. At least he was off the clock now; no client was getting billed an additional $180 an hour so he could stare out the window. Idly, he opened the book on his lap. He scanned the table of contents, bemused by how few of the titles seemed familiar.

Then he saw one that was staggeringly familiar. At first he was unable to concentrate at all, as thoughts and images tumbled about in the confusion that enveloped him. Then, with a velocity that outstripped the plodding logic he knew he would have to work through later, he understood the implications of what he saw before him on the page.

He looked up sharply at Falk, who casually turned the page and read on. He had to get away. Now. He needed to think things through. He had to leave.

Abruptly, Matthew looked at his watch and stood up. "Oh, shit!" he muttered. "Look at the time. I forgot. I promised to meet my girlfriend ten minutes ago. I'm sorry, Rowell. How about if I just leave it with you and we talk after you've had a chance to check out the changes?"

When Falk looked up from reading, Matthew was already

moving toward the door. "Well," said Falk, scowling a little, "I guess that's all right. I hope, though, that you'll give some thought to what took place here today. There could be some interesting developments." Falk arched one eyebrow to tantalize his listener.

"Oh, I will," said Matthew from the door. "I'm gonna give it a lot of thought."

He would indeed.

Robert Frost had written a poem called "Bursting Rapture."

*Institutional failure, my ass,* he said to himself as he walked out the door.

# 46

---

# Backtracking

Matthew walked hurriedly after leaving Falk's office. Voices and other sounds throbbed around him without registering as he made his way up the stairway and back to the litigation department. Someone—he thought it might have been Robolawyer, he didn't really notice—addressed him, but Matthew pretended not to hear and rushed on by without responding.

He had circumambulated his way to his office and put one foot across his threshold when Sally's voice startled him.

"Matt, wait!"

He looked back at her, but she was now speaking into her telephone. "Here he is now," she said. She lowered the phone and covered the speaker with her right palm. "It's Laura. I'll transfer."

Matthew nodded, then went on into his office and shut the door. He picked up the ringing phone as he rounded the desk. He dropped the book of poems in his in-box.

"Laura," he said, sitting down. He was relieved to hear from her. Their relations had been strained since the meeting with Felch, and they hadn't gotten together in the last two days.

"Hi," she said. "I thought I'd check to see if your paranoia was in remission yet." Her tone was arch, not angry—thank God.

"Everybody thinks I'm paranoid. It's a plot."

"I missed you," she added, more softly.

"I'm glad," he said, smiling. "I missed you, too." Matthew felt a rush of affection and gratitude, but his agitation still percolated within him.

"How about," Laura said, "we shack up at my place tonight? Ply me with a bottle of wine, big guy, and I'll let you eat your Thorazine out of my navel."

Matthew laughed in spite of himself. He felt the familiar thickening of tissue at the back of his throat. Does blood also rush to the larynx when you get aroused?

"It's a deal," he said, "but I have to warn you. My paranoia is even more inflamed. Engorged, you might say."

He heard her sigh. "You're not gonna hit on any reporters this time, are you?"

"No. I promise. My paranoia is running in different channels. And I need to think through where it might take me."

"What does that mean? What 'channels'?"

He told her. "Robert Frost wrote a poem called 'Bursting Rapture.' "

There was silence on the line for a moment. Then she said, "And Edgar Guest wrote a poem called 'It Takes a Heap of Living to Make a House a Home.' Am I missing something or what?"

"No, just forgetting. That an entity called the Bursting Rapture Realty Trust owns a small share of One Adams Place. And that Rowell Falk is a big, big fan of Robert Frost."

Laura hesitated again, but when she spoke she sounded less certain. "Yes, I remember now. The little one. Bursting Rapture owned, what, two percent of the deal?"

"One and a half."

Her tone turned dismissive. "But it's a coincidence, surely. You said yourself the name sounded Oriental. That might still be the best explanation for where the name came from."

Matthew shook his head. "I don't think so. I think its more likely provenance is Falk. Lo Fat is Falk's client, after all; and it stands to reason that Rowell would have been the one to structure the legal entities that would own pieces of Adams Place. In fact, I spotted this little 'coincidence' while thumbing through a copy of Frost's poems in Falk's office."

"That," she said, her skepticism ascendant again, "could be true but entirely meaningless. Just an innocent bit of draftsman's whimsy in naming the trust. It doesn't mean he knew anything about who was getting the money."

Her point was a good one, and Matthew mulled it over.

"Maybe," he said. "And maybe not. Because Falk had a motive."

"Maybe," continued Laura, not hearing him, "the poem itself may give you a clue. You're the English major. Why don't you check it out?"

Matthew's eyes fell on the volume of Frost's poems in front of him. He smiled.

"Well," he said, picking up the book, "Mr. Falk *was* good enough to lend me his copy. Why don't we just take a look?"

He hunched the receiver to his ear and opened the book to the table of contents. He ran his finger down the list of titles, searching for "Bursting Rapture."

"If I hear any English major crap about deconstruction or symbolism," said Laura, "I'm hanging up."

"Jesus!" Matthew exclaimed. The telephone receiver lost its tenuous purchase on his shoulder and tumbled onto his desk. He heard Laura's voice call his name as he stared at the page in front of him. Finally, he picked up the receiver again.

"Did you drop the phone or something?"

"I found another one."

"What? Another what?"

"Another poem. By Frost. This one's called 'The Gold Hesperidee.' The trustee of Bursting Rapture is a company called the Hesperidee Corporation. There's nothing Oriental about that. It's *got* to be Falk's work."

"That," said Laura, "you can check."

"What?"

"It's a corporation, isn't it? Their creators leave more

tracks than those who set up a realty trust. For a corporation you have to file articles of incorporation with the secretary of state's office. With the names of the incorporator and officers and directors. Plus you gotta make annual filings to keep the office from dissolving it."

"You're right!" said Matthew, excited now. Then he frowned. "Except it's a Maine corporation, not a Massachusetts one."

"So, what's the capital of Maine? Do you know anybody there?"

"Augusta. Of course! Karen Indelicato. An old girlfriend of mine from law school. She's the administrative aide to some state senator up there."

Matthew started flipping through his Rolodex.

"Old girlfriend?" said Laura. "I must say I don't care for the name."

Matthew found the card. "Look," he said, "I gotta run this down. I'll come by tonight when I get out of here. OK?"

"Call me back and keep me posted," said Laura. "I don't want you losing touch after hooking up with old girlfriends."

Matthew chuckled. "I will. And I promise to bring that bottle of wine."

"Don't forget the Thorazine."

Matthew laughed as he hung up. He never had gotten around to telling her about Falk's motive.

A few minutes later he hung up again after a short conversation with Karen Indelicato, who promised to fax him everything she could find out about the Hesperidee Corporation at the Maine secretary of state's office.

He sat back and carefully read the two poems, but nothing in the text of the poems told him anything. Someone had just lifted the titles and applied them to the entities in question. He closed the book and pushed it to the front of his desk.

What did it mean? It seemed very likely that Falk had set up and named at least two of the entities that received profits generated by Adams Place. But Laura was right. He could have been a lawyer innocently doing his job on behalf of Lo Fat, with no knowledge of Vu's role in the deal. And the one and a half percent of the profits paid to Bursting Rapture was probably too small to be Vu's anyway. The man would want a bigger cut than that if he had infused cash into the deal to bail out a struggling Lo Fat as the project was getting off the ground.

Which meant Vu's share was still likely to be the eleven percent that went to the 27 Fayette Realty Trust. The trust of which Danny had been the nominal beneficiary, he still believed. And the trustee of that trust—Sinon, Inc.—had the same mailing address as Morrissey's firm. He had assumed all along that it was Morrissey's firm that had drafted the 27 Fayette Trust documents. Had it?

Matthew reached behind him and pulled the Danny file off the shelf. It was a rust-colored accordion file that held everything he had gathered on the case since Danny's death. He untied the ribbon that bound it and, lifting the flap, slid the file's contents onto his desk. He riffled through the papers until he found what he was looking for. Two typed documents. Both were declarations of trust, one for 27 Fayette and the other for Bursting Rapture. He laid them side by side and compared them.

They were absolutely identical. In every respect except as to title and name of trustee. If they had not been drafted by the same person, the drafters had both slavishly followed the same form of agreement.

Matthew stood up and retrieved a black vinyl-clad three-ring binder from the top shelf behind his desk. The binder's spine bore a typewritten title: DAPHNIS & CLOONEY— CORPORATE FORM BOOK. It had been given to him shortly after his last performance review, when he had accepted Falk's invitation to try doing some corporate work. Opening it, Matthew quickly found the firm's form for realty trusts.

It, too, was indistinguishable from the instruments establishing 27 Fayette and Bursting Rapture.

*Hold on*, Matthew told himself. *Not too fast*. Maybe trust declarations were so standard everyone, including D&C, took them from some commercial form book. Lots of such books were published and used by Massachusetts lawyers. But as he read from the trust instruments, Matthew knew that was not the case. The prose was clean and fluid, unblemished by the kind of mindless legalese—like "the said trustee" and "shall notify same"—that usually disfigured legal documents lifted from commercial form books. These trust instruments exhibited precisely the clarity and elegance on which D&C's corporate department prided itself. And it had always been Falk himself, the consummate draftsman, who had led the charge in this respect. These instruments, Matthew was convinced, had been drafted right here at Daphnis & Clooney.

He returned to the pile of documents and replaced the trust declarations. He spun his chair toward the office window and, clasping his hands behind his head, he leaned back. Looking down across the rooftops of the buildings on the other side of High Street, he noticed that the weather had changed. An autumn rainstorm seemed imminent.

Matthew felt confused. Could he have been mistaken about Fleishman all along? Now that he thought about it, he had to admit it was more likely that the lawyer with the closest connection to Lo Fat at the time the financing for the hotel project was arranged would be the one to know the implications and consequences of Danny's sudden appearance as a police informant. That suggested a corporate lawyer, not a litigator like Fleishman. And Falk, as a member of the Management Committee, was also privy to Danny's identity. Why hadn't that occurred to him before?

He had been led astray—if, indeed, astray he was—by that business with the OA credit. Fleishman should have disputed Matthew's claim to being the originating attorney for Danny's case. He didn't, and Matthew's suspicion had been aroused. And he still couldn't explain Fleishman's uncharacteristic neglect of his entitlement to the credit. Why hadn't Fleishman complained?

Or was that the right question? Why was Fleishman entitled to the OA credit on Danny in the first place? Danny had come to the firm, Fleishman had told him, at the suggestion of Lo Fat. Would Lo Fat have advised Danny to call Fleishman in 1992, when he first ran into trouble with the restaurant? Did Lo Fat even *know* Fleishman then? Or was Lo Fat Fleishman's client all along? Maybe he should be asking who the OA was for Lo Fat.

And why had the original new case form for Danny gone missing?

Matthew turned to his computer and attempted to bring up the conflicts data base. The system was down. Great. He drummed his fingers on the desk and thought for a moment. He got up and left his office.

Mrs. Beadle, smiling coldly, was at her station. She clasped her hands together and set them on the counter in front of her.

"Good afternoon, Mr. Boer," she said. "How can we help you."

Matthew smiled. "Good afternoon. I'm afraid I have a somewhat unusual request."

"I'm getting accustomed to the unusual from you, Mr. Boer." Mrs. Beadle, holding her thin smile, arched an eyebrow.

Matthew chuckled apologetically. "I'd like to look at all the cards on a client named Lo Fat. Have you heard of him?"

Mrs. Beadle lost her smile. "Heard of him?" she snorted. "I should say so. That's like asking a librarian to give you all the books by Dickens."

He gave her a propitiating shrug. "You don't actually have to pull the cards. Maybe you could just let me thumb through the card catalog to see if I can find what I'm looking for."

"And what would that be?"

"I'm not exactly sure," Matthew said, "but I promise not to disturb anything. Just a peek."

Mrs. Beadle hesitated while he smiled at her as innocently as he could. Then she pulled open the counter-high saloon door that afforded access to her domain. "This way," she said, "and I will hold you to your promise."

"Thank you," said Matthew as he followed her to the cabinet that held the cards. As she walked back to the counter, he pulled open the drawer labeled E–F.

She was right. There were a lot of cards under Lo Fat's name. He counted forty-six in all. The oldest one, a yellowed card bearing a date in 1984, identified Falk as the originating attorney. So Lo Fat was, as Matthew had assumed, Falk's client. He flipped forward looking for other names, but the next dozen or so all listed Falk as originating and responsible attorney. Then a card indicated that a litigation matter had been opened in 1993. For that case, Ben Fleishman was named RA, with Falk retaining the OA designation. Which all made perfect sense, of course. As a corporate lawyer, Falk could hardly be the responsible attorney for supervising a litigation case. Matthew held the dog-eared card between his left thumb and forefinger while he transferred the information to a blank sheet on his pocket diary.

Finished, he was slipping the diary back into his coat pocket and preparing to close the drawer when a new thought made him stop. Fleishman was listed as OA on Danny's first case, which Fleishman had said was a referral from Lo Fat. That case had been opened in 1992. Yet Fleishman's tracks did not appear on a Lo Fat card until 1993, when he was first made the RA on a Lo Fat litigation matter.

How had Lo Fat known to tell Danny to call Fleishman?

Perhaps Lo Fat had called Falk about Danny, and Falk had suggested he call Fleishman directly. But even then, Falk would have been entitled to claim the OA credit. Or maybe Fleishman had met Lo Fat earlier, either socially or as someone kibitzing with Falk on a case that never blossomed into litigation, and Lo Fat had simply suggested that Danny call the litigator.

Pulling open the drawer labeled L–M, Matthew's fingers walked their way to Li and stopped at the card for Danny's first matter, the one for the Lotus Blossom case in 1992. A shiver ran through him when he saw the card. It was not the information on the card that chilled him, for it was identical to that on the photocopy of the card in the file back in his office.

It was the condition of the card.

The card was crisp and white. Its corners were not dog-eared or smudged by almost four years of thumbing perusals.

Matthew sneaked a look over his shoulder. Mrs. Beadle's attention was directed to a computer screen a few feet away. Matthew plucked the card from the drawer and tucked it into his pocket. Then he did the same with the one that first listed Fleishman as responsible attorney. The dog-eared one from 1993.

"There's a fax for you," said Sally when he reached his office again. "It's sitting on your desk."

Matthew closed the door behind him and eagerly pored over the papers filed when Hesperidee was incorporated. He was disappointed. He recognized none of the names of its officers and directors, and its mailing address was a post office box in Blue Hill, Maine. A sure dead end, the address, and he wouldn't know where to begin in checking out the names. None of them was Oriental, at least. But aside from that, the papers told him nothing.

Then he spotted a familiar name and his heart raced. Howard Ramseth. He was listed as the incorporator, the person who had filed the papers with the secretary of state's office to establish the corporation. Matthew knew Howard Ramseth. He had been a senior associate at Daphnis & Clooney up until two or three years before, when he had left to become in-house counsel to a large real estate development company.

Matthew called Howard Ramseth. They spoke for ten minutes. When he hung up he felt a dark anger begin to burn inside him, a sizzle at the back of the brainpan. He sat still for several minutes, mulling over how to proceed.

Then he asked Sally to get a copy of a document from Ben Fleishman's secretary.

Then he called Barry Golden. He hadn't seen him since Ira's birthday dinner at Aporia, but Barry knew more about computers than anyone he could think of, and Matthew had a question for him.

"You're talking about a network now, not a dedicated computer?" asked Barry.

Matthew assured him he was.

"Then there'd be a trail. Ever hear of a system log?"

Matthew had not. He listened to Barry for several minutes. Then he called Ira and told him.

Then he left the building, bought a bottle of wine, and went home to Laura's apartment. He had homework to do, but he was looking forward to enjoying a quiet time with Laura first.

He wouldn't get it.

# 47

---

## Dim Sum

They were all over each other before Matthew even opened the wine.

"Wait a minute," Laura said when he kissed her at the door, but she was soon swept up in the moment.

"Wait," he protested himself, as she loosened the knot on his tie. "I gotta tell you what I found out in Central Files."

"Central Files?" she asked, with a mocking smile, her lips brushing his. "Ooh, I can hardly wait." She dropped the tie on the floor and started on his shirt buttons. "But like I said, I missed you. Tell me later."

"But it's really—"

She cut him off with her kiss as her hand slid inside his shirt and along his chest. He felt a jolt and gave it up. He put his arms around her and pulled her closer to him, his hands gliding up the smooth skin of her back under her sweatshirt, past where the bra strap should have been. They lurched toward the couch.

Their kiss broke when they landed heavily on the couch, Laura on top, and she smiled at him.

"Want to tell me now?" she murmured teasingly. She ran her hand up his thigh.

"Like you said, it can wait," he said thickly.

They kissed again, and Matthew could have sworn he heard chimes.

Laura broke off the kiss abruptly, tilting her head to one side to listen, and Matthew realized he *had* heard chimes.

It was the doorbell. It was ringing again.

Laura took a deep breath and blew it out noisily. "Hold that thought, lover. I'll be right back."

Getting to her feet, she shook her shoulders and straightened her sweatshirt. Matthew eyed her hungrily as she made her way to the front door. She pulled aside an edge of the lace curtain over the window in the door and peered out at their intruder. She let go of the lace and, turning back to smile knowingly to Matthew, she opened the door.

A teenage boy in a windbreaker and baseball cap stood on her stoop. With a smile, the kid handed Laura a small white shopping bag. The words "Hunan Palace" were printed on the bag in red letters, just above a pair of crossed chopsticks.

"All paid for," said the boy in response to Laura's unvoiced question. He ambled down the steps as Laura looked after him. Then she turned back to Matthew.

"So," she said. "Chinese. A little surprise to make up for being such a jerk the *last* time we had Chinese?" She brought the bag to the dining area just behind the couch and placed it on the table. She parted the handles and peeked into the bag.

Matthew was at a loss. "I didn't order it. You mean you didn't?"

"Nope." She reached in and extracted a large white takeout carton. Chinese food. She set it down on the table and opened the flaps.

"Would Ira do this?" she asked.

"I don't know why," he said, pulling himself to his feet. "I told him I was headed over here, but I don't know why he would have sent food."

He walked over to stand next to her. They looked into the open carton.

Inside was a roundish object, the size of a softball, but flatter. Its outer cover was a deep olive-green, streaked with black, and the object itself was neatly bound with butcher's cord.

"What is it?" asked Laura.

Matthew gave a smile of recognition. "It's sticky rice. You know, the kind they serve when you have dim sum. It's delicious."

*Must be Ira after all,* he thought, recalling his friend's passion for dim sum. But why just a single serving of rice and nothing more?

"What's this green stuff around it?" she asked as she worked the cord off from around it.

"It's a lotus leaf." He watched as Laura began to unfold the leaf. "That's what they steam it in." He checked his watch. "I wonder if Ira—"

Laura shrieked and pulled back sharply, knocking the carton over on its side. She clutched him.

Together they watched in horror as blood oozed out of the carton and made a tiny puddle on the surface of the table.

Matthew started to step forward, but Laura held him back. "Let me look," he insisted. She released her grip.

He restored the carton to its upright position and looked inside. He caught a glimpse of bloody flesh. His heart racing, he peeled away a little more of the lotus leaf.

"What is it?" she asked, looking over his shoulder. "It's awful."

Fully unwrapped, it looked like a narrow section of thick red muscle, tapered at one end, crudely hacked off at the other, where the tissue had blackened. Bloody and lifeless, it was coiled obscenely in the center of the lotus leaf. One surface of the thing was more gray than red, and it appeared to have a curious texture, as if dotted with tiny bumps. Matthew reached in with his index finger to feel it there.

"Don't!" snapped Laura, grabbing his arm.

But he ran his finger along the surface of the muscle, feeling its abrasive texture.

"Jesus," he said, scared now.

"What *is* it?" Laura demanded more insistently.

"It's a tongue. Part of one, anyway."

"A tongue?"

"Yes. Probably a pig's."

Terrified, he thought back to Morrissey's advice. And the knowing look he had seen in Herman Vu's stare.

"Why's somebody sending me a tongue?"

"I think it's meant for me," Matthew said. "It's a message. To tell me to shut up. And to scare the shit out of me."

"Well, it works for me," she said emphatically.

"Me, too," he agreed.

He staggered back to the couch and sat down heavily.

She was still standing by the table. "I don't get it," she said. "I know you told me Morrissey warned you off, but why send it *here*? Why my place?"

Matthew shrugged. "Who knows? To show how much they know about me. And that they can reach me anywhere they want. Maybe to make the point that I should be concerned for *your* safety, too."

"Christ," she said, taking a seat beside him. "This is too much. You think we should call the cops?"

Matthew considered this. "And tell them what? That somebody sent us some raw meat? It wouldn't make any sense unless I told them what I found in Lo Fat's files. I don't want to do that."

"Suddenly you're getting protective of client secrets?" she asked sardonically.

"Fair enough," he admitted. "But I think I'd just get myself in a whole lot of trouble—with the firm and the bar— and the cops wouldn't be able to do much about it all anyway. It's not like I've got evidence that could get anybody arrested."

"But if you tell, it'll all be out there. There wouldn't be any reason to threaten you then."

"Oh, sure," he said wryly. "You can't just holler, 'Allie allie in free!' They'd want revenge. That's the whole *point* of a threat, don't you think? To bring home the consequences of going public."

They were both silent, thinking.

"No," Matthew said at last. "It has to be the other way around. They have to know that the only way to keep it from becoming public is to leave me alone."

Laura looked up at him and frowned. "Well, that seems to be the gist of the message. It's what they want you to do. So you're going to drop it?"

He shook his head. "I can't do that. Not after what I found out today. I mean, I know I can't do anything about Herman Vu and Lo Fat. They're untouchable. I *always* knew that. But I know who fingered Danny for them, and I can't let the bastard get away with it. I just can't."

She grabbed his hand and squeezed. "Matthew, this is scary."

He stared straight ahead. "I have to find a way."

He spent most of the rest of the night working on it. And preparing, as if for trial.

# 48

## Pluto

Given how good she was at this, Sarah Kerlinsky seemed unusually stiff in front of the jury. DeMarco supposed he should be grateful for that, at least, as he watched Sarah enter the home stretch of her summation. Unlike him, she spoke from notes, which she consulted too often in his view, and she was droning on in an unpleasant voice that was barren of affect. He knew she could be stunningly persuasive on her feet, especially on cross, but this morning she seemed tied to her script and she had established little rapport with the jury. She came across like the tough old spinster who drilled irregular verbs into you in junior high school. Even when she remembered to look up at them, they must have felt she was checking up on them. Are we paying attention, class?

They were, and intently. As if they feared everything she said might be covered on the final exam and they wanted desperately to get it right.

Because she was killing him. He could feel it. His boss couldn't, of course. Sitting beside him at the counsel table, Jackie Crimmins listened to Sarah with visible delight. After

DeMarco had finished his closing argument, Jackie had squeezed his biceps and whispered "Superb!" Now his articulate features signaled his poor opinion of Sarah's performance with wry smiles and grimaces for DeMarco's benefit.

But Jackie *was* with him, after all, and even if it was politics that had quickened this ceremony of support, he was grateful for it. Would Jackie also be there when the jury returned? Or would he wait upstairs for word of the verdict from one of the court officers, lest he end up being too closely identified with the failed prosecution of a cop killer?

When he was being honest with himself, DeMarco admitted he had a very bad feeling about the case. He had felt it start to slip away from him the afternoon Sarah told him about Carvalho's daisy chain of affidavits, and he had striven frantically to seize control of it ever since. How could you hope to rehabilitate the testimony of a guy like that? And it had only gone from bad to worse. If the cop expected DeMarco to put in a good word with the AG, he was sorely mistaken.

But DeMarco still had a shot. A good one. He listened carefully for something—a turn of phrase, an unfortunate simile, perhaps—that he might turn to advantage on rebuttal. Resting his elbows on the table, he made a cage of his fingers and rested his chin on his thumbs as he watched Sarah. Bless her heart, she was now practically reading her argument to the jury.

"Take a hard look," she was saying, "at the witnesses the Commonwealth would have you believe. The prosecution has only four people who can connect Michael to the murder. The three men who were arrested with him, and his cellmate at the Charles Street jail. And what a foursome they are.

"Let's start with Liu, Cheng, and Huong. Although their testimony is shot through with contradictions, the general thrust seems to be the same: Namely, that Michael, and Michael alone, had been selling drugs out of the third-floor apartment for the last month or more. That he alone was in the third-floor apartment when the shots were fired, and that he alone came running down the fire escape and climbed in through the window into the second-floor apartment. Carrying the gun, which he then handed to one of them. That

Michael then snatched the gun back and shoved it under the mattress. And sat down to wait for the officers.

"Now, these three can't even keep their joint story straight. According to Mr. Cheng, Michael handed the gun to Liu. Mr. Huong says Michael handed it to *him*. And Mr. Liu can't remember who took the gun—he can't even remember if he himself ever held it.

"They also claim that Michael alone worked out of the third-floor apartment. This is directly contrary to the information in Detective Carvalho's affidavit. Everyone agrees that a man named John dealt drugs out of the apartment. There's no question of Carvalho inventing John. He was there. The only question is when. The Commonwealth's witnesses claim John hadn't been around for some time before the shooting. Mr. Huong, in fact, insists that John hadn't been around for at least a month. Yet the police source mentioned in the warrant affidavit—whoever you think he is—placed John in the apartment—had him *living* there, in fact—just two days before the shooting.

"In addition, you have the records of their extensive criminal activity. Loan-sharking. Gambling operations. Extortion. These are not the kind of people you would trust to make change for a five-dollar bill. Mr. DeMarco wants you to trust them with a man's life. And don't forget, they have been promised dismissal of all charges and other favors in exchange for their testimony. These men have every reason, in other words, to tell you exactly what the prosecution wants you to hear."

Sarah halted and lifted her head to look in the direction of the jury box. "For some reason, these three men have decided to pull together, to turn upon and incriminate Michael. Maybe they singled him out because he was the newest addition to their drug business. He was the stranger in their midst, an illegal immigrant. With no one to protect him. You heard testimony, and you just heard Mr. DeMarco tell you, that their operation was probably part of a larger organized crime network. Maybe they were told to finger Michael. We don't know. But we do know they lack any claim to credibility.

"Now, Mr. DeMarco would have you believe they could

not have cooked up so consistent a story. We've already seen that it's a far cry from 'consistent.' But he stresses that they first began to tell this story while they were still in jail, when, he says, they were segregated from one another—before they had an opportunity to discuss their testimony among themselves and get their stories straight. Does he really expect you to believe that word does not travel from prisoner to prisoner in the Charles Street jail? *That* one I leave to your common sense.

"But Mr. DeMarco also neglects to mention another critical link in the chain of communications among these three men. All of them, remember, are represented by the same lawyer. And that man, James Morrissey, visited all three of them on numerous occasions. That's communication enough to fashion a common story, especially one as full of holes as this one."

As she turned over the page in her binder, the paper snagged on one of the binder rings. DeMarco listened to the crinkle of paper while she shimmied the page to free it. Smoothing it back, she read from her notes silently for a moment, then raised her head again.

"Which brings us to the fourth and last witness who can tie Michael to the shooting. I refer to Mr. Flores, the gentleman Michael was so fortunate to share a cell with at the Charles Street jail. A rather large man, you may recall, with a long police record for violent crime, including assault and battery, assault with a deadly weapon, assault on a police officer, and other lesser blemishes. You saw him: a great big bruiser, a scary-looking fellow. Not exactly the approachable type. Not a man whose appearance invites easy intimacy. And you heard him: not a native English speaker. You also heard uncontested testimony that Michael has a poor command of the English language himself. Please, take a look at him now."

At the defense table Michael Chin started as jurors turned in his direction. He appeared baffled by their sudden scrutiny.

"Talk about the odd couple," Sarah continued. "Put to one side for the moment all the many reasons that make Mr. Flores such an untrustworthy witness in the first place. I ask you, ladies and gentlemen, how likely is it that Michael—a small man, with little English, a frightened alien in the terrifying jailhouse environment—would swagger up to someone like Mr. Flores and volunteer that he had 'done a cop'? Now, those aren't my words. Those are the words Mr. *Flores* insists Michael used. 'Done a cop.' How likely is that? Does that even make sense?"

Sarah made a vague gesture of dismissal with her right hand before flipping the page again. But she did not look down at it. Her eyes swept across the faces of the jurors while she waited. She returned to her notes.

"So much for the witnesses. Let's now take a look at the physical evidence on which the prosecution relies. Yes, one of Michael's fingerprints was found on the gun. But so was one of Mr. Huong's. So that doesn't really advance the case very much. Does it come as a shock that there would be guns in a place where drugs were sold? Of course not. And the only reason to believe that Michael was the shooter and Mr. Huong was not is if you credit the testimony of these four very incredible witnesses. One of whom, of course, is Mr. Huong himself.

"But there is another piece of physical evidence that Mr. DeMarco would like very much for you to forget all about. The police quickly conducted gunshot residue tests for traces of gunpowder on Michael's hands. This would indicate whether he had fired a gun recently. They found nothing. No traces. You heard the Commonwealth's own expert, Dr. Keevers, testify that sometimes these tests aren't all they're cracked up to be. But you also heard him acknowledge, finally, that you can't always trust a positive result from a gunshot residue test. That's because there are other substances, besides the barium and antimony in gunpowder, that could trigger a false positive. But a false negative? Where the test fails to pick up traces that are actually there? Very rare indeed, as Dr. Keevers admits. And that's what we've got here.

"But in his argument, Mr. DeMarco tells you the test results *must* be wrong. They must be wrong, he tells you, because *nobody* tested positive for gunpowder. All four people arrested in the second-story apartment tested negative. Including Mr. Huong, the other man who left his fingerprints on the gun. Since the murderer, according to the prosecution, had to be one of the four men arrested in that apartment, and none of them tested positive, then the test results must be meaningless."

She let them consider this for a short time. Then, moving around the lectern, she took a step toward the jury box. She laid her right arm across the lectern and clutched the upper edge in her hand.

"You know what Mr. DeMarco's argument reminds me of, ladies and gentlemen? I hope you won't think I'm going too far afield if I tell you a little story."

She smiled at them. It was a real smile, DeMarco observed, not one of those rictus grins that had seemed scripted into her argument. This one was warm and confiding, as if she were taking a personal risk and begging their indulgence.

"It's about astronomy. An event in the recent history of the science. It was about 1900 and astronomers were observing the orbit of the planet Neptune. Taking measurements, stuff like that. Complicated mathematical calculations made with the finest, most advanced instruments and telescopes. And something just didn't add up. The scientists kept detecting, in their calculations, a slight deviation in one segment of the arc of Neptune's orbit. A wobble, if you will.

"Because it wasn't supposed to be there, you see. It fit no theory regarding the behavior of Neptune—or of the solar system in general. The scientific community was convinced there was some error in their mathematical models. Or some defect in their instruments. Everybody was frustrated and confused.

"Now, you know the saying, 'It's a poor workman who blames his tools.' Fortunately, there was an astronomer who took that saying seriously. So he asked himself a simple question. What if the wobble is real? What could cause such a phenomenon?

"His explanation seems pretty simple in retrospect. He theorized that there must be another object capable of exerting a gravitational pull on Neptune sufficient to put that wobble in its orbit. An object so far from Earth it could not be detected by existing instruments, but close enough to Neptune, and big enough, to interfere with the course of its orbit.

"Something like another planet.

"Of course, it was just a theory, and it remained one for some time, until the development of the radio telescope permitted scientists to verify it. Then, in the 1920s, astronomers picked it up. Right where the astronomer predicted it would be found.

"We know it as the planet Pluto.

"Notice, ladies and gentlemen, that all it took to escape the box those astronomers found themselves in was to change one of their assumptions: that there were only eight planets in the solar system. But imagine a ninth, and everything could be explained. Not proven, of course, at least not until Pluto was discovered in the distant sky by means of a technical advance. But even before it was proven, it provided a consistent explanation for a phenomenon that otherwise had scientists scratching their heads and blaming their tools.

"Now, Mr. DeMarco," Sarah continued, "wants you to scratch your head like him and to blame his tools because he has no other theory that allows his case to hold up."

She pivoted slightly in DeMarco's direction and scratched her head, her eyebrows arched for the jury. What could he do? He had to smile back, and the jury joined him.

"But you, too," she said, "can change one assumption and eliminate the wobble in Mr. DeMarco's thinking." She grinned. "Well, maybe not *all* of the wobble." There was scattered chuckling throughout the courtroom. "But enough to get him out of his box.

"So let me give you a different scenario, ladies and gentlemen. Imagine a fifth person. Someone who fired the shots through the door, ran down the fire escape, handed the gun to Michael or Mr. Huong, and then fled out the front door of the second-floor apartment.

"What was to stop him? The arresting officers testified that there was no one guarding that door. And there was no one guarding the front of the building itself. The only policeman outside was Detective Kelleher, and he was watching the building from the back. The killer could have stepped out into the night and disappeared without even breaking a sweat.

"It's not a perfect theory, I admit it. It doesn't explain why the other four didn't disappear with him. But then, even if the fifth man didn't exist, we can't explain why the four men who *were* arrested didn't do what I just suggested. They could have walked out. But they didn't. Maybe they didn't know they could escape. Maybe only the shooter was desperate enough to risk it. But it's a reasonable alternative, ladies and gentlemen. And it accounts for the absence of gunpowder traces without having to blame the tools."

For a moment there was no sound at all in the courtroom. Then a ventilation fan kicked in and its drone seemed to prod Sarah to continue.

"A fifth man. Call him Mr. X, if you like. Or you can call him Pluto." Another brief pause as she smiled. "I prefer to call him John. Because that's what IT called him. He described John as a tall, thin Chinese male in his late thirties. As I said, everyone acknowledges that John exists. And that he dealt drugs out of the apartment from which the shots were fired. Mr. DeMarco's unholy trinity of drug dealers want you to believe John was no longer around. But IT says he was. IT is the fellow who could tell us about John. IT is the man who has, from the beginning, posed the biggest threat of all to the prosecution's case against Michael Chin. IT is *the* most critical witness for the defense."

Sarah lifted her hands above her shoulders and opened her eyes wide. "So where is he? Look at the lengths to which these people have gone to keep you from hearing from him. First, the prosecution refuses to identify and produce him. So we ask the court to compel them to do so. And the prosecution opposes us. 'Oh, don't do it, Your Honor. He's too valuable an informant.' But the court issues the order. And then? The police claim they can't find him. They pretend to look for IT. They lie under oath about their search. Fortunately, Judge Doyle was unconvinced and threatened to deep-six their case for good. And, like magic, in the nick of time, the prosecution comes up with Danny Li. He's IT, Your Honor. But Danny Li ends up dead before he can say a word to anybody. And then, with Danny not around to contradict them, the policemen suffer a belated attack of conscience, a church-door conversion, and Detective Carvalho tells us there never *was* an IT. IT was really Danny Li—except, of course, that IT never existed. Can we believe *anything* that comes out of Carvalho's mouth? All his *sworn* testimony? I tell you, that man could swear a hole through a skillet."

Sarah crossed her arms and examined her audience.

"Reasonable doubt?" she asked wonderingly. "Ladies and gentlemen, this case is so flimsy, I'm almost embarrassed to bring up that standard, the standard by which you are to weigh the evidence—as Judge Doyle will explain in his instructions. The prosecution's case was crippled from the outset by the lack of an eyewitness, by the amount of time it took the officers to reach the second-floor apartment, and by the pathetic quality of the witnesses they were forced to rely on.

"It's understandable, I suppose, when you have a murder like this. A fine policeman cut down in the line of duty. A horrible event, full of tragedy and anguish for everyone involved. But all that righteous fire, all the pressure, the understandable drive to catch and convict the murderer—these things have distorted the Commonwealth's perception of the case.

"And the police? Well, maybe we shouldn't damn them too harshly. They may believe, sincerely and fervently, that Michael killed their colleague. But they have embarked on a course of obstruction, perjury, and abuse of power—all in an effort to prop up the prosecution's sagging case against Michael Chin.

"Ladies and gentlemen, this case was dead before it began. I beg you, kick out the last props and let this absurd contraption fall to the ground. Where it belongs. A tragedy, yes. Anguish, yes. But it's been a tragedy and a source of anguish for Michael as well.

"End his nightmare."

She waited a moment: "I am confident that when you weigh all the evidence, such as it is, you will agree that the Commonwealth has fallen far short of its obligation to prove, beyond a reasonable doubt, that Michael Chin fired the shots that killed Detective Dunleavy. I ask that you return a verdict of not guilty."

The only sound in the courtroom was a soft slap as Sarah closed the vinyl-clad covers of her binder. She carried it with her back to her table, offering an encouraging smile to her client.

DeMarco placed both hands on his own table and pushed himself lightly to his feet. He sidled around it and loped to the lectern in four swift strides. Gripping its edges firmly, he surveyed the jurors. A tiny smile traveled across his features. Then he leaned forward, his head cocked slightly to one side, and said with mock wonderment:

"*Pluto?* Did I hear her mention Pluto? Are we talking outer space here?" A few of the jurors smiled, expecting fun. "Ladies and gentlemen, we gotta bring this thing back to earth."

Suddenly he was very serious. "I just want to make three points here, before you go off to do your deliberations. Just three simple points.

"First, this fifth person." Raising his eyebrows slightly as he uttered the numeral, he couched it between two tiny pauses. "People, there is no evidence—I mean *zero* evidence—that another person was present on the day of the murder. In fact, Ms. Kerlinsky conjures this person out of the very *absence* of evidence. Out of the absence of gunpowder traces. Talk about a wobble.

"Just consider what you would have to believe, in order for such a person to exist. That the four men arrested in the second-story apartment heard the gunfire. That they watched Mr. *Pluto* pop into the lower apartment, drop off the gun, and run out the front door. That they sat there listening, immobile, as the police bashed away at the steel door in the room above them and eventually came crashing down the fire escape toward them. And then, despite having watched Pluto escape so handily, they just sat there and waited for the police to climb in the window and arrest them." He shook his head in mock sadness. "Ladies and gentlemen, anybody who'd believe that would buy swampland from Detective Carvalho."

They all smiled; several even laughed.

"No, there's no 'wobble' in the prosecution's case that needs to be explained by inventing a fifth person. There's just a crack in the lenses of Ms. Kerlinsky's telescope. Blame *her* tools, not mine.

"My second point is even simpler. Is *everybody* lying here? Think about it. *Everybody?* Because that's what Ms. Kerlinsky is asking you to conclude. That on the important details of this case, every witness we've put before you is lying to you. Mr. Liu. Mr. Cheng. Mr. Huong. Mr. Flores. All the policemen. Even Dr. Keevers, from the state lab. How likely is that, ladies and gentlemen? That everyone is lying? I submit to you that it's very unlikely indeed. So unlikely, she has gone so far as to insinuate that the lawyer for the three Chinese witnesses conspired, somehow, in the fabrication of testimony before you.

"The evidence you heard is not like a chain, where the weakness of a single link is enough to snap the whole thing. It's not like that at all. It's really more like a steel cable, where the testimony of each witness is a strand of wire, each one wound around the others and reinforcing the strength of the whole. Even if you were inclined to think that one strand or another is a bit, well, frayed, it cannot be the case that *all* of them are no good. Yet that is what the defense argument requires. It requires that you believe no one. And *that* defies common sense."

DeMarco stepped back from the lectern a half-step. He shoved his hands in his pants pockets.

"And third. Please. Let's keep this business with the police in perspective. Detective Carvalho did not exactly cover himself with glory in the way he handled this case. He was no saint. And neither was his friend Piscatello. They did and said things no police officer should ever do or say. I'm not asking you to condone it.

"But for all his flaws, Detective Carvalho was not fabricating evidence with an eye to ensuring Michael Chin's conviction, as Ms. Kerlinsky would have you believe. Nor did he destroy evidence that might have exonerated Michael Chin. Everything Carvalho did sprang from a single—and serious—error in judgment. He took a shortcut to get around the technical requirements for obtaining a search warrant. He swore out an affidavit that he had heard certain things from an informant about drug dealing at sixteen Tyler Street. And bear this in mind: everything he swore was true, except for one thing: it was Detective Dunleavy, not Detective Carvalho, who heard those details from an informant.

"Everything Detective Carvalho did wrong *after* that had one motive and one motive only: to shield himself from the consequences of having sworn that false affidavit. Not, mind you, to help the prosecution's case. On the contrary, he almost got it thrown out of court. No, he was not lying to convict Mr. Chin. He lied, as he himself admitted, to save his own skin.

"So he said he couldn't find his informant. He pretended to look for him. When he learned that Danny Li was Dunleavy's informant, he tried to scare him out of testifying because that would expose his lies. He did this even knowing that we desperately wanted the informant to assist us in this prosecution. These were not the acts of a policeman who plants or destroys evidence to assure a conviction. Quite the opposite.

"Eventually, Carvalho came to see that he had to come forward and tell the truth. Better late than never. But at no time did he lie to you about any matter that has a bearing on the guilt or innocence of Michael Chin. Detective Carvalho is not hiding his informant. He had none. And if IT existed, believe me, I'd be the first to want to put him on the stand. So I could cross-examine him on what he claimed to know about this John character.

"Consider this, if you will, for a moment. If Detective Carvalho was just making all this up—about Danny being the real snitch and IT not existing—so he could help convict Michael Chin, why didn't he testify that he had made up that business about John as well? Think about it. John has been the linchpin of the defense's theory of this case since day one. First, because IT's account of John's presence at the scene just before the murder conflicts with the testimony of the prosecution's three witnesses, who say he wasn't. And second, because Ms. Kerlinsky started hinting wildly that John might have been the actual murderer. Well, if you're Carvalho and you want to invent testimony that would help the case against the defendant, why stop at pretending there is no IT? Why not say you made up the business about John as well? What could be easier?

"And *why* didn't he do that, ladies and gentlemen? Because it wasn't true. He had every incentive to deny John's existence, and he did not. For that matter, he had every incentive to *maintain* the existence of IT, which he could have done by simply keeping his mouth shut. He did not. He came forward.

"That is not the conduct of a man who is seeking to frame Michael Chin. That is the conduct of a fallible human being who eventually came forward and told the truth even though he knows it will bring him a mess of trouble. IT does not exist. No one is keeping some mystery witness away from you."

DeMarco stopped and ran his hand through his thick mop of hair as if he were suddenly very weary. He stared down at the bare lectern.

"Please," he said, lifting his head slowly to engage them again, "do not judge this case by the conduct of the police officers involved. Do not let that conduct deflect you from your sworn duty, which is to weigh the evidence fairly and determine whether that man, that man *there*"—and he swung himself around and pointed at the defendant, who blinked back at him in surprise—"shot Detective Francis Dunleavy. Frannie was a policeman, too, remember. He was the one who asked Carvalho to get the affidavit for him. Apparently, the officers viewed these arrangements as business as usual. Don't get me wrong: I'm not condoning it. But he does not deserve to have his killer walk out of here, free as a bird, just because he and his fellow officers made mistakes.

"Mistake or no mistake, Frannie Dunleavy was trying to do his job. It's a very, very tough job. One in which the bad guys go free if you make a mistake. Frannie gave his life to do his job. Tonight, when you return to your homes and families, you're a little safer, a little more secure, because men and women like Frannie do their job. Remember, too, that in Jamaica Plain tonight, there'll be a modest little triple-decker with its lights burning. There's a bike on the porch and a battered station wagon in the driveway. And inside, a mother and three children are without a husband and father because Frannie was doing his job. That's all they will have to console them, that he died like that—as a hero, doing his job.

"They deserve more than that meager consolation. They deserve *justice*." DeMarco's voice rang in the hushed chamber. "*Frannie* deserves justice. Don't let anyone talk you out of that. The overwhelming evidence presented at this trial, from every witness you heard, proves that Frannie died because Michael Chin shot him down to avoid arrest. Michael Chin heard the banging of the hammer on the door and he made a choice. Michael Chin chose murder. Justice demands that he answer for that choice.

"Now it's time for your choice. Ladies and gentlemen, there is only one possible verdict here that fits the evidence and does justice for Francis Dunleavy. And that is a verdict that the defendant, Michael Chin, is guilty of murder in the first degree."

# 49

---

## The Boat Room

The morning after receiving his delivery from the Hunan Palace, Matthew was up before first light, having slept less than two hours. The morning broke clean and cold, its chill a warning that autumn was about to give way to winter. Leaving Laura's apartment, he decided to make the long walk from the South End to his office. The cold air cleared his head, and a brisk pace kept him warm despite the sharp wind bearing down on him from the direction of the harbor. He walked north on Tremont.

At the last minute he decided to cut through Chinatown. Even at this hour Beach Street was bustling with activity, as men hurried by with barrows filled with foodstuffs, and vegetable hawkers loaded their sidewalk display cases. Coffee shops and bakeries were already open for business, and men clustered on corners smoking and laughing, some drinking tea. Cars were scarce; it was hard to believe that the streets would soon be so choked with traffic that driving through Chinatown would be unthinkable.

When he passed the Skydragon he kept his eyes directed straight ahead of him.

He stopped at the corner where Tyler Street began its southerly course toward Kneeland. Looking down Tyler he could see the steps below the entrance to the tenement where Dunleavy had been shot. He could just make out the spalling on the corner of one of the steps. He was struck by how long ago that event seemed to have occurred, and how many emotional bridges he had crossed—and burned—since then.

A Dodge Caravan filled with Asians turned in front of him, cutting off his view, and he thought of Danny again. He, too, once had left Chinatown for the suburbs each morning in a van loaded with waiters and cooks and busboys, all headed for the Lotus Blossom. Probably illegal immigrants, most of them, for whom the long hours and low pay—much of it cash and under the table—had seemed their ticket to a better life. As, no doubt, it had seemed to Danny as well. And perhaps to Michael Chin?

He stepped across Beach and headed toward the colorful pagoda arch known as the Chinatown Gateway. A gift to the city from the government of Taiwan, the arch was losing its paint and needed restoration. He glanced idly at the Nankin on the corner to his left and wondered if Julie still worked there.

Passing through the arch, he made his way north up Kingston Street and turned right to march up High Street. Looming in front of him, a few blocks ahead, was the Trifle Tower. In the early morning sunlight its pink granite panels were suffused with a lambent glow, and even the phony Palladian windows, transmuted magically into glittering mirrors, drew him to them. He had never seen the Tower in this light, and for the first time he wondered if he had been too hasty in dismissing its architectural claims. The thought saddened him, for he was reminded that he was unlikely to be working in the Trifle Tower much longer. Assuming he lasted out the day.

Daphnis & Clooney was a tomb at this time of the morning. He was in his office before seven, poring over his Danny file. He spent most of the morning continuing his preparations. On his instructions, Sally allowed only a single interruption, a call from Ira, which he finally received about nine-thirty.

"Ira," he said, picking up the phone.

"Well," said Ira, "he wasn't too happy about it, but Ike finally agreed to give me fifteen minutes. They'll expect me about twelve-fifteen. Just before they get their feed, so they'll probably be getting pretty snappish."

"That's great, Ira," said Matthew. The fear washed over him again when he realized it was actually going to happen. Then he felt gratitude for his friend's support. "Ira," he said, "I want to thank you. For sticking your neck out like this. It's an act of friendship."

Ira guffawed. "More like an act of self-destruction. But, like I said before, I don't like it when somebody diddles with my law firm. Especially when it's one of my partners."

"Should we meet outside the Boat Room? Do they know I'm coming?"

"No. I didn't want to push my luck. I'll swing by and pick you up a few minutes before. And Matt?"

"Yes?"

"Be brief and get to the point early. These guys are going to take a lot of convincing."

"I will, Ira."

Matthew hung up. He was surprised how scared he felt. Even his hands were shaking. He shook his head once, hard, and forced himself back to work.

The Boat Room, so called because its walls were hung exclusively with prints of sailing vessels, was a semi-circular conference room just across the reception area on the thirty-ninth floor of the Trifle Tower. At eleven each Thursday the Management Committee of Daphnis & Clooney entered this windowless space and gathered around its oval conference table, a massive structure fashioned from a single sheet of granite and trimmed about its circumference in chamfered oak. On the table Mrs. Beadle would place flowers and a silver coffee set with white china cups and saucers. Before the chairs for each of the five members she would arrange a pad of paper and the week's agenda, to which were affixed all the documents needed to make business decisions for the running of the firm.

At precisely twelve-fifteen Matthew followed Ira into the

Boat Room. The committee members, who were clustered together at one end of the big table, looked up at Ira with mild curiosity, then surprise when Matthew appeared. They recovered quickly and smiled indulgently toward Ira.

The four men were in shirtsleeves. Ike Rosenthal, the chairman, sat at the head, with Rowell Falk to his right and Ben Fleishman on his left. The fourth man, Lindsay Wolsey, sat next to Fleishman. Wolsey was almost as large as Ira, and his bullet-shaped head was home only to the cotton fluff around his ears and a neatly trimmed beard. A bankruptcy lawyer, Wolsey was a blunt-spoken man who was respected for his business judgment. The only woman in the room, and the firm's only African-American partner, was Petina Stong, who wore a gray suit over which she had draped one of her trademark scarves. She was a striking woman with high, prominent cheekbones, and her scarf's brilliant colors— splashes of crimson and azure—sparkled gaily against her dark brown skin.

As chairman, it fell to Rosenthal to break the ice. "Well, Ira, we've made some time for you, but I confess I'm a little nonplussed." By twitching his eyebrows in Matthew's direction, he left little doubt as to the source of his discomfiture.

Ira said, "Thank you, Ike." He swept his gaze around the table. "Let me thank all of you for allowing this intrusion. And for permitting me to violate your sanctum by bringing an associate with me." He smiled at them.

"Spare us the stand-up comedy, Ira," said Wolsey grumpily. "What the hell is this about?"

Ira dipped his head in a slight bow. "I'm sorry, Lin. I'll get right to the point. I asked Ike if I could come here because I have information which strongly suggests that a member of the firm may have been involved in criminal misconduct."

"What?" It was Falk who leaned forward and stared at him incredulously. Feeling himself bristle with anger, Matthew noticed the fear had left him, shooed away like a noisy child out the door. He was now itching to get started.

"Please, Rowell," Ira continued. "Just hear us out." He looked at Rosenthal. "May we sit down?"

Rosenthal paused, then nodded. They sat down at the far

end of the table. Matthew laid his stack of exhibits in front of him.

Ira said, "I'm here because I knew you wouldn't even listen to Matt otherwise, let alone credit what he's about to tell you. Also, because I think his accusation has merit. Since it was Matt who figured it out, I'm going to ask you to listen to him. Matt?"

Ira smiled at him encouragingly. Matthew placed both hands on the surface of the table and looked at his listeners. His gaze lingered briefly on Falk, who showed him nothing.

"I have uncovered evidence," he began, "that a partner in this firm—a member of this committee, in fact—has engaged in what can only be described as a conspiracy to commit murder. The murder of a firm client. My client, Danny Li."

Shocked, his listeners said nothing. Only Fleishman seemed to react, as he rolled his eyes up and to one side in exasperation.

"Please," Matthew continued. "Hear me out before you dismiss me as some guilt-stricken paranoid, as Ira did for some time—until I got lucky. Just ten minutes is all I ask."

Rosenthal gave him a curt nod of grudging indulgence.

"Like everybody else, I assumed that Danny was killed because I screwed up at his bail hearing by disclosing information his killers used to determine his identity. Then, among documents gathered for the *Felter* case, I discovered a very strange sheet of paper. Buried in Lo Fat's files relating to the ownership of One Adams Place. It was a schedule of beneficiaries for an unidentified realty trust. It listed only one beneficiary: Danny Li."

He passed copies of the schedule to Ira, who handed them around the table.

"A coincidence? Possibly. Li is a common Cantonese name, I'm told. But it got me curious, so I looked harder and I found what I believe was the trust that went with the schedule." The declaration of trust followed the schedule around the table.

Fleishman spoke up as the papers went around. "How did you get access to these documents?" he asked suspiciously.

For a moment Matthew feared they would get sidetracked on the issue of access and he'd never get to make his case.

He said, "You forget, Ben. They were in my office for weeks before you had them hauled off and locked up."

The statement was true as far as it went, Matthew told himself, and a frowning Fleishman apparently accepted the false inference it invited.

Matthew continued. "That trust instrument is for something called the Twenty-seven Fayette Realty Trust, and, from what I can tell from the other documents, it is entitled to receive eleven percent of the profits from the hotel project. Twenty-seven Fayette happens to be the Waltham street address of the restaurant Danny once owned. I knew this because I represented him in a lawsuit over his ownership of that restaurant. During a deposition in that case, Danny told me he feared he would get killed if he answered questions about his ownership of interests in any real estate.

"In addition, the mailing address for the trust was a law office, the office of the lawyer—a guy named Morrissey—who just happens to have represented the three men arrested with Michael Chin after Dunleavy's murder.

"Now, this was getting to be just too much of a coincidence. Danny as the sole beneficiary of a trust that owned eleven percent of Adams Place, with the checks to be mailed to the office of the lawyer who represented defendants in a case on which Danny was wanted as a material witness? Too much.

"Danny was a small-time hustler. Eleven percent of Adams Place? This was way out of his league. It had to mean he was a straw for somebody else. Somebody whose name couldn't be on the papers."

"Are you suggesting," Petina Stong interrupted him, "that he was a straw for someone in the firm?"

"No. I believe he held it for Herman Vu. But I can't really prove that. But I discovered *another* trust in those files, one whose significance I did not appreciate at the time because its stake in the project was small. It's called the Bursting Rapture Realty Trust. Bursting Rapture gets one and a half percent of the profits. Its trustee is a Maine corporation called the Hesperidee Corporation."

He handed copies of the trust agreement around.

"And then, just yesterday, I happened to discover that the

name of this trust, and the name of the corporation, were both taken from the titles of poems by Robert Frost. And it occurred to me that the biggest fan of Robert Frost I knew was Lo Fat's lawyer. Rowell Falk."

Falk leaned forward, a bemused look on his face. It was Fleishman who snorted his disbelief.

"*This* is your evidence?" he demanded, his jutting eyebrows massing as he scowled at Matthew.

"No, sir," said Matthew. "It was just what piqued my curiosity. That, and the fact that both trust agreements are obviously drawn entirely from the corporate department's form book. So I figured someone, probably Rowell as Lo Fat's lawyer, had drafted the trust agreements for Bursting Rapture and Twenty-seven Fayette. But that could have been entirely innocent. I mean, the entities had to be named *something,* so why shouldn't he indulge his hobbyhorse in picking the names?

"But then I did something I should have done long ago. I got a copy of the articles of incorporation filed for the Hesperidee Corporation. Up in Maine. And I discovered that its incorporator was one Howard Ramseth. You remember him? He left a couple years ago to take a job as in-house counsel? So I called him up and, yes, he remembers setting up Hesperidee. And Rowell had him do it."

"But that," Wolsey said, "could have been just another part of the legal work he was doing for Lo Fat."

"But it wasn't," said Matthew. "Hesperidee was set up more than a year before the One Adams deal got started. And it was set up for another reason entirely, according to Howard.

"Howard says it was established to hold the deed to Rowell's Maine vacation home. His island."

The room was still as the implications of this information sank in. Matthew resumed.

"I haven't checked it yet, but I'm sure Howard has it right. If someone were to run title on Rowell's island, you'd find the Hesperidee Corporation on the deed. That means that Rowell directs Bursting Rapture, and he's been getting one and a half percent of the profits from One Adams Place.

"Now, owning an undisclosed stake in a client venture has

got to be a violation of the firm's partnership agreement, not to mention a breach of his duties to his partners anyway. However you slice it, he's been raking in secret profits from a venture with a client of the firm."

None of the partners looked at Falk, who stared impassively back at Matthew.

Rosenthal said, "This may be a matter for the partnership, but you're still a long way away from conspiracy to murder."

Matthew said, "Let me tell you what I think happened. Then you can decide for yourself. Let's go back to 1990, '91. Lo Fat has embarked on his dream, his grandiose project to build One Adams Place. He gets approval from the city's redevelopment agency to proceed. But the commercial real estate market has cratered. Construction lenders are skittish. Money is scarce and tight. Lo Fat desperately needs an infusion of capital.

"So desperately, in fact, that he goes to Herman Vu and the Tung On for it. They cut a deal. For bailing him out, Vu gets eleven percent of the net. His participation must be hidden, of course, and Rowell arranges cover through a shell game of realty trusts and limited partnerships—and even when you get to the bottom of those, the trail stops at Danny Li. Danny agrees, for some unknown consideration, to act as straw for Vu. And that's how Vu gets his money out. By check paid to Twenty-seven Fayette, sent care of Morrissey's law firm, and no doubt paid back out by a different check to Danny. Danny in turn gets the cash to Vu somehow. And everybody's happy.

"That's why Danny couldn't afford to discuss his real estate holdings during his deposition in 1992. And that's why, when the DA was breathing fire at him, he refused to accept protection. He said he had irons in the fire. Twenty-seven Fayette was his iron.

"Meanwhile, back in 1991, Lo Fat's illiquidity makes itself felt here, too. At Daphnis and Clooney. He can't pay his legal bills. Rowell is busy setting up the paperwork for compensating Lo Fat's new silent partner, so he suggests they just do the same thing with the legal bills. Give Rowell a piece of the action in exchange for his forbearance in pressing for the payment of his fees. One and a half percent. He sets up Bursting Rapture to receive it. And names as its trustee the Hesperidee Corporation, which he had already set up to own his island.

"That was his mistake, of course. His participation would have been virtually undetectable if he hadn't used Hesperidee. Because his fingerprints were all over that entity. I suppose he figured no one would ever have cause to look in the secretary of state's office way up in Maine.

"Anyway, things change. The market sweetens and Adams Place turns gold. It proves to be a big moneymaker. Lo Fat and Vu get rich. Rowell muddles through on his one and a half percent.

"Fast forward to 1995. Francis Dunleavy gets murdered. The DA wants a snitch. Danny comes back to me for help and I open a new file. Rowell gets my confidential memo and recognizes Danny's name. And he grasps immediately that Vu's straw is an informant. He probably figured he was a drug addict into the bargain, given the kind of informing Danny was doing.

"This was not a stable situation. To have the secrecy of your client's relationship with a gangster in the hands of a junkie who provides information to the police. And who's about to become an extremely public person. Very unstable indeed. Plus, if Vu's relationship with Lo Fat is made public, could it be long before someone discovers Bursting Rapture? And the man who's behind the Hesperidee Corporation?

"All it took," Matthew continued, "was a phone call. Probably to Lo Fat. Who gets word to Vu. Bang. Danny's history and everybody's secrets are safe.

"It was Rowell who made that call."

Matthew quailed briefly as he felt the force of their implacable, if unvoiced, hostility to his claim. Falk may have been pocketing funds for years from Lo Fat, funds that should have been assets of the firm, but he remained one of them. Whatever his peccadilloes, they resented Matthew's accusation that their partner was a criminal. Falk himself was a mountain of imperturbability, vouchsafing no reaction beyond a tiny smile that twitched at the corners of his mouth.

Again, it was Fleishman who pressed him. "That's one hell of a leap, Matt. You better have more than that."

Matthew breathed deeply and went on. "I do, Ben. Take a look at how he responded when I opened the case—the new one in which I would be representing Danny as a material witness in the *Chin* prosecution. You see, I screwed up the new case form when I opened the case. I listed myself as originating attorney. By chance, some time later, I learned I had no right to claim the OA credit. It should have gone to the lawyer who was the OA on the very first matter Danny brought to the firm. For the restaurant litigation.

"Now, my discovery came on the heels of learning Danny's role in Lo Fat's project. I was coming to suspect that someone in the firm might have tipped Danny's killers. This OA business made me even more suspicious. Paranoid, Ira thought."

Matthew smiled at his friend, who did not smile back. *Get on with it*, read Matthew.

"Why, I asked myself, didn't the *real* OA demand his rightful credit? After all, Danny had just paid a five-thousand-dollar retainer and the case looked like a complicated piece of work, so there were going to be some dollars made, a good chunk of which would end up going to the OA. That chunk couldn't come to me, of course; I'm just a salaried employee, not a partner sharing the fees. So why didn't the real OA stand up? Did he just miss it?"

Matthew answered his own question. "No. He was a member of this committee, and therefore privy to my confidential memo naming Danny as the client. The memo also mentioned the work I had done for him on the restaurant case, so the OA *had* to have realized he was entitled to the credit. But he said nothing. Again, why?

"Because he didn't want to draw attention to himself and his connection with Danny. Remember, he's about to tip Danny's killers to his identity. If something happened to Danny, someone might start looking for who had tipped. So why invite needless scrutiny by making a fuss about his rights to Danny as a client?

"Of course, things worked out far better than he could have hoped. I screwed up—and big-time—at Danny's bail hearing. Everybody blamed me. So did I. But then I saw Danny's name on that schedule of beneficiaries and I began to wonder why Ben didn't bitch about the OA credit."

"Me!" Fleishman craned his neck forward. "What are you talking about?"

"You, Ben. Central Files has you down as the OA for Danny's first case. And you didn't complain."

"Buddy," said Fleishman, "you've really got your head up the old wazoo. I was not Danny's OA."

"I know that, Ben."

"I'm the OA." Falk spoke for the first time. "I bring in more business than anybody in this firm. I can't be expected to remember every nickel-and-dime client I bring in the door."

"Maybe so, Rowell," said Matthew. "But Central Files has Ben down for it anyway. On the cards as well as the computer. And that fact had me suspecting Ben for quite a while."

He turned his attention to Fleishman. "I'm sorry, Ben. But you were the one who first sent Danny to me. You were the one who fired me from the *Felter* case and then arranged things so I wouldn't have access to the documents where I might stumble onto Danny's tracks in Lo Fat's files. Plus, I figured you were trying to ease me out the door by getting me to take a public reprimand from the Board of Bar Overseers."

Fleishman stared at him in disbelief.

Matthew continued. "I was wrong, Ben. And I'm sorry. No doubt my judgment was affected by how pissed I was at you for dumping me."

"I did what I thought was best for everyone involved— especially you," said Fleishman.

"I know that now, Ben. But, again, it was that OA business that kept me from seeing that. Until, that is, I looked through Rowell's Frost collection and discovered Rowell's tracks all over everything. That started me thinking about Lo Fat's connection with Rowell. So I went back to Central Files to pull the cards to see when it was that you and Rowell came to represent Lo Fat.

"Of course, I learned Lo Fat was Rowell's client, first coming to the firm in the mideighties. I also discovered that you weren't listed as a responsible attorney on a Lo Fat matter until 1993. This caught my attention. How, I asked myself, would Lo Fat have known to call you in 1992—a year before you ever represented him—and ask you to help out his friend Danny in a squabble over the restaurant?"

"He didn't," said Fleishman. He twisted his head slightly to look at Falk for the first time. Falk, who kept staring at Matthew, did not meet his gaze.

Falk spoke, a sour grimace on his face. "It was an obvious transcription error. Someone typed 'BF' instead of 'RF' on the new case form. The initials are pretty similar to begin with. Come to think of it, it was a litigation matter in Ben's department. It would have been *his* secretary who typed it wrong in the first place."

Matthew smiled. He was enjoying this now.

"It's too bad we can't confirm that with Central Files," he said. "The original new case form is missing from their files. Mrs. Beadle was quite disturbed, in fact. It never occurred to her, of course, that someone might have taken it. You see, I did a bad thing." He smiled. "Please don't tell Mrs. Beadle, but I stole that 1993 card that first listed Ben as RA. I also lifted the 1992 card for Danny's first case, the one that showed Ben as OA."

He pulled the cards from his inside coat pocket and, leaning out over the table, laid them side by side in the middle of the granite slab for their inspection.

"Notice," he went on, "how beat up the 1993 card is, especially the upper corners, which are soiled from so many thumbs. And then see how pristinely preserved the 1992 card is. I'm no expert on this stuff, but I'm willing to bet you the 1993 card is older than the putative 1992 card."

"Putative?" asked Rosenthal.

"Yes, putative. Rowell pulled Danny's real 1992 card and replaced it with a new one naming Ben as OA. Just in case somebody wondered—as it turned out I did—who the real OA was supposed to be. And he knew I was likely, based on painful past experience, to check the cards as well as the computer data base."

"And you base this allegation on the condition of the cards?" Rosenthal was clearly unimpressed.

"In part. I also have the new case form."

"I thought," said a puzzled Petina Stong, "you said it was missing."

"I said Mrs. *Beadle's* was. But as Rowell has reminded us, it would have been typed by Ben's secretary, and in his capacity as chairman of the litigation department, Ben would keep a copy of that form. So I asked my secretary to get it from his office. As you can see," Matthew said as he handed Ira the copies for circulation, "Rowell's initials identify him as the OA. That means it was not a transcription error."

"No, it doesn't," said Rowell, sounding angry now. "It just means the transcription error occurred in Central Files, when they typed up the cards."

"And the computer?" asked Matthew. "It also names Ben as OA."

"Obviously," Falk explained, as if to a child, "the data entered into the computer was taken from the cards. You're clutching at straws, Matthew. Who could have changed the computer entry, six years after the fact?"

"*You* could, Rowell. Your prowess on computers is hardly a secret. Christ, you've been reviewing my work before I can even get it printed out. With your computer skills and your position as a top administrator, you would have had supervisory-level access to the computer network. Access and knowledge, in other words, that would have allowed you to bypass the read-only command protecting the conflicts data base from mischief."

Falk shook his head. He glanced at his partners to his left, but Rosenthal's attention was fixed on Matthew. Fleishman did catch his eye, but it was not a friendly look.

"There's a way to verify all this, you know," Matthew went on. "I called this friend of mine, Barry Golden. He's a whiz with computers. Barry tells me there is something called a system log in the network. I don't understand it myself—though Rowell might. Anyway, the system log captures all activity on the system by date and time. All you have to do, my friend says, is dump the system log into a program capable of searching by key word, and you can establish the date and time of changes made to the data base."

He added with a smile, "I'll bet you a nickel the change was made after I sent you guys the confidential memo identifying Danny as the missing snitch. And probably in the wee hours of the morning. I mean, who else but the original OA would have a reason to make the change?"

"*You* would," said Falk acidly. "To cast suspicion elsewhere—anywhere but where it belongs: on you for fouling up and getting your client killed. From what we've heard today, it's plain you're not entirely rational."

"Jesus, Rowell. Talk about grasping at straws. And such a curious choice of words, given these trusts and all. But there's another little wrinkle to the system log I didn't get to yet. It can actually identify the *user* who made the change. How about it, Rowell? Will we find you made the change from your own computer?"

For the first time, Falk looked frightened, his eyes widening, and Matthew knew he had him. The others seemed to notice, too, for they remained silent. Matthew pressed on.

Matthew said, "I have a couple questions for you guys. Ben, whose idea was it to dump me from the *Felter* case? Was it Rowell's?"

Fleishman frowned. "No, as a matter of fact. I got a call directly from the client. He was concerned about appearances, given his position in the community."

"But did he suggest the rationale? My relationship with Laura, I mean?"

"No," said Fleishman, sliding his eyes in Falk's direction. "That was Rowell's idea."

"And the Chinese wall? To screen me away from the files? Was that Rowell's idea, too?

Fleishman was looking squarely at Falk now. "Yes. He even insisted they be locked up."

"To make sure I never made the connection between Danny and Lo Fat. He believed the files had been sanitized, but you can never be sure with so much paper. And he was right. The schedule of beneficiaries was filed out of sequence and went unnoticed."

He looked at Ike. "One more question. Who suggested that you send me that memo when I opened the case? The one that told me to let you know as soon as Danny was arrested?"

Rosenthal's eyes never left Matthew's. "Rowell did," he said.

Matthew sat back in the plush conference chair and breathed deeply. He waited for their reaction. He had convinced them, he was sure of it. But what would they do with it?

It was Wolsey who spoke first.

"This doesn't make sense. Why would he do it? What motive could he have? Just to keep us from discovering his little skim from Adams Place?"

"That's one reason, though not, I grant you, a very compelling one. No, I believe Rowell had bigger ambitions. Jackie Crimmins keeps dropping these hints about putting Rowell on the bench. At first I pooh-poohed them. I couldn't imagine Rowell on the trial court. But then I heard Jackie talk about him in the same breath as the SJC, and it came to me. Rowell wants a seat on the Supreme Judicial Court. It would be the crowning achievement of a distinguished legal career. I always wondered why he was such a big booster for Jackie Crimmins. I mean, he's a man whose politics and style otherwise would have curdled the blue blood in Rowell's veins. Especially Jackie's stand on the death penalty. It clashed so loudly with Rowell's proud tradition of supporting civil liberties. But if Jackie becomes governor and owes Rowell a big favor . . . ?

"So Rowell starts writing that article on state constitutional law. *Criminal* law, for Christ's sake. This wasn't some nascent passion, coming to the fore in his maturity. It was a calculated maneuver to broaden his scholarly credentials, to show himself off as something more than a business lawyer.

"But let the press get wind of his dealings with Lo Fat, and Lo Fat's connection to organized crime, and you can kiss good-bye to his prospects for a seat on the SJC. Danny threatened all that, and Rowell did what was necessary to end that threat."

There was a glumness in the room now. Falk slowly looked about him, as if taking stock.

"You don't really expect," he asked contemptuously, "a prosecutor to take any of this, this *crap* seriously, do you? All this silly business about compensation credits?"

"No, Rowell," said Matthew. "I doubt they could even get an indictment with what I've got, let alone a conviction. And

I doubt there's much more evidence to find. You've been pretty careful. I'm not here to suggest that the committee call the cops."

"What *do* you want?" asked Rosenthal. "Just what is it you expect us to do with this information?"

It was Ira who answered, raising his voice.

"I want him outa here! I don't want somebody like this as a partner."

"In your dreams," Falk said flatly.

Rosenthal stared back and forth at the two of them in horror, visions of years of nasty and scandalous litigation dancing luridly before him.

"I want more than that," Matthew interjected quietly. "I want him out of the practice. Let him live on his income from One Adams Place. And if you guys don't back me on this, I'll take it so public the firm will never recover from the stink. Eddie Felch would just lap this stuff up. I've had the good fortune to make his acquaintance recently."

He watched Rosenthal stiffen in anger at this threat to his firm. Before he could compose himself and respond, Fleishman jumped in.

"You do that, Matt, and you'll be finished. And I don't mean just at D and C. Everything you know about Lo Fat's business dealings is a client secret. Secrets you have an ethical obligation to maintain. You go blabbing that stuff to the press and your present difficulties with the Board of Bar Overseers will seem downright trivial. They'll pull your goddamn ticket!"

"Thank God," said Matthew, "for the Board of Bar Overseers."

From the smile on his face, they could see he was not being sarcastic.

"You forget that ethically I can reveal client secrets to defend myself against a charge of misconduct," Matthew continued, still smiling. "In order to justify a harsh sanction, they're claiming my ineptitude at that bail hearing caused Danny's death. Well, everything I've told you today is evidence that I did *not* cause his death. I might have to *insist* on a public hearing."

"You're asking for a lot of trouble, Matt," said Fleishman.

"I think there'll be enough to go around for all of us."

"Not for me," said Wolsey harshly. He turned to face Falk. "I'm with Ira. Rowell, you're out."

A starchless Rowell Falk stared at the blank pad of paper in front of him. He said nothing as Wolsey stood up and made for the door. Then Rosenthal stood up as well.

Before Wolsey reached the door, however, it swung inward and Mrs. Beadle wheeled in a cart heaped with sandwiches and fresh fruit. She seemed surprised to see Wolsey standing in front of her, but he mutely made his way around her and disappeared. Rosenthal followed him. As Fleishman and Stong rose to join their departing colleagues, Mrs. Beadle noticed Matthew and Ira for the first time.

"I don't think anyone will be wanting lunch today, Mrs. Beadle," said Ira.

"Is it because of the news?" she asked, turning her head to look after the retreating lawyers.

"What news?" asked Ira.

Mrs. Beadle seemed befuddled. "About Michael Chin," she said. "He was acquitted. They announced the verdict a few minutes ago."

"Well," said Ira, looking over at the slumping figure of Rowell Falk, "I guess one out of two ain't bad."

A moment later Matthew realized that Ira and Mrs. Beadle had gone and he was alone with Falk. The man still had not moved. He still seemed to stare at a spot in the center of the granite table before him.

"You know," Matthew said, "I don't suppose I'll ever know the real reason why you took me under your wing after my performance review. Making me your coauthor and all. Did you really want to work with me, or did you just want to keep tabs on me?"

Falk raised his eyes only and peered at Matthew over the tops of his reading glasses.

"No," said Matthew, shaking his head. "I don't think I want to know. I should thank you for one thing, though. For suggesting to Ike that he send that memo telling me to inform him when Danny was arrested. You gave him a chance, didn't you? In the hope the DA would never find him. It took a certain amount of courage on your part. The safest move would have been to make your call as soon as you learned he was the snitch. To have him taken out immediately. But you held off until I reported that the police had him in custody. Hoping you wouldn't have to finger him for murder. For that little bit of grace, I suppose I should be grateful. But I just can't summon up the gratitude. You know why?"

He stared into the hollow of Rowell Falk's eyes.

"Because I don't think Danny would see it that way."

He left the room.

# 50

---

## The Poor Son of a Bitch

Sarah fooled herself into thinking she felt relaxed and rested, in her chinos and open-necked blue blouse, as she sat across the table from Matthew. But she knew her accumulated exhaustion hadn't left her just because she'd had a good night's sleep two days in a row.

They met at a popular seafood restaurant on Beacon Hill, a short walk across the Common and the Public Garden from her office in the Statler Building. She had agreed to take a break from catching up on the paperwork she had neglected during the trial.

After they ordered Matthew raised his wineglass in salute. "Congratulations, Sarah. They were out less than three hours. It must be very satisfying."

She smiled and raised her own glass. "Thank you," she said. "But you know, ever since I filed that motion to produce the informant, things kept breaking my way. They practically handed it to me, the cops and Jerry. Even when Doyle reinstated the indictment, I was sure I was going to win, only with more panache. When you come to think of it, I won just about every major battle along the way. Except near the end, when Doyle wouldn't let me mention the missing drugs in my closing."

"Why not?"

"Not enough foundation, he said. Too speculative. No proof there ever were any drugs to go missing. What crap! But that just gave me an issue for appeal in case the jury went nuts. So even that was OK."

"Well," said Matthew, "You were just terrific. Really. I loved the bit about Pluto. I didn't know you were a student of astronomy."

"Are you kidding?" She took a sip of wine and smiled broadly. "I made all that up. About the discovery of Pluto. I suppose something like that must have happened. But it just came to me, right there in the middle of my closing, and I couldn't resist." She cocked her head and grinned at him. "You won't tell on me, will you?"

Matthew laughed out loud. They fell silent as a waitress laid steaming cups of seafood chowder in front of them. Matthew tore open his package of oyster crackers while Sarah filled her spoon with the creamy liquid.

"What next?" he asked. "Another criminal case?"

"Oh, I'm not finished with Michael yet. He still has his civil rights claim against the city for the beating he took in jail. Looks like it will settle, though." She sipped noiselessly from her spoon.

"Sounds like Michael made out like a bandit."

Sarah halted her spoon on its way back to the bowl, then smiled. "So tell me," she said, "all these things you said you discovered."

He told her.

By the time he finished, her soup bowl was still half full and her broiled scrod lay untouched and cooling on the plate next to it.

"Amazing," she said softly. "Even *I've* heard of Rowell Falk. He's leaving the firm? For sure?"

"I think he's toast," said Matthew. He speared another one of his scallops.

"The business with the compensation credits was so *stupid*."

"Well, you're right that it couldn't withstand much scrutiny. He must have known that. But if anyone noticed the case was carrying the wrong OA, he probably figured he could just blow it off as an error in transcription. That's what he tried on the committee. It would have worked, too, if it hadn't been for the computer evidence. That killed him."

"What if it hadn't worked? I mean, suppose they had all stuck together. Would you really have gone public with the whole thing before the Board of Bar Overseers?"

Matthew feigned a shudder and, elbows tucked into his sides, waggled his fingers in front of him. "Are you nuts?" he said with a grimace. "After getting my mouth-watering delivery from Herman Vu?"

"Things got a little sticky?" Sarah couldn't help herself.

"Especially the rice," he said, smiling with her. "I don't think I'll ever get Laura to eat dim sum. No," he went on, serious again. "It was all a bluff. All I wanted was to nail Falk. If that hadn't happened, I'd have just folded up my tent and gone home. Fortunately, it did work. If Vu wants me to hold my tongue—so to speak—I will. They can have my silence now."

"And you think you're safe."

"I don't see why not. They wanted me to butt out. Well, I have. Except for what went on in that Management Committee meeting. And you can be sure Daphnis and Clooney isn't gonna want to make any of it public. Neither will Falk. Plus I did something to give me a little bit of an edge with Vu. A counterthreat."

Sarah smiled. "A counterthreat?"

"Yeah. I wrote up everything I knew about the whole mess and stapled all the documents I had to it. I gave it to somebody to hold for me. And just to see that the right people know about my package, I sent a copy of the whole thing to Jimmy Morrissey."

Sarah raised her eyebrows at the mention of the name.

"Hey," Matthew explained, "who else could have told them I was onto something they would want me to butt out of? So I sent it to him, with a little note explaining that the package would be delivered to Eddie Felch if anything the least bit untoward ever happened to Laura or me."

"I like it," Sarah said. "I like it a lot."

"It's not perfect. Except for Falk, they still get away with it. But at least I got Falk. I owed Danny that much."

Grim-faced now, Matthew turned away and gazed in the direction of the raw bar, his scallops forgotten. Sarah watched him carefully for a moment, then made up her mind. She waited until he turned back to her.

"I'm going to tell you anyway," she announced. "Michael will be deported soon, so I can't see how it could hurt him."

"What can't hurt him?" Matthew asked, dipping his head to one side.

"Let me tell you a little story, Matt. It's about Pluto. Not the planet this time, but the man. The fifth man in the room. And *this* one I'm not making up."

Once upon a time, she told him, after enduring many trials before and after reaching this country, Michael Chin finally found steady and gainful employment. Nothing fancy, mind you. He was a gopher, an errand boy for the Tung On. He did things like collecting envelopes filled with protection money from merchants. Or gathering the TO's cut of gambling receipts at the social clubs. But eventually he gravitated to the drug trade. Sometimes he manned a retail outfit, like the apartment where Dunleavy was shot. Other times he made small deliveries. It wasn't exactly what he'd dreamed of when he left Hong Kong, but it beat the hell out of bussing dishes.

Then, one cold night in February, he and Warren Liu were told to meet a car that would stop for them on Kneeland Street. They were to accompany the driver to Charlestown. Michael never knew the address, but he thought it was near the old Navy Yard. When they got to Charlestown, the driver—Pluto—removed a shiny metal attaché case from the trunk and led them into a house. There they met three men, who had a briefcase of their own. An exchange took place. Money was transferred from Pluto's briefcase to theirs, and several large plastic bags full of white powder were tucked into Pluto's briefcase, which he promptly locked.

The three of them went back to the car, restowed the briefcase, and drove to Chinatown. They parked just east of the arch, on Surface Road, the southbound feeder to the Southeast Expressway. Pluto took his bag from the trunk and they proceeded on foot through the arch into Chinatown. They then walked to 16 Tyler Street. They went up to the third floor, where Pluto rapped on a heavy steel door and identified himself to a man behind it. Dai Cheng let them in.

Pluto dropped the bag on the bed and introduced Michael to Cheng, who sat down at a table in the middle of the room where he resumed rolling small quantities of powder into lottery tickets. There was a large gun lying on the table.

To Michael's surprise, someone entered the room from the window across from the apartment door. It was Lai Huong, who had come up from the apartment below when he heard them arrive. Pluto explained to Michael about the little double-floor suite and how it functioned, with retail sales made out of the upper unit through the hole in the door, and backroom operations in the room below. He also told the four of them they were to break down the cocaine into smaller lots and see to it that all of them got delivered to their proper destinations before morning. It would be safest to do this work right there in the upstairs apartment because of that steel door. He was just beginning to detail the various destinations for the repackaged product when the hammering began.

The noise of the hammer on the steel door was deafening in the little room. And things happened so quickly Michael never could piece together everything that happened. He did remember, however, that Pluto looked terrified, staring around in all directions like a trapped rabbit. Then he snatched up the gun from the table and started firing at the door.

A few seconds later the five of them scrambled back down the fire escape to the second-story apartment, where they were all soon screaming at one another. Eventually, Pluto took charge again and started giving orders. He told them all to stay right there, in the apartment, no matter what, while he went to see if there was a way out. If there was, he'd return. And if he didn't return, they'd know he'd been arrested. Then he handed the gun to Michael and left by the front door. Someone eventually stashed the gun under the mattress.

"So there was a John after all?" Matthew interrupted.

Sarah smiled sweetly back at him. "Who's John?" she asked.

Matthew blinked, uncomprehending. "The guy mentioned in Carvalho's affidavit. I mean, wasn't he Pluto?"

Her smile disappeared. "You don't see it yet, do you, Matt?"

"See what?"

"Pluto was Danny."

Matthew gaped at her.

"Danny?" he said at last.

"Yes," she said firmly, her eyes level on his.

"What—I don't get it. I mean, when did you learn this?"

"The first time I interviewed Michael. He told me his name. But of course, I didn't know he was the snitch until after he was dead. Remember, your client's identity was a big secret at the time of the bail hearing, and Michael was not brought up from the jail for it. So I didn't know Danny was your client until the newspapers published his name—after his murder."

Matthew shook his head in bewilderment. "I still don't get it. Why would Danny arrange to have himself raided and then shoot it out?"

"Well, he probably never had much of a choice," Sarah said. "I think we can extrapolate what happened. Dunleavy and Carvalho must have been pressuring him pretty hard to come up with the skinny for a juicy bust. And given what you've told me about his other dealings with Vu, Danny felt he had to keep the narcs happy so his possession beef would go away. Somehow he got word to Dunleavy that the dope had made its way to Tyler Street. How, I don't know. We do know that Dunleavy got a call at the Blue Diner just before the bust. Maybe Danny had somebody helping him, someone who made the call when he got back to Chinatown.

"Anyway, Dunleavy got his call. The diner, remember, was only a couple blocks away. Kelleher testified that Dunleavy said his caller wanted them to wait a bit so the snitch could clear out. But Carvalho was too impatient and the cops showed up early.

"Danny must have had a heart attack when the hammering started. Maybe he feared the cops would give him away in their surprise to see him there. He was just supposed to be a snitch, remember. A purveyor of information. The cops didn't know he was an actual player in the very transaction they were busting. So he panics and starts firing."

"And runs, leaving the others there."

"Exactly."

"But then what?"

"We don't know for sure, but I figure he went to his superiors and gave them an edited version of what had happened. And they sent Jimmy Morrissey to represent the four men who were arrested. Michael says Jimmy pumped him for information for the better part of an hour. Jimmy files some discovery demands and goes through the motions of trying to get bail. Fat chance there. Anyway, the next thing I know I get a call to represent Michael."

"Who from?"

She hesitated. "That I can't tell you," she said. "But it doesn't affect the story."

But Matthew knew who it was. It had to be one of Vu's people.

"You see," she continued, "I learned the other three had turned on Michael, naming him as the shooter. And Michael tells me he's been told to keep his mouth shut, not to testify, and everything will be all right. The whole thing has Jimmy Morrissey's fingerprints all over it. You want to know what I think happened?"

Matthew nodded.

"I can't prove any of this, but I believe Jimmy figured out pretty fast, after talking to his clients and looking at Carvalho's affidavit, that there was no John. His clients never heard of him, and two of them worked out of that apartment on a regular basis. Now, Jimmy, being a savvy old veteran of the war on drugs, figures there was no IT either. The whole affidavit, he decided, was a Cinderella, created out of whole cloth by Carvalho just to get his search warrant. So Jimmy decides to turn that to his advantage. He drops Michael as a client and has his remaining clients swear it was Michael who did the shooting. Jimmy manages to get a deal from DeMarco in exchange for their testimony.

"Now, as to the claim that Michael was the shooter—well,

he knew his clients weren't the most believable sort, and they'd get cut up real bad on cross trying to keep their phony stories straight. And the forensic evidence against him was weak to begin with. No gunpowder traces.

"But what he really had going for him was the affidavit. Jimmy knew that any defense counsel worth her salt would demand, and get, an order to produce IT. Who, Jimmy was convinced after talking to his clients, couldn't exist. And that would put the police and the prosecution between a rock and a hard place. Put them, that is, in precisely the situation they found themselves in as events unfolded. Of course, it worked out far better than Jimmy could have dreamed. He couldn't have *scripted* it any better. For the affidavit, I mean. Fifty-two warrants!

"And, then, just to hold everybody's interest in the affidavit, Jimmy gives it all a liiiiittle twist." She squeezed the pads of her fingers together and gave her hand a quarter turn, like a screwdriver. "He tells his clients not to deny John's existence. Just say he hadn't been around for a while. That way he'd have the prosecution in knots trying to straighten out whether IT existed or not, and who worked out of the third floor and who didn't. Diabolical, don't you think?"

"Ira told me he was crafty," Matthew mused. "But I never expected anything like this. He suborned perjury."

"I said he was savvy. I never claimed he was ethical."

"But how could you go along with it?"

She laughed at him. "I didn't go *along* with it, dear heart. There was nothing else I *could* do. Everything I knew—or suspected, to be more precise—was based on privileged communications from my client. So I couldn't disclose what I had figured out. And besides, do you think Jerry would have believed me if I went to him? Not. He'd think it was *me* being the clever one, trying to blow smoke to muddle up his big cop killer prosecution. No, Matt, I had a client charged with a murder he didn't commit. I did my job."

She spoke with fervor. She knew she was right. DeMarco had held on to his case against Chin with the tenacity of a snapping turtle. He would never have believed her.

Matthew said, "So Morrissey found a way to get all the defendants off."

"Including Danny, don't forget," added Sarah, raising a forefinger to stress her point. "Because he also eliminated the need to search for a fifth man. In fact, one of the beauties of his scheme was that it gave DeMarco a compelling interest in denying the existence of a fifth man. His case would collapse if the jury gave the notion any credence. Which, thank you very much, they did.

"But," she went on, "alas, for Danny's sake, Jimmy was in the dark on one thing. He didn't know that Danny was IT. It's the one piece Jimmy couldn't have known and Danny couldn't tell him. Even so, everything worked perfectly until DeMarco learned who Dunleavy's snitch was."

"Then," said Matthew miserably, "Danny was in the soup and none of us could help him. Especially with Falk tipping off his bosses. Why didn't he run? The poor son of a bitch never had a chance."

"Hey, Matt," said Sarah. "Don't lose *too* much sleep over the guy. He was a dealer and a killer, remember. That's why I'm telling you all this. I thought it would help."

Matthew shook his head. "A dealer, I grant you. But not much of a killer. He was a little guy who got squeezed between the cops and the mob, and he panicked."

Sarah retrieved her purse from the back of the chair next to her. "I guess you knew him better than I did," she said as she extracted her wallet. "I just wanted you to know you weren't grieving for some innocent lamb." She slapped a credit card down on the little tray that held the check. "I promised this lunch would be on me, Matt. Now I'm gonna go earn my fat contingent fee from the bastards who beat up *my* little lamb."

She smiled at him and he did his best to smile back.

Then his eyes widened.

"Wait a minute!" he exclaimed. "What about the drugs? You said he put the briefcase on the bed. What happened to them?"

Sarah gave him a pitying look as she handed the tray to the waitress. "That's what I was trying to bring out at trial, but Judge Doyle wouldn't let me." She turned back toward him as the waitress walked away. She held her hands open before her. "It was the cops. Obviously. It wouldn't be the first time, you know. I figure Carvalho reported an empty briefcase after filching its contents."

Matthew looked down. "That's what Eddie Felch said, but I didn't believe him. I didn't believe him when he told me Danny was a dealer either."

"Right," she said, smiling wryly. "Well, Danny was a dealer and Carvalho was bent. I'm sure he'll manage just fine without his departmental pension."

Matthew stared into her eyes, as if looking for something there. But he wasn't seeing her, she was sure. He was thinking, furiously, groping for something. It was as if she could see the wheeling machinery of his mind, watching as the tumblers turned on their well-oiled spindles and then clicked deftly into alignment and some secret came unlocked.

"Of course!" he said, grinning back at her. "Of course!"

Sarah said good-bye to Matthew at the door and watched him make his way down Park Street in the direction of the Trifle Tower. She wondered briefly about the curious excitement—exaltation, even—that had seized hold of him just before they parted. He had left her with a sense of fixed purpose, but whatever had fired it he hadn't shared with her.

The sunlight was dazzling after the gloom of the restaurant, and she squinted into it as she descended the steps from Beacon Street and into the Boston Common. She would take the long loop back to the office. Reaching into her purse for her sunglasses, she felt a thick packet that puzzled her for a moment until she remembered the four airline tickets to Albuquerque. She swapped glasses and smiled. A day or two to clear up Michael's civil case, and she and her family would be basking in the sun in New Mexico.

She kicked through the leaves on the Common, reveling in the gorgeous autumn afternoon. Squirrels ran before her, couples lingered on benches, and office workers sat on the grass eating their lunches under the watchful eyes of milling pigeons. She was vaguely cognizant of how bone weary she was and knew that the fatigue would swamp her within a couple hours. But right now, with the sun on her face and the smell of damp leaves and humus in her nostrils, she felt as crisp and vibrant as the day itself.

Then, as she stepped into the shade of a gigantic copper beech, the exhaustion kicked in earlier than she had expected, and she felt her body sag under the load. She made her way to a bench and sat down. Closing her eyes, she let the weariness wash over her. After a moment's pause, out of nowhere and unsummoned, a whispered phrase shimmered across the screen of her consciousness.

*Good job.*

Eyes still closed, she smiled as she allowed herself to appreciate what she had accomplished. She *had* done a good job.

Damn good.

She stood up and retraced her steps across the Common. She was headed for Park Station and the subway.

And home.

# 51

---◆---

# Welcome Home

Carvalho swirled the rye around the lip of the shot glass for a second before tossing the whiskey to the back of his throat. Then he picked up his beer and took a sip from the bottle. He got mostly foam at first, followed by enough liquid to drown the gag reflex triggered by raw whiskey on an empty stomach. As the nausea ebbed he waited for his hands to stop shaking.

"Another one, Trubs," he called out tentatively, unsure whether to trust his voice.

"Hey, look at that, Ray," said Trubs, his back to him as he faced the overhead television. On the screen the dour face of Jeremiah DeMarco was mouthing soundlessly. "They're calling you a rogue cop now. Are you a rogue cop, Ray?"

The bartender was grinning at him, no malice in his question.

"Suck one dick and you're a cocksucker for life," Carvalho answered bitterly.

The bartender chuckled appreciatively as he filled his shot glass.

"That's some shitstorm you're in, Ray. You gonna be all right?"

"Sure."

He took a small swallow this time. He looked into his bartender's hard gray eyes, hooded like a reptile's. He detected little there, just mild curiosity. As the bartender turned away and walked up the bar, Carvalho realized with a jolt that Trubs was not his friend—and certainly not someone he would leave himself open to. He had been a regular at the Cork for eight, nine years now, and Trubs had always been behind the bar, but Carvalho knew nothing about the man. Nothing at all. It had never occurred to him to inquire. For his part, Trubs had listened to Carvalho and his friends, to their bruising raillery and the terrible tales of what they had seen and done on the job. But he was not his friend.

*Come to think of it,* he thought, *do I have any friends?* Frannie was dead. And Sal? He hadn't heard from him since that weasel Weiss showed up in Joyce's office. That left only Donna. And she—he noted glumly, as he checked his watch—was late.

He emptied the shot glass. It lay more tranquil on his stomach than the first one, and the shaking had almost disappeared completely. He asked and received another refill.

The relief and exuberance he had experienced after testifying had forsaken him in less than twenty-four hours, only to be replaced by a paralyzing sense of dread and a black depression. Downright joyful company, he was. No wonder she was late.

He wondered what Piscatello was thinking tonight. Did he still think he'd made a smart move, going to the AG the way he had? If he did it to nail Frannie's killer, it sure was a bust. Michael Chin was off the hook and, according to Gogarty, he was likely to pick up some coin from the county for getting beat up. And what did you get for yourself, Sal? Huh? Fuck all. Dorothy McGuire, the assistant attorney general who was hounding them, had made it pretty clear she would seek indictments against both of them. Much to DeMarco's satisfaction, which he had been voicing to every reporter who would listen. The only guy who didn't seem to be out to fry his ass was Jackie Crimmins. He had made that little speech to the press right after the verdict, about the pressures on cops trying to do a tough job with a net of technicalities thrown over them. Nice, but face it. It was just politics.

It wasn't until he had finished off his fifth whiskey that he noticed what was happening. There was nothing there. Nothing. All the booze did was stave off the dry heaves and the shakes. But there was no high. He could not get drunk.

The shit didn't work anymore.

Carvalho's heart began beating rapidly, and he could feel his pulse jumping in his temple. It pounded so hard he was racked by the sudden conviction that his heart would rupture at any moment. Panicked, he whirled his head around, as if looking for help, but no one seemed to notice his plight. He raised his glass and hollered at Trubs. The man ambled back in his direction, taking his sweet time before picking up the bottle and refilling the shot glass.

The bartender noticed something, for he asked, "Are you OK?"

Carvalho nodded, once, hard, and Trubs moved away again. He downed the whiskey and waited for the familiar click.

Still nothing. His heart continued its hammering and he was about to call out to Trubs again when he felt a hand on his arm. Jerking his head in the direction of the touch, he saw Donna's pretty face smiling up at him.

"I'm sorry I'm late, Ray. The traffic was murder."

She slipped off her jacket and laid it across the back of the adjacent barstool. Removing her stocking cap, she shook out her hair as she sat down. Then she looked over at him again and picked up the expression on his face. Her smile evaporated and concern took its place.

"Ray, what's wrong? You look gray."

He rubbed his eyes hard with his thumb and forefinger, leaving them there, pinching the bridge of his nose. The ferocity of the hammering had subsided somewhat and he felt less terrified. But the whiskey still wasn't working.

"Let's get a booth," he croaked. "Trubs! Can we have the bottle over here?"

She tagged after him to the booth, her eyes never leaving his face. They took seats across from one another. He crossed his arms, squeezing his hands under his armpits.

"What is it, Ray? Are you sick?"

He looked at her. "I don't know. The whiskey's not working. It scared the shit out of me for a second."

She looked at him quizzically. "What do you mean, it doesn't work?"

"I mean it's not getting me high. I've had half a dozen shots and I feel nothing. Zilch."

She placed her fingertips on the edge of the table and leaned forward a little. "So why waste your money on it?"

He exhaled harshly. "I 'waste my money' because it clears my fuckin' head. And stops the shakes. But it's not giving me the lift I need."

Trubs arrived and set the bottle on the table. "Anything for you?" he asked Donna.

She waved him off, then said, "Wait. Bring Ray something to eat, will you? You want a burger, honey?" she asked him.

"Yuck. Forget it, I'm fine."

Trubs lingered.

"You should eat something, Ray," Donna pressed.

He raised both hands and made as if to push Trubs away. "Nothing! I'm fine, I said."

Trubs shrugged at Donna and left. She turned back to Carvalho.

"It's the booze, Ray," she said softly.

He straightened up and eyed her with exasperation.

"Well, *duh*!" he spouted angrily, bobbing his head for emphasis. "What the fuck do you think I've just been telling you? It's not working."

He poured himself a shot from the Seagram's bottle. He drank it down in two swallows.

"No, Ray. That's not what I mean. I've heard about this. It happens. It means you've reached the point where you have to keep drinking just to stay afloat. Just to stand still. 'Cause it's killing you. You gotta give it up, Ray."

Carvalho stared at her wordlessly. In every cell of his being he knew she had to be wrong. But his whole fucking life was in the toilet and the rye he had just downed was doing nothing at all.

"Ray, why don't you go back to those meetings? How could they hurt?"

"Those meetings," he said with disgust, staring down at the bottle. "All they do is sit around and *talk*. It's *all* just talk."

"I still don't see how that could hurt." She smiled. "You're quite a talker yourself, you know."

She placed her hand over his and he looked up at her. Her eyes glistened as she smiled at him. He knew he didn't stand a chance without her.


The first thing he spotted, as he made his way down the steps to the church basement, was the no-smoking notice above the door to the meeting room. Which pissed him off. Even fifteen feet from the doorway he could make out the banners pinned up like Cub Scout pennants on the bulletin board to the left of the empty podium. He'd seen them all before, of course. Except for one. YOU ARE NOT ALONE, it said. Horseshit, he thought.

Grinding out his cigarette under his foot, he paused a few feet from the door. He closed his eyes for a moment. There was a tremendous pressure on his chest but he did not know how to relieve it. His palms felt damp. He wanted more than anything to get the hell out of there. The meeting hadn't started. He could still leave. Yes, he would leave.

He had turned on his heel to make his exit when he heard the voice behind him.

"Hi there. Welcome."

He hunched at the sound. Slowly, he turned back to see a small woman smiling from the doorway to the meeting room. She looked to be in her middle fifties, with salt-and-pepper hair and smile lines radiating out like spokes from steady eyes that never left his. Behind her he heard people laughing together in the room.

"Hi," he said at last.

"Welcome home," she said. Then the woman saw something in his expression. Her smile lines evanesced and her face softened.

Something was wrong. He could feel the shakes again. But this time it was more than his hands. He could feel the shaking seize hold of his diaphragm, his chest. The feeling was vaguely familiar, but he could not place it. What was happening to him?

The woman pivoted slightly to one side and she spread out her right arm to invite him in.

"Welcome home," she said again, softly.

Raymond Carvalho realized that he was crying.

# 52

## A Good Enough Excuse

The entrance to the apartments at 21 Harrison was not secure. Though there had once been a buzzer system, it had obviously been out of order for some time, and no one even bothered to lock the inner door anymore. Matthew ran his eyes over the mailboxes below the buzzer buttons until he found Danny's name. Apartment 413. He stepped through the deserted vestibule, pulled open the unlocked door, and headed for the elevators. Out of order, a handwritten sign needlessly reported; the elevator doors were open and the floor of the car was littered with trash. He took the stairs to the fourth floor.

He shuffled along the worn orange carpet until he found the door to number 413. He inhaled deeply, breathed out, and knocked. Immediately, he heard the sound of footfalls from inside the apartment. The door swung open and there, like magic, she stood.

"Hello, Julie."

She seemed confused by his unexpected appearance, but she nodded in silent greeting.

"May I come in? Just for a moment. I wanted to tell you

a few things I found out about Danny's death."

She said nothing. He was sure she would refuse him.

He said, "I know Danny fired the shots that killed Dunleavy."

Her eyes narrowed slightly, then she stepped aside to let him enter.

In contrast to the building itself, the living room was surprisingly homey. The furniture—a couch, a floor lamp, a coffee table, three cane chairs—was inexpensive department store stuff, but it was in good condition and the room was tidily kept. A photograph of the two of them, with Danny beaming delightedly at her, sat on top of a television set.

Matthew took a seat on the couch. Julie took one of the cane chairs, crossing her legs. She looked quite self-composed, as she had at the trial, now wearing beige chino slacks and a blue shirt. Just like Sarah at lunch earlier, he thought.

She said nothing, waiting for him. There would be no small talk. He decided to get right to it.

"To be honest with you," he said, "I really came just to ask you a question that's been nagging me."

"Yes?" she said.

"Yes. Did Danny arrange to get arrested by Dunleavy or did he just capitalize on the opportunity created by his arrest?"

There was no sound in the apartment for some time.

When she spoke she enunciated carefully. "I don't understand," she said, but Matthew had detected her almost imperceptible flinch at his question.

"Yes, you do. He couldn't have done it alone. You had to know. Because he needed your help. Where are the drugs now? Here in the apartment?" He looked about him rhetorically. "No, that would be too risky, wouldn't it?"

"I'm sorry," she said. "I still don't understand what you are talking about."

Matthew stood up and walked over to the television set. He picked up the picture and studied it. Still holding it, he turned back toward her.

"Look, I could take my suspicions to Jerry DeMarco. He'd have to find them interesting enough to investigate. And we both know that, if he did, Vu would find out and he'd put it together—just like I did."

He glanced at Danny's picture again.

"You know," he continued, staring at Danny's picture as he spoke, "when I was trying to convince Danny to consider witness protection, he told me it wouldn't work. He said if these people wanted to find you, they would."

He looked up at her. "You both understood that from the beginning. The scheme had to be so good Vu wouldn't look for you. Because if he did, he would find you. No matter where you ran to."

She stared at him.

He restored the picture to its place on the television and said, "Please, understand me, Julie. I don't care about the drugs. I do not want Herman Vu to discover he has a score to settle. With you *or* me. All I want is to know the truth. I just want to know what happened. You tell me and I'm out of your life."

She continued to stare at him. They remained like this, their eyes locked on one another's, for what felt like minutes, though Matthew knew it could only have been a few agonized seconds. Then he shrugged.

"OK," he said, turning toward the door. "I wish you luck. You'll need it."

"Wait," she said. "All right."

He turned back to face her. She waved him back to the couch and he obliged her.

"Ask your questions," she said when he was seated again.

He smiled. She was not going to make it easy.

"I already asked one. Was Dunleavy's bust a setup?"

"Yes. He chose Dunleavy very carefully. He was known to be a man who kept secrets."

"So let me see if I've figured it right. He decides to rip off his employer. He knows Vu will have to think he knows who did it, but if he thinks it's the police, well, what can he do? He has to lump it. So Danny arranges to get busted. Jesus, and I thought he got picked up trying to feed your habit."

He shook his head as he recalled how, when he met her on the street near Downtown Crossing, she had let him leap to the wrong conclusion that she was a junkie. Let him? Hell, she *led* him. No wonder he had been so bewildered by her miraculous "transformation" at trial.

"I *told* you I had a cold," she said, a tiny smile at the corners of her mouth.

"Sure. So Danny tells Dunleavy there's going to be a very big drop in Chinatown, one Danny just happens to be handling himself, and he arranges to have the cops come down on sixteen Tyler. Except the drugs never make it to sixteen Tyler. He switched bags. How did he do that, by the way? His escort never left his side"

Her smile was gone. "He had two bags in the trunk. No one could see in the dark."

"Of course. But he still had to tip Dunleavy that the drugs had arrived. That was you, wasn't it? How did you work it?"

"I sat in the window of a teahouse on Beach Street. When I saw him come through the arch and walk past me with the bag, I called Dunleavy."

Matthew picked up the thread again. "And they all go on to the apartment. Danny will give them some excuse for leaving the apartment for a few minutes—a *very* good excuse, I hope—and while he's gone the police are to show up and bust everybody. They seize an empty briefcase, but Vu believes otherwise, because he's got four trusted lieutenants to swear a bag full of dope was there when they got arrested. How am I doing?"

Julie gave him a minuscule bow.

"What was his excuse going to be to get out of the apartment? I can't imagine anything that would work. I mean, there could never *be* an excuse good enough to convince Herman Vu that Danny's absence just happened to coincide with his shop getting busted and Herman Vu getting taken for God knows how much cocaine. How could Danny have hoped to swing that?"

"They gave it to him themselves," she said. "He was supposed to call them and tell them that the drugs made it to the apartment. There was no phone there and Vu doesn't trust cell phones. Danny would have to use the pay phone in the Jade House. It's the restaurant across the street. He was going to wait there until he saw the police. Then he would call."

Matthew smiled. "That's pretty good. A perfect alibi, in fact. He'd be on the phone to one of his bosses when the cops arrived. He could even broadcast the play-by-play as it happened. Add a little drama to the proceedings.

"But he didn't count on Carvalho. And Carvalho is a cowboy. He got antsy. He didn't wait to give Danny time to split, and Danny finds himself in the upstairs apartment when the bust goes down. He knows the cops are going to be awfully surprised to see him. They might say something that would give him away. He loses it and starts shooting. And we all know what happened after that."

Matthew relaxed and leaned back, his right elbow resting across the arm of the couch.

"Didn't it ever occur to him that the cops might open the case in the presence of the guys who got arrested? And that they would see that it was empty?"

"No," she said. "But it occurred to me. So I picked the case. It took me a long time to find the right one. It was made of metal and felt heavy, even when it was empty, and the lock was *very* strong. We did not think the police would be able to open it in the apartment without a key."

"Turns out you were right," he said, recalling Carvalho's testimony. "They needed a chisel." He shook his head slowly. "Jesus. And I thought Danny's 'irons' were his cut for being Vu's straw on One Adams Place."

Her eyes widened with surprise at his knowledge.

"Oh, I know all about that," he said. "That was the other clue that made me suspect Danny had to have cooked all this up. Whatever he was getting to be a straw beneficiary for Vu could not have been enough to risk his life to keep it. That deal was not his iron in the fire. Once I learned he was a dealer for Vu, I knew it had to be bigger than that. It was the coke.

"So what were you planning to do then?" he asked. "Wait for a while and then leave town with the dope? And where to?"

"We would have waited a few months," she said in a monotone. "Then I would leave. Danny would tell everyone we had broken up and I was going to my sister's house in Montreal. Danny would stay longer."

"Yes, he would have to find a way to ease himself out of his position with the TOs."

They were both silent for a while. He stared at Danny's photograph across the room.

"It's *still* hard to know," he said, as if to himself, "what to think of him. I liked him, you know." He looked up at her and her dark eyes were on his. "Was he dirty all along? I mean, was he working for Vu from the start? Was he fronting for Vu at the Lotus Blossom, too?"

"No," she said, shaking her head sadly. "It was his dream, the restaurant. Lo Fat helped him get it started. It was Lo Fat who arranged for him to become a partner in the hotel. That was why they lent us the money for our share of the restaurant. But when it failed, he had to go to work for Vu. It was the only way he could pay back the money we had borrowed. You *have* to pay them back, you know. You see, he believed he was a failure. To have to work in the Tung On."

There were tears in her eyes now.

"I'm sorry, Julie. I tried my best to help him with his troubles at the restaurant."

The tears were falling steadily now. She made no attempt to wipe them.

"I really wanted to help him," Matthew said softly. "It seems that everything I do brings you pain. I regret that. But I do wish you well. I hope you get a whole *pot* of money for the cocaine."

He stood up.

"Where will you go now? And don't tell me Montreal, because I know you'd never try to take that bag through customs."

She cleared her throat. "I have uncles in Los Angeles," she said hoarsely. "They will know how to help me."

He nodded. But he didn't believe her.

# 53

---

# In the East

The four of them were gathered in the Teitelbaums' kitchen on Fisher Hill once again, Laura's hand in his under the table, Hannah sitting across from them cradling a mug of coffee. Ira loomed over the butcher-block island on which he was smartly disjointing a chicken. Matthew described once more, for Hannah this time, his conversations with Sarah and Julie. Through the kitchen window the setting sun was bleeding orange into the horizon, spreading cozy warmth through the little room.

"That," said Hannah when he had finished, "is a terribly sad story." Her brown eyes were large and earnest.

"Sad!" barked Ira savagely, cracking the breastbone in half with his hands. "He was a hustler from the git-go. He finally got too ambitious. That's what did him in." He picked up his boning knife and severed the filaments of clinging membrane that held the two chunks of meat together.

"Well, I still think it's sad. And poor Julie! It must be horrible."

Ira lowered the knife and scowled at his wife. "She was an accomplice, Hannah. She set out with her boyfriend to rip off the mob. And she still plans to peddle the dope where it'll end up ruining other people's lives." He picked up the chicken's back and snapped it loudly like a dry stick.

"I'm not sure what to think," said Matthew. "Morrissey tried to warn me about him, you know. He told me I didn't want to know the answers to my questions. I owed Danny nothing, he said. Grieve and move on. I thought he was just warning me about some rough customers, and he was. But he knew about Danny. He knew he was the killer. And he knew that was an answer I wouldn't want to learn. He was right, too."

They fell silent. The only sounds in the room were made by Ira's knife.

"And yet," Matthew resumed, "most of the time I feel the way Hannah does. That Danny did what he could, given the limitations of his world and his own uncontrollable dreams."

" 'Men are as the time is'?" Ira asked, his voice heavy with irony.

"Some are, Ira. Some can't rise above that. I guess I'd put Danny in that category. I always had the feeling, with him, that he was living life by ear, you know what I mean? Like nobody ever taught him how to sight-read. And he just had to make it up as he went along. That's something I can identify with."

His voice was low and serious. Laura squeezed his hand under the table.

"Well," said Ira, "I'm sorry. I don't buy that innocent-babe-in the-woods schtick. Your very first contact with him involved his jailbait scheme to commit tax fraud. He was as phony as a rainbow on an oil slick."

He piled the pieces of chicken on a plate and pushed it to one side. He picked up a red bell pepper cut in half length-wise.

Hannah said, "How did you know it was Danny? Who stole the drugs, I mean?"

"It was just a hunch," Matthew explained. "When Sarah explained about the shooting and kept insisting Carvalho had taken the coke, it just didn't make sense. Stealing the drugs minutes after watching his best friend die. He didn't strike me as that cold-blooded. But if it wasn't Carvalho, who did that leave? Then I remembered that change in Julie. How she had talked like she just got off the boat the last time I'd seen her, and how crisp and articulate she was on the stand. Something didn't add up. And a large quantity of cocaine seemed like a more plausible iron for Danny than being a cutout for Vu. So I went to see her."

Again, they lapsed into a silence broken only by the click of Ira's knife on the cutting board.

Then Laura asked, "What about Falk? Will he leave without a fight?"

"He better," Matthew said grimly.

"Oh, he will," said Ira, dicing the pepper. "The partners will see to that. We may know Matt was just bluffing, but they can't take the chance he won't go public. That kind of media coverage—seeming to protect Falk—could destroy the firm. So Falk's history. And good riddance, I say. Whatever we think of Danny and Julie, Falk is worse. He's an embarrassment to all vertebrates."

Matthew and Laura laughed.

"So," Laura asked Matthew, "will you tell Falk? About Danny being the killer?"

Matthew smiled, feeling a tiny ember of malice billow in his soul. "No, I don't think so. Besides, I promised Sarah not to tell anyone. Present company excepted, of course."

"Let him eat his liver," said Ira.

"What makes you think he will?" asked Laura. "*He* seems pretty cold-blooded."

Matthew said, "I think he's a lot worse than Danny, that's for sure. But he's no monster. Not like Vu. Vu seems like a parody of the rest of us, some parallel species pretending to be human. But not Falk. When he was sitting there, all crumpled and defeated in that conference room, it seemed plain to me he understood the enormity of what he had done. It wasn't just that he'd been found out. I started to ask him a question about our relationship, his and mine, whether there was anything to it, but I stopped him. You know why? I was afraid he'd tell me it was real, and I didn't want to hear that. I was afraid I'd believe him."

A silence settled around the four of them. The sun sank lower, burning its way beneath the rooftops below Fisher

Hill. Ira was at the stove, his back to them. He was dredging the chicken pieces in flour and laying them to brown in a smoking skillet.

Hanna said, "What do you think you'll do now, Matt? I can't imagine you'd want to stay at Daphnis and Clooney."

Ira barked a harsh laugh from the stove. "You might say he's aborted his career at D and C."

"I'm gonna call in gone," said Matthew with a grin.

"And then?"

"I'm not sure. Maybe look for a teaching job in one of the law schools. Or work in a state agency."

"You wanna be a fucking bureaucrat?" Ira asked in disbelief, still facing away from them.

"Ira," said Matthew, grinning, "what do you think *you* are? You're a freelance bureaucrat. What else is a lawyer these days?"

"You're swearing off private practice entirely?" Laura asked him.

"Oh, I don't know. I admit it even got exciting there for a while. Falk routed and all. But I also feel like I've been schooled in disillusion. Law firms don't teach. They deform. Being a lawyer is hard enough, but a lawyer in private practice is whipsawed between wanting to do what's right, which you can't do if it's not in your client's interest, and making sure you don't do something that's wrong, because that's forbidden. So what does that leave? The unwrong? We do whatever we are legally permitted to do on behalf of a client, no matter how despicable, in the faith that somehow the whole system will work things out for the best.

"In fact—" Matthew stopped, catching himself starting to orate—a sickening prospect, but he continued anyway. "In fact, it's like Jackie's discussion of theodicy. The belief that some mysterious power or higher purpose can justify the apparent evil in the world. He ridiculed something he calls psychodicy. Well, maybe the legal system is sustained by our faith in jurodicy—the curious faith that the localized, permissible evil we do on behalf of our clients will dissolve in the mystery of the higher justice served by the adversary system. Like Sarah in this case, manipulating everybody else's perjury. This time she had the unusual luxury of knowing her client wasn't guilty. Well, right now I don't have a lot of that faith to nourish me."

Ira had turned around now to face him.

"Now *that's* got a truly scholastic stink to it," he said. "You're ready to write off the whole adversary system because of the likes of Jimmy Morrissey and Rowell Falk?"

Matthew conceded the point to his friend. "No, I'm not. Not really. I'm just a little beat up right now and I need a rest from it all. It'll probably all make sense to me again after a while. But not right now."

"It won't be the same at the old shop without you," said Ira, his voice softer.

Matthew forced himself to smile. "We used to be together at the top of the Trifle Tower, Ira. But I was respectable in those days. Now they wouldn't even let me up."

Ira laughed. "Goddamn English majors." Then he dropped his fork on the counter and turned off the stove. Turning back toward the table he said, "You're not gonna go back home to the Midwest and the 'real snow,' are you? Isn't that your next line?"

"No," answered Matthew, his compressed lips smiling into Laura's pale gray eyes. "In the east my pleasure lies. This is home."

At that moment the last rays of the sun caught her hair from behind, and a nimbus of fire flared about her. His heart settled and was still.

# Epilogue

Suffolk County, which manages the Charles Street jail, settled Michael Chin's civil rights claim by agreeing to pay him $270,000. Sarah Kerlinsky received one-third of that amount as her fee.

The attorney general obtained indictments and convictions against Raymond Carvalho and Salvatore Piscatello for perjury. Both officers lost their jobs and pensions, and both served nine months in the Billerica House of Corrections.

The family of Francis X. Dunleavy brought a wrongful death action against the landlord who owned the tenement at 16 Tyler Street for allowing a dangerous activity—drug dealing—to take place on the premises. At trial, the plaintiffs were able to demonstrate knowledge of the activity through evidence that agents of the landlord (a realty trust of which, Eddie Felch later reported, Lo Fat was a principal beneficiary) had collected the rent through the hole in the steel door. A jury returned a verdict for the plaintiffs in the amount of $185,000. The Supreme Judicial Court eventually overturned the verdict, finding that the risk of getting shot through the door was not reasonably foreseeable.

Rowell Falk resigned from Daphnis & Clooney and retired to his island home off the coast of Maine. Not long afterwards, Sarah Kerlinsky had a long lunch with the bar counsel, an old law school chum of hers, and the Board of Bar Overseers suddenly lost interest in Matthew Boer. Bar counsel's investigation was terminated without discipline.

Ira Teitelbaum ran for Falk's seat on the firm's Management Committee, but he was handily defeated by Robolawyer.

The *Felter* case settled on the eve of trial for $3.4 million; the hotel contributed $800,000 to the settlement.

Sarah Kerlinsky was appointed to the bench of the Superior Court not long after her victory in the *Chin* case. This pleased both her father and her uncle, and it delighted her husband, who welcomed a judge's more manageable work schedule.

Jeremiah DeMarco left the district attorney's office to take a position as a partner in the firm of Royce & Bell, where he devoted his practice to white-collar criminal defense.

Laura Amochiev was elected a partner in her law firm. Awed by the ethical acuity behind her decision to withdraw from the *Felter* case because of the conflict raised by her relationship with Matthew, her partners appointed her to chair the firm's legal ethics committee. She moved in to live with Matthew.

Julie Soo quietly left Boston and was not heard from again. Wherever she went, Matthew was certain only that her destination was neither Montreal nor Los Angeles.

And Jackie Crimmins, like a child who plunges without looking into a crowded thoroughfare and emerges untouched on the other side, was elected governor of Massachusetts. Matthew Boer took a position in the new governor's legal office.